E. E. HORNBURG

THE
FOREST'S
KEEPER

THE CURSED QUEENS, BOOK THREE

THE FOREST'S KEEPER

E. E. HORNBURG

CITY OWL
PRESS

THE FOREST'S KEEPER
The Cursed Queens, Book 3

CITY OWL PRESS
www.cityowlpress.com

Digital and Paperback Cover Design by MiblArt. Hardback Cover Design by JV Arts. All stock photos licensed appropriately. Map Design by Cartographybird.

Edited by Tee Tate.

For information on subsidiary rights, please contact the publisher at info@cityowlpress.com.

Paperback Edition ISBN: 978-1-64898-300-9

Hardback Edition ISBN: 978-1-64898-427-3

Digital Edition ISBN: 978-1-64898-301-6

Printed in the United States of America

Praise for E. E. Hornburg

"*The Night's Chosen* is a fairytale-like fantasy romance about the burden of duty and following your heart. From the characters to the prose, the fairytale vibes are strong in this book. The world building pulls you in immediately. I look forward to reading the rest of the series!" – *Gabrielle Ash, author of The Family Cross and For the Murder*

"Fantastic world building! Mystery and deception. People are more than what they seem. I could not put down, *The Shadow's Heir*! I was totally captivated right from the start. I knew that Myra and Alvis' story was going to be truly special, and I was not disappointed! The characters added color and flavor to the story. Unique in their own way. This is a series I highly recommend and has fast become a favorite of mine. Enjoy retellings with a twist? These books are for you. Take a chance. You won't be disappointed! I give this 5 stars." – *The Literary Vixen*

"This stunning fantasy debut swept me away. *The Night's Chosen* offers up a delectable blend of intrigue, magic, and romance all wrapped up in fresh takes on fantasy tropes and themes. The author's vivid, lyrical writing is perfect for the story and brings to life a world of wonder in the most divine of ways to create an immersive experience sure to completely transport the reader. Hornburg's story is a total page turner that will keep you guessing through twists and surprises." – *Kat Turner, author of Hex, Love, and Rock and Roll*

"E. E. Hornburg has invented a world with several charming aspects. Her vision of a free-thinking society with fewer sexual hang ups is refreshing. Her pantheon of deities offers cultural variation, and her main character's devout nature is an admirable trait… The value in Ms. Hornburg's story-telling lies in the smaller touches which are sprinkled like stardust throughout the pages." – *InD'tale*

For Dale, the Cal to my Rose.
And I hope you enjoy the swamp zombies.

Chapter One

ROSE

WIND WHIPPED AROUND ROSE'S RED HAIR AS SHE STARED AT THE mountain where Luana's castle should be located. The air had a bite to it even though it was close to the summer solstice. At the top of the Paravian Mountain peaks there were hints of crisp snow still collected. A reminder that this was not Rose's realm. It sent a shiver down her spine and a twist of unease into her stomach.

She needed to see Eira.

Rose thought she was prepared but standing before the mountain she knew nothing was further from the truth. She gripped the reins so her knuckles turned white. There'd been many adversaries in Rose's life before. A mountain was a first.

How in the deities' names were they supposed to get inside?

The journey took far longer than she'd wanted, filled with stops and visits to the villages along the way so the people could greet the new future queen and she make connections with the local leaders. Pretending that she was excited to take on the role Eira had left.

Everything was *not* fine.

How was it possible for everything to be fine when Eira and Father didn't speak to each other? When Eira was living in the mountains doing deities knew what? When Rose had to act as though she were the heiress to the Cresin throne when it was the last thing she wanted? When the only communication Rose had with Eira was through letters over the last several weeks? Each piece of correspondence was a frail whisper of the long conversations the two of them once had when they were younger.

Sometimes they were apart. It was only natural. When Eira left for university or Rose was on a mission, and when Eira journeyed to the Paravian mountains in the first place to find the cure for Father's curse. That time, Rose would have gone with her, but she ended up trapped inside of Amelia's mirror instead.

Now, Rose was in a different yet still awful trap.

She needed to see her sister.

The caravan paused their horses in front of the mountain showed on the map, but it looked like any other mountain. Weeks ago, Eira sent a letter and asked Rose to join her in the Paravian mountains for a summer solstice tournament. Delighted, Rose wrote back right away to let her know she would be there. Now if only she could figure out how to get into the mountain where Lunana's castle stood.

On his horse at Rose's side, Cal looked at the mountain with furrowed brows, his sharp blue eyes taking in the area and strong chin firm. He messily tied his dark blonde hair back since he'd grown it out some over the last few months now that Amelia was gone. He said she liked it when her men were "clean cut" and growing it out was his minor act of rebellion and freedom. The hair wasn't unkempt or wild - not like Rose's unruly curls - and still manageable. Rose liked it more now that she was used to it. It made him look rugged and husky. She told him this once, and he only rolled his eyes and told her to mind her own business. But she swore she saw a small smile tug at his lips.

He loosened his grip on the reins and looked over to Rose. "How are we supposed to get in?"

Rose shook her head. "I don't know. Eira failed to mention that tiny detail."

The rest of the people in the caravan, a small group of knights and courtesans from Faren Castle who wanted to join the festivities, murmured among themselves. It was just another thing to add to their ever-growing list of reasons Rose was a terrible future queen. She wasn't even able to get them to another castle's event. The tournament was going to take place in Paravia, and the priestesses secured rooms for them to sleep in. Still, some were curious about Luana's castle, and Eira in her kindness said a small number could come for a night.

Believe me, I agree with you all. I'm terrible at this, Rose wanted to tell them. But knew that wasn't possible. Eira needed Rose to hold her ground, at least for a little while longer. But they needed Rose to lead them *now*. Despite the summer solstice coming, as they were so far north and in the mountains, Rose was glad to have her mother's red cloak around her shoulders.

She fiddled with the fastenings as she tried to think of what to do. She'd never asked Eira how to get inside a mountain.

There was a tiny sliver of a crack in the mountain wall that didn't fit with the rest of the rocks and stones. A slight glow came from it. Rose leaned forward to see what it was. Floating out of the crack were tiny sparkles of light, like stardust, and little by little it opened wider. On Rose's other side, her close friend and lady-in-waiting, Lady Evony, gasped.

"Oh, Rose,I think we found it!" she squealed, then elbowed Priestess Cynth. "I told you Rose knew what she was doing."

Wonderful. Even Priestess Cynth had been doubting.

The crack in the mountain wall opened even further and from it, Eira and Cadeyrn came walking through, stardust floating around Rose's older sister in silver clouds. Her long black hair fell across her shoulders in waves and her silver tunic flowed like a gown.

"You're here," Eira squealed and all of Rose's doubts and worries vanished, even if for the moment.

Rose grabbed her crutch that was attached to the saddle and slid off the horse. The two sisters met halfway and collided together in a bone-crushing hug. Everything was going to be fine.

"I'm sorry I didn't tell you about the entrance," Eira said once they broke apart. "I wanted you to have a surprise."

"You did that," Rose said. "But was not sharing how to come inside the best way to welcome everyone?"

Eira looped her arm through Rose's and leaned toward her. Her voice was low so others didn't hear. "It's not ready for the tournament. I'm glad only a few of you are staying tonight."

Rose stilled. Not ready? What did she mean by *not ready?* "It's not?" She tried keeping her voice light but wasn't able to hide the panic behind those two words.

Cadeyrn clasped Rose's shoulder. "Don't worry. The tournament will be in town as planned. We'd hoped the castle would be ready for people to come visit, but outside of this group we won't be able to. We'll explain everything when we get inside."

Rose's shoulders relaxed, and she nodded. At least the tournament wasn't off. Still, her mind filled with questions. Wasn't part of the point so people would see Luana's castle? Then they would believe Eira's story about being touched by the goddess and let her take her place as heiress to the throne again. Eira could return home in peace.

Eira broke away from Rose and faced the group, a wide and dazzling smile across her face. She glowed as she spoke. "Welcome, everyone. We're so pleased you made the journey here, and I can't wait to greet each one of you. Luana's Castle may not be what you expect, but I hope you can see the beauty and wonder in this place and grow to love it as we do."

She faced the mountain and Cadeyrn joined her and together they placed their hands over the long-cracked stone. After a few moments, light spread from their palms across the mountain wall and the crack opened large enough for a person to walk through, light pouring out of it.

Evony gasped. "Their love opens the door," she cooed.

Cal only rolled his eyes. "At least we can get inside now."

"You're such a grump," Evony told him. "It's romantic."

"It's a clever barrier to keep people out."

Cynth nudged Evony with her elbow. "Ignore him. I'm sure he's just *frustrated*." She winked.

Evony giggled, and the group followed Eira and Cadeyrn into the mountain while Cal seemed to growl at them. He never was one for romance and grand gestures. Cal was practical and jaded with relationships. Rose assumed it must have been from his work with Amelia and seeing the way she manipulated her own trysts and affairs.

Actually, Rose couldn't remember the last time Cal was interested in someone. They'd been so focused these days on Rose adjusting to her new role and Cal being second in command on the guard. They didn't have time for romantic endeavors.

One by one, they all walked through the mountains opening. The tunnel widened enough to fit each person and their horse, and the soft, sparkling moon rock walls brushed against Rose's shoulder. Even if the castle was ready for more visitors, she had a hard time picturing crowds of people using this entrance to come for the tournament. Even if it was amazing.

Cal appeared to be more hulking than usual with the walls surrounding all around him. In fact, Rose couldn't remember the last time she and Cal spent any time together outside of duty and responsibility. It was possible there was someone in his life and he hadn't bothered to ask him about it. Her shoulders slumped at the thought. In fact, she had spent little time with Evony or Cynth either. Some friend she was. Maybe this trip would be helpful for all of them to get away from the troubles of Farren Castle and rekindle their friendship again.

The tunnel opened into a vast cavern filled with stars and sparkling streams, with shimmering green-blue grass. Rose gasped. Eira described in her letters what mountain looked like inside, but seeing it was something no one would have been able to prepare her for. A shooting star flew overhead across the grand castle ahead of them.

At her side, Cynth's horse paused, and her chin quivered. A single glistening tear glided over her dark cheek, and the light of the shooting star caught in the circlet around her shaved head to make it glimmer. "It's beautiful. I can feel her. I can feel Luana here."

Against her better judgement, Rose wished high priestess Nyx had joined them. She was one of the most vocal about Eira not becoming queen and Rose was sure her opinions had swayed the Council. She should have been here to face the truths she tried to deny. It may have been petty of her, but Rose hoped once people saw the castle and everything Eira was doing there, Nyx would be ashamed of her behavior. Besides, if Nyx believed Eira, it would be one step closer to Eira coming home and Rose not having to be playing this charade anymore. She hoped the stories people would share once they returned home would be enough to convince her.

Eira hired some people from the village to help around the castle, and it was clear she'd made the correct choice. Luana's castle was in various states of disrepair. Some areas were clean and polished and shone with stardust. Others were void of color, with ragged tapestries with crumbled stone walls, as though a storm blew through and rid the place of any care or love. For months, Eira had been living here trying to break a curse put on by the goddess Luana centuries ago when Aytign experimented with death magic and it killed his lover and destroyed the temple in the castle and left the rest of the building in disrepair. When Eira received Luana's magic, it bound her to Aytign, the dragon who lived there. With her magic, Eira was supposed to restore it to its former glory, and in time, break the curse.

Then she could return home, claim her throne, and everything would go back to normal. The way things should be.

Rose could only hope.

Chapter Two

AMELIA

Swamp witch...

Amelia jolted upright from her bed and looked around. A green glow from the swamp shone through the window like a cursed candle. Blonde hair plastered to her neck with sweat and blankets kicked off to the ground.

That voice. But the room was empty. She slid off the bed and lit the candle on the table. The old wooden, almost rotted, floors creaked beneath her feet as she tiptoed over to the cradle where the baby lay. He slept peacefully despite the sweltering heat of the swamp. Praise Yla for that. Amelia didn't want to have to deal with a screaming child at night.

If the baby was still sleeping, what woke her? It didn't sound like Mother or Charis either, and Amelia checked to be sure they both were asleep while she crept through the cottage, the single candle guiding her path.

She'd heard the voice in the past. While trapped in the mirror, it haunted the dreams she had of this swamp. It beckoned to her. But it always sounded distant, like an echo of a memory. Not tonight. Tonight, it was right there by her side while she slept. As clear as a bell, as though they hovered over her bed. Maybe more of a banshee than a siren.

Amelia...

She paused mid-step. There it was again. It was deep and mesmerizing and sent a shiver through Amelia despite the suffocating heat. It was a man. She was sure of it. A silent chuckle escaped from her. Amelia knew how to deal with a man. This time, the voice didn't come from above or in a dream. It was outside.

The old door groaned when she opened it, and a pool of fog swarmed around her ankles. It was a stifling summer night in the swamp, but a cool breeze swept through her hair. Tree branches rustled overhead and the hum of the bugs and croaking of the frogs sang along with them.

Come to me…

Amelia looked out into the swamp with her candle outstretched to see better. Not a single person. Unless the voice wasn't a person. Not caring about having bare feet, or that her white nightdress clung to her like a second skin, or could barely see past her extended arm, she walked over the balcony and down the stairs to the green waters in a trance.

Amelia blew out the candle and watched smoke slither into the air like a charmed snake, then set it on the porch to take a night swim. The water was warm on Amelia's feet and legs as she stepped in. Every day she swam and floated in the swamp, letting it restore her weak and worn body and spirit drained from living in the dry land of Oxare. An ocean, lake, or river would be preferable, but the swamp was enough for Amelia to connect to her water powers again.

Her nightgown floated around her thighs as she walked further in until she was waist deep. The voice was silent now, but she could feel it there with her still, ever present the way the thick fog hovered around the cottage.

Instead of the pitch black and thick algae making it impossible to see through the water, there was a light. Tonight, a pale green light glowed through the slime, and she could see scaled and fanged creatures swimming across the water.

"What is that?" Amelia asked no one but herself, or perhaps she hoped the voice heard her.

The glow grew brighter the closer Amelia came and was as though an invisible string attached to her and pulled her forward. She was shoulder deep, and the glow grew brighter and bigger with each moment.

Come to me, Amelia.

She could only obey. She never took orders, but she was this voice's to command. At least for now. It was a relief to not be the one making the decisions. Something else showed the way.

Amelia took in a deep breath and walked under, her skin shifting into her sorceress form with shimmering green and blue scales along her arms and legs and over her cheekbones. A sharp pain pierced her neck, and she cried out, bubbles escaping her lips. She gripped the wound. There was no blood or injury found. Only the thin gills her fingers slid into. She'd always been able to hold her breath underwater for long periods of time, but never able to fully breathe. Her hand ran over the gills a few times to convince herself they were real.

All around the green water, creatures of all shapes and sizes swam past her. Some were as small as her fingernail, and others the size of a house with thick claws and pointed snouts. But none of them paid her any mind. In fact, she could see them clearly, as though she weren't underwater.

It was a magic she'd never seen or experienced before.

Through the green water and mist, a figure appeared in the distance. He walked toward her across the bottom of the swamp as though he were marching on a dry dirt road. His tattered robes floated the way a cloak would, his black braided hair wild and unkept and resembled seaweed tangled around his head. He should have been a peasant and begging for food and clothing. But he walked like royalty.

"Amelia."

She had heard his voice in her dreams for months. Now, he was here in the flesh. Amelia stepped toward him, amazed at how easily she could walk through the water the way this man did. Then, when she saw him up close, she had to hold back a gasp.

He was there in partial flesh.

Bits of skin held onto his skull, the same green color of the swamp where he walked. Various fungi had grown on his arms and legs and neck. It was as though his body was slowly rotting and turning into the swamp itself.

Amelia wanted to step away. She wanted to return to the surface and go as far away as possible and never return. Forget her plans of revenge and power. But she couldn't. After hearing his voice all those weeks and seeing the swamp in her dreams, she had to know why she was called here.

"You've finally found us," the man said. "We've been searching for you."

"We?" Amelia asked.

The half man ignored her question and continued to talk. "Each day you swam here but never saw what waited below. I had to summon you."

"You've been summoning me for months," Amelia corrected. She pinched her brows together in disgust. As if this thing couldn't have brought her here whenever he wanted. He'd been haunting her for so long, she barely remembered what a peaceful night's sleep was like. "Who are you? What do you want with me?"

He outstretched a skeletal arm toward her and moved his hand in a beckoning movement. "I am called Dusan. Follow me."

She wanted nothing more - and nothing less - than to follow.

Dusan turned his back to Amelia and walked away, and she trailed after him. As disgusted as she was, she needed to know what was here.

The swamp turned brighter as they walked until they reached a cavern as tall as a tree and as wide as her cottage up on land. The rotting man guided Amelia. She focused on moving forward to stop from gagging. Her eyes watered from the stench of rot infiltrating her nostrils.

The green glow was brightest here and along the walls were etchings and crude sketches of the water god Colma and sorcerers and sorceresses. Some in battle, some in peace, some with wealth, and some in poverty. They wore the same type of robe, but theirs were in one piece. They were simplistic and plain, so much different from the gowns Amelia wore in court.

"This image must be ancient," she observed.

"As am I."

A shiver ran down Amelia's spine, but she kept her head held high.

She couldn't let him see any sign of fright or nervousness. She was a queen.

Or at least she used to be.

They walked through dark and narrow corridors. The earlier glow faded behind them and barely left enough light to guide their path. The ground was muddy and sticky, and things grabbed out at Amelia's ankles. She jumped when something cold and clammy grasped her leg and kicked whatever it was to the side.

Eventually, they entered a large room. The center of it was empty save for two seats overtaken with growth from the swamp. Shelves filled with bodies laying on them the way you would a bed and covered the walls from floor to ceiling. Amelia's heart raced and when she looked down at the ground, she was awed to see she no longer walked on just sand. It was littered with bones.

Death. It was a place of death. As it was in a swamp and from the images on the cavern walls, Amelia assumed this placed belonged to her god, Colma. But no. This was Stula's realm. It must have been.

The deities were calling her to her death as a punishment for her deeds.

Amelia's hands shook, and she grasped the sides of her nightdress to stop them. No. Don't show him any weakness. If she was strong, she could get her way out of this. She'd been in tighter spots than this.

Maybe.

"What is this place? Where have you taken me? Who are you?"

Amelia wished more than ever she had a weapon with her, but she rarely ever carried one. Water was her weapon and was usually all she needed. But this man - creature - whatever he was - lived in the water. What use would her powers do against him?

Dusan walked in a circle around Amelia and gestured to the cavern. "This used to be a burial ground for Colma's sorcerers and sorceresses. But Eral Forest took over it. Kutlaous's followers made this place theirs. The swamp was once lake for us and our eternal rest. Then they claimed it, and our souls have been in anguish for a millennium. Our despair has turned the lake into this, and we want rest."

Amelia took in a few deep breaths and steadied herself. Now the shock was gone. She inspected the surrounding corpses. The same shining blue and green scales on Amelia's skin covered them, too. They were in various stages of decomposition and turning into the swamp itself. Not unlike the man who stood before her. A few even had their eyes open and watched her.

She swallowed. Those eyes would haunt her next, she was sure.

"What do you want me to do about it?" she snapped. "You woke me from a good night's sleep and took me away from my baby. It better be for a good reason."

Dusan chuckled, a dark and unamused sound. "Me taking you away from that screaming child and your complaining companions was a favor. You'll take any excuse to get away."

Well, at least someone understood her. He may not have been much to look at but was the first person in months who didn't chastise for her frustration whenever the baby cried. It was possible he'd been better looking in life. She squinted and tried to imagine him covered in skin and without the fungi growth. There were sharp cheekbones and maybe once full lips. Yes, perhaps a thousand years ago he might have been reasonably attractive.

She crossed her arms over her chest. "You still didn't answer my question. What do you want me to do? I have other important things to attend to."

"Such as getting your revenge on the royal family? Putting that child on the throne so you can control the kingdom through him?" He shook his head. "I can get into your dreams. You don't think I can see what you have planned and your doubt about them? If this is what you want and that's why you've been doing nothing?"

Amelia felt the blood drain from her face. He couldn't possibly know that. But he had been haunting her dreams and thoughts. Was it so improbable he saw inside her mind? She kept her face calm, even though her heart was pounding. He might have seen into her dreams, but that didn't mean he had to see what she felt and thought now.

"I know what you want." He crossed over to the chairs and sat in one of them sideways with one leg hanging over the armrest. "You want freedom. Just like we do. That's why you have done nothing in weeks. The swamp is the first taste of freedom you've had since before you can remember. But you're not free, are you?"

The corpses along the walls shifted and moved as the two of them spoke. Some reaching out to Amelia liked they wanted her to join them. She wanted to flinch and shoo them away and run back to the cottage as fast as possible. But she wouldn't give the man the satisfaction of knowing he frightened her.

"And?" she asked, keeping her voice casual and bored.

"We're not the only unhappy ones around here, and we've heard about what you did in Farren. We've been waiting for the right sorceress to come along, and I think we can help each other, and there are others who'll join us. You need allies to get back to the castle, and need to have certain people out of the way, yes?"

She would. When she was queen, Amelia was able to get what she wanted through her power and manipulation and using people's fears against them. But now, people knew who and what she was and saw her as an enemy. Getting back into the castle wasn't going to be easy. It was another reason it made sense to be here in the swamp. Eira was now even more powerful than before thanks to her encounter with the goddess Luana, and Rose was the next to be queen and a fierce warrior. With already having assassination attempts on them by Amelia, it wouldn't be as easy to get to them, and they had powerful people on their side.

People such as their grandmother, Renata, Kutlaous's Minister. She resided in Eral Forest, and Amelia knew if she wanted to get to the princess, she needed to get to Renata first.

Working with corpses wasn't something Amelia expected, but they obviously had power. Amelia had plenty of that on her own, but she wasn't in a position to say no to an offer that could help her. Anything to get out of this situation she was in and go to a life where she didn't have to listen to the whims of others and do as she pleased.

For too long, people made her choices for her. Her mother for being engaged to the king when it wasn't who she wanted to marry. King Brennan for choosing her to marry in the first place and she left her child behind. The court and needing to play nice by their rules. Trapped by Eira in the mirror unable to do anything. Now, even here when she was away from everything, she still was controlled by the screaming of the crying child and the complains of Mother and Charis.

And it all came down to the royal family. If it weren't for them, she'd be back in the Dravian Islands and none of this would have happened. She gripped her arms tightly, and her heart pounded, all the memories and rage flooding back in waves. It'd been foolish to be waiting here for so long. It was time she stole back the life they took from her.

And it would start with taking their lives.

A slow smile spread to her lips. "Tell me what to do."

Chapter Three

ROSE

Eira gave Rose a room with a view of the moon and shining silver bed covers, and all was in good condition. From the work Eira had done so far, it was obvious the castle would be glorious. Even so, Rose couldn't help but admit Eira made the correct choice in having the tournament take place in the village instead of the castle. They wouldn't want pieces of wall and ceiling falling on their guests.

Rose worked on settling into her room, when a knock came to the door and Eira poked her head through, her long midnight black hair cascading over her shoulders. "How is everything?"

"It's a beautiful room." Rose beamed and waved her sister inside. Eira closed the door behind her and took a seat on the bed. Rose couldn't help but feel like they were young again at home and sneaking into each other's rooms to talk and play games when they were supposed to be sleeping or working on their lessons. She took a seat at the vanity stool and stretched her twisted leg out, then laid out a roll of arrowheads on the table to be polished.

Yes, they would be dirty and possibly bloody by the time the tournament was done, but that didn't mean she shouldn't take care of them. She needed to impress her opponents after all.

"Will anyone be able to see the castle?" Rose understood why more guests didn't stay at the castle. But part of the point of this whole excursion was for them to see everything Eira did and experienced here. Or at least so Rose thought.

Eira looked at the canopy over the bed before answering. "Maybe? Things haven't progressed the way I'd hoped. Malle has made things difficult."

Thankfully, Rose hadn't encountered the disturbed spirit yet. She still shivered as though it was here in the room with them. Human opponents were one thing, but spiritual ones were another. Unless they were sorceresses of course. The sting of not being able to defeat Amelia this past autumn and being trapped in a mirror for several weeks still lingered. She should have been able to handle it. Instead, she discovered Amelia wasn't human at all, but a sorceress whose skin turned to scales and human means couldn't kill her.

Rose tried to research how to kill a sorceress since then but had little luck. She hadn't been good at digging through the library. Sorcerers and sorceresses could live longer lives than humans, but they weren't immortal. She worked on not trying not to dwell on her failure that day, but the memory of the shock, the powerful water Amelia retaliated with, and the weeks trapped in the mirror ate away at her. Rose clenched her hand around one arrowhead. She just needed to kill Amelia.

With a deep breath, Rose released her hold on the tiny weapon. It'd been weeks since Amelia escaped the Golden Palace in Oxare, and no one had heard a word from her. Rose couldn't help but wonder if it was the calm before a terrible storm. The soldiers from all the kingdoms were searching for her. She wished she could be out there with them, but she couldn't. Rose's new duty was to stay at Farren Castle and play the role of heiress. She grimaced.

"Rose? Are you all right?"

Eira's voice brought Rose back to the present, and she shook her head as though it would help her get rid of all the worries and memories. "Yes, I'm fine. Sorry. I must be tired from the trip. So, they haven't come? I thought you said Alvis and Myra were going to help you."

Her sister pinched her brows together in a look that said she didn't

believe Rose, but she wouldn't push it. Eira knew when to leave
something alone and didn't push hard subjects. A skill Rose should learn
from her.

"There are some things Myra needed to take care of at her father's
estate, and they're warming up Oxare to having a former servant and
Stula follower as their future queen." A coy smile played at Eira's red
lips as though she were remembering something from her visit to Oxare.
"And I think they're wanting some time together. I couldn't deny them
that."

"Don't you think they'll have enough time together once we find
Amelia and you break the curse and you're back in Farren ready to take
your place as queen?"

No, Rose hadn't learned the skill of not pushing difficult topics until
more appropriate times or in more appropriate ways. Eira put her head
to the side and smiled at Rose.

"Tell me how you really feel, Rose."

Rose covered her face with her hands and twisted in her seat, which
only made her already tired leg cramp. She groaned. "Sorry, I promised
myself I wouldn't bring all that up so soon. I wanted us to enjoy
ourselves at least a little."

Eira pushed herself upright and off the bed. She'd always been the
graceful one. But, after her encounter with the goddess Luana, even
standing up from a bed looked like a dance. She grabbed an extra stool
that stood to the side and slid it over next to the vanity.

"Well, we can't avoid it forever. Besides, Amelia and this curse is the
whole reason you're here anyway. If it weren't for her, we wouldn't be in
this situation at all," Eira said. She patted her lap, and Rose propped
her leg up so Eira could massage it. After only a few moments, Rose felt
herself relax and leaned against the vanity. During the journey she
didn't use her leg much for walking, but keeping her balance and
directing the horse still made her muscles ache. Few people instinctually
knew when Rose needed the help, and there were even fewer people
Rose let help her without asking first.

It was then Rose realized it wasn't just playing at being the heiress to
the throne and the weight of what Amelia might do next that hovered

over her. She couldn't remember the last time she'd felt so relaxed with someone. Not even Cal.

It was a depressing realization.

And more reason Rose needed to talk to her sister.

"The tournament should be a move in the right direction. You can gain more allies and prove you deserve the crown. I'm sure it's been awful."

Eira finished massaging Rose's leg and set it back on the floor. She bit her bottom lip. "The curse is a challenge, and we worry about Amelia, and I would like to have the kingdom's trust again…" Her voice trailed off, and it made Rose pause. She didn't like the tone in Eira's voice. As much as she was afraid to, Rose egged her on.

"But?"

"But…" Eira pushed her hair over her should and looked around the room. Her gaze fell on the window looking out over the view of the glimmering lake outside the castle. Stars glimmered against the mountain walls beyond them, and it was as though Eira got lost in their light. "Is it terrible that I don't always hate it? Malle's spirit is horrifying. Aytigin is a pain in my side most days, and the thought of Amelia out there somewhere haunts me. But I've never been so free."

Eira looked happy oddly enough. There was a lightness about her that had nothing to do with her star and ice magic. She floated through the world. It was good to see her sister so happy like this. As selfish as it was, Rose envied her a little.

Rose shook her head. "No, it's not terrible. We still have the matters at hand to resolve."

Eira's shoulders fell. "I know, and the more allies I build, the more help we'll have at tracking Amelia down and breaking this curse."

"And killing her."

Eira took in a deep breath through her nose. "Maybe."

The world paused around them, and Rose could have sworn her heart stopped. Did Eira really just say "maybe" with killing Amelia? It was only a few months ago when Eira herself gave Rose the order to kill her. Her jaw tensed and it felt as though the room closed in on her, trapped back in the mirror with Nell again. "What do you mean, maybe?" she managed to get out.

Something changed in Eira then. She didn't change positions or facial expression. A wall went up around her, and the sister here to greet Rose was gone and a future queen sat in her place, ready to give instructions to one of her soldiers. "I'd think with everything we've seen Amelia do, we'd have learned by now that killing people doesn't always resolve our problems."

"And trapping her in a mirror and keeping her alive didn't either. Look where that left us. I know we preserved the life of the baby, but the child should be born by now. What reason has she given us to protect her life when she's shown no regard for anyone else's?"

Eira kept her composure, as she always did, but her shoulders and jaw were rigid. "And I will not stoop to her level and only focus on revenge. I'd advise you to do the same."

"It's not revenge, it's justice!" Rose's voice grew louder with each word. She should know how to keep her calm and tried to remember the ways to ground herself. Deep breaths and clenching and unclenching her thighs to focus on something else. But no matter how much she practiced those things, sometimes it didn't help. "But what about all she's done? The people she's hurt. What she did to…"

Me.

What Amelia did to Rose.

If the roles were reversed, Rose would have stopped at nothing to be sure justice was served. But not just Rose, but to Eira too. She'd hunt her down and put her to sleep. The way she almost killed Father. The way she had hundreds of innocent people killed in her pursuit of Eira. How she trapped her down daughter, Nell, in the mirror for eleven years. Rose's blood boiled at the memories.

"How can you not want justice?" She lowered her voice, but the words were sharp.

"And how can you only want blood?" Eira asked back. She straightened her shoulders and smoothed out her skirt. "I want justice as much as you do, Rose. I do. But we need to look at the bigger picture. I refuse to be the type of queen Amelia was where killing people is the only answer."

Rose always admired how noble and peaceful Eira was, but sometimes it was plain foolishness. "But you will be queen someday,

Eira," she pointed out and grasped her crutch. "And you can't always avoid blood on your hands."

"I have blood on my hands!" Eira's voice grew louder, and stardust floated all around them in shimmering clouds. "People are dead because of me. You think I don't know that? We need to think it through and not jump. Besides, do you know how to kill a sorceress?"

Rose swallowed the lump forming in her throat, and her grip on the crutch was so tight her knuckled turned white. She took in a few deep breaths, determined to not let her emotions get the better of her. "No. I don't."

She pushed herself up and grabbed her satchel that held the straps for her ankle. She slung it over her shoulder and made her way to the door.

Eira stood from her seat and followed. "Rose, where are you going? You can't just walk away."

She turned back to face the future queen, the stars still reacting to Eira's emotions and swirling in the surrounding air. "I'm going to go practice for the tournament. I can't talk about this anymore. You need to think about what you're doing. While you're living in an enchanted castle with your lover and magic and freedom, the rest of us are living with the results of your actions and searching for Amelia."

"Rose…"

Rose shook her head. "I'm standing in your place as the next heiress. I'm holding my side of the bargain. But you need to help us too Eira, and that might mean making choices you don't want to. You know I would rather be out there, finding Amelia and protecting our kingdom and you, but I'm staying put out of loyalty to you. I'd think you'd want to do the same for me."

Eira opened her mouth to speak, but Rose didn't want to hear it. All she wanted was a sword in her hand. She stormed out of the room.

Chapter Four

ROSE

IDEALLY, ROSE AND CAL WOULD MEET AT THE TOURNAMENT GROUNDS
back in the village to look and get a lay of the land. Unfortunately, the
trek from the castle to Paravia was too long to make in one afternoon.
Especially when they'd already been traveling for so long. Instead, she
met him deep below the castle in the armory. There were people from
the village who supported Eira, who asked about learning how to fight,
so Cadeyrn volunteered to train them. Sometimes he went to Paravia,
but other days they came to him in the mountains where they could
easily access Aytigin's hoard of weapons and supplies. Along with
cleaning and organizing them.

They lit the star lanterns, and the two of them stopped in the
doorway to take the sight. The metal of the weapons glistened in their
light. Set before them was an array of swords, bows, hatchets, clubs, and
daggers. Piles and displays of weapons ranging from ancient and worn
to new and sparkling, and mundane to magical. There were items Rose
didn't even know what they were. She could have cried.

They stepped inside, and Rose wandered the space in awe. She
wanted to touch everything in sight, while feeling like she shouldn't out
of respect for the pieces of destructive art. Aytigin and Cadeyrn said
they could use anything if it wasn't the pieces blocked off in the back.

Aytigin was protective of these items and only wanted people touching them under his supervision. It was exactly where Rose went first. They drew her to them as though a string pulled her along so she could see.

A shimmering line of stars circled a few choice weapons that floated in the center. A long sword floated in the middle and on either side was a dagger and a bow and arrow. Jewels and engravings of the gods Aros, Kutlaous, and the goddess Stula were encrusted into the metal. There was something radiating from them, almost like a hum or a song beckoning Rose to reach out and grab one. She caught her reflection in the sword's shine's blade, then a flash of yellow eyes appeared where hers should be in the image.

"The Shadowslayers. I didn't know they actually existed."

Rose jumped when Cal approached and blinked. When she looked at the sword again, her yellow eyes were gone.

"Didn't mean to scare you." Cal looked at her out of the corner of his eye, and the corner of his lip hinted at a grin.

She barely registered his words as she looked around the room. Those yellow eyes. She hadn't seen them since she'd traveled with Eira to Eral to seek a cure for their father. Eira said she didn't seem them, but they were the same color as that wolf's eyes, Rafe. Rose could have said those were what looked out at her. But no one was here but her and Cal. Something in Rose's stomach sank at the realization no one was there. Relief too. But she'd hoped… She didn't particularly like Rafe and didn't trust him. But if he served Stula, maybe he could help her defeat Amelia.

Cal's smile faded as he watched Rose look around. "Is everything okay?"

Rose blinked a few times and shook her head. "Sorry, I'm fine. I thought I saw…"

But it was ridiculous. She never mentioned the yellow eyes to Cal.

"Saw what?" Cal's voice was sharp as he turned into the role of a royal guard. He looked around the room like Rose did.

"Nothing," Rose said. "Don't worry about it. My eyes are playing tricks on me, I'm tired from the trip, and I fought with Eira."

Cal narrowed his sharp blue eyes that penetrated through her and she knew he didn't believe her, but what could she say? I think someone with yellow eyes, possibly a wolf that works for the goddess of death, might watch me but he's not here? He would think she'd lost her mind. So, instead, she ignored his wary look and put her focus back on the magical weapons.

"Did you ever think you'd see the Shadowslayers in person? It looks like everything that supposedly was a myth exists," Rose said and looked at her reflection in the sword's blade. Only her reflection, nothing else.

"They exist here at least," Cal added.

True. Luana's castle wasn't supposed to exist. Gallis's Chalice wasn't supposed to exist. These weapons weren't supposed to exist. What else were they told were myths and the truth was they existed somewhere in this world? Probably here in the very castle they stood in.

"Do you believe they can do what they say?" Rose asked. "A sword that can slice through even the hardest of stone, arrows that fly faster than light, and a dagger that never misses its mark?"

"Maybe kill a sorceress."

Rose couldn't keep her smile off her face as they locked eyes. Their friendship hadn't been the way it was since before he'd attacked him and Eira, thinking it was the only way to keep his sister Myra safe. Not because Rose hadn't forgiven him - she had. But because life got in the way and so much happened, she didn't know how to act around him sometimes. Then there were moments like these where it was like he could read her mind.

There was a dangerous excitement in Cal's gaze, and it made Rose's chest tighten. She tore her eyes away from him and searched for another weapon. If she didn't, she'd steal away with the Shadowslayers and Aytigin would have her head. Which would only make matters worse between her and Eira. She didn't blame Aytigin for being so protective though. She'd be the same way.

She found a short sword with a slight curve at the end of the blade and a simple hilt wrapped in leather. Nothing fancy, but it could slash through someone's armor well enough. With her free hand that wasn't holding her crutch, she swished it through the air a few times then pointed it at Cal. He didn't even budge. The image of pure trust. And probably the knowledge that without the straps around her ankle the likelihood of him beating her in a fight was stronger.

"I wish I was out searching for Amelia with them. If we were and not stuck in Farren Castle, we'd have found her by now," Rose said.

Cal chuckled. "Maybe."

Rose raised her brows at him. "Maybe? With our skills? You know we'd at least have made more progress."

"Why are you so focused on getting Amelia?" Cal leaned against a table with an array of daggers laid across it. He picked one up and examined the blade.

"Shouldn't I be?" Rose asked back. "I'd think she should be everyone's top priority."

"I'm not saying it's not, and I want justice for all she's done as much as you do. If not more."

Rose's chest tightened again. Of course he did. He and Myra had more reason out of anyone to want Amelia captured after how she'd treated them.

"You don't have to do it. It's not your sole responsibility. You have other things you can focus on too," Cal added.

Rose pressed her lips together and tried to breathe through the anger rolling through her belly. "Right, like being the 'future queen.'" The idea made her sick and want to laugh at the same time. How anyone played along with it was beyond her.

"Yes, exactly."

Rose raised her brows. "You remember it's only until Eira gets her title back, right?"

He shrugged. "*If* she gets her title back."

Her grip tightened around the hilt of the sword. She should pummel him right there for those traitorous words against Eira. Even if she was angry at her sister at the moment, it didn't give anyone the excuse to speak against her. "What did you say?"

He held his empty hand out in a sign of peace. "I'm not saying I don't want Eira to be queen, and I think she can get her title back. But she has a long way to go. She'll only get her crown if she can make them believe her story. Even if she gets it back someday, that doesn't mean you can't use this position, and you should be prepared for anything."

Rose shook her head, refusing to even consider the possibility that

Eira wouldn't be on the throne someday. "But I don't want to be queen. I'd be terrible at it anyway."

"You don't want it, or you're afraid of it?"

Her heart stopped at his words. Afraid? Of being queen? The idea of her sitting on the throne was preposterous, not frightening. Admitting she wouldn't be good at the role didn't mean she feared it.

"I'm not afraid. You're being ridiculous."

Cal tossed the dagger back and forth between his hands then set it back on the table. "All I'm saying is you can do more than serve on the guard. If you wanted to be queen, you could. If you want something else, you could do that too. Your whole life you've been following and protecting Eira, but now you're in a place you don't have to. Don't allow other people to run your life if you don't have to."

His words stung, and Rose wondered if it was residual resentment from his life serving Amelia. Eira never controlled Rose or forced her to do anything she didn't want to. Rose was on the guard and served her sister because it was her choice. For years she'd seen the pressures of being Luana's Chosen on Eira and how she always had to put the kingdom and deities before her own wants and needs. Rose believed with everything in her that Eira would be the best queen for Farren. Still, it didn't mean Rose wanted the same life for herself. She didn't mind serving the kingdom, but sitting on a throne wasn't the way she would do it. On the guard, she could protect Eira while still being herself and not needing to be in the center of attention the way Eira was. But these days it felt more and more as though they dragged her through the situation and needed to play along even if she didn't want to be.

"Eira would never do that," Rose said quietly, almost as though she needed to convince herself and not Cal.

"I know she wouldn't. You just can do so much, Rose, don't sell yourself short."

Rose put the sword away and swallowed the lump in her throat. Cal was a man of few words, so when he talked this way, it must have been something he'd been thinking about for a long time. She had her back turned, but could feel his eyes on her. She rolled her shoulders to ignore the sensation, even as she could feel her cheeks warming.

Cal cleared his throat, breaking the momentary silence and tension filling the room. "But I understand. I want to be out there too. Maybe I'll get Aytigin to let us take the Shadowslayers with us, and we can hunt her down ourselves."

Rose turned to see a playful grin on Cal's face. "We'll show them at the tournament. Eira won't have a choice but to send us out there."

"Let's get to practicing then." Cal found a sword to his liking and swished it around in the air with satisfying swipes. "Show these people how it's done."

Chapter Five

AMELIA

"WELL, IT'S ABOUT TIME WE DID SOMETHING OTHER THAN SIT AROUND this pathetic cottage." Amelia's mother, Mariah, paused her pacing in front of the bedroom window and pushed aside the torn curtain with her finger to look out over the swamp. The trees and fog made it difficult to see the sunshine. "Which has hardly been suitable for any decent living being."

Amelia let the complaints roll off like waves on the seashore. The truth of it was, she didn't mind the cottage. It was run down, but maybe in time she would find one of Gallis's Restorers to make it more suitable for residence. She couldn't be here permanently, but it was an excellent spot to hide away from the world.

She looked in the dirty and cracked mirror before her and ran a brush through her golden locks. Even she had to admit, it wasn't ideal for receiving visitors and didn't give the sort of intimidating atmosphere she'd prefer. But it was what they had. Amelia applied some kohl to her eyes. She would have to be intimidating enough to make up for it.

"I've said it before and I'll say it now. You're welcome to leave, Mother."

Amelia would prefer it. For years, she'd been away from her meddling mother. One of the few joys of living in Farren Castle. Now it was like she was a young girl, not able to move or breathe without her mother criticizing everything Amelia did. Mother played her part in getting Amelia out of the Golden Palace and the mirror, but now she needed to go back to the Dravian Islands. Soon.

"Someone needs to keep you focused and in line. You've forgotten the purpose of you being in Cresin." She turned on her heel toward Amelia, her shoes clicking over the wooden floors and arms crossed over her chest.

Despite the sweltering heat, Mariah kept her silver hair in a perfect twist on top of her head, and her lightweight dress floated around her like a cloud. The tattoo of waves on her collarbone was on display for all to see. Like Amelia, she didn't need the tattoo in order to access magic. But it helped people believe she was only a human, not a sorceress, and Mariah saw it as a point of pride. A way to show off which deity she served. For all her complaints about their surroundings, it didn't prevent her from looking like the regal sorceress she was.

She stood behind the mirror, making it impossible for Amelia not to see her. She looked down over her pointed nose at her daughter's reflection. "I didn't do all this work for you to ruin it. If it weren't for me, you'd still be in that mirror from the mess you made."

Amelia's blood boiled, but she'd had plenty of practice at hiding her true thoughts and emotions. She refused to give her mother the satisfaction of getting under her skin. Besides, things were looking up. Amelia had a plan. She smiled sweetly. "And if it weren't for you, I'd have my daughter - whom you failed to capture for me."

There was a knock at the door. Then Charis poked her head through the door and held the baby in her arms. Asleep, miraculously. "Sorry to disturb, but… something is happening in the water."

Amelia didn't wait for Mother to move and pushed her way past and out the door so she could get a better look at what Charis was talking about. It was only a couple of days since her encounter with the ancient burial ground and she hadn't told either of them what happened, only that she had a plan, and someone was to visit the cottage soon.

Mother and Charis followed Amelia and met her out on the balcony, where they could clearly see the green water bubbling and swilling. It rolled in a circle, then opened into a giant hole. From the center, two forms appeared and rose out of the water. One was tall and broad with smoky black robes and a hood which covered their face. The other was lanky, and while he wore all black as well, his clothing wasn't a set of robes. His dark hair was shaggy, and his clothes seemed made of leaves and linen. Both people were barefoot.

Charis let out a wordless squeak. She must have put the baby down in the cradle because her arms were empty. "What in the deities' names?"

Half her body was on the other side as she leaned over the railing. It creaked and groaned beneath the weight, then cracked. She squeaked again as she tumbled and caught her balance. She whipped her head around so fast toward Amelia, her hair hit Mariah on the other side. "Who are they? What do they want?"

"Calm yourself," Amelia said, a little disappointed Charis didn't fall into the water. "They will help you out of here."

The swamp water closed behind the two visitors as they walked toward the cottage built into a tree. Amelia moved and stood at the top of the stairs. She imagined she was back in Faren castle with a crown on her head and soldiers on either side. But as the visitors approached, the surrounding water reacted to Amelia's mood and stance, stilling itself in peace and calm. She remembered she didn't need those things to be powerful and to intimidate those around her. Amelia was enough on her own.

"Welcome." Amelia looked down on them and inwardly grimaced that they didn't bow before her. People would bow before her again soon. There was still fear behind the lanky one's deep brown eyes. There was something else too, though. A hint of rebellion. "I see you received my message, servant of Stula."

The priest in the robes removed his hood, revealing a pale, shaved head with large black circles around their eyes. "It was quite the intriguing message, sorceress. I wasn't aware we had a mutual adversary."

Mother and Charis looked at Amelia but said nothing.

"Come join me inside where it's a bit more comfortable, and we can discuss how we can help each other."

Amelia turned to go back inside, forcing the others to follow. At the sound of footsteps behind her, she knew everyone followed. She'd arranged chairs in the main sitting room as best as she could and placed the sturdiest and tallest armchair in front near the fireplace. It wasn't lit. They'd all melt in the summer heat. It was still the most powerful location in the space and Amelia waited next to it for the others, refusing to sit until the others took their own seats. No one would look down on her.

Satisfied, she placed herself in the chair and crossed one leg over the other. The slit in her dress slid to the side to reveal her thigh. She leaned back and could picture herself being back in the throne room. "Now, tell me why you want Kutlaous's Minister killed."

Charis audibly gasped. "The *Minister*?"

But Mariah's only reaction was a raised eyebrow. Amelia was sure she'd hear thoughts later.

The priest held his hands in front of his face and strummed his fingertips together. "The Minister has evaded death for years. Stula gave us premonitions that her day has come, but time and time again she seems to continue on. It's against the ways of nature and Stula's will." He paused his strumming and looked at Amelia square on. His pitch-black eyes were pools of darkness as deep as a starless night sky. "And there are many in Eral who feel as though it's time for the torch to be passed."

Interesting. Very interesting.

Amelia rocked her crossed leg up and down in thought. "Who is unhappy with Renata?"

The priest waved his hand toward a window like they were all waiting there for them outside. "There are a few select groups. The ogres being the most vocal. They've had complaints against the Minister and her family for several years. Something about an arranged marriage gone wrong. A new chief has come into power, and she's very driven to give the ogres a new position in society."

It was Amelia's turn to be surprised. The ogres rarely got involved in politics or other groups in and out of Eral. Most people and creatures preferred it that way, and they all kept their distance from the ogres. They weren't a group Amelia particularly wanted to work with, either.

Hearing they held a grudge against Renata, and members of her family, was new information. But, if they were unhappy, she could use that.

The priest continued. "Besides, she's getting older and losing her touch. Eral has not been as strong as it used to be. The Minister cannot keep up with it forever."

"That's not how everyone feels," the other visitor said. His voice was low and quiet, but not fearful as Amelia expected. "Many in Eral would miss her presence."

Amelia cocked her head and observed him. Instead of cowering under her gaze, he sat straighter and looked up at her as though he was surveying and judging her right back. His brown eyes were steady and observant. Still, that rebellious, maybe even playful, look was behind them. Like a puppy. A puppy that could turn into an attack dog. "And who are you? Are you one who would miss Renata?"

"This is Rafe," the priest introduced for him. "He is a unique servant of Stula."

"I spend a lot of time in Eral, but I do not fall under The Minister's jurisdiction since I don't belong to Kutlaous."

Amelia sat forward again and kept her gaze on Rafe. "Well, as it doesn't affect you, what does it mean to you, anyway? Besides, Renata may be his hand here in the world, but that doesn't mean she *is* a deity. She's only mortal. Which means she'll need to move on eventually."

"I can ask the same of you. What is *your* grudge against the Minister?" the priest asked. "I wouldn't think you'd have an interest in Eral or those who follow Kutlaous."

Amelia shrugged. "Perhaps it would seem that way. But I assumed you were smarter than that and would have figured it out by now. Her granddaughters are the princesses Eira and Rose. I need to get rid of them, and I cannot do that with their powerful grandmother in the way. Besides, I wouldn't mind having some influence on who is the next Minister. I think the two of us could help each other, don't you agree?"

The priest smiled, if you could call it that. The corners of his lips hinted upwards, and there was a dark glimmer in his black eyes. In her peripheral vision, Amelia watched the reactions of her mother and Charis. The latter had gone silent, but her face was a ghostly pale white and her blue eyes wide in shock. While Mother watched Amelia like a curious shark waiting for her moment to attack.

The priest gestured to Rafe. "I had a feeling my companion would be useful today then."

She'd been wondering why Rafe was there, but he intrigued her so she didn't question it. Perhaps she should have. "And how will he be useful?"

"Rafe, show her who you are."

Rafe looked at the priest out of the corner of his yellow eyes and took in a deep breath. Within moments, his body shifted. Black fur grew over his body, his clothes ripped and shredded to the ground as his bones and muscles popped and cracked until he turned into a giant wolf. So large he could have a person ride on his back like a horse.

Charis pressed herself against the wall as she cried out. Even Mother let out a small gasp. Meanwhile, Amelia took in a breath and kept her own surprise in her head. She didn't expect a wolf to appear in her cottage. But he was impressive.

"Rafe is a special servant of Stula's and assists her in… difficult… cases such as these. If we give him a command to take care of someone, he will carry it out. No matter what," the priest explained.

This Rafe was becoming more interesting and appealing with each minute. She circled around him, inspecting like she would if she was picking out a new dress. "If we needed to have the Minister killed, you could do it? Even though she serves Kutlaous?"

The wolf nodded his head once. "If I'm given the command, it will be done."

His deep voice made the cottage tremble.

Amelia's heart skipped a beat. This was some of the best news Amelia had heard in a long time. It was tempting to give him the order for the entire Farren royal family. Alas, she was selfish and wanted those kills for herself. She'd earned them. She met Rafe's eyes and smiled. He didn't smile back. But it didn't matter.

"Give the command."

"As you wish, my lady." The priest stepped forward and placed his plans on Rafe's side. "Follow my lead."

Under other circumstances, Amelia wouldn't follow orders.

However, this was going to get her what she wanted. So she approached Rafe's other side and put her hands on his black fur. As large and intimidating the wolf was, his fur was soft.

The priest closed his eyes and chanted in a language Amelia didn't recognize and around them the cottage went dark with dark purple fog filling the space. The wolf's fur was warm to the touch, but Amelia didn't let go. His voice wordlessly rumbled, and he growled, baring teeth as long as a knife. The wolf blinked and his eyes turned a glowing red and, with a final shake of the cottage, he howled.

Chapter Six

ROSE

Rose groaned as she went through the flaps of her preparation tent and sat on a stool. She tossed her braid to the side and rubbed the back of her neck. Barely halfway through the day and already pieces of her wild red hair stuck to her head with sweat, and some unruly strands escaped from her braid and coiled into frizz.

The first few rounds had gone well. Archery and the joust, which were always her best because she didn't have to use her ankle as much. Next was swordplay. She was exhausted, but in the best way possible. A thrill went through her she hadn't felt in months from having a bow and arrow in her hands again.

The scent of caramel and butter from beyond the tent filled Rose's nostrils, and the call of vendors selling food and flags representing favorite knights boomed over the chatter of the people. Minstrels and bards commissioned by Efarae played their lutes and sang songs, telling tales of the eternal love Ray had for Luana, which had created their world.

Lady Evony walked through after Rose, a wooden bowl of water in her arms and a towel draped over her shoulder. "Your final blow to Sir Filbert was incredible!" she gushed as she took a seat next to Rose and dunked the towel into the water bowl, then wrung it out.

"Thanks," Rose said with a smile and took the towel from her. She lay it behind her neck and groaned again at the cool relief from the summer heat. It was cooler at the top of the mountains and in Luana's castle, but here in the village of Paravia, summer certainly had arrived. "It felt incredible."

Evony sighed. "It's too bad. He was handsome, though. Maybe you can tend to his wounds later." She wagged her brows.

Rose scoffed and leaned over to one of her sacks to dig out her straps. With swordplay being next, she needed her ankle strong and sturdy. "I'm not here to find companionship, Evony. I'm here to win a tournament and remind Eira I'm more valuable with a weapon in my hand than sitting on a throne."

"Who says you can't do both?" She wiggled her shoulders and walked over to the tent entrance. She lifted the flap and looked around outside. "What is the point of being a warrior if you can't have fun?"

It had been too long since she had that type of fun. While Evony never missed an opportunity to point out who she found attractive and who she thought would be a good fit for Rose. Rose enjoyed a handsome man as much as the next person. But her relationships were few. These days, she was so focused on trying to find Amelia these days; it was almost like she'd forgotten men existed.

"I guess it doesn't hurt to look," Rose admitted. Maybe she'd go seek Sir Filbert at the banquet that evening.

She slid her boot off and rolled up her pant leg to reveal the twisted limb underneath. There was never a time Rose didn't have this misshapen leg as it was an injury because of complications during her mother's pregnancy and giving birth. A birth which led to her mother's death. It wasn't something she thought about often, her mother. Rose didn't remember her since she was only a baby. She was told Father wandered around the castle, a shell of the man he used to be. When she was a child, the few times she saw Grandmother, there was something about the way she looked at Rose that made her feel guilty. Maybe like it was Rose's fault her daughter was gone. The daughter who was supposed to be Kutlaous's next minister and live in Eral Forest.

Rose resolved those thoughts years ago, and Father returned to his normal self, and she loved visiting Grandmother in Eral. It was no one's fault there were complications. When she wore Mother's red cloak, she found strength and comfort in it. But while Rose wrapped up her ankle and watched the surrounding tattoo straighten from thorny vines to Aros's sword surrounded by white and red roses, she wondered if maybe some of those feelings still lingered. Why she still felt the need to prove herself. Once done, she shoved the pant leg down again as though it could hide not only her leg, but the memories and feelings attached to it. Rose asked who he was up against for the next match.

Evony turned back to Rose but didn't face her and instead fixed her wavy dark brown hair, conveniently blocking her eyes.

"Evony?"

She pulled out from her pocket the most updated bracket and handed it to Rose, who grabbed it and unfolded the parchment. Her words were crooked and hastily scratched across the page, but legible and still with Evony's signature dramatic swirls and loops she used for all her correspondence. Which usually was a party invitation. The name of Rose's next competitor was clear. Rose folded it again and handed it back to her.

"Cal. It's fine. I've fought against him before."

Evony finally looked at Rose again and pocketed the page. "I know. Do you think competing against each other makes things more complicated?"

Rose tested her ankle to make sure the straps were tight. She bounced up and down on her heels. "Complicated? What do you mean by that?"

Her friend placed her hands on her curvaceous hips. "Are you telling me you don't see the way Cal looks at you? He's crazy about you."

"What? Cal isn't crazy about me. He's my best friend."

"Oh, please. Everyone knows it but you, apparently. I would have sworn you did, too."

Rose stretched one of her arms over to the other side. "That is the most ridiculous thing I have heard." But as the words came out of Rose's mouth, they sounded hollow. Maybe there were moments she caught Cal looking at her, but they were friends. Surely there were times she looked at him without him realizing it.

Evony raised a brow. "Why do you think he's stayed at Farren Castle even though he doesn't have to? He's not threatened by Amelia anymore. He could have gone off and done whatever he wanted or gone to search for her. But he stayed."

Rose switched to the other side in her stretch. "They offered him a position on the guard. It made sense."

Evony shrugged. "Maybe. And you don't have any feelings toward him at all?"

"I care about him obviously, Cal's my friend. He's like my br…" But she couldn't finish the sentence. It made sense for Rose to see him like a brother but saying it out loud didn't feel right.

Rose wanted to take it back because of the smile on Evony's face. "I thought so."

Rose finished her stretching and went over to her weapons to get her sword. "Weren't you wanting me to seek Sir Filbert? Now you want me with Cal?"

"Well, who says you can't have both?"

Of course, that would be Evony's answer. Rose should have known. She grabbed her sword and hooked it to her belt, then unsheathed the blade.

"Just think about it, will you? And if you determine you don't see Cal that way, I'd tell him sooner rather than later so he can get a move on his life. Diar knows he's been pining for too long."

Rose gripped the hilt and pursed her lips. "He hasn't been pining."

She gave the sword a few practice swings, and in a flash, yellow eyes appeared, then vanished from the metal. Rose dropped the sword and it thudded to the ground, making Evony jump.

"Are you okay? What's wrong?"

Rose turned the sword back and forth so that she could see the blade. But the eyes were gone. Was she seeing things? This was the second time now. She must be seeing things. No one was around but her and Evony. Let alone a shape-shifting wolf that may or may not serve the goddess of death. She shook her head.

"Nothing, just lost my grip for a second."

Evony raised a brow but said nothing. Even if she wanted to, she would have been interrupted because the trumpets sounded. It was time to prepare for the next event.

Rose took in a deep breath. "Well, here we go."

They ventured back out into the heat of the summer day after she sheathed the sword.

People filled the seats, ready to cheer for their favorite warriors. Even children joined in and wore the colors of their favorite knights and guards and painted their faces to resemble their banners.

Rose tried to push the image of the yellow eyes and her conversation with Evony out of her head as she greeted spectators and mentally prepared for her fight with Cal. She needed to focus on winning this event and showing everyone what she could do. Rose's goal was twofold. One, help people to trust Eira and her judgement of whom to ally with. Two, to show Eira where she was most useful.

This was not the time to be wondering about beings she hadn't seen or spoken to in months or potential romantic endeavors. No. Not potential. Nonexistent. Evony didn't know what she was talking about.

Rose hoped.

"Your highness?" A tiny voice rang out from the crowd. At Rose's side stood a little girl dressed in a blue and silver tunic with a crescent moon on the front. She looked up at Rose through shining brown eyes and coiled black hair that fell into her face.

Rose smiled at her. "Hello there." She crouched to see the child eye to eye. "And what is your name?"

"Abigail," the little girl answered, her voice still soft and light like a bell. She held something behind her back and pulled it out. It was a small doll with curly red hair, freckles all over her nose, and a set of white straps wrapped around her ankle. A lump formed in Rose's throat. "Would you sign her for me? You're my favorite."

Rose's heart warmed. Evony had told her there'd been dolls made in her likeness, but she hadn't seen one before and thought it was a fib to encourage her in tournaments. "I would love to." Abigail handed Rose the doll along with something to write with, and Rose propped it on her knee as a makeshift table to sign the doll's white ankle straps.

"Thank you, your highness. I think you're going to be a wonderful queen," Abigail told her once she had the doll handed back. She hugged it close to her chest, then hurried off to where her parents were waiting. The mother and father dipped into a bow and curtesy, and Rose nodded her head to them.

Her face flushed and her head spun a little, but glad Abigail left before she had the chance to say anything more. Poor thing. She did not know how terrible Rose was going to be as a ruler. When Eira took the throne, she hoped the child wouldn't be disappointed.

She crouched to the ground at the end of the fighting circle. A dwarf with a gray beard that almost touched the ground scribbled on a scroll longer than he was to take bets, and children stood in line to have their faces painted by an Efarae artist.

Across the way, Cal paced around, and his Kudo flew overhead. Usually, Cal had scores of fans lined up at these things, ready to greet him. Women threw their favors at him and asked for his signature on various parts of their bodies. Today, there were none. Odd.

Rose harrumphed as she stood again. The straps may have straightened her leg so she could stand, but if she knelt or crouched for too long, her knees ached. Only in her twenties and she had the aches and pains of Grandmother.

Rose tried not to pace in front of her bench to not wear out her straps prematurely while a tall fae with curly black hair and a flowing green dress announced her and Cal, but fidgeted with her gear and sending sporadic prayers to Aros, the god of war and hunting. She should have prayed to him earlier. Ah well, too late now.

She approached the ring and looked at Cal. His mouth was a thin line, and he gave her a slight nod, his knuckles white on the hilt of his sword. The sword of Aros on his arm glowed in anticipation. It made his already muscular arms grow even larger, and he took in a deep breath.

He wasn't the only one with Aros's magic, though. Rose closed her eyes and felt for her own powers, and her tattoo shone through the fabric of her pants. In moments, she could feel her muscles growing stronger, waves of energy pulsing through her body, and new air filling her lungs.

The horn sounded, and they circled one another. Rose made the first move. Block. Jab. Lunge. Dart. She predicted each move before he made them, knowing his habits, which side he favored, his favorite tricks. In fact, she barely broke a sweat.

That couldn't be right.

Some days, simply warming up with Cal was difficult, let alone training with him.

Aros curse him and stick an arrow in his ass.

Their swords clanged together, and Rose pushed Cal with all her strength until he fell onto his back with a thump. She knelt with her knee on his chest and held her sword against his neck. He was barely putting any pressure against hers. She could throw it out of his hand easily.

"What are you doing?" she hissed.

Cal furrowed his brows. "Fighting."

"You're not fighting, you're playing at fighting and letting me win."

Cal pursed his lips together. "What are you talking about?"

Rose put more pressure on his sword. "Make me fall—swear—yell —do what you always do." She looked around at the cheering crowd until she saw Eira in the top box next to Cadeyrn. "Do you want Eira to be embarrassed by our performance? Give her something to be proud of so she knows which side is stronger. Give yourself something to be proud of. When you lose, lose knowing you deserved it. Not the weak thing you are now."

Cal gritted his teeth. "I'm not weak."

Rose raised an eyebrow. "Are you sure?"

She slid across the ground to the other side of the ring after he shoved her off his body.

Much better.

Rose couldn't rise before Cal went at her again. She fought while still on her back until she saw an opening and wrapped her leg around his and twisted so he fell. She jumped to her feet as Cal did. The crowd went wild. This was what they came to see. A polite duel between friends wasn't entertainment. But two warriors pitted against each other, equal in strength and skill. That was something to watch. Cal may have been larger, but she was quick. Cal used all his strength and skill now. Rose's leg was trembling from the use, and her arms shook, but her heart pumped with pure adrenaline. It was hard, but exhilarating. They fought and sparred until sweat poured over their faces. Rose tried to wipe some off her face when something in the crowd caught her eye.

Or someone. With yellow eyes.

He was there, and Rose wasn't seeing things. Rafe, the thin and lanky wolf shifter with shaggy black hair, stood in the middle of the crowd and his eyes were directly on hers.

What was he doing here?

Cal's sword hit hers, and it flew out of her hand.

Rose expected for a roar of cheering to fill the stands, as Cal was usually such a fan favorite at tournaments. Instead, there were a few leering jests coming from the crowds. Someone boo'd Cal and made a rude hand gesture. She blinked a few times and shook her head. She must not have been hearing or seeing correctly. Thankfully, Cal didn't seem to notice as he circled around her, swinging his sword back and forth.

"Fuck," Rose said under her breath. She ducked and dodged his blade until she was at the edge of the ring, unable to go any further, and his sword tip hit her chest. His heavy breathing matched her own—he was as tired as she was. The horn sounded, announcing the end of the duel. Cal had won.

Cal lowered his sword and sheathed it. He raised an arm, calling to Kudo, who flew to them and landed on his shoulder. Cal looked over to Rose, who limped over to her sword.

"I hope you're happy," he said, and stormed away.

Rose let out a wordless cry and sheathed her sword again. Hardly anyone in the crowd was paying attention to her anymore, and as she looked around, Rafe was nowhere to be seen.

Chapter Seven

ROSE

That night at the banquet, Rose had to go back to using the crutch and a leather brace. She'd worn out the straps during the tournament and didn't have time to rest. It wasn't as though she was a wonderful dancer with them on anyway, but without them she was atrocious. Dancing with her crutch didn't go over well either.

Rose downed the remaining wine in the bottom of her goblet and let her leg rest, propped on a chair, as she watched her older sister, wishing they could speak. Rose knew she wasn't seeing things when Rafe appeared in the crowd, but now he was gone, and she hadn't seen him since. She should tell Eira what she'd seen. Since finishing dinner, Eira hadn't sat. Either she was dancing with someone or was bending an ear to a nobleman with a request, handling each conversation with grace. But now Eira was dancing with Cadeyrn and laughing. Rose wanted to go to her so they could talk but couldn't bring herself to interrupt her happiness.

"Care to dance?" Cal stood over Rose with a hand extended out to her.

Rose raised an eyebrow and wiggled her ankle. "I wouldn't be a good dance partner this evening."

Cal rolled his eyes. "It's a slower song. We barely have to move if you don't want to. "

Rose watched as the guests glided along the dance floor. They were all so graceful. It would be impossible to hide her limp and to dance with… Cal. She scowled, remembering the duel.

"I know you're mad but you should at least dance to one song, so people don't assume the future queen of Cresin is a boring wall flower," Cal said.

Rose scowled at the suggestion, but he had a point. If she was supposed to be helping Eira gain allies, she couldn't do that sitting down. She needed to attempt to look like she was having fun.

"Fine." She lowered her leg and went to grab her crutch, but Cal stopped her.

"We'll be fine without it. Let me help you."

"Don't carry me."

He'd carried her in the past when she over-exerted herself at practice, but always waited until no one was watching. Once, he dared when the other knights were around and Rose gave him a verbal lashing. He never tried again after.

"I won't."

With a gulp, Rose stood. Cal put an arm around her waist and led her to the edge of the dance floor. He held her so most of her weight was on him and Rose's sturdy leg, so she wouldn't have to worry as much about tripping. They swayed back and forth and made tiny circles. It wasn't anywhere close to how the other couples were dancing, but Cal was gentle and tried to help them move as gracefully as possible.

"It won't kill you to look at me," Cal whispered into her ear.

With a grimace, Rose looked into his pleading blue eyes. "You went easy on me."

"And you told me I was being a dumbass, and I gave you a proper fight," Cal pointed out. He left out how she had lost. Wisely so.

"I shouldn't have had to convince you to," Rose snapped. "Why would you do it? Was it some kind of charity? A way for you to seem like some upstanding gentleman? Did you think I wouldn't have a chance if you didn't?" Her voice rose, and the other guests were staring.

"Of course not," Cal hissed, trying to keep his voice low. "You know, I know you're a good fighter."

"So, why?" Rose asked, forcing her volume to match his. "I panicked. What was I supposed to do? You're the future queen. If I won, I was the jerk who beat you. If I lost, I would be…" He looked at the ground, trying to figure out what to say next. "They all love you, Rose. You know they do. Me? They hate me already. I beat you…" He shook his head. "It was selfish, and I'm sorry."

Rose jerked her chin back. "They what? They don't hate you."

Stunned, Cal stopped dancing and stared at her. "You can't possibly not realize they do. You heard them during the fight."

She had. Of course, she had. Rose just didn't realize Cal heard them too. She squeezed his shoulder and rested her chin on it. "How long has that been going on? You didn't have people asking for you signature either."

His arms wrapped around her tighter and they rocked back and forth in time with the slow music. There were two of them, no one else.

"I've always had people who haven't liked me and considered me their enemy. They knew who I worked for and didn't think I was trustworthy, which I understood. Things have changed now that the entire kingdom knows I served Amelia. If I won, they'd only hate me even more, and I'd never gain their trust. If I lost, they'd still disrespect me, but at least you'd have a win and make them happy. They need to love and respect you more than they do me."

They were silent for a moment, and Rose held onto Cal even tighter. He always said he didn't enjoy court or felt he fit in well, but it never bothered him. What did they think matter? She trusted him more than anyone else, and Father trusted him too. Cal was part of the guard and would do anything for Cresin.

"You're my friend. I want to be sure everything is all right between us." Cal finally looked back at her, and Rose met his gaze. "Are we all right?"

"Of course we are," Rose told him, even if she didn't entirely understand. Besides, she'd never let a stupid thing like a duel get between them. There was something different about this one because of the change in her status. Then the discussion she'd had with Evony must have gotten in her head more than Rose realized. It was done now, though. "Besides, you won fair and square. I got distracted when I shouldn't have."

Damn Rafe. When she met him so many months ago, she and Eira joked that she'd skin the wolf and use his fur for a cloak. The idea still sounded appealing.

Cal gripped Rose as he turned her in time with the music. "Yeah, what was that? You usually have good focus."

She debated if she should tell him or not. She hadn't mentioned Rafe back then and wasn't sure how to bring it up now. Someone needed to know and help her figure this out. Beyond Eira, Cal was the person Rose trusted more than anyone. "Do you remember the day you tried to kill us?"

Rose wanted to kick herself for the question. There wasn't a good way to bring up the subject of the day he tried to murder her.

Cal gulped, and his jaw stiffened. "Yes. What about it?"

"The reason Eira and I were there was because we'd gone to Eral Forest and saw a priest of Stula to find the cure for Father," Rose said.

"I remember."

"Well, while we were there, we met a wolf. He was a shape shifter named Rafe. I think he works for Stula, and he'd helped us find the priest and got us back to the edge of the forest." She took in a deep breath. "I saw him in the crowd. He has bright yellow eyes, and I thought I saw them in the armory. Then, while preparing for our duel, I saw them again. Then during our fight, he was there in the crowd. He was staring right at me."

Cal looked around like he could see the wolf there, too. "Why didn't you mention him before?"

Rose shrugged. "I don't know. I didn't think it mattered, and I haven't seen him since then."

"Why do you think he's here?"

She could only shrug again. "I don't know that either. By the time the fight was done, he was gone again."

Rose looked around the way Cal had, wondering if Rafe followed them there too. "I wanted to talk to Eira about it, but she's been busy."

The two of them were quiet as the other guests danced around them. Cal's grip was firm around Rose's waist, so she could allow herself to relax, even if it was just for the moment. Cal was always the person she could be around to relax. They were getting back to that place, and it was a bigger comfort than anything else.

She placed her hands on his shoulders and rested her chin on them, so the two of them pressed together even closer. So much she could feel his heart beating against hers. Rose swallowed, thinking about what Evony said earlier. Cal's firm hands shifted on the small of her back and she shivered.

Was Evony right?

No. She couldn't be. Cal wasn't a man of many words, but if there was something important, he brought it up. He would have told her. Right? Rose bit her lip. It wasn't as though she knew what sort of response she'd have, anyway. Her stomach fluttered at the thought.

"Cal…" His name was out of her mouth before she could think of what to say next.

He adjusted his stance so he could look at her better. "Yeah?"

"I…" She tried to form a thought, but when she lifted her chin from Cal's shoulder, a pair of yellow eyes appeared at the door. Rafe stood there, casually leaning against the frame wearing a black tunic with matching black trousers, his dark hair falling in front of his eyes, which were staring right at Rose as though he knew her thoughts. Rose straightened and met his gaze. An entirely different sort of shiver ran through her now. "Rafe is here."

Cal tensed and his fingers clenched around Rose's dress before letting go and turning to where she looked. Rafe pushed himself off the doorframe and jerked his head backward, showing he wanted Rose to follow.

"Let's go," Rose said.

Cal helped Rose back to her seat so she could grab her crutch. Then they made their way to the hallway where Rafe waited for them. He was a dark and smoky cloud lurking in the shining corridor filled with shimmering images of Luana and the stars. They made everything of stardust, marble, and glass. It made Rose worry that if she took the wrong step, she'd shatter the entire building. Having Rafe there only made her nerves even more on edge, seeing someone so dark occluding the space.

Rafe's yellow eyes darted from Rose to Cal. "Who's this? I wanted to talk to you alone."

"This is Cal," Rose answered, nodding to her friend. Cal stood at her side, his arms flexed and folded over his broad chest, giving a perfect view of the sword hanging at his hip. In comparison, Rafe looked like a twig Cal could easily snap in half. "Whatever you say, I will tell him anyway. What are you doing here?"

Rafe practically growled at them and something dark clouded his eyes, then vanished. But he switched his focus, so it was only on Rose, his brows furrowed together and body as tight as a bow's string. "You're needed in Eral."

Chapter Eight

ROSE

Rose's heart stopped for a beat at the darkness and intensity of Rafe's tone. Or maybe it was the slight desperation in his face. She shifted her weight from foot to foot and leaned more on her crutch. "What do you mean? What's wrong? Is it Grandmother?"

"Eral Forest is sick."

Rose and Cal exchanged looks. They could see the edge of it back home from Farren Castle, and from that view, at least it looked fine when they left. "What do you mean by sick?"

Rafe scratched his ear. And it looked like he was trying to explain it. "The trees are wilting. The ground is always wet, and there are mushrooms."

Rose's shoulders slumped, and she blinked a few times. Wet dirt and some mushrooms? That's what all this fuss was about? "So, you've had some rain, and there are always mushrooms. The fairies and pixies love them."

Rafe groaned and rubbed a hand over his face. "But it hasn't rained. And there are mushrooms… everywhere. And they're turning strange colors and the fairies, they're not the ones you once knew. One day they'll be bright and colorful and going about their usual tricks, and the next, they've changed. They're darker somehow."

Rose frowned. She was still doubtful, and from the look on Cal's face, he was too. Still, something didn't sit right about what he was saying.

"It's almost like Eral is drowning in poisoned water."

Drowning. Poison. Rose's eyebrows shot up, and she and Cal looked at each other. "Amelia," they said at the same time.

"Amelia must be hiding somewhere in Eral," Rose said. She gripped her crutch to contain her excitement. Finally, they might have a lead. "I know we've sent people out there, but they aren't familiar with Eral and how it's supposed to look, and it's so large and changes so often. It would be easy for Amelia to evade anyone searching for her."

She turned to face Rafe, whose face had paled a bit. "Do you think Amelia is hiding in Eral?"

Rafe shrugged and shook his head. "I'm not sure. We don't get involved the politics of the kingdoms. I suppose it's possible. But then, there are the ogres."

"Ogres?" Cal repeated. The way his stance shifted and stiffened, Rose could tell this caught his attention. "What have they been up to?"

"They're growing restless and there have been more run-ins and trouble with them than usual."

But if the situation was so dire, and it could be Amelia who was causing it, there was still something off about the situation. Out of all people, Rafe wasn't the one she'd expect to reach out to her about it. Rose strummed her fingers on her crutch. "Why hasn't Grandmother told us anything? Why are you the one out here? She could have written or come to visit Farren."

Grandmother's visits were rare, as with her position as Kutlaous's Minister. She was bound to Eral Forest and could only leave for short periods of time. It was like the way Eira and Aytigin were bound. But if there was something amiss, surely Grandmother would have at least sent a letter.

"Is my grandmother well? She's not sick or harmed or anything is she?" Rose asked.

"She's fine. But she isn't getting any younger." There was a hint of a tease in Rafe's voice and a small smile on his thin lips.

"She's not that old," Rose shot back right away. But, when she thought about it, Grandmother wasn't particularly young either, and it wasn't like life in Eral Forest was easy. It would be only natural for such a lifestyle to catch up with her. She lifted her ankle a couple of inches off the ground and rotated it back and forth. Cal did his best to be sure she didn't put too much weight on it while they danced, but it was still sore from the whole day of activity.

"You'd be amazed at how many times she's had to get out of a few rough pinches," Rafe told her. "She's not as resilient as she used to be. Not that she would admit it."

Wasn't that the truth?

"I need to sit." Rose scanned the hallway and found a bench off to the side and walked over to it. She took a seat and stretched her leg out in front of her. It wouldn't do any good for her to be sore and tired during this conversation, even if it meant Rafe stood over her now. Cal took the space next to Rose and, to her surprise, Rafe crouched lower so he was more at her eye level.

She ignored his considerate actions and kept going with the issue at hand. "What am I supposed to do? I don't know why you need me."

"You're the minister's granddaughter, her last relative. Don't you have her magic?" Rafe said it so matter-of-factly for a moment Rose felt silly for asking in the first place.

"Rose and Eira," Cal pointed out. "And Eira has the support of a dragon and one of Oxare's strongest warriors. You could have sought her out."

Rafe scratched behind his ear. "Princess Eira would be of help if she were willing. But her gifts from her fae bloodline have always been weak, I've been told. With all the power she now has from Luana, I'm sure she hasn't taken the time to strengthen them and has gotten weaker. Rose, you might have more access to that magic and be able to assist."

Rose leaned back against the glass wall and could almost feel the stardust inside of it. She and Eira both had been born with fae magic. This was true. It came from their mother and grandmother's line. But they were only a fraction of fae, so their powers were weak as it was. Rose may not have had an encounter with a deity the way Eira did, but she was dedicated to Aros. Which meant her focus and practice went to that magic, and not of that from her bloodline. If she'd dedicated herself to Kutlaous, it would have been a different story. Grandmother had chastised them both about it for years.

"But you know I'm dedicated to Aros," Rose said.

"Which would be more helpful in this situation than star magic anyway."

Cal nudged Rose with his shoulder. "He has a point."

The two of them watched Rose as though she were the most fascinating being they'd ever seen. She looked back and forth between them. Rafe with his shining yellow eyes, intense and almost desperate. Then Cal, facial expression impossible to read to anyone but her. He took a seat next to her on the bench, thick brows furrowed over his blue eyes, waiting for her call but patient.

It was her call, and the thought made Rose want to squirm in her seat. Even on the guard she reported to the captain, and while she was acting as the next in line for the throne, her father, King Brennan, was still the one who reigned. She never wanted to be the one making the ultimate decision. If it was something that affected her and no one else, that was one thing. But those other choices that would impact other people and maybe even the kingdom? It was too much pressure. Too many expectations. Expectations, she was sure no matter what she did would hurt or disappoint someone else, and Rose wasn't sure if she could handle that.

The truth of it was, though, she wanted to go. Something deep inside of her knew she needed to go to Eral and at least check in on Grandmother to be sure everything was all right. Besides, if what Rafe was saying was true, not only would Rose be able to help Eral, she also might find Amelia, and show everyone where Rose truly should be. With a sword in her hand and not on a throne.

Rose balked at her own indecision. It wasn't even a choice. Of course she was going to go. There was no question.

She rolled her shoulders and grasped her crutch to stand. "We'll tell Eira and return to the mountain to prepare and leave as soon as possible."

Rafe's smile grew wide, showing off his pointed canines, and even Cal had a glint in his eye. It was all she needed to feel even more confident about her choice.

Now, it was just a matter of telling Eira.

———

PRIESTESS CORVINA WAS KIND ENOUGH TO LET EIRA USE HER PERSONAL study to meet with Rose, Cadeyrn, Aytigin, and Rafe, where they told her about Rafe's message. Rose's heart sank further and further into her stomach with each word, making it more real than it felt before. Eral was sick, the ogres were growing restless, and Grandmother hadn't told either of them a thing. Eira tapped the tips of her fingers against her thumbs, a habit she picked up when trying to calm herself.

"Cal and I are going to go help," Rose said once they finished telling Eira the situation. Her sister's eyes grew wide, and her mouth opened in surprise. Rose hated to leave so soon and to disappoint Eira like this. Especially after their argument the day before. But they needed to go. "We think Amelia could be behind it. We could find her, Eira. If she is the one behind it, we can not only put an end to whatever ails the forest but also capture her for good."

Eira swallowed and nodded, leaning into Cadeyrn, who placed a palm on her back. "Of course you're going to go. I wouldn't dream otherwise."

"We plan to return to the mountain tonight to gather a few things, then leave as soon as possible," Cal added. He remained standing strong near the door, one hand on the hilt of his sword, as though he were prepared to defend them against attackers at any moment. He turned to Aytigin, who was inspecting the bookcases with one of his long claws. "If we could make use of your armory, we would appreciate it."

Aytigin only raised a brow like they bore him with the conversation. But Rose could tell by how taught his white wings here that while he pretended to be uninterested and examined Priestess Corvina's book collection, he'd been listening in on every word. From what Eira told her, Amelia manipulated and used him the way she had the rest of them. She used his dedication and obsession with the goddess Luana to trap Eira there and promised Eira would break the curse for him. Which Eira was going to do so. But not because of something Amelia did.

The dragon tore himself away from the books and stood in front of Cal, arms folded across him. He was lean and lithe in comparison with Cal's arms the size of tree trunks and broad chest, but with the impressive wingspan and long tail with ancient calculating ice-blue eyes, Rose couldn't help but wonder which of them would win in a battle if pitted against each other.

"Which did you want to take?" he asked.

Cal opened his mouth, but Rose beat him to it. "We want to take the Shadowslayers."

The room went silent, and even Rafe, who'd been reclining against a windowsill during the entire conversation, perked at the announcement. Rose almost saw his shaggy black hair stand straighter.

"You have the Shadowslayers?" Rafe asked.

Aytigin snapped his head toward Rafe so quickly Rose thought his neck might break. "And you will not take them. No one will. They're the most powerful weapons in existence and if anyone will use them, it'll be me, and I will not be joining you in my circumstances being what they are. Don't even think of getting them on your own. I have spells on them you won't be able to break and if you did, I'd know."

Rose doubted he would go with them, anyway. Even if it weren't for him and Eira being bonded, she couldn't imagine him wanting to leave Malle's spirit. She rolled her neck to ease some of the tension gathering there and prayed to Aros Eira would talk reason to Aytigin and they could bring them. If the Shadowslayers were as powerful as legends claimed, they could solve killing Amelia. Surely, Eira would see things from her side.

"I agree with Aytigin," Eira finally said. Rose's heard dropped, and she gripped her crutch even tighter when Eira refused to look at her. "If Aytigin and I went with you, that would be one thing. But since we won't and we don't know what they do, I have to agree. I can't risk you getting hurt. I'm sorry. Besides, if you find Amelia, I want you to bring her to me alive."

Rose felt her face turn as red as the flower she was named after. "Eira, we don't know what's out there. We need to use any tool necessary."

"I assure you, we would do everything in our power to protect them," Cal added.

"You can use any other weapons," Eira told them in a lowered voice. "I'm sorry."

Cal gave Rose a small shrug of his shoulders, unhappy but accepting of the situation. His blue eyes pleaded with her to let it go, and her stomach twisted. Maybe if they brought Amelia to Eira, they could use the weapons then. What other options did they have at this point? She sighed and nodded. "Fine. And you want Amelia alive? What if she escapes again?"

Snowflakes and stars floated around Eira and a new icy expression came over her older sister's face. "Don't worry, she won't."

Chapter Nine

ROSE

AYTIGIN FLEW ROSE AND CAL BACK TO THE MOUNTAINS, WHILE RAFE turned into his wolf form to run the way there. At least Aytigin and Eira could be at least that far apart for short periods of time. Rose had never ridden on the back of a dragon before, and wished the experience was under different circumstances. She sat behind Cal, wrapped her arms around his firm torso, and rested her cheek against the back of his shoulder. Beside them, Cal's hawk Kudo soared through the air and let out a gleeful screech.

Cal looked behind him at Rose. "You don't get a view like this back home."

She shook her head. They really didn't. During the journey to Paravia, Rose saw the landscape and appreciated how gorgeous it was. But viewing the peeks of the mountains from above with their white tips and the green trees and valleys and creeks below, even at night when there was only the moon and stars to light the scenery, she could have looked at it forever. It was moments like these when Rose felt the most in touch with her fae side. Something deep within her she barely recognized jittered and buzzed with excitement.

When the ride was calm, Rose pushed herself to sit straighter and arched her back with arms outstretched, letting the night air blow through her hair. Kudo let out another screech and flew loops and swirls around Aytigin. It was like riding a horse through an open field. Like it was only you in the entire world. Only better. Instead of the wide field, there was the endless night sky. If only it wasn't Aytigin, the dragon she was riding on, the old grump. Eira claimed he was getting better and hoped Rose could get to know him better. Oh well, plans changed.

But Aytigin didn't seem to mind because he couldn't have gotten away fast enough. Almost the moment Rose and Cal set foot inside the mountain, he was off in a whoosh, leaving a trail of smoking ice in his wake. The two of them stood there, looking at the space where he once stood, and caught their breath. It wasn't as though they expected him to stay long. The bond between Aytigin and Eira not only affected distance but also time. It still surprised Rose at how easily Aytigin could leave them at his beloved castle without him.

Rose and Cal looked at each other, shrugged, and headed into the castle. Their footsteps echoed against the walls in a way Rose hadn't noticed before while they walked through the entrance. No one was there to greet or assist them since Eira let the workers have the time off to enjoy the tournament.

Rose shivered and looked around for any sign of Rafe since he claimed he was going to meet them there. But it was only her and Cal, from what she could tell. It was like a haunted castle she'd read about in a book her governess used to read before bedtime.

An icy wind blew through the hall, and a soft cry was heard in a far-off room. Rose shivered again. It was possible this castle inspired all those tall tales.

At her side, Cal shook his head and Kudo flew around him, then landed on his shoulder. "I say we gather whatever we can and leave as soon as possible. This castle isn't my favorite."

"If we don't see this place until after Eira breaks the curse, I won't be sad."

Cal nodded, and they took quiet steps to their rooms. They may have been the only living people there, but Rose still didn't want to disturb anything. Eira had worked too hard to get so far in breaking the curse. And she didn't want to disturb the frail peace Malle was in at the moment. She hadn't encountered the spirit yet, but she'd been told Malle's fury was something to avoid at all costs.

Rose's hands almost shook with excitement as she threw together a pack. It'd been ages since she'd done something like this. She would travel with her family and carry out tasks with the guard before everything changed. There wouldn't be much she needed to bring. Rafe was going to get them to Eral Forest, so it would not be the days' long journey Eira and Cadeyrn had. They would stop at Grandmother's cottage first, so if there were any extra supplies they needed, it would be easy to get them there.

Among her things lay her mother's red cloak. In the summer heat, she wouldn't need its protection from the cold. But it helped her stay cool. Mother must have enchanted it to adjust to whatever season it was. She reached for it and slung it around her shoulders, her body relaxing under its protection.

Next, it was time for the armory.

Cal met Rose down there with his own small travel sack and Kudo still perched on his shoulder. They stood side by side looking into the armory and the vast array of weapons that were welcome to them. Anything they wanted from blades to knifes to bows and arrows to hatchets. There were weapons Rose had never even seen before and wouldn't know what to do with. Whatever they could ever wish and dream for.

Except for the ones Rose really wanted.

The Shadowslayers stood there in the back of the room, marked off from the rest, and when Rose saw them, her heart sank. She didn't understand it. Why didn't Eira see how necessary they could be?

"Rose… you're more than capable without them."

Rose blinked a few times and saw she'd gone toward the Shadowslayers without realizing. It was like they put her in a trance, and she lost all sight of anything else once she set her eyes on the shining steel. At least this time, she didn't see those yellow eyes. She shook her head.

"I know," she answered Cal and looked over her shoulder at him. He was already inspecting swords and comparing them. "They're just so pretty."

She smiled to make it seem like she was joking and not contemplating going against Eira's and Aytigin's wishes. To distract herself and get to what they were really there for, Rose went over to a table of knives and looked at her options. There was one small blade with vines etched into the metal and had the look of tree branches for the handle that would fit perfectly in the pouch Rose had on her crutch. She picked it up and inspected it for a moment before storing it away.

"I thought you wanted to take them too," Rose commented.

Cal practiced a few moves with a long sword around and the sound of it's swooshing through the air sang in Rose's ear.

"I do," Cal answered. "But I also don't want to cause more tension with your sister. Besides, we're both more than capable of managing without them."

"But what if they can kill Amelia?"

Cal stopped his testing and sheathed the sword, then strapped it along his back. He tugged the strap tight across his chest, maybe a little too tight, and paused. His fingers gripped around the leather strap, and she could tell scenes and moments were playing out in his mind. There was a haunted look in his blue eyes when he was thinking about his past employment with the former queen. He cleared his throat. "Then we'll be sure Aytigin and Eira allow them to be used when we bring Amelia back here. Eira wants her captured alive, remember?"

Unfortunately.

Rose grimaced and turned away. He was right. She knew he was. But something still tugged at her when the Shadowslayers were near, and she didn't know how to shake the feeling away. They each gathered what they wanted with minimal conversation after that, only discussing details of what they planned to do when they arrived in Eral. Before long, they both had as much as they could carry and went back out.

Something tugged at Rose and when she got to the door, she turned and got one last look at the Shadowslayers. They almost seemed to glow.

"Why don't you just take them?"

Rose jumped at the fresh voice and let out a small cry. Even Cal grasped for one of his swords. Outside of the armory, Rafe stood there, leaning against the wall with arms crossed over his chest.

"They left the two of you here all alone. It's like that dragon was asking you to take them."

Rose and Cal both breathed sighs of relief and removed their hands from their weapons. Kudo offered the wolf a small disapproving caw.

Cal took a step toward him and gave him a piercing stare. "Because they trust us, and we will not betray that trust. We have orders."

Rafe raised a single brow. "Such a loyal lap dog, aren't you?"

"As though you're one to talk."

Rose wanted to roll her eyes. Men.

"It doesn't matter," Rose said. "We have enough and need to get going. I want to arrive at Grandmother's before morning if we can."

They could have rested, then left in the morning, but they all were too awake and eager to leave. There was no way Rose could get a moment of sleep and knew Cal felt the same way.

Rafe ignored her and pushed past them and went into the armory.

"Hey, didn't you hear me?" She gave Cal an exasperated look, then followed Rafe. "How did you get in here, anyway? Eira and Cadeyrn had to let us in before, and then Aytigin."

"I follow my own rules," was his only answer, and he didn't even look at them when he said it. He stood in front of the Shadowslayers and looked at them like a dog would with a long stick found in the woods he could play with. He waved an arm in front of them and the air around the weapons wavered like the ripples in a pond.

He took a step back and his yellow eyes roamed over the scene. "I might be able to get them. It'll hurt, but it's possible. Some warriors the two of you are, not even trying."

He might? Rose's heart skipped a beat. The idea made her more excited than it should have. If Aytigin was telling the truth, if they could get through the protections, he'd know they took them. He'd be furious and Eira betrayed. But... something hummed beneath Rose's skin, thinking about holding them. She took steps forward toward them and away from Cal.

"Rose, you can't be seriously thinking about it."

She tore her gaze away from the weapons, a feat more difficult than she expected, toward Cal. He was in the armory again too, arm outstretched toward her, his jaw tense and blue eyes piercing. There was a gleam in them, though, the one he had when he was about to do something dangerous but thrilling at the same time. He was thinking about it. What the two of them could do.

"Aren't you?" she asked.

Cal swallowed, and his arm slowly lowered to his side. "We can't."

Rafe finally shifted his stance so he could see the two of them, a sly half grin across his elfin face. He reached out toward the weapons again and the air wavered some more. The surrounding space turned a blue color and frost spread across his hand. But he was closer to them than he was before. "Are you sure about that?"

Magic beneath Rose's skin hummed. A little frost on her hand? If she used her Aros magic, it could be more tolerable. And she had her mother's enchanted cloak. A little cold she could handle.

Rafe moved so fast Rose barely saw him enter the warded off circle. He snatched the dagger, and he was back at Rose's side, a thin layer of frost covering him from head to toe in a harsh shimmer. His whole body shook from the cold, and tiny icicles hung from his nose and eyelashes and it plastered a wide blue lipped grin on his face. He tossed the dagger back and forth between two hands.

"Easy as can be." He stepped aside and bent at the waist in a mock bow, his arms outstretched toward the remaining weapons in a gesture inviting Rose to go next. "Will I be alone in this endeavor, Princess?"

"Rose…" Cal's hesitant voice made her pause, and Rose looked back and forth between him and Rafe. Cal was so loyal and dedicated, even if it went against what he wanted. He was good like that.

Rose never had been very good.

She gave Cal a smile that matched Rafe's and tightened her cloak around her shoulders, then stepped through the wavering air. The cold air made her gasp, and her lungs caved in on themselves. It wasn't just cold, it was freezing her down to her bones. A cold so deep she couldn't think or feel anything else. Far worse than even the harshest winters in Cresin. She thanked the deities for the cloak, otherwise it would have been far worse. Something bumped into her, making Rose lose her balance, and Rose saw Cal at her side, his lips already blue. He put an arm around her shoulder to steady her and they locked eyes.

Cal was also good like that. Even if he didn't agree, he was still on your side.

"I can't believe we're doing this," he said through chattering teeth.

"Believe it. Together?"

He nodded once. "Together."

They both reached for the other two Shadowslayers. Call took the sword and Rose the bow and arrows. Rose's skin zinged and warmed at the touch, and a flash of yellow eyes appeared in the arrow heads then vanished. They stepped out of the area, back into the warm armory, and Rose could have fallen to the ground in relief to be out of the frozen space. It was amazing. It didn't even look cold by the weapons. And they had no hint of frost or cold damage on them.

Rose looked at the bow in her hand and turned it back and forth, trying to convince herself it was really there. Magic inside of her sang in a way it never had before and it melted all the frost that had formed on her body off in moments. It was like holding it strengthened her muscles and senses sharper. The sensation was like how her Aros magic felt when she summoned it, but there was still something different about this. Like pieces of her magic were missing and now that she had this in her hand, it was complete.

Cal was staring at his weapon in awe, too. Did he feel the same way Rose did holding it? The frost melted off him into a small puddle on the floor, and he swished it back and forth a few times. Watching Cal with a sword always looked like a dance, and now it was pure art and magic.

"Pretty amazing, aren't they?" Rafe asked. He pretended he was jabbing someone with the dagger, then flipped it in the air and caught it by the handle. "I'd say worth the wrath of a dragon."

"At least if he comes after us, we can fight him back," Rose said. She handed her crutch to Cal, balanced herself on one foot, took one arrow, and notched it on the bow. She aimed it toward a practice target on the back wall and fired. The arrow soared through the air with a whoosh that almost sounded like a song, and it landed right in the middle of the target with a quiet thud. She lowered the bow and admired her handiwork. She barely even had to aim. "Incredible."

The word was barely out of her mouth when there was a low rumbling beneath her feet. Rose grabbed onto her crutch again to keep from losing balance. Cal and Rafe lowered their blades as the room shook. Weapons all around them trembled and hovered into the air.

Rose's stomach dropped. Oh no. Of course, it had been too easy.

The trembling weapons rose higher until they were at eye height, then they all turned and pointed directly at Rose, Cal, and Rafe. The three of them crept closer together into a tight circle, the Shadowslayers at the ready. Rose took in a deep breath and prepared herself for the worst. Rafe grabbed her arm.

"Run," he instructed.

They needed no more encouragement and took off out of the armory as the other weapons flew toward them. Rose quickly fell behind and she cursed, not having the sense to have put on her straps earlier. Knives and arrows flew past her, and one scraped against her arm, leaving a thin slice of red across her sleeve. She hissed and dove to the ground, belly down, and crawled away on her elbows and holding her crutch. A sword flew overhead and aimed right toward Cal's back.

"Cal!"

He looked behind him and dodged away in time. Then, seeing Rose on her stomach crawling along, he turned around and ran toward her. "Get on my back," he said.

Rose shook her head. She'd only weigh him down. Her theory of staying close to the ground helped, but it wasn't fast enough. The cloak helped protect her too, though it wouldn't be enough. They needed a quicker way to get out. She and Cal dodged another knife, and she propped herself up. "Rafe, you need to shift!"

Rafe tossed the knife to Cal, who caught it with one hand, then transformed into his wolf form. He dodged flying weapons with easy leaps and bounds when he turned around and made his way back to Rose and Cal. They climbed on top of him like a horse, Rose behind Cal, and she struggled to strap her crutch to her back so she could hold on with both hands. As she did, an arrow soared past and scraped her shoulder. She hissed, but it didn't seem to be a deep wound. Something she could take care of once they were back to safety. At least now they were all together and could make a quicker escape. They ran through the door of the armory, Rafe sliding along the way. Rose screeched as she and Cal held on for dear life. "Someone close it!"

Cal jumped off and slammed the door shut. All the weapons that hadn't escaped with them slammed against the door so hard Rose thought they would break it down. But it stayed shut and only a few other weapons that escaped with it flew out and down the hallway, giving the three of them a moment to breathe. Rafe and Cal and various scrapes across their arms and hands- or paws rather, in Rafe's case - and Cal had a red mark over his cheek. Rose had the scrapes on her shoulder and another on her arm.

Cal's breathing was heavy, and he placed his hands on his hips like a legendary hero. "All things considered, that could have been worse."

Then, the stone floor shook beneath them, and a cold fog rose from their feet. A piercing shriek filled the air that sent a whole other type of chill through Rose.

They'd woken Malle.

"I wouldn't speak so soon," Rafe told Cal.

Malle's spirit floated through the wall and hovered in front of them, her eyes blazing. "You took them. You took my love's weapons."

Her words were quiet yet seethed with a rumbling fury. The castle trembled again and Rose gripped Rafe's black fur. They could drop the weapons right there and leave them be. Maybe it would calm Malle down. She felt a warmth on her back from the bow and arrows like they were telling her to not let them go, to keep them as close as possible.

"You will pay!" the spirit yelled. She stretched out her fingers and arm so some stray pieces of stone floated in front of her and shoved them toward Rose and Rafe.

In a flash, Cal was in front of them, his tattoo blazing to give him extra strength and speed, and a shield to block the flying stones.

"I'm getting really tired of shit flying at me," Rafe grumbled.

Still using the shield to continue blocking the flying stones, Cal climbed back on Rafe's back, and they ran down the hall. The castle shook all around them, and paintings and statues came alive to reach out toward the trio of thieves and stop them from leaving. Cal lowered the shield and traded it for the sword while Rose got out her bow and arrow. They struck and aimed toward each opposition, clearing them all out of the way with ease. All the while, Malle flew behind them, keeping the air as cold as winter, making Rose's teeth chatter.

"Do you think you can outrun her?" Rose asked Rafe, needing to raise her voice over the sound of the trembling castle and Malle's shrieks.

Rafe chucked, and the feel of it rumbled beneath Rose. "Put away your weapons and hold on."

They did as they were told, and Rose wrapped her arms around Cal's torso as tightly as she could while he gripped Rafe's fur. Black smoke filled the area around them, and the castle turned blurry. Then Rafe shot forward. Rose let out a wordless yell of surprise, but something stifled as soon it as it released, they moved so fast. Everything was a blur, and she couldn't even tell where they were. The speed took her breath away and made her stomach turn and clench. Crashing and shrieking and yelling rang in her ears. Still, she buried her face in Cal's back and held on.

Finally, Rafe skidded to a halt. Rose looked up, and it took a moment for it to feel like the world stopped spinning around her. Once it did, she saw they were outside of the mountain. Somehow, Rafe got them out of the castle and down the mountain in a matter of minutes. She and Cal's chests heaved from having the wind knocked out of them.

Cal leaned over so he could look at Rafe. "Any chance you can get to Eral Forest that fast?"

Rafe's tail wagged behind Rose, and it brushed past her hair.

"That was the plan. We don't have time to waste. As long as it's okay with our leader."

It took Rose a moment to realize they were talking about her. She blinked a few times and looked out toward the mountains. Eral Forest wasn't visible from that vantage point, but she could almost feel it calling out to her the way the weapons did. She took in a deep breath and nodded, even though Rafe and Cal probably couldn't see her.

"Let's go."

Chapter Ten

AMELIA

AMELIA TRUDGED THROUGH ERAL FOREST, FOLLOWING THE DIRECTIONS the Stulan priest gave her. She was traveling further away from the swamp and deeper into the forest proper, but the ground still squished beneath her feet and there was still a humidity in the air that made her clothes stick to her skin. Behind her, Charis slid and stumbled through the forest terrain, the mud making her lose her footing almost every other step.

"I thought when we left the swamp, it would be dryer," she grumbled. "At least in the cottage I can stay out of the water."

Amelia referred to the notes on where to go and let Charis catch up a bit. Even if it was tempting to lose the girl somewhere in the forest and be done with her. "I thought you wanted to do something other than wait in the cottage. You've been complaining for weeks."

"Well… yes. But maybe something closer to proper civilization?" Charis tripped on a protruding tree root and landed in a circle of mushrooms. The tiny pixies hiding in there swarmed up around her in a tizzy, their wings fluttering like a hummingbird with black and blue shimmering dust trailing behind them.

Charis swatted at them like they were flies, which only made the situation worse. They buzzed in anger and took grabbed strands of her hair and pulled. She shrieked and stomped her feet and turned and flailed her arms around. Amelia folded her notes and stuffed them back in her pocket and laughed, which only made Charis stomp her feet more.

"It's not funny!"

This only made Amelia toss her head back and laugh more. At least Charis was useful for one thing. To keep Amelia amused. Unfortunately, they needed to get a move on. Once she calmed herself, Amelia stepped up to the scene and had to bite back another laugh at the sight of the pixy biting Charis's earlobe. That only made Charis wail even louder.

Amelia clapped her hands and a douse of water poured over all of them, soaking Charis and the pixies to the bone, but also stopping the miniature attack. The pixies all turned to face Amelia in unison, their beady black eyes blinking at her. The lot of them were a pale sickly blue with dark black circles around their eyes. Odd. Usually, pixies came in a range of colors. It was rare to find two that looked alike side by side, and here was a whole swarm that all looked exactly alike.

Someone else's problem.

"Good, now that I have your attention and you've stopped attacking my companion, you will show me where I can find the ogre camp, or I'll make a constant downpour over you for the rest of your miserable little lives, which I'm sure will make them even shorter since you'll likely drown in it."

That silenced them even more. One of them, a minuscule male from the looks of it, hovered forward and with a jerk of his head directed Amelia where to go. They all followed him in a black and blue shimmering cloud and Amelia and Charis went with them.

"Did you have to get me wet, too?" Charis asked as they walked, wringing out her skirt, which had a layer of mud caked on the hem.

"I got them off you. Be grateful."

The pixies led them through more of Eral Forest, and when Amelia took the time to notice, there were gatherings of mushrooms around each tree. All of them are green and black and blue with growths on top of growths. The blue shimmer of more pixies flitted between the mushrooms and up into the fungi infested trees. They could barely walk without almost stepping on a mushroom, which surely housed a pixie or two. It was a wonder they hadn't bothered them until now.

"You're a sorceress. I don't understand why we have to walk through the forest like this," Charis complained. Amelia held in a grimace. Did she never stop moaning and groaning? "Aren't you supposed to fly us around on a broom or something?"

Amelia laughed. "That's ridiculous. Don't listen to children's stories."

It didn't matter that they had to travel though, because before long, the sound of drums and laughter echoed off the trees. Ahead was a small clearing with a circle of carts and tents and half-built huts with a blazing fire pit in the middle. Tall ogres, at least a head taller than any man Amelia'd ever seen, stood between all the entrances. Amelia covered her nose to block the stench of mud and sweat and alcohol and blood that infested the air. Ogres were disgusting creatures.

But beggars couldn't be choosers. As much as Amelia hated to admit it, when it came to allies, she was a beggar. And having something big and ugly and brutal on your side had its uses.

She waved off the pixies. "You may go, and I won't drown you. This time."

The pixies chattered and flitted away, back to whatever mushrooms they could find to make a home in and dance the night away.

Charis's jaw had dropped, and she let go of her wet skirt. "Ogres. You want us to visit ogres. I won't, I can't, we can't…"

Amelia ignored her babbling and walked forward, her heart pounding. She'd never gone to an ogre camp before and knew they hated humans. While Amelia wasn't entirely human, she was close enough. She'd rested all day before and didn't use a piece of magic until her minor threat to the pixies to be sure she had enough energy to sum up any magic she needed to face them should the need arise. She never had an issue with energy before, but she didn't want to risk it.

"Get your flute out," Amelia instructed, and Charis complied. This was the real reason she brought the girl with her. Not for company, for Amelia would have preferred to go alone. But because she'd done wonders with putting the guards at the Golden Palace to sleep while aiding in her escape with the flute.

Amelia beckoned to Charis, and they crouched behind a tall bush, two guards in their view. They looked even taller up close, with sharp fangs protruding from their lower lips into their green skin, and Amelia took in a few deep breaths. She was a queen and a sorceress. She could handle a few ogres. "Play the sleeping spell."

Charis's hands shook as she put the instrument to her lips, and the first few notes were shaky, but it did the trick. As the song went on, the eyelids of the guards grew heavy, and they leaned against the sides of the huts. Little by little, they put more of their weight on the stick walls and slid to the ground fast asleep.

Once Amelia deemed it safe, they tiptoed their way between two huts thatched together with sticks, mud, and grass, Charis still quietly playing her song. It was like water sliding between rocks.

They entered the camp and all around the bonfire were tall, muscular, green ogres eating and drinking. Some danced along with the sound of the drums, while others sat on large logs slobbering down on a piece of meat, and others showed off their huge clubs and weapons. Amelia scanned the area to find who she truly was looking for. But it didn't take long. The water magic flowing inside Amelia splashed and swirled with excitement. She smiled.

There in front of the fire was a large stone chair, almost throne-like with its thick arm rests and engravings and soft cushion, sat the chief, Kartek. She lounged on the throne with one leg propped on an armrest, and ate from a string of grapes, her short leather skirt showing off her muscled legs. A necklace of fangs hung around her neck, the longest in the middle landing directly on her cleavage that was only covered by a thin leather piece wrapped around her. White tattoo stripes covered her body, and she shaved half of her hair on one side that showcased her pointed ears. Her jewelry and tattoos flickered in the firelight. A queen in her own right.

Well, Amelia was a queen too. And she knew Kartek wanted something, and Amelia was the one who would give it to her.

Amelia straightened her shoulders and stepped away from the protective shadows of the huts into the firelight. A few notes from Charis's flute wavered, but Amelia could still hear it in her ear, so knew the young woman was still behind her, even if she was nervous. She and

Charis had taken a small tonic before leaving to find the camp, so they were immune to the flute's song. One by one as they walked in, ogres fell to the ground asleep in loud thuds. But it didn't take long for them to be noticed, which was fine by her.

Kartek raised her head and shoulders from their reclining position and looked through the crowd.

"Who's there?" Her voice boomed through the camp, and all the ogres stopped what they were doing to look. When Kartek saw the invaders, her yellow eyes narrowed. "Come to me."

The camp all turned to where Kartek was looking and stared at Amelia and Charis. A weak note that sounded more like a squeak played out of the flute, but nothing that could put anyone to sleep. Amelia gestured to Charis to lower the flute, and she did.

Amelia stepped forward and all the ogres parted for them to walk through, obeying their queen's orders. But Amelia could see the hatred and bloodlust in their eyes and in the way they gripped their weapons. Some puffed out their chests, showing off the fangs on their jewelry and tattoos, displaying their strength and how many kills they had. Charis whimpered at Amelia's side, but they kept walking, Amelia's head held high.

She wasn't tall and muscular, but she had a few kills in her past, too.

Kartek chuckled and sat upright on her throne, both feet on the ground now. "Well, well, well, what do we have here? A disgraced sorceress and…" She grimaced, looking at Charis. "A fancy lady? Whatever did I do to earn such an honor?" Sarcasm dripped from the words, and a cruel smile played on her lips.

Water boiled within Amelia. How dare she speak to them in such a way? She clearly knew who Amelia was, and yet she still dared to disrespect her like this. Amelia could drown this ogress from the inside out. Did she know that? Water flowed out from Amelia's fingers and into orbs around her hands.

The only way for an ogre to take someone seriously was through force. It was a good thing this was something Amelia was intimately familiar with.

"I wouldn't mock us if I were you," Amelia said and threw out a hand toward one ogre standing at Kartek's side. Within moments, he gurgled and choked. He dropped his spear and held his hands against his throat while water trickled out of his mouth. Kartek watched with her chin propped up on one hand as though she were bored, but Amelia knew better. There was a glint in the ogress's eyes of interest and curiosity.

Kartek leaned back in her seat. "That's enough. I understand your point."

But did she? The ogre was in Amelia's grasp and power now. Amelia was in complete control, something she hadn't been in for so long. Her heart sped at the sensation of it.

"Enough!"

As much as she didn't want to, Amelia let go of her hold. The ogre collapsed on the ground, making the whole camp shake, his arms catching him. He coughed and wheezed as he tried to fill his lungs with air. Killing one of Kartek's people wouldn't be the best way to gain her trust, anyway. But at least she gained some respect.

"Disrespect me again, and I could do the same to you," Amelia said.

Kartek raised an amused brow. "I'm sure. Now, sorceress, what are you doing in my camp?"

"I have a proposition for you," Amelia answered. "It is my understanding your people have been unhappy for some time and hold a personal grudge against the royal family of Farren. I've heard you been destructing part of Eral Forest because of it."

Kartek crossed one muscular leg over the other and folded her hands over her stomach. Amelia couldn't read her expression. This ogress was smart to not let Amelia see what she was thinking. If what she'd heard about ogres was correct, most weren't that way. They would just rip her head off. "Some ogres would say we're taking back what is ours. As for the grudge you mention, yes, there are some of us who would say they have denied us something."

"And what do you say?" Charis asked. Her eyes went wide and her face paled, as though she was as shocked as Amelia that she dared ask the question.

Kartek still looked amused but closed off. "I say, I do what's best for myself and my clan. Other chiefs hid us away but then would kill anything they wanted, and, getting themselves killed. Did you know I'm the third chief within a year to sit in this seat?"

Amelia shook her head. "It doesn't sound like a steadfast way to rule."

"I agree. The ogres should be more and do more. I want us to have respect."

There it was. The way Amelia could get in. "I can get you respect."

Kartek took a handful of grapes and poured them into her mouth. "Oh, really? How would a disgraced sorceress and former queen do that?" she asked as she chewed.

Amelia kept herself from cringing. Perhaps if the ogress learned some manners, she'd be more on her way to gaining respect. She took in a deep breath to focus. "I have it under a good authority that Eral Forest will change hands soon and will need a new Minister."

The entire camp stilled at her words, and she could feel every eye on her. Kartek lowered the vine of grapes and leaned forward.

"Is there something wrong with the current Minister?" she asked. Her voice remained low and casual, but there was a hint of nervousness behind it.

"She will not be with us much longer," was all Amelia said. "And I understand many can lobby for the position. There's a competition of some sort?"

"Yes, but no ogre has won it."

"What if I can promise you will?"

Kartek leaned back in her seat and strummed her claws on the edge of the armrests. Her yellow eyes narrowed as she stared and considered Amelia and Charis. "You can ensure I win and become the next Minister?"

Amelia nodded. "And when you are Minister, the two of us can take our revenge on the Farren royal family. There's just a couple of small things I need you to do that will help us both."

Chapter Eleven

ROSE

THE WORLD PASSED BY IN A BLUR, LEAVING ROSE WITH A TURNING stomach and spinning head with the echoes of a roaring dragon ringing in her ears. Aytigin must have known the weapons were gone because as they ran out of the mountains, his roar bounced off the mountain walls and there was a trail of ice across the ground. Thankfully, they reached the end of the distance Aytigin could have between him and Eira before he did and found a place to rest for the night.

They went the rest of the way the next day, but not at the fast pace on the run from Aytigin the way they did before. But it still amazed Rose at how fast Rafe could run. By nightfall they stood there facing Grandmother's cottage. Rose tried to catch her breath to soothe her nausea, and in front of her, Cal's chest heaved. They slid off Rafe's back to go into the cottage.

Everything looked the same as the last time she'd been there. The same circle of water around the tiny peninsula that housed Kutlous's Minister's home. The same enormous tree that towered over them, with a tall and narrow stone cottage in front of it. When Rose peered up into the branches of the tree, she could see the windows of all the rooms that had expanded from the cottage into the tree. The same silver haired grandmother stepping out of the door in her floor length green dress with a smile on her face.

Rose breathed a sigh of relief. The first she felt her shoulders relax since she saw Rafe in the crowd at the tournament. Grandmother was here, and they were here now. They were going to take care of everything.

Cal nudged her with his shoulder and pointed to the ground. "Is that normal?"

Rose looked down around them and couldn't believe her eyes. Mushrooms covered the normally red path that led to the cottage. Everywhere. The largest clusters were near the bottoms of the trees, growing and piling into little towers all around and up the trunks. But when there wasn't any more room there, they grew and spread out across the forest floor. Tiny sparks of blue and green danced around them like fireflies. They'd barely be able to take a step without crushing a mushroom and possibly a pixie or fairy hiding underneath the rim.

"Don't disturb them!" Grandmother called from the edge of her island. "They get angry if you do. Now come on before your tea gets cold!"

The terrain of Eral may have changed, but Grandmother didn't, and the thought of her sweet purple tea lifted more worries off Rose's shoulders. She grinned and moved along the path that led to the cottage, Cal close behind her. When they arrived, Grandmother was there with open arms and a wide smile to embrace them in a warm hug. Even Cal, whom she'd only seen a few times when she visited the castle.

But that was Renata for you. Everyone and anyone was always welcome. It was the way of being Kutlaous's Minister, for you could only find her cottage if you needed her help. She was the one constant in the ever changing and evolving forest, and all who lived there knew if they were in need Renata would be there with a smile and a cup of tea, and usually, a solution.

"What a treat and surprise! I didn't know you were bringing a man with you," Grandmother said with a twinkle in her green eyes. She patted Cal on the shoulder and a soft blush rose to his cheeks. Rose bit back a laugh. "Why haven't you brought him sooner?"

"He's my friend, Grandmother," Rose answered. "You've met Cal, and Rafe is here…"

But when Rose turned around, Rafe was gone. She looked around and past the pond to see if he was somewhere behind a tree, but he was nowhere to be found. There weren't even paw prints to show he'd been there at all. He did the same thing the last time she'd met him. He was there one moment and gone the next. Rose pinched her brows together. "He was just here."

Grandmother guided them into the cottage, but a bit of the spark in her eyes dimmed. "Rafe was with you?"

They stepped inside, and the comforting atmosphere of the cottage warmed Rose's senses. While it was hot and sticky outside, it was cool and dry here, even though the fireplace flickered and danced with flames. She breathed in the scent of the herbs and spices hanging from the ceiling and closed the door behind her.

"And what is that you're carrying?"

Rose looked over her shoulder to see Grandmother eyeing the bow and arrow set, then the sword strapped to Cal's back. Of course, she would recognize the Shadowslayers. Grandmother's eyes went wide the more she looked at the weapons.

"Do you have the knife, too?"

Rose pulled the knife out of the strap around her waist and showed it off, its shine even more dazzling in the fireplace's light. "Aytigin had them in the armory."

Grandmother raided a brow. "And he let you take them?"

Rose and Cal's eyes met.

"Not exactly," Cal answered. "But we thought their use would outweigh Aytigin's anger."

Grandmother clicked her tongue and shook her head as she went to the kitchen and poured each of them a steaming cup of tea. She shooed them away to sit down, then followed with her tea kettle and hung it over the fire. "If an angry dragon comes knocking at my door, I'm feeding the two of you to him first."

They all settled in around the fire and as Rose sipped her tea, more of her worries and anxiety melted away. She propped her foot up on a cushion and let herself relax. She'd only been to her grandmother's cottage a handful of times as Grandmother usually came to visit the castle. Each time she was here, Rose felt as though she had never left. It was where she sensed her fae blood the most, like it would awaken there in Eral and near Grandmother. On the table next to Rose's chair sat a small green plant with round leaves, and as Rose drank the tea, a tiny red sprout of a flower bloomed like it wanted to say hello to the unknown visitor.

"Now, tell me what brings you here. It's quite the surprise," Grandmother said. She stood from her seat and took the teakettle to refill their cups.

"But you always know when we're coming to visit, even if we don't tell you," Rose said.

"I knew, but the moment I sensed you enter Eral, you almost were already here. I usually have more time to prepare," Grandmother explained. "And while I might know you're coming, I don't know your intentions."

Once they all had their cups refilled, she sat again in a soft cushioned chair and looked at Rose and Cal with a single eyebrow raised. "As much as I would like to believe this is just a friendly visit, I know there's more to it. Especially if Rafe brought you."

Not able to avoid the topic any longer, Rose dove into the story of what had brought them there. Rose shared everything, even about the yellow eyes and how Rafe was in the crowd at the tournament. Grandmother's face didn't reflect any shock or surprise at the information Rafe had brought to them and kept the same watchful and gentle look while she listened. Rose couldn't help but notice at how gray and thin Grandmother's hair was becoming, and the way the lines around her eyes and mouth were more pronounced than she last remembered.

Grandmother had long silver hair that went all the way down her back for as long as Rose could remember. And did she seem to move a tad slower than normal when she served the tea? Rose rubbed her thumb over the side of her teacup while she talked to keep her focus on the task at hand, and not worrying.

"Is there any truth to what Rafe told us?" Rose asked when she and Cal were done.

"There was an excessive number of mushrooms outside," Cal added. He was sitting forward in his seat, a large chair with big pillows all around. It was his first time here, but with his rugged hair and traveling leathers, he looked like he'd been born in Eral.

Grandmother sighed and leaned back. Her gaze fell to the little plant and its newly sprouted flower, then back at Rose.

"He's not wrong. Things in Eral have been changing lately, and I'm doing what I can to stop it." She stood and went over to a workbench nestled against the wall overlooking a window, and Rose and Cal followed. All over the wooden table, which looked almost more like an altar with its candles and flowers and a miniature statue of Kutlaous with his coiled horns and long goatee, were the remnants of Grandmother's experiments. Herbs and seeds scattered across a deep green cloth, bowls with wooden spoons contained black and green potions, then stacks and stacks of books piled in the corners, along with several of them open. Rose peered over and noticed the pages covered in Grandmother's handwriting in the margins.

"At least near the cottage, I've been able to dry some of the ground and keep things at bay. But there's only so much one person can do. Even if she is Kutlaous's Minister," Grandmother explained, a deep ache in her voice that made Rose's heart break a little. She rubbed one horn on the Kutlaous statue. It was turning gold from being rubbed so often. His eyes pierced through Rose and she had to look away. "I've been praying to the god for help, and hoping he would come to our aid, but I haven't seen or heard him yet."

"Why didn't you tell us?" Rose asked. She walked around to the side of the table to look at more of the books and the various ingredients Grandmother used. "You don't have to go through this alone."

Grandmother smiled. "I was planning to soon, but Rafe clearly got to it first. But I was avoiding it, yes. I know the burdens you, Eira, and your father have on your shoulders now, and you need to be focusing on that. You'll understand once you have your own kingdom to rule."

Rose couldn't return the smile and grimaced. She had no intentions of ruling anything if she had any say in it.

Cal stood on the other side of the table opposite Rose with his hands resting on it. "We're here now, Minister, and happy to be of service however we can."

"Which I'm grateful for." She pulled one book on the table forward. It was thin and covered in black leather with silver writing. She thumbed through it until she found the page she wanted. "This book has been helpful, and there's a certain spell I think that can help. I can gather dirt and leaves and pieces of the forest and lump them together with my magic. I can aim it toward the source to soak up the water and prevent it from spreading further." She extended a hand over her worktable where dozens of dirt piles lay. "But I'm not how I once was. Even as Minister, I'm growing weak."

It was a confession that didn't sit right with Rose. But all the more reason for them to have come to her aid.

"And we think Amelia might have something to do with it," Rose added.

For the first time since they arrived, Grandmother's face lit up. "I agree."

She hurried over to another side of the cottage where a large tapestry that displayed a map of Eral hung. She waved over the east side of the map. "This is where the water and mushrooms are the most prominent. Many of the creatures living here have moved west and northward because it's become inhabitable for them. There are some over there for me to contain it, but they keep falling asleep and have little to report, and our concoctions don't come to use."

Rose huffed. A sleeping spell. Amelia was becoming too predictable. "So she must be over in that area somewhere."

Grandmother waved a finger and shook her head. "Close, but not quite. My suspicion is she is just south." She pointed to the lower southeast end of the map where the images tapered off, and where the edge of the Cresin and Marali borders would meet. "I don't think she's hiding in Eral, but just south of it in Marali. There's a prominent swamp there. But it's cursed. Hardly anyone gets in or out alive, and it isn't visible on any map. I didn't want to tell your father or Eira until I was absolutely sure because of it. Your kingdom has lost too many lives due to Amelia, as it is, and I wasn't about to send your father's soldiers in on a suicide mission."

Rose strummed her fingers on the side of her crutch in excitement. Amelia could be close then. She was hiding herself in a swamp no one could find and might die in, but those were minor details they could figure out. Especially with the Shadowslayers at their side, and now teaming with Kutlaous's Minister, and possibly a shape shifting wolf if Rafe ever returned, it was in the realm of possibilities they could actually get Amelia.

"What do we do first? How do we get in?"

"And what about the ogres?" Cal added. "What have they been up to exactly?"

Rose's heart sank. She'd almost forgotten about them. But they had the Shadowslayers with them. Surely, they'd be able to handle any ogres if they ran into any. Then again, Rose never met an ogre before. She'd heard they were brutal beings.

Grandmother sighed and gestured toward the northwest corner of the map. "They're camped out here at the moment, as the mud and mushrooms don't bother them as much. They like to keep to themselves and don't get along with the other creatures of Eral much, so, as long as they don't unnecessarily harm anyone, I leave them alone and they do the same for me. It's been many years since they've gotten along with our family, and we all prefer to keep our distance."

They didn't get along? Rose blinked a few times. No one particularly got along with ogres, but this was the first she'd heard of a specific grudge. Especially with her own family.

"Have I never told you this story?" Grandmother asked.

Rose shook her head. "I don't know what you're talking about."

"Well, it's all your mother's fault. If she wasn't so stubborn and just let me handle it, we might have a better relationship with them."

Rose's jaw dropped, and Cal's brows raised high. Her mother? She could barely get out a single word in response. "What?"

"Oh, yes. Years ago, when your mother lived here in Eral with me, I was training her to be the next Minister. It wasn't a guarantee, of course, with the Trials, but more often than not, someone related to the current Minister and had training won. Lennox was on track to do well. Knowing this, one ogre wanted to marry her and raise the status of their clan."

Rose gulped and leaned harder on her crutch and blanched. She knew Mother was in line to be the next Minister, and it was part of why Grandmother and Father didn't get along well. Once she married the future king of Cresin, her destiny to be Minister was gone. But an engagement to an ogre? This she'd never heard of. Across the table, Cal scrunched his nose like he smelled something foul.

"Oh yes, it was not an ideal situation," Grandmother agreed. "And of course, Lennox refused to marry him. I was working on a plan to be sure she didn't have to, but I told her to go along with it in the meantime to maintain peace." She laughed to herself, but there was a note of sadness to it, as though she were reliving bittersweet memories. "But she didn't listen, and we had countless arguments about it. Then, only a few days before the Winter Solstice in the middle of a snowstorm of all times, she ran away to Farren Castle. That's when she met your father, and well… the rest is history, I suppose."

The tale knocked the wind out of Rose, and she rested her back against the wall. So that was how they met. She knew it was at the Winter Solstice, and they had a whirlwind romance, but Father never told her or Eira the details of how it all happened. She would need to ask him about it when she returned home.

"What are the Trials?" Cal asked.

His question snapped Rose out of her shock. Come to think of it, she also didn't know what these Trials were.

"Now that is very secret information. The details of the Trials and how someone comes to be the Minister is something those of Eral and the followers of Kutlaous keep close to their heart," Grandmother answered. She took a step back and contemplated Rose and Cal for a few moments. Her gaze landed on Rose, and her face softened. Maybe more memories came to mind because her green eyes clouded over. "I can't tell you everything, but I suppose you can know the general idea."

She led them through the cottage to a hall and along the walls was a giant mural of Eral Forest. Scattered among the trees, there were tall ogres, elegant fae with their pointed ears, stocky dwarfs, and even a tiny pixie in their midst. Below each image was a range of dates, and in the background, Kutlaous looked forward as though he were watching over everything.

"Each minister of Kutlaous has a connection to magic. It is rare when a human becomes the Minister because they need to have magic in their blood and not just a tattoo for the deity they serve. Kutlaous didn't want his creatures to be ruled by a single family the way most humans do in the kingdoms and their rulers, so he created the Trials. It is a series of tests that challenge their magic, mind, and strength to prove they can handle the responsibility of the Minister. The winner then is bound by Kutlaous and Eral to serve until they pass into Stula's realm."

Rose and Cal walked side by side through the hall, looking at each previous Minister. Some had time spans that ranged from a few years and others centuries. All came from different species and groups. They listened in silence to Grandmother's words and continued to walk in silence once she was done. There was something still and reverent about this hall like she was in an ancient temple.

"Do Ministers ever have partners or spouses?" Cal asked. Rose jumped at the question. Not only because the sound of his voice in the silence startled her, but he never talked about marriage or anything of that sort.

Grandmother shrugged one shoulder. "Occasionally. It's a difficult and sometimes lonely life as Minister, and many times the Minister outlives their partners, so they are part of the life of Eral for a very short amount of time in comparison. Although, it's rare, but some choose to bind themselves to Eral as well."

"What do you mean?"

"Few make this choice, for not all spouses or partners want to be bound to one place that way. But for some, they can undergo a similar process as the Minister, binding their magic and life to the Minister, and they're also connected to Eral. They can assist in the Minister's duty as well as have a slightly elongated lifespan. Some see it as romantic, others as a great sacrifice." She gave Rose a sad smile. "Your grandfather was gone by the time I came to be Minister and never had to make that choice."

Rose nodded. That story she knew. He'd been a fae warrior and died in a fight when Mother was a child. Grandmother raised her on her own and became Minister not long after.

The last image on the mural was of Grandmother with her long hair and green dress. A staff was in her hand and her hair was a soft red. She also lacked the lines around her eyes and mouth Rose was so used to, but recognizable as the current Minister none the less. Rose looked at it for a while, then noticed the date near her name. It was one hundred and fifty years prior. Rose blinked and looked again, worried she had misread it. That couldn't be possible. That would mean Grandmother was… and even her mother…

"Do children of the Minister become bound to Eral too?"

Grandmother turned to Rose with pinched brows, then noticed where Rose was looking. She nodded in understanding. "No, they do not. Being part fae, your mother would have a longer life than most humans as well. She didn't look it, but she was much older than your father when they met." She gave Rose a wink.

Rose must have known this deep down, but since she never met her mother having died in childbirth, it wasn't something she thought about much. "Eira and I are part fae. Does that mean we'll also live longer?"

"Perhaps," Grandmother answered simply. "The lifespan shortens with each generation and as bloodlines mix. Your mother had fae blood both from my family and her father's, while you only have it from mine. You may live a little longer than your average human, but I don't imagine it would be significantly so."

Rose nodded but wasn't sure how she felt about that. There was so much about her own family and history that she'd never asked about, and now she felt silly for being so ignorant.

Grandmother let out a long yawn and stretched and rolled her shoulders. "I fear it is getting late. We can discuss our plans in the morning."

Yet another surprise. Rose couldn't remember ever there being a time when Grandmother went to bed before anyone else. She only nodded again, though. "I think I'll stay up longer. But we'll see you in the morning."

Cal bowed his head to her. "Good night, Minister, and thank you for everything."

Grandmother smiled and patted Cal's cheek. "You can call me Renata. We're practically family."

Cal blushed a bit. "It's an honor."

She gave Rose a hug and a kiss on the forehead. "Don't stay up too late," she whispered in Rose's ear. "Although with this handsome one at your side, I wouldn't blame you if you did."

Rose pulled back and let out a small gasp. "Grandmother!"

The Minister only smiled and gave an innocent shrug, patted Rose on the shoulder, and went off to her room, leaving Rose and Cal to contemplate all they learned.

Chapter Twelve

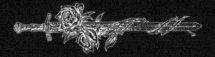

ROSE

Not yet feeling as tired as Grandmother, Rose and Cal made their way back to the main room of the cottage, found something in the pantry to eat for dinner, then made themselves comfortable in front of the fire. After a long few days filled with travel, the tournament, stealing weapons, and all the information Grandmother had given them, Rose was grateful to relax for a little while and let her mind rest. It was swimming with all the new information she'd learned and even if her body was exhausted, she knew her mind wouldn't be able to shut off for a while. At least it seemed like Cal felt the same way and stayed up with her.

"Can you believe she's been Minister for 150 years?" Rose asked Cal. She lounged on the chair sideways, her knees falling over the armrest. Cal was on the couch next to her.

"I'll admit, I didn't realize she was that old," Cal answered.

"Neither did I," Rose mused, almost to herself. "And then my mother and the ogres and the swamp…" She pressed a hand to her forehead like if she held it there long enough, she could absorb everything she found out better. "I need a drink."

She hopped up out of the chair, grabbed her crutch, and made her way to the kitchen. With the trees outside blocking the moonlight, all they had were some candles and the fireplace to light the room, but she still rummaged around through the cabinets to find some of Grandmother's liquor. She looked over her shoulder and called to Cal. "Found it! Do you want any?"

She turned back to the cabinets before he could answer, set the bottle on the table, then began her search for cups. The couch groaned as Call stood and made his way over to her. His footsteps came closer, making the wooden floors creak. "I'll help with the cups."

Rose could have carried them over herself even with the crutch, but it was likely at least a little would spill, so she didn't complain about his offer. Once she found them, Rose handed Cal two short clay cups and carried the liquor with her free hand back over to the fireplace. He helped her stay steady as she sat on the rug and rested her back against the couch. Once she was on the floor, Cal took a seat beside her. After pouring themselves a glass, they clinked cups in a small toast and took a sip.

They talked more about everything they learned and tried to come up with plans on how to access the swamp without getting killed. Cal found a couple of Grandmother's books she already had out on her workspace about the subject, and they tried to read, but their eyes were too tired and glossy to soak up any of the information and make a plan. Eventually, admitting they were too tired to make any genuine progress, they set the books aside and talked about other things as they continued to pour their glasses. Life at home, what Myra's most recent letters to Cal said, some of the gossip Evony had told Rose about the courtiers, and anything else they could think of.

With a content - and slightly tipsy - sigh, Rose leaned back and rested her head against Cal's shoulder. While she didn't like the way it came about, she enjoyed having this moment with him. It felt like it used to be before evil queens and curses and dragons took over their lives. They were Rose and Cal again. Able to talk and laugh and relax however they wanted.

She felt Cal tense when her head met his shoulder, but he immediately relaxed again and patted her hand. He was so good to her; she realized. He always helped when needed, made her relax and smile, and was always there when she needed him.

Yes, there was the time this past autumn when Cal tried to kill both her and Eira. But he thought Myra was being threatened and couldn't go through it. She shuddered at the memory.

"Are you cold? I can get you a blanket. Where does Renata keep them?" Cal asked.

There he was again. Being thoughtful. It made her want to snuggle up against him even more. How rude of him.

She shook her head. "No, I'm fine. I was just thinking about when you tried to murder us."

Cal shifted so he could look at her. "Must you to bring that up?"

"I've forgiven you, if that's what you're worried about," Rose said and tugged on his arm so he couldn't get away. He was just so comfortable. They should outlaw for a man to be so comfortable. Like a big warm muscular pillow she could bury herself in for days.

He chuckled. "I'm glad, otherwise this would be a very compromising position you have me in. But maybe I should check you for knives."

Rose yawned and waved her arm over where her red cloak and weapons they discarded hours prior on a stool near the door. "They're all over there."

"Well, good. I can rest easy tonight."

And Rose *had* forgiven him, oddly enough, she realized. For a while she was bitter and frustrated, but ultimately Cal hadn't been able to go through with it and helped her and Eira escape from the castle and try to kill Amelia. He ended up in the dungeons and tortured by her for it. She squeezed his arm even tighter. It wasn't a time Rose liked to think about. She was in the mirror then and did not know what Cal was going through, otherwise she would have tried to help him escape.

Cal shifted again, but this time he slid his arm out of the hold Rose had captured it in, then put it around her shoulder, giving Rose even more space to rest her head against. She laid it on his chest and let herself listen to the beat of his heart. Not thinking about what she was doing, Rose looked up at him.

Diar bless it, he was handsome. Especially now that he had grown out some stubble and his hair was more unkempt. Cal always was attractive, Rose never denied it. You'd have to be blind to not know he was handsome. In fact, she had a hunch even blind people knew how good looking he was. It was as though Diar themself had taken a magic wand and doused him in handsome magic.

Which really wasn't fair, because now all Rose could think about was kissing that handsome face and how maybe Evony and Grandmother had a point. He looked at her back with those startling blue eyes, and Rose swallowed a lump forming in her throat. She bit her lip.

She'd thought about kissing Cal before. Of course she had. Who wouldn't if they spent as much time with him as she did? They'd have to be an idiot. But maybe, just maybe, he'd thought about it too?

The thought never occurred to her until Evony brought it up at the tournament. Now, when they were alone for the first time in forever and with the fireplace going and liquor coursing through her veins, it was all she could think about. She should kiss him, even just to get it out of the way and see if there was any validity to Evony's claims. Then she would know for sure.

Rose leaned up and forward, hardly believing what she was doing. His lips were right there. She could almost taste them. They probably tasted amazing.

As her mouth almost brushed his, she felt Cal back away and move his arm from around her shoulders.

"It's getting late. We should probably go to sleep."

Rose's heart sank into her stomach. He didn't let her kiss him. She'd read the situation all wrong. But he was looking at her too. She swore he was. There was no way she misread this. She pushed herself up and her magic rolled and boiled within her, and the tattoo on her leg had a soft glow through her leggings. It'd been a long time since she let her anger control her magic, but this was outrageous.

"What was that?" Rose blurted out.

At least Cal had the sense to not pretend like he didn't know what she was talking about and narrowed his eyes at her. "It's late, and we should get to bed. And you're drunk."

She felt her face grow hot, and she twisted around to grab the crutch that was now lying on the ground. It took a few flails, but finally Rose grabbed it and with her other hand tried to push herself up onto the couch. "I - am - not - drunk!" she spouted but kept slipping with each word.

All right. Maybe she was a little drunk. But she wasn't admitting it to him.

Cal grabbed her arm and helped her get to her feet. "Fine, whatever you say. Let me help you get to bed."

This was not the time to play the nice guy, and she pushed him away. "I'm fine! You're the one who has a problem. I thought you wanted to kiss me! But no, you just wanted to make me look like an idiot!"

After slipping to the ground a couple of more times, Rose finally let Cal assist her to her feet, but once she was firm enough, she tried pushed him away again. Still, he grabbed her free wrist.

"Rose, we can't."

The intensity of his voice made her pause and looked into his steady gaze. So he did want to kiss her. But it still didn't make sense.

"What do you mean, we can't?"

"You know what I mean. You're…. You. And I'm me." He shook his head like it would make his words make more sense. "You're the heiress to Cresin, Rose. You need to focus on that, and I need to focus on me. It wouldn't work."

Heat roared within her, and she tore her wrist away from him. Her magic kept flowing, making her balance steadier and the ability to move on her own easier. "I'm not the heiress, not the real one. And you're you? Whatever. I'm going to bed."

"Rose, don't be angry…"

Don't be *angry*? Didn't everyone know saying that only made the person even more angry? She scoffed and stormed out, her crutch thudding on the wood floor. Thankfully, Cal didn't follow her.

Making her way through the cottage, Rose managed her way up the winding stairs and found a room whose door had a red rose and a sword engraved in the front. This one must be hers. She balanced herself and pushed the door open with the foot of her crutch to reveal a bedroom with a fourposter bed with a nightgown laid out across the red quilt. At least getting ready to sleep would be easy enough.

She slammed the door shut and tossed herself onto the bed. After changing into the nightgown and throwing her other clothes onto the floor, she tugged the quilt down and buried herself underneath it. Only then did she let hot tears well in her eyes, but she blinked them away.

This was ridiculous, and she was being silly. Plenty of women had been rejected before. This was no reason to be so upset.

But… it was Cal.

The times Rose allowed herself to imagine anything of that sort with Cal, that was not how she thought it would go. How could she have misread it all so much? But she hadn't. He didn't say he didn't want to kiss her too. Only that they couldn't. It was nonsense.

Rose tossed herself on her side and squeezed her eyes shut, forcing the tears to stay inside. She was drunk and tired. That's all this was. Everything would be fine in the morning. She'd put her focus back on finding Amelia and saving Eral forest, and all of this would just be a faded memory.

Chapter Thirteen

ROSE

The smell of roasted coffee and freshly baked rolls woke Rose up the next morning. She rolled herself out of bed, pulled on a fresh pair of leggings and a light sleeveless tunic with a brown belt, and part walked and part stumbled down the winding stairs where Grandmother was already busy preparing for the day.

A pair of pixies, one pink and the other yellow, perched on the windowsill and spoke with such quick and high-pitched voices Rose could hardly understand what they said. Grandmother must have, though, because she patiently nodded while she listened to their chatter. A coffee kettle hung over the fireplace and a tray of mugs sat on a stool next to it, so Rose made that her first destination.

While preparing jars of butter and jam, Grandmother smiled at Rose as she walked by. "Go have a seat, dear, I'll be there in a moment. I have a busy day planned for you."

Rose only nodded and made her way to the fireplace. After pouring herself a cup she nestled into one of the big chairs and listened to the chatter of the pixies. Now that she was more focused, she come make out at least a few of the words. Something about the mushrooms covering the forest floor and the color blue. Not wanting to eavesdrop on their conversation, Rose instead tried to focus on other things in the room. Like how Cal wasn't anywhere to be seen. It wasn't likely he was still in bed; he woke up earlier than anyone Rose knew.

But maybe seeing him first thing this morning wouldn't be the best idea, anyway. Her face warmed at the memory of how foolish she'd been the night before. She tried to kiss him? Rose shook her head and took a sip of coffee. Maybe he'd been too drunk to remember. She could only hope.

"He's out chopping wood." Grandmother came over to Rose with two plates filled with sausages, biscuits, butter, and jam. She handed one to Rose and sat next to her with her own. Rose lowered her face onto her plate, hoping Grandmother wouldn't notice her warm cheeks. "He was up ages ago and noticed my piles were growing low, so after his breakfast, he went out to get more. He's so helpful. Why haven't you brought him here before?"

Rose smothered one of her biscuits in butter, followed by jam, and sighed. Why did she want to talk about Cal? It was like she knew it was exactly the topic Rose was avoiding. "I didn't need him to… there was no reason… I just didn't."

"Well, how long have the two of you been courting?"

Rose placed her plate on her lap in a huff. "We're not! Did you pester Eira like this when she brought Cadeyrn here?"

A playful smile came to Grandmother's lips, and she took a sip of tea. "Maybe a little. But I know I've seen Cal in your father's court a few times. I would have sworn the two of you…" She waved her hand back and forth a little.

Rose groaned. "It's not like that. Cal…" She tried to search for the words. "He… we… I don't think that's what he wants," she finally settled on, but as the words came out of her mouth, they felt wrong. Like when you're trying to think of someone's name, you don't quite remember and say something you know right away it doesn't fit.

"Have you discussed it with him? Is that what he's told you?"

Rose opened and closed her mouth, then grimaced. "Sort of?"

Grandmother looked at her out of the corner of her eye, and Rose wanted to groan and shrink back. It was like she was an adolescent again and Grandmother had to lecture her about losing her temper or not being patient enough or something. It was odd how some habits and attitudes you think will get better as you get older, but they still hang onto them. Rose may have been twenty-four now, but most of the time, she hardly felt like an adult. Why was it so many people assumed once you hit certain ages, suddenly you were mature and ready for the world? There were moments she felt like she was, then others, like this. She may as well have been fourteen throwing a tantrum over something silly.

"Did you let him explain when you 'sort of' spoke?" Grandmother asked.

Rose shifted in her seat. "I'll admit, it wasn't my best timing. Or moment."

Grandmother chuckled and leaned over to pat Rose's hand. "With matters of the heart, sometimes there's never the perfect timing or moment." She let out a deep breath. "You're a passionate woman, my darling. So much like your mother was, where sometimes she wouldn't listen to reason. But she knew what she wanted, and didn't let herself sway from it, and while it was messy, she ultimately did the right thing. If Cal is the man I think he is, he knows and understands this about you. Your passion is a beautiful thing, but don't let it cloud your eyes from what's there."

Passion. That was a friendly word for temperamental and emotional. It didn't mean she didn't have a point, though. Alcohol and Rose's temper were a terrible combination, and they collided the night before, where she made some poor decisions. The least she could do was talk to Cal to smooth things over. Then she could lick her wounds of rejection in peace.

The door flew open, and Cal appeared in its entrance, his arms full of newly chopped logs. Sweat dripped off his brow and glistened off his muscles, being shown off by the rolled-up sleeves of his shirt. Rose swallowed and bit her lip. Life would be so much less complicated if her best friend wasn't so gods-damned attractive.

Grandmother clapped and went to greet him. "My hero, you can go put them over there by the fire."

Cal nodded and made his way over there and knelt to drop them with a thud in the wood box. The sweat and his tight-fitting shirt did little to hide what was underneath. Rose tried to keep her focus on breakfast but couldn't help but let her gaze follow his movements. He looked at her once the wood was in place and she quickly lowered her head to her biscuit and sausage. She was in so much trouble.

"Morning," he said, and Rose's stomach flipped.

Clearly, alcohol wasn't what caused Rose's attraction. If she thought it was welcome, she would have jumped across the space between them and kissed him right there. She cleared her throat and tried to act as calm as possible. Especially since she was supposed to still be mad at him.

And she was mad at him.

Obviously.

"Morning," Rose answered, and let her eyes look up at him through her lashes. He didn't stand up again, leaving him almost at eye level with her. Their gazes locked, and all they did was look at each other for a moment or two. She should say something. Anything.

"Rose, I-"

"All right, you two! We have a lot of work to do this morning," Grandmother announced.

The moment broke between them, and they both turned to see Grandmother with a pile of books in her arms. She swayed like a tree branch in the wind, and Cal jumped to his feet to help. He took the pile from her arms as though they were merely a few pillows and put them on a table near the chairs and couch by the fire.

"What are these?" Rose asked. "I thought we were going to prepare to leave and find the swamp."

"And you will," Grandmother answered as she took a seat on the couch and flipped through the books. "But you haven't spent time in Eral like I have, and you don't know its ways. You don't know what's out there, so I want you prepared." She handed Rose a book with a green leather cover. "This morning you'll read, then you and Cal can do some practice outside. Then, after dinner, I have some concoctions I want you to learn."

Rose placed her breakfast plate on the ground and paged through the book Grandmother handed her. It was a reference to all the creatures that lived in Eral with bookmarks made of ribbons and flowers and scratch papers tucked between the pages and notes scrawled in the margins. "I cannot learn about every species who lives here in a day. And I don't need to. We'll be fine."

Grandmother only tsked and handed Rose another book opened to a specific page. This one was a bread recipe. Rose raised her brows. "I'm an awful cook. And what does bread have to do with anything?"

"Take down this recipe and keep it safe. While you're gone, I need you to find one ingredient. I have the rest of it and I've been meaning to, but…" She trailed off and shook her head. "Never mind why I didn't now. But it's very important."

"Renata, with all due respect, don't you think we need to find the swamp and Amelia sooner rather than later?" Cal flipped through another book on the pile.

"Yes, but you won't make it far without preparation. If the royal guard were on a mission, would you go in without a plan or training?" Grandmother was already backing up and moving around. She went to her worktable and tinkered with the different vials and concoctions spread across it. "And Cal, I have other chores for you as well. Now, get to reading."

So, the rest of the morning, they did as they were told. Rose and Cal sat side by side and looked through all the books Grandmother had brought them. She didn't read them cover to cover but tried to note the portions heavily notated or bookmarked. It was like Grandmother was punishing them for stealing the weapons. It was worse than when she was a girl with her tutor. Eira was always better at lessons and being studious. Rose didn't mind it to an extent but would rather learn by doing instead of reading about it.

The Shadowslayers stood near the door, propped against the wall, shining and begging to be used. Rose looked at them longingly and let a book page slide along her finger to the next without her bothering to read what was on it. Renata had stored them away for so long, it was a shame to not be using and practicing with them as often as possible. She couldn't wait to get her hands on them again.

Meanwhile, Grandmother bustled around the cottage, seeming to never stop. The cottage was a flurry of creatures coming in and out of the doors, asking her for advice or helping wherever needed. All the while, when she had a moment, she putzed around at her worktable, mixing this and stirring that.

After a couple of hours of reading, Grandmother was outside speaking with a faun, and Rose stretched out her back and leg and pulled out the recipe for bread. She knew little about baking, but many of the ingredients seems commonplace to her. Yeast, butter, flour, etc. Renata had checked them off along with some others such as rays of sun at dawn, starlight caught at midnight, mushroom, and pixies dust, and she assumed it meant Grandmother already had those. The only one not checked was the ashes of a phoenix after it ended its life and before it rose again.

Rose crinkled her nose as she read through the recipe. She didn't know how someone would gather these things, let alone bake and eat them. She nudged Cal with the edge of a book and handed it to him. He grunted but took it anyway.

"Have you ever heard of bread like this?" she asked.

He shook his head as he read the ingredients, then pointed to one ingredient at the bottom. "Swamp water," he said. "At least we can get more of that if she needs it."

"In theory, and if we make it out there," Rose said. "This bread sounds disgusting. I wonder why it's so important."

Cal shrugged. "Maybe it can poison a sorceress?"

It was a possibility, and one Rose liked. If that was the case, she would find the last ingredient as soon as possible.

They sat not speaking for a few moments, the only sound being that of the crackling fireplace. Cal placed the recipe book down on a table and leaned back in his seat.

"Rose, are we all right? After last night…"

She inwardly cringed. They'd gotten so relaxed, she'd forgotten about her embarrassing rejection for a little while. "Yes, we're fine. It would have been nice to have a little more of an explanation, but you were right to an extent. I was a little drunk."

"A little?"

She sighed. "Fine. Maybe a lot."

"It took me by surprise," Cal confessed. He shifted in his seat so he faced more toward her and ran a hand through his hair, their knees almost touching. "It's not as though I haven't thought about it."

Rose's stomach tightened. "You have?" She sighed and leaned back. "I was thinking I was crazy."

"No, you're not crazy."

"So, it was just a surprise?"

"Well-"

The door burst open, and Grandmother paraded through with bushels of vegetables in her arms. "Here we are! I don't know about the two of you, but I am exhausted."

Cal was on his feet in moments yet again. "Let me help you with that, Renata."

Rose curled her lip. For someone who wanted her and Cal to be together, Grandmother certainly had a way of ruining the moment.

Chapter Fourteen

AMELIA

NOTHING WAS HAPPENING. AMELIA STRUMMED HER FINGERTIPS ON THE
porch railing and stared out into the dark green and foggy swamp. The
slight glow in the distance helped illuminate the swamp in the night,
and she could see small bubbles and ripples moving through the water.
It'd been days since she'd recruited Kartek and her clan, and there was
not a single sign in Eral that the Minister was dead. There was no word
from Rafe or the Stulan priest either. Everything was supposed to be
coming together and now… nothing.

Off to the side, Mother sat in a rickety chair reading a book by
lamplight and rocked back and forth. The rocking of the chair against
the rotting wood of the porch made a loud and sharp creaking sound
that grated on Amelia's last nerve.

"I've told you not to trust ogres and Stulan followers," Mother told
her. "The only ones we can trust are other sorceress and sorceresses.
This is what I've been telling you ever since you were a child. Why
you've gone back on my advice now of all times is beyond me."

Amelia held back a snarl and gripped the railing as though it was
Mother's neck and if she squeezed hard enough, she could shut her up.
"I am working with other sorcerers. I've told you this."

Mother laughed. "You were sleepwalking it more sounds like. I thought I'd raised a more intelligent daughter than that. One who could tell the difference between dream and reality." She sighed and set her book on her lap. "Maybe I should return to The Dravian Islands."

"Yes, maybe you should," Amelia snapped. Get her jabs and criticisms far away from her as possible. "All of this is your fault anyway."

"My fault?"

Amelia turned on her heel to face her mother who sat there with a look of feigned shock. "Yes, your fault. I wanted none of this. But you insisted I marry the king and be the one to bring respect and power back to the sorcerers even though I was pregnant with someone else's child."

"Of course I did!" Mother shoved herself up from her chair and let the book crash to the floor with a loud thunk. "What else would you have done? Married a low born sorcerer who owned a tea shop? You are one of the most powerful sorceresses in generations. It would have been a waste, and you know it."

Amelia hadn't thought about Nell's father in years. She'd never entertained the idea of marrying him. Either. Allowing herself to be with child was what she thought would get her out of the engagement to King Brennan. It was the foolish and unthought out plan of a desperate young woman. The only thing she'd been thinking about was taking back control over her future and not pulled into the political and power-hungry plans of her mother.

Ironically, it turned into Amelia's own plans of power. Power and revenge.

Perhaps it was time she included Mother in those plans of revenge.

"And look where it's gotten us." Amelia spread her arm out to the bubbling and foggy swamp. "Don't you love our kingdom where we sorceresses can live in peace?"

Mother lifted an accusing finger at Amelia and stalked toward her. "Don't you dare speak to me like that!"

But Amelia didn't back down. She hadn't needed to answer to her mother outside of letters in years, and she wasn't about to start now. "I will speak to you however I want. You can no longer shame or scold me. I am a queen."

Mother stopped her stalking and lowered her arm. She leaned back slightly and chuckled. "You used to be a queen, and we both know whose fault it is that you aren't any longer. You-"

She let out a shriek as something pulled her to the ground. Amelia jumped and almost fell herself then caught herself on the rail. A boney hand covered in swamp slime and mold grasped around Mother's ankle. Another hand pounded onto the porch floor and whatever it was, pushed itself up out of the swamp water. All at once the swamp grew cold and clammy, making Amelia shiver.

Dusan rose out of the water, a swamp-covered specter there to haunt them, and Mother shrieked again. She clamored against the floor to get away from him, but he only tugged her closer, so her legs hung over the side and her eyes met his. She visibly shook, and the sight thrilled Amelia. Served her right.

"Don't call us a dream," Dusan seethed. "She will restore our grounds. We will finally rest in peace."

Mother's face paled, and she slowly nodded. For the first time in Amelia's life, the woman was speechless.

Seeming to be satisfied, he released his grip on her, and Mother scrambled away back to the rocking chair. She stood beside it as though it could protect her from any other swamp creature attacks.

The part-man continued to push his way up onto the porch until he stood there towering over the two of them. There was something different about Dusan than the last time Amelia saw him. More skin had grown over his bony face, and flesh gathered on his bones. He was still part skeleton, but with a hint of humanity. His focus was now on Amelia, and she shivered again as he turned to face her. He barely moved but his whole body rotated around to look at Amelia as though it was on some sort of floating platform.

"Why is the Minister still alive?"

She wouldn't let him know that she'd been wondering and worrying about the same thing, or that he made her stomach roll and tighten. Instead, she gave him a casual shrug. "How am I supposed to know? Ask that wolf the priest gave me. You told me to recruit him. We did his silly ritual, and it was supposed to be done."

The ancient sorcerer snarled. "He's avoiding it. But he only can for so long if the ritual was performed correctly. And what of the ogres?"

"They're willing to work with us. They already have a phoenix and once the Minister is gone, they'll have the rest of it."

"And the rest of their task?"

Amelia shifted her shoulders, trying to release some of the tension with no one noticing. That piece was almost as important as killing Renata. At least for her. They needed to find Finley to get back the mirror. "Well, what do you expect from ogres? They're land creatures you're expecting to capture pirates. What did you think was going to happen?"

Dusan clenched his fists and the swamp water around them bubbled and rolled in reply. The fog thickened and trembled around them like thunder. A small whimper came from Mother's direction, and Amelia shot a glare at her. They couldn't show too much weakness.

"The pair are on land, and they're close. I can feel it," he said. "Get the mirror and kill the Minister. I don't care how you do it."

His bossing her around was getting under Amelia's skin. Her own water magic waved through her veins, and she wanted to send a wave at him to push him back into the swamp where he belonged. Droplets of water pooled around her fingertips, and she let them hover for a moment. With a deep breath, she calmed her magic and her skin soaked up the water again.

No. She needed the sorcerers and sorceresses hurried beneath the swamp. She needed to play nice for a little while longer.

"If you didn't trust me to get the job done, then perhaps you shouldn't have dragged me down to your grave with you," Amelia told him. "You've waited this long, a little while more won't kill you." She smiled. "Oh wait, you're already dead."

The sorcerer took three gigantic steps to Amelia, so they stood nose to nose. She didn't blanch or gag at his moldy swamp stench but stared at him back. "Care to join us?"

"Thank you, but the glowing green water isn't my style."

"Could have fooled me." He took a step back and lifted his chin, so he looked down on her even more than before. "Don't expect me to stand aside and watch if you fail. I'll have no regrets dragging you or anyone else down with me."

The fog thickened and swirled around him, bringing swamp water up to engulf the sorcerer. It poured down over him and he melted back into the water and rolled off the porch. Wind whipped around Amelia, and she shivered, then it stopped, and the swamp was even more still and peaceful than it had been before.

Amelia stood where the sorcerer once was and glared out toward the water. How dare he come to her in such a way and threaten her? Amelia was perfectly aware things had stalled yet again and didn't need the reminder.

Mother's squeaky footsteps sounded, and she stood next to Amelia. Her skin was covered in bumps and her hand trembled. Amelia raised a brow. "Yes, just a nightmare from sleep walking, don't you agree, Mother?"

Chapter Fifteen

ROSE

After two days of reading, practicing with the Shadowslayers and working with Grandmother, Rose and Cal were finally deemed prepared enough to venture out to find the swamp Amelia was hiding in. Along with the ingredients for the all-important bread Grandmother wouldn't let them forget about.

Grandmother squeezed Rose so hard in a hug as they prepared to leave, she thought her ribs were about to snap. She straightened Rose's tunic and the sack of supplies wrapped around her, then swiped away dust that wasn't there off her shoulder. She was like a mother, sending her child off to school for the first time.

"Now remember what I've told you, be careful of this new ogre chief because she's clever, don't drink the swamp water, and-"

"Don't eat the mushrooms," Rose finished for her. They'd only been told every hour since they'd arrived. There was a time Rose could tell which ones were safe to eat, but now none of them were.

Grandmother smiled, and her shoulders relaxed a little. "I wish you sister were here with you to see the two of you working together."

The bow across Rose's back seemed to dig in deeper at the words. As much as she tried to ignore the way she betrayed Eira's trust, it still haunted her if she let herself think about it. But the result would outweigh the means. They were finally going to capture Amelia.

"I'm sure she would be here to help if she could," Rose said. And it wasn't a lie. If it wasn't for being bonded to Luana's castle, Rose was confident her sister would be there at her side. And she wouldn't have stolen anything.

Cal went to Grandmother next and wrapped her in an all-consuming hug. "We'll take care of your forest, Renata. We can promise you that. Thank you for everything. It's been an honor."

She patted him on the shoulder; her face tight like she was holding back tears. Something in Rose's stomach knotted. Things must be bad if she was emotional like this. All the more reason for them to stop it.

"We should get going," Rose said, but surprised at how her voice shook at the words. Oddly enough, part of her was sad to go. She had limited time with Grandmother, and she hated to end it. "But we'll be back soon."

Grandmother waved her hands, shooing them away. "Yes, yes, go, go, go. Do what you need to, but hurry back once you're done. I want to see you one more time before you return to Eira."

Still, Rose gave her one last hug before heading out. Then it was time. Grandmother waved to them from the door and they were on their own.

Rose and Cal stood shoulder to shoulder, the Shadowslayers strapped to their backs, and sacks slung over shoulders. Eral Forest loomed before them, a green haze around the trees and hovering over the mushrooms and shrubbery. Tiny blue specks danced across the forest floor, beckoning the pair to join them. Or maybe warning them to stay away. A shiver ran through Rose. This wasn't the Eral Rose once knew, but the two of them would bring it back.

There weren't any other options.

THE MAP DIDN'T MAKE SENSE. ROSE LOOKED AT IT, THEN OUT AT THE path three times before finally lowering it with a frustrated huff. She thought they'd been following it exactly, but this looked nothing like what she was told.

Cal leaned against a tree off to the side and took a swig of water from his canteen. "Admit it, Rose, we're lost."

"We're not lost," she snapped back. They'd been walking all day, and only a little while ago did they venture out of the areas Rose was most familiar with. "The map is just wrong."

Cal heaved a sigh and snapped his canteen closed. "Whatever you say. I'm going to find water, I see more animals gathering, so I think there's a stream nearby. Do you want any?"

Rose was getting thirsty, and her canteen was painfully low already. She whipped it off and handed it to him. "Fine. I'll wait here and figure out where to go."

"If I'm not back in ten minutes…"

"I'll come find you."

She found a log to sit on and took a seat to make sense of the map Grandmother gave them. Eral couldn't have changed that much, could it? Fungi covered the log, but she found a small empty spot to perch on, and a cloud of pixie dust flurried into the air when she did. They'd gone through the knoll, and past the rabbit glen, and over the hills exactly as the path showed and where the map led. But she couldn't figure out where they were.

Something cawed overhead and Rose lowered the map to look. Kudo swooped and soared over her and landed on the log. "Kudo! What are you doing here?" she asked the bird.

In the rush they had to leave the Paravian mountains, they'd sadly had to leave Cal's hawk behind. The bird was excellent with directions, so she was glad he was here.

Kudo extended his leg out to her, and a piece of parchment was attached to it with a string. She untied it and rolled out the paper. It was a letter from Eira. Rose would know her swooping handwriting anywhere.

Rose,

I can't believe you took the Shadowslayers after we specifically asked you not to. Don't you know how dangerous it could be? And Aytigin is furious. It's going to take a lot of convincing for him to allow anyone in the castle again. I know why you wanted them, and I understand why you took them, but I'm still hurt you did it even when I asked you not to. Beyond that, the castle is a disaster because of it.

I'm working to calm Aytigin and Malle down, so when you return, it's in peace. But please, be careful. It's only because I love you and am worried. Who knows what those weapons can do? I wish we'd had more time so you could have at least practiced.

But I hope this letter finds you well and safe. Kudo was pestering us non-stop and wanting to return to Cal.

I know this is important, and I'm glad you're helping Grandmother, but please don't do anything else so reckless. We need to save Eral and find Amelia, but not at the cost of you endangering yourself.

I hope to see you soon, happy and safe. I know it's been a difficult time, and thank you for all your patience. We will defeat Amelia and put things right again. I promise.

Love you,

Eira

"What are you doing?"

Rose jumped and Kudo cawed in her ear as Rafe swung from a branch above her. She frowned. "Must you always do that?" He had a terrible habit of leaving her behind, then appearing out of nowhere and startling her. He chuckled.

"But it's so much fun." He let go of the branch and landed perfectly on the log Rose was sitting on, making Kudo fly over to another tree branch. He handed her a sack of berries. "I found these."

As much as Rafe irked her sometimes, he had his uses. Rose was fairly familiar with Eral and could figure out where to find the good food. But Rafe still knew it far better than she did. Rose opened the sack once she'd put the letter away and ate. "Where am I exactly?"

Rafe opened his own sack of berries and ate as well. "In Eral Forest."

Rose's shoulders slumped. Of course, he wasn't actually going to be helpful. She was wondering if this whole thing was a waste of time. Or at least that they had recruited a guide of some sort. Maybe she could befriend some of these pixies and fairies if she managed to not destroy their mushroom homes. "Is this whole thing pointless?" she asked.

Rafe paused and looked up from his snack. "Why would you say that?"

"Because I've only been out here for a day and already don't know where I'm going or what I'm doing."

"What did you think this was going to be like?"

Rose stretched out her legs and looked out at the forest. She reached and plucked a purple leaf hanging from a branch, almost ready to fall to the ground on its own. It wasn't anywhere close to autumn, but all the trees had different color leaves than she would have found back home. But there was something different about them. The colors faded, like someone was stripping it away. It wasn't as though she didn't like being in Eral and exploring it. In fact, she loved it. But she hated the feeling of being useless.

"I'm not sure," she admitted. "But more than this."

"Well, buck up, little princess. Eral doesn't like to reveal all its secrets at once. When it feels you are ready, it will help guide you where you need to go," Rafe said.

"When I'm ready?" Rose asked. "What is that supposed to mean?"

Rafe shrugged. "Eral is picky and changes all the time. I've lived here my whole life and still don't know all its secrets. Like your grandmother's house, for instance. Kutlaous hid it within Eral's magic, but for those in need, it will be sure they find it. If you are in search or in need of something, Eral will find a way for it to be delivered to you. But you can't always demand what you want from it."

"I'm a princess. I'm accustomed to making demands and people complying." It was not as if she made many. But when she did, she never had trouble getting what she wanted. Or at least she used to. Rose never realized how spoiled she truly was. Kudo let out a small caw, and she glared at him. "No one asked you."

"You'll find Eral doesn't care about such titles."

Rose twirled the leaf between her fingers. "Why do you care? You left us without a word. While you and my grandmother are familiar with each other, she is wary of you. You also seem to not care much about politics. So why are you here with me at all?"

It was a question she'd wondered for some time now. He'd told her why he sought her help, but it felt hollow, or like he was leaving details out. Or for him to have led her and Eira to Grandmother's when they'd been exiled to the forest. Rafe didn't seem the sort to help someone else unless it was for his own gain. She was grateful, of course, but it made little sense.

"You were in the home of my mistress. It was a sign I should help you," he answered.

Rose let go of the leaf and let it float to the ground. "Your mistress?" she asked. "You led us to my grandmother's house, and you don't seem keen on one another."

"The cave," he clarified.

Rose paused and thought for a moment until she remembered the first time they met. It was back in the autumn when she and Eira sought Stula's priest. "The cave… but it's an ancient temple for Stula."

Rafe nodded his head deeply and cocked it to the side with a sly smile. "Stula is my mistress. Did you not know?"

Rose sat across from him, stunned. It made sense, and she assumed something connected him to Stula in some way. Yet, he was in Eral. "But… but you yourself have said you've lived in Eral your whole life. I assumed you were a child of Kutlaous."

"Have you seen his mark upon me?"

"Some have theirs in places… one cannot always see. And some don't have a tattoo at all. The Fae and many other forest dwellers don't."

He chuckled again and rolled the sleeve of his left arm. On it was a large tattoo of a black skeletal hand holding a rose. Stula's mark. Rose leaned forward and grabbed his arm to examine it.

"I used to be a child of Kutlaous, I suppose. Years ago. But I never had a kinship for the god. There are many of us who don't follow the religious traditions of those in town. You should know, coming from fae heritage, where you are born with your own powers. There are sects who don't believe their power comes from the deities, but themselves."

"But Grandmother follows Kutlaous. She's his Minister," Rose pointed out.

"Yes, but didn't she teach you about the ways of some of the other fae?"

Rose had to concede on that. Even Father taught them the other beliefs of those who differed from them because he wanted her and Eira to have a thorough understanding of all who lived in Eral and the surrounding kingdoms.

Rafe continued. "I was in one of those sects. As a young man, I evaded death several times, but one day a frozen river took me. I got myself out, but barely alive. Stula found me and took pity. She gave me the power to turn into a wolf and live forever for my allegiance. I have served her ever since."

Rose released his arm from her grip and took another handful of berries. A servant for the goddess Stula. Many people were superstitious about Stula's followers, and even she had to admit the priest they'd met in the cave sent shivers down her spine. But Cal's adopted sister, Myra, they'd recently learned, was a dependent of Stula. She was one of the kindest and strongest people Rose ever met.

Rafe rolled down his sleeve again. "To answer your question. I saw you in her cave, which put you under our protection. So, I helped. I stayed because I found it interesting, and it is refreshing to do something else for once. Besides, once a wolf finds he likes someone, he becomes loyal to them."

"What? Oh." Rose blushed. He *liked* her. That was… odd, and she wasn't sure what to do with this information. "Well, thank you."

Rafe bowed his head again. "You're welcome."

"Does that mean you'll help us figure out where we're going?"

The shifter rocked his head back and forth like he was considering it. "I suppose I can take some time out of my schedule to show you around."

Yes, she was sure he had many events he needed to attend to during his day. Then again, he served the goddess of death. Who knew what sorts of tasks Stula gave to him? Rose shifted in her seat. Maybe he was more like Myra than the few priests Rose had encountered in the past.

Cal's heavy footsteps crunched and squished through the area, and he stood before them. His eyes lit up when he saw Kudo. "Hello there, friend."

The hawk flew toward him and landed on his shoulder. Cal rubbed the bird under its chin. "What brings you here?"

"He brought a letter from Eira," Rose answered. She then gestured to Rafe. "And Rafe found us too. He said he'll help us find our way around."

"Glad to have the help," he said, but there was a slight harshness to his voice that made Rose wonder how glad he was. He handed Rose her canteen. "Water?"

She took it gratefully and gulped some down. "Thank you, that's perfect."

They made camp in a nearby clearing that night, and Rose looked at the stars as she tried to rest. Eira knew all the constellations' names and used to tell her the stories when they were children and could not sleep. Rose remembered only a few. She tried to recall them to quiet her mind, but all she could think about was what Rafe had told her. He was in wolf form now, curled in a ball near the fire. The revelation was shocking enough, but there was a piece of the story which didn't make sense. He claimed he helped them because he found them in the cave. But it was a set of yellow eyes which led them there, and Rose had always assumed it had been Rafe. Which meant either he was lying - or there was someone else watching her.

Chapter Sixteen

ROSE

"And now Daisy is getting sick too," the little pixie moaned. Her long purple hair fell over her eyes, and she pushed it back, sniffing away tears.

Rose, Cal, and Rafe had been traveling for a few days now, and there was no sign of the swamp anywhere. Granted, she'd barely even covered a quarter of Eral forest, and it was difficult to tell how much progress she was making. It seemed to grow larger with each step she took. But she had made several friends with the forest dwellers and word spread quickly Rose was associated with Renata, which made them come to her with their woes when she was in the vicinity.

"What are the symptoms?" Rose pulled out some of the herbs and concoctions Grandmother packed for her.

"She was really tired, but we didn't think anything about it other than she needed to sleep. She loves to stay awake later than the rest of us. The others who have gotten sick have started to turn blue but... Daisy is already blue so we couldn't tell it was the same," the pixie answered. "But she started to get dizzy and now she's mean and gets so angry at us. She's even become violent."

"Is she nauseous?" Rose asked. A few of the other forest dwellers expressed the same sickness. Fatigue, dizziness, turning blue, fever, loss of appetite, and finally they would completely switch and turn angry and violent. In the bad cases, Rose heard of them screaming out of nowhere, and fall silent again. Then, one day, they'd be dead.

The pixie shook her head. "I don't think so."

Rose mixed together a few of the ingredients Grandmother had provided and handed a tiny vial to the pixie. "Give Daisy this and see if it helps."

"Is it a cure?" the pixie asked hopefully.

"No," Rose answered. It was a sickness none of them had seen before, and they needed an Attendant to visit the forest as soon as possible because it seemed to be spreading. But this concoction Grandmother created helped a bit. "But it might help her get some energy and stall the progression. Rub some upon her forehead twice a day."

The pixie took the vial and nodded. "Thank you!"

"You're welcome," Rose said.

The little thing flew away in a blur of color and Rose leaned against the trunk of the tree she was sitting in. She may not have been able to find the swamp yet, but at least she could be of some use in Eral. Even if it wasn't exactly what they needed. She hated waiting around and searching and couldn't help but wonder what Eira was doing in the mountains.

Cal, who'd been off to the side watching the scene, stalked up to the tree where Rose was sitting and leaned against it, looking up at her with his shining blue eyes that made her stomach flip. Kudo cawed overhead and flew off in search of who knew what. This had been like a holiday for the hawk, and he hunted everything he could get his claws on. In spite of not having luck finding the swamp yet, and forest dwellers searching out Rose each moment they had and needing to dodge the muddy and fungi infested terrain, their few days in Eral had been pleasant. Rose felt more relaxed than she'd been in a long time.

"You're getting good at that," Cal told her. Word spread quickly about Renata's granddaughter being in Eral, so as they traveled several forest dwellers came to her for assistance. At first, it took Rose by surprise, but after the first few she welcomed the change of pace. It made her feel like she was doing something useful.

"Thanks." She smiled down at him and beckoned him up with a wave of her hand.

Cal's tattoo glowed and he swung himself up with the ease of a monkey in the jungle. Rose scooted over and they sat side by side, their feet dangling in the air and swinging like they were two children playing.

"Where's the wolf?"

Rose shrugged. "I'm not sure. He likes to vanish then reappear a lot."

It was a habit that made her want to shake him and tie him to one place so he couldn't move. But for all she knew, with his Stulan magic he could disappear in a puff of smoke.

But right now? With Cal next to her and the peaceful forest around them, Rose rather liked it that Rafe was gone for the time being. Cal pushed his shoulder against hers and kept it there and it made everything inside of her turn into warm mush. She'd had these girl-like crush feelings around him before, but never like this. Now that it could be a reality, it was like every ridiculous thought or emotion she had about him came to the forefront and she couldn't push it away.

"I'm glad to have the break from our companion."

"I am too." Her voice was surprisingly quiet. She cleared her throat. "You know, we never got to finish our conversation the other day. At Grandmother's."

Cal raised a brow. "We didn't?"

She shook her head slowly. And it got slower and slower until her head stopped as Cal gazed at her. An amused smile played on his lips and a joke only he knew danced in his eyes.

"I thought my feelings about it were clear," he said and put his hand around her waist. With a short tug he pulled her closer to him, and their noses almost bumped.

Rose bit her bottom lip and felt the inside of herself melt and burn with want. The truth of it was, it wasn't clear. One day he acted like the idea of kissing her was the worst in the world, and the next he said how he did want it, and now he looked at her like he wanted to kiss her just as much as she wanted to kiss him. "I might need you to make it a bit clearer."

His hand moved from her waist and made a trail up her spine until the back of her head was cupped in his palm. Safe and secure in his hand, but he held it tight and gripped her curls between his fingers. Strong and powerful and safe, but there was still something dangerous about his grasp. He pulled her face toward his, and all thought and reason left Rose as their lips joined.

For a moment, Rose was almost surprised at the kiss, this new thing entering their relationship. Then she sank into it, letting his lips massage hers in soft and slow movements, his tongue mingling with hers. What surprised her even more was how natural it was now they were there. It wasn't strange or unusual. Instead, it was like this was what they should have been doing all along ever since they met as young adolescents. Kissing Cal was as natural as breathing. Like being home.

Cal groaned as though in pain, and Rose almost pulled away, when he grasped her hair even tighter. She took in a sharp breath, clutched onto him, and sank in deeper until she felt dizzy. She swayed and only then did she remember they were sitting in a tree. Cal's arm grabbed hers in a swift moment Rose could barely see with his magic from Aros still coursing through him, preventing her from plummeting to the ground.

"I got you. I won't let you fall."

"Promise?"

"Promise."

Once they were back upright, Cal leaned in again. His face was pale and blue and black lines ran down and over his arms. She pulled back and grabbed his wrist to examine his arm. "Cal! What is this?" This wasn't like the color of the pixies turned when they ingested too many mushrooms. Instead, it was as though whatever was coursing inside of him was taking his life-force away.

He tugged his arm away from hers, but Rose wouldn't let go. A sharp and burning sensation shocked through her arm, and Rose gasped at the pain. The same lines crept over her body, starting at her fingertips and reaching up her hands. She looked at her transforming skin in horror. "What's happening?"

"I should have controlled myself," was the only answer Cal gave her.

"That's not an answer." Rose tugged his arm even harder and ran her fingers over the blue and black lines that were already fading from both of their bodies. They vanished as quickly as they'd come, and the pain subsided. "What aren't you telling me? That night, at Grandmother's, you said something about how we couldn't. I was me, and you were you... that wasn't just because I'd been drinking a little."

The way Cal's face twisted and hardened, Rose immediately hated herself for bringing it up. There was something he wasn't telling her, and clearly it affected them both, and now she almost didn't want to know what. But she did mention it, and if she didn't find out the not knowing would drive her madder than if she did.

"What was it, Cal? What were you talking about?"

He rolled his shoulders and the glow of the tattoo faded away. "Rose, think about it. Think about who you are and who I am. You're the princess and next in line for the throne, and I'm..."

Rose groaned. "I am not next in line for the throne. It's only temporary."

"You don't know what will happen in the future. There is the possibility that Eira will never get her title back."

Heat filled Rose's chest and she clenched her fists. This was ridiculous. This is what Rose got for not letting things go; she ended up in stupid conversations. "I can't be on the throne."

"And why not? You would do better than you realize. I wish you would see that."

"But I don't want it! And what does that have to do with us? With this?" Rose shot back and gestured to their arms.

"I'm Amelia's lackey! Do you really think she would have let those of us who worked for her have any sort of happiness? You saw how people treated me at the tournament. Can you imagine what the reaction would be if you and were to be together?"

The harshness in his voice took Rose by surprise, and she leaned back slightly. The confession was so ridiculous and at the same time so obvious, it never occurred to her that this would bother Cal. "That's what all of this is about? Who you used to work for and what other people think? Who cares?"

Cal rubbed his face with his hands and groaned. "You don't know what I had to do for Amelia in the past. The people, the court, your father, the council, they would never allow me to court you. I've never liked living in court or fit in."

"Like I do?"

"It's different, and you know it. I would never be able to gain people's trust. You need someone the people would approve of. And even if I did, Amelia would never allow it."

With a sigh, Rose pulled one leg toward her chest and wrapped her arms around it, letting the other one dangle and swing back and forth on the branch. The truth of it was she could see his point. Even so, what did it matter? She was only sitting as heiress until Eira got her title back, and then Rose could go off and do what she wanted. She couldn't imagine Eira refusing it. And he still wasn't explaining the blue and black lines or the pain they felt.

"I'll be with who I want," she told Cal. "It doesn't matter what they think, and it shouldn't matter to you either."

Cal gave her a look like he knew she was an idiot. A look she was far too familiar with from him from when she made stupid moves on the training grounds. "Rose, I know you're not that naïve. Even if you don't inherit the throne, you'll still have expectations and standards to live up to."

"But what about Eira and Cadeyrn? Or Myra and Alvis? They're marrying who they want." She stopped cold at that last statement and felt her cheeks burn. Even Cal had to look away for a moment. Only a couple of kisses and already she was bringing up marriage? They were the most amazing kisses Rose ever had, and her feelings for him were something more intense than anything she'd felt before, but even she had to admit it was far too soon to mention marriage. Cal was already scared enough as it was.

"It's different for them," Cal said in a low voice. "Cadeyrn and Myra at least have titles. My father was woodcutter."

Rose wanted to yell and scream and tear the world apart. It shouldn't be so complicated. This was why she always hated court. Nothing was ever straightforward, and people always had other motivations and there were so many rules to follow.

"And even all of that aside, Amelia would never allow it."

Rose shook her head and flexed her fingers. "What does that matter? You don't work for her anymore."

"No, but she made sure we would never be happy. Especially us men." He took in a deep breath, then grabbed the top of his shirt. Pulling it down, he revealed a large black spot with blue lines that looked like veins protruded out of it on his chest over where his heart would be.

Rose's jaw dropped. How had she never seen this before? She'd seen Cal shirtless countless… no. Wait. She never had. Without shirt sleeves, yes, or with his back turned when he changed, but never completely shirtless. She'd assumed he was overly modest. Even if he had no reason to be. The man was built like a god.

She extended her hand then pulled it back. "Can… can I touch it? Will it hurt you?"

He nodded and wrapped his fingers around her wrist to lead it toward his chest. He pressed her palm against the black spot, and where she should have felt warm soft flesh there was an emptiness. Her hand didn't go through his chest into his body, but into air or a dense fog. Almost like nothing was there at all.

Rose's own heart twisted, and she swallowed. "What did she do to you?"

Cal kept her hand where it was and rubbed it with his thumb in soft reassurances even though his words were nothing but. "Amelia is a possessive woman. She didn't want to share any of her men. She put a cloud over our hearts, and if we ever were with someone and were truly happy with them, it would turn to thunder and lightning."

Rose swallowed and closed her eyes, trying to get the image of Amelia and Cal out of her mind. "Did she… did you and she ever…"

She opened her eyes to see Cal shaking his head and it was as though a weight was lifted off her chest.

"No," he answered. "But it didn't mean she wanted me around other women and enjoying myself either."

Rose removed her hand and rubbed her eyes. "I mean, it didn't hurt that badly. Maybe you're just being overly cautious…" She knew she was being senseless, but there had to be a way around it.

Cal rubbed Rose's knee and she looked up at him. Her heart twisted again at the look on his face. "There was one woman, once, years ago. It didn't end well, and how I felt about her is nothing compared to you."

Rose swallowed. If she remembered correctly, there was a young woman in the village Cal had taken to. The women he courted were so few and far between, it wasn't difficult to narrow down who it was. Rose always thought the woman left the town. "Is she all right?"

"As far as I know, she is now."

She nodded. Good. That was good. Sort of.

"Then what was this?" She waved her hand back and forth between them. "We could both be terribly hurt, but yet you thought it was the right thing to kiss me in a tree in a cursed and dying forest?"

He raised a brow and gave her a crooked devilish smile. "I don't always do the right thing. I might be strong, but you can't expect me to resist you forever. You're my weakness, Rose. You always have been. I hoped maybe because I didn't work for Amelia anymore, maybe the curse would subside."

Inside, Rose burned. Knowing she was his weakness and he wanted to try with her, it made her happier than it should have. "Well, I've always lived on the risky side. Maybe we could try again? We can figure something out."

As they leaned toward each other, the tree they were in shook and they each grasped onto the branch. Rose looked over her shoulder to find a giant green ogre shaking the tree trunk. He smiled up at them, a crooked and toothy grin.

"Or you can get down here with me and we can have some real fun."

Chapter Seventeen

ROSE

The ogre looked up at them with a stupid grin and continued to shake the tree, threatening to throw Rose and Cal out of it onto the muddy forest ground. Rose gripped the branch as tightly as she could and lowered her body against it so she could wrap her arms around it. Doing so, on the other side of the tree was another ogre, its eyes almost meeting hers, helping to shake the tree. If they shook for any longer, they'd uproot the tree right out from the soggy ground. Rose had a feeling the ogres would succeed in their task sooner rather than later.

Had they really been so engrossed in their romantic endeavors they didn't notice two giant ogres coming to attack them? She felt like an idiot. This was why it was good to avoid romance sometimes, it just distracted you from other more important things.

Rose looked up and Cal was doing the opposite of her. Instead of getting closer to the tree, he held one hand against the trunk and grasped the Shadowslayer dagger in the other and got to his feet. His tattoo glowed while he gained his balance.

"Cal, what …"

Before she could finish her sentence Cal jumped off the branch onto one of the ogre's back. The beast was at least two heads taller than him, and his arms the size of Cal's torso. The ogre let out a roar, a sound that made the forest tremble. It wasn't only from the surprise of Cal jumping on him, Rose realized, but there was a small streak of blood on his shoulder from where Cal jabbed him. It wasn't enough to severely injure the ogre or delay him, but at least distracted him.

The other ogre chuckled, but it sounded more like a thunder's rumble. He gave her what would be a toothy grin if he had more than a handful in his mouth. What made Rose pale was the necklace of fangs around his neck. "Hello, little princess."

"Jump, Rose!" Cal yelled.

She didn't need to be told twice. Feeling for her magic, the tattoo on Rose's leg glowed, and she grabbed onto the branch with both hands and swung herself down. She hadn't put on her strap that day, so she landed on the ground in a lump. Cal and the ogre he fought struggled back and forth. But the one mocking her crouched to the ground as she giving Rose nabbed her crutch and sack, along with the other Shadowslayers. She cursed at herself for not putting her straps on that day because now she only had one leg and arm to use to fight back.

He reached out for her, but she swatted at his hand like he was a giant buzzing fly. The magic and strength coursing through her body gave her hits an extra boost where the ogre looked at least a little irritated. She pressed her free hand to the soggy dirt and dug deep inside for her fae magic to summon vines and branches of the forest. The ground glowed and pieces of the forest crawled to her and wrapped themselves around her ankle. It wasn't the same as her straps, but it was faster and would have to do for now. She would at least be able to balance on two feet.

She grabbed a low-hanging branch and bent it toward her then snapped it to the ogre. It hit his stomach with a satisfying thwack and gave her a moment to see how Cal was doing.

Cal had gotten his ogre further away from the tree and was fighting with both feet on the ground now, but only had the dagger as a weapon. The Shadowslayer sword still stood off to the side where their belongings were stashed. Rose took up the bow and arrow and balanced herself on one leg, her bad foot on tip toe. She took in a deep breath and shot an arrow toward the ogre. It flew through the air with a whistle and thudded into its shoulder.

The ogre roared again and looked over his shoulder; with an annoyed snarl he ripped the arrow out and threw it on the ground. At least Cal was able to run back to Rose and grab the sword. Side by side, the two of them warded off the pair of ogres attacks. Rose with the arrows, and Cal using the sword. But they were no match for the strong ogres and their swinging clubs. They jumped and dodged their opponents, guarding the other when they were down then ducking low as a club swung at them.

Rose hadn't had much experience with bludgeoning weapons. Luckily, her arrows struck where they were aimed as promised by the legends, and even splintered through the clubs. Pieces of wood showered around them. One swung at her and Rose ducked to the ground. From her boot, Rose pulled out the dagger and slashed at one of the ogres calves. Thanks to its magic, the cuts went deeper than they should have through his thick skin, and he hissed.

A dark fog came over the area, and it made Rose shiver. Even the ogres paused for a moment at the sensation and looked around stupidly. Then, with a whoosh Rose could barely see, a dark cloud flew toward one ogre and lashed at his neck.

Rafe was back, and Rose had never been so relieved to see him.

The black wolf snarled as he bit at the ogre's neck, and he howled and yelled. The ogre grabbed Rafe around the torso and threw him off. Rafe didn't cry out but growled as he landed on his feet, yellow eyes blazing and fangs bared.

Rose, Rafe, and Cal all stood back-to-back in a tight circle, prepared for the ogres. For the first time she'd been able to notice Cal again, and he had multiple bumps and cuts on his body from hits. Rose's Aros magic prevented her from feeling the pain of her own injuries too terribly, but she was sure she would be sore in the morning.

Her ankle was weakening. The vines and branches weren't enough to keep Rose's leg upright for long, and as she aimed an arrow toward one of the ogres, she felt it give away and she fell to the ground, her cheek landing in a pile of mud and fungi. In the fog, an ogre approached and swung, and the world went black.

ROSE AWOKE TO SOMETHING SOFT AND WET RUBBING HER FACE. SHE blinked her eyes open and when they adjusted, saw a wolf's pink tongue coming toward her.

"Ugh!" Rose lifted her arm to protect her face from the assault and pushed herself away with her good leg. "Rafe, get off of me!"

Rafe stepped aside and sat back, his head tilted to one side. "Took you long enough to wake up."

She pushed herself into a seated position and wiped her face off with her sleeve. Not that it was much cleaner, considering she was sitting in an over-watered forest. "Did you have to do it that way though? Gross."

Rafe's black tail swished back and forth a few times, and he moved his shoulders in what Rose could only interpret as a wolf's way of shrugging. "You were out for a while. I had to do something. Are you okay?"

Her head pounded, and she rested it in her hands. Ogre clubs were no joke, and she swore she would practice defense against bludgeoning weapons as soon as possible. "Yeah, as well as I can be. How's Cal? How did you get the ogres away?" She looked around and the ogres were gone. No thanks to her and her ankle though.

Rafe hung his head and looked up at her. "I couldn't protect the two of you. I'm sorry."

Rose's stomach dropped; her headache forgotten. Everything around her stilled at his words. "Where is he?" She was almost too afraid to ask but had to know.

He gestured his head toward the east, toward the direction of the swamp. Or at least that's where Rose thought he was gesturing toward. She was a little turned around. "They hit him, too, and took him that way. They tried to take you along, but I wouldn't let them."

Rose took a survey of the area and was glad to see that her sack and crutch were still there. Tossed off to the side and the contents of her sack scattered, but everything important was still there. Crutch, straps, knife, bow and arrows. She crawled over to her things and collected them together. Her body was screaming she needed to rest, and the throbbing in her head made her eyes go buggy. But she would have to deal with it.

"Do you think you know where they took him?"

"I have an idea of where their camp is, yes," Rafe answered.

"Good." Once her things were together, Rose pushed herself to her feet with her crutch. "Show me. Let's go."

Rafe walked over to her and surveyed her up and down. "Are you sure about that? You should probably rest."

She shook her head. "We're getting Cal back."

"Cal is a big boy, I'm sure he can take care of himself."

"I'm going with or without you."

Rafe sighed. "Their camp may be near the swamp. Let's go."

Chapter Eighteen

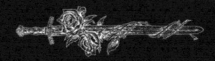

ROSE

RAFE LET ROSE RIDE ON HIS BACK AS THEY JOURNEYED THROUGH ERAL Forest in search of the ogres with Kudo flying overhead. Thankfully, being large and clumsy creatures, ogres left a messy path of broken and shredded branches in their wake with large footprints in the mud. When those weren't to be seen, Rafe could smell their path.

By nightfall, Eral Forest was almost pitch black, and this was when they normally would set up camp as it was almost impossible to see and continue on. But off in the distance was the soft glow of a bonfire. A light green fog hovered over the forest, and Rose was grateful Rafe was the one doing the walking because the ground was so soggy and filled with mushrooms, it would have been almost impossible for Rose to navigate with her crutch.

A circle of tents and poorly patched huts with wagons and carts made a large circle around the ogres' camp. Kudo found the sturdiest hut available and perched on top with a caw. The bonfire cracked and lit the dark forest night, and the scent of their meal filled the air. Rose slid off Rafe's back, and he shifted back into his human form. They tip toed around the camp and hid behind one cart. They peered over the top of it to see a group of ogres around the fire.

Rafe groaned. "That smells amazing," he said. "We haven't eaten like that in days."

"We cook our food," Rose said.

"Not well."

"Well, keep your stomach in check, we don't want to look like we're desperate when we go in there. Desperate people do desperate things and can't be trusted," Rose said as she raised her cloak hood. "Maybe we can negotiate and get Cal out of there. See what they want to get them to calm down to help Grandmother some. Then, we can decide how we will proceed. If we can, we bargain."

She didn't want to waltz in there intending to fight. There were too many of them, and Rose was still recovering from the the attack.

One ogre approached the fire and threw some sort of liquid upon the food they were cooking, and a fresh odor filled the air. Rose and Rafe covered their noses and stifled groans.

"Why did they have to ruin it?" Rafe grumbled.

"What is it they put on their food?" Rose asked, unable to distinguish what exactly the pungent smell was. She rubbed her eyes with her palms.

Rafe sniffed the air and grimaced. "Mud, blood, mucus, and some sort of plant I don't recognize."

This time, Rose couldn't contain her groan and rubbed her eyes again.

"Ogres," she said. "They're the only creatures I know of who would find it to be a delicacy. Or even edible for that matter."

Sure enough, upon closer inspection, the ogre tending the fire in its light appeared to be green with large teeth protruding from its lower lip. Rose's stomach turned. She'd only seen ogres a few times in her life, for they liked to keep to themselves. Once a few of their leaders met with Father a couple of years ago. Eira met with them as well to learn for her own future dealings with them. When Rose questioned Eira about it later, she learned they were gruff, rude, loud, and violent. The meeting didn't go well, and they hadn't heard from them since.

Ogres were also almost always hungry.

Rose gulped and straightened her shoulders. If they didn't go now, she'd lose her nerve. "No time like the present. Don't you agree?"

"If you're sure," Rafe said.

Rose cried out, and the sound echoed across the trees. "My leg!"

The ogre standing at the fire paused and turned, and a few others followed suit.

Rafe stood and hoisted Rose into his arms. She cried out again but gave him a look while doing it. He was supposed to help her limp to the camp, not carry her. But this made it more convincing.

Rafe approached the edge of the camp as Rose bit her lip. "Make way for the princess! Please, can we rest by your fire while I tend to her? We offer food for your table in gratitude."

A tall ogre approached them, almost taller than the ones they fought. He crossed his arms over his broad chest, showing off his tree trunk arms and the white marks which covered his green skin. "The princess?"

Rose peeked out from under her hood and gripped Rafe tighter. "I fell and something in my ankle popped."

The ogre eyed the three of them, but his gaze fell upon the sack Rafe was holding. He nodded to it. "What did you bring for our table?"

"A few rabbits I caught this morning," Rafe answered.

The ogre looked doubtful but grabbed the sack out of Rafe's hands anyway.

"Let them in," a deep and raspy female voice said from further in the camp. "We shouldn't let the granddaughter of Kutlaous's minister have to fend for herself in Eral. She and her companion may sit with me."

The hulking male led them through, and Rose grasped Rafe even tighter than before. Each ogre appeared larger and stronger than the last. They scattered their axes and clubs through the camp, gleaming in the firelight. They devoured their meals and picked at their large, pointed teeth. Rose no longer needed to force tears from her eyes to complete her ruse. The stench of their dinner did the job fine.

The ogre led them to the female who sat on a stone chair next to a phoenix cage. Rose wasn't sure which surprised her more, the flaming red, yellow, and orange feathers of the phoenix, or the female ogre before her. She was tall, muscular, and lounged on a stone throne, licking her fingers clean off whatever poor creature she'd had for dinner.

Strips of brown cloth covered her chest and pelvis and over them she wore a thick fur coat. The flames of their fire reflected in the large silver belt strapped around her waist signifying her station in their clan.

"I'd heard someone in a red cloak was wandering the forest. You've become quite popular," the chief said. She extended an arm to her side where another male ogre sat upon brown cushions. "Have a seat and we'll bring you something to eat."

Rafe set Rose on a brown cushion as the captain clapped her hands twice. In moments, the two of them had plates of food in front of them. Rafe did not have any trouble digging in and Rose carefully picked at her meat. Maybe she could blame her injuries for her lack of an appetite. Even if it looked appealing, she had a hard time trusting what was in front of her. These ogres attacked her then kidnapped Cal, and now they welcomed her with open arms? Something wasn't right here.

The chief sat straighter and stared at Rose with her orange eyes. "What? Our food not good enough for you?"

Rose grimaced and took a small bite. It took everything in her to not spit it right back out but chewed and swallowed as quickly as possible.

The chief chuckled darkly. "You're braver than you look. Is your ankle truly hurt?"

Rose glanced at Rafe who only raised his eyebrows. "My ankle has trouble, yes, but not at this moment."

The ogress's dark black hair slid to the side as she glanced at Rose's twisted foot. She'd shaved half her hair off and designed it with swirls and the rest was straight and spiked. "At least part of your story is true. What is your name?"

"I thought you already knew."

The captain chuckled again. "Very well, if that's how you're going to be. Yes, I know who you are, granddaughter of Renata, Kutlaous's Minister. But since you refuse to tell me your name, I'm going to call you Red, and my name is Kartek. I'm in charge of this troupe of miscreants. Enjoy your meal. We will discuss other matters later. I hate having to discuss politics over dinner. This is my belt claiming celebration after all."

She snapped her fingers, and someone brought her a plate of something big, bloody, and foul.

"Belt claiming?"

Kartek smiled as she bit into a piece of meat, blood dripping down her chin. "I won my title a few weeks ago. We've been celebrating ever since."

"How did you win it?" Rose dared to asked.

"I smashed the other chief's head into the ground until his brain splattered across the dirt," Kartek answered. "Then I ate it."

Rose's stomach turned again.

The ogres ate and drank into the night. They sang loud songs and danced around the fire, reveling in whatever victories they'd had through the day. It was sickening and entrancing at the same time. It was unlike any gathering Rose had witnessed at home. They were louder, devoured more food, and took no care for what others may see. Couples and groups of them kissed and caressed one another as though they were behind closed doors. The Cresin court was open about their relationships and who they shared beds with, but even in the most outrageous of parties they still saved some things for when they were alone.

But it was not only that. It was the necklaces of teeth around their necks. The bones they carried with them and banged together like musical instruments. The way a fight broke out, and they all watched and cheered. They'd had small brawls on the practice field with the guard, of course. But once things got out of hand, the captain quickly broke them apart. Kartek didn't bother to stop the violence but urged it on.

Rose lowered her gaze to her plate of mostly untouched food and saw Rafe was doing the same. How long would this go on? The eating, drinking, dancing, and now fulfilling their other desires and impulses? And where was Cal? Rose wished Eira was there. She would know how to handle the situation and find a way out without making it appear they were ungrateful to their hosts. Rose could only sit there and avert her eyes. She looked toward the sky instead where Kudo was flying about. He hovered over each hut and tent, maybe to discover which one Cal was in.

At least Kartek didn't have anyone join her at her seat and mostly observed the goings on of their clan. Kartek glanced over to Rose and Rafe and nodded. "Come join me."

She stood, the necklace of teeth around her neck jangling and her silver belt shining and walked away from the party to a nearby tent. Another female and male followed. They must have been her second and third.

Rafe helped Rose to her feet, and she could limp over to the tent with her crutch. Her straps needed to be at full power soon.

They sectioned the inside of the tent off into three makeshift rooms divided by curtains. One curtain was left open to show three people tied to wooden pillars. Two females and one male. One female had long wavy blond hair, and a wide-brimmed hat with a purple feather sticking out of it napped peacefully in the corner. The other rose her head when they entered, her short black hair falling over her eyes. She peered out at them with narrowed lids. Her gaze met Rose's then darted away again toward the napping woman. Rose held in a gasp. To the side Cal sat there, his head slumped down and shoulders sagged. Bruises and cuts were all over his arms and legs, but he was there alive and breathing.

Kartek sauntered over to a table on the far end of the tent and poured herself something to drink. "This is Arag," she said, gesturing to the other two ogres with her. "Who is your companion, Red?"

Rafe bowed his head. "Rafe."

Kartek smiled at them as though she knew what he was going to say. She leaned against the table and stared at Rose. "I have heard a young woman with a red hood has been wandering the forest helping its dwellers. Is this true? Has your grandmother taught you some of her knowledge?"

Rose weighed her options. Sharing too much could be dangerous, but if the captain needed Grandmother's skills, perhaps it was something Rose could use to barter with.

"To an extent, yes," she finally answered.

"Do you have her same skills?"

Rose shrugged. "I have some of them, and a few of my own as well."

"What do you know of this sickness which is spreading through Eral? The one where they turn blue." Kartek snapped a finger at Arag and pointed to a wooden chair. He grabbed it and brought it over to Rose's side. Rafe guided Rose into the seat then stepped to the side. He crossed his arms in front of him and kept his yellow eyes sharp on the ogres, ready to pounce at the first sign of danger.

"Not much. The infected mushrooms have caused it from what I can tell," Rose answered. "I don't know of a cure."

"But you have helped forest dwellers with it?"

Rose crossed one leg over the other, a nervous finger tapping against her knee. "A few. There are some remedies which seem to calm the victim. But nothing cures them."

Kartek snapped her fingers again, and Arag drew open a curtain for the third room of the tent to reveal another female ogre laying upon a cot. Her green skin had a blue tint to it. Her orange eyes opened and closed and looked at the ceiling, not acknowledging anyone else was in the room. Kartek stood by the female ogre's side and for only a moment a hint of softness filled her eyes. "Her name is Zorar. Help her, and I will consider listening to your petition."

"We didn't say we wanted anything," Rafe said, the hint of a growl in his voice.

Kartek raised a single brow at him then stepped away from the bed and sauntered to the tent entrance. "No one would dare approach my camp unless they desperately wanted something." She nodded back to the bed. "As I said. Help Zorar, and I'll consider helping you."

Rose looked back and forth between the scene at the sickbed and Cal slumped off to the side with the other two prisoners. The woman in the hat was still sleeping, but the other one kept glancing over at Rose out of the corner of her eye. Something about the pair of them struck a cord in Rose's mind, but she couldn't figure out what. But even more important was Cal.

"Untie him," Rose blurted out before Kartek could get too far.

The chief turned back, and her orange eyes blazed at Rose. "I doubt you've helped Zorar yet, unless your magic is more powerful than you let on. It's not time for you to lie out requests at my feet."

"I'm not saying you need to free him yet," Rose quickly added. Freeing Cal was her request, but she couldn't let him stay tied up there. Surely there was something else they could use the ogres help with.

"And it's not my only request. I just need him to move about in the tent and camp to assist me."

Kartek let out of a single chuckle. "Are you so weak a woman you need two men to assist you?" She looked Rafe up and down and then at Cal. "Or maybe you're so fabulous, the two of them can't help themselves and bow to your every whim."

Rose bristled at the comment and shook her head. "I'm neither. I'm just trying to do the right thing and assist Zorar the best I can."

The ogress considered this for a moment. "I doubt that. But very well." With a single nod of her head, the other two ogres returned and cut Cal's bonds free. The dark-haired woman didn't bother to look their way in hopes they'd free her too, and a pang of guilt hit Rose.

She'd learn about them too, and maybe they all could escape.

"But I'm doubling the guards around the tent," Kartek said. With that, she walked away, leaving them in peace. In moments, the stomping of ogre feet surrounded the tent, and Rose could see guards' shadows all around them.

Rafe turned to her and shook his head. "I can't tell if you're incredibly brave or incredibly stupid. What else do we need from them?"

"I'll tell you later," Rose said. She didn't want to say anything in front of these other prisoners until she knew if they were trustworthy. "Help me get over to Cal."

Rafe went over to her side and let her sling her arm over his shoulder and he helped her limp over to where Cal sat. She knelt next to him and brushed his muddy hair off to the side so she could see his face better.

"Is he your lover?"

It surprised Rose to hear the soft voice of one of the other prisoners. Despite being tied up in an ogre camp, the dark-haired woman's voice was soothing and melodious. Rose looked over her shoulder and saw her bright eyes looking at them with an intense curiosity, like she could see something Rose couldn't.

"Not that it's any of your business, but no… it's complicated," Rose answered, not sure why she gave the woman even that amount of information.

A small smile played at the corners of the woman's mouth. "Usually, it is. Then again, usually it isn't either. We just like to use that word as an excuse to avoid how things truly are."

Rose pressed her lips together in a tight line and ignored her statement. Whatever the status of the relationships between her and Cal was, it wasn't any of this woman's business. Rose eyed her, then pulled a cloth out of her sack to wipe the dirt and grime off Cal's face. He murmured something wordlessly and rocked his head back and forth. At least he was conscious.

"And is she your lover?" Rafe asked the woman. He gestured to the other prisoner sleeping off to the side.

The woman smiled even wider now. "She wishes. But I don't take lovers. Romantic relationships never appealed to me much. But she is my best friend." She leaned over and nudged her companion's shoulder. She whispered something into her ear and the other woman stirred.

With an enormous yawn, the other woman rolled her shoulders and pushed herself up into a seated position. She straightened her hat and pushed her long blonde hair aside. Her blue eyes brightened at the sight of Rose, Rafe, and Cal. "Well, well, well, Ai, looks like we have a party."

Chapter Nineteen

ROSE

Ai rolled her eyes, but there was a fond amusement in them. "We can't have much of a party tied up here."

The other prisoner gave her a sly smile and wiggled her shoulders. "Depends on what sort of party you want if you ask me. I have fond memories of being tied up." She winked at Rose.

Rose raised her brows and searched for some ointment from her sack to tend to Cal's wounds. Things had gotten a little rearranged during their fight with the ogres. "Sorry, I'm not interested in women."

In what she could only describe as a pout, the prisoner stuck out her bottom lip and sighed. "Ah well, your loss."

"Finley is interested in anything and anyone who'll give her the time of day," Ai told them.

The other prisoner, Finley, tossed her hair to the side as though she were a lady in a palace showing off for a suitor instead of a prisoner in an ogre camp. "And who wouldn't?"

Rafe walked around the tent, inspecting the pieces of furniture and objects lying around like he was bored and looking or something to do. "And she's so humble too," he muttered.

Finley shot him a glare from underneath the rim of her hat. "No need to be rude."

"Ignore him," Rose told her. "We usually do."

"Unless you need saving," Rafe said over his shoulder.

"I still think you'd make an excellent cloak!"

Cal groaned from where he slumped over, and his head moved back and forth. Hope fluttered in Rose's chest that he might be awake and paused her search. His blue eyes batted open and were glossy as he glanced around the room. They then focused on Rose and a new clarity and softness came to them. "Where are we?"

He pushed himself up and groaned, so Rose put a hand behind his back to assist. "We're in the ogre camp. They knocked you out and took you back here, so I came after you."

"Rose, you came after me? And you got in without them harming you?" he asked, an air of amazement in his voice.

"Don't get too excited, Cal, we're trapped and there's something I have to do."

As they talked, Rose couldn't help but notice Finley looking back and forth between the two of them. She tried to ignore it, but she wasn't particularly keen on these other prisoners spying on her reunion with Cal.

Finley's blue eyes grew so large it looked like the entire ocean lay in them. "Rose and Cal." She squealed and clapped her hands. "You know Myra!"

Rose and Cal's heads turned in unison to look at Finley and Ai, who both wore large and excited smiles.

"And how do *you* know Myra?" Rose asked.

Cal rubbed his head a bit like he was trying to get his bearings. "Are you two the pirates she told me about?"

Finley squealed again and moved to sit next to him, only to be stopped by the rope tying her to the floor of the tent. She tugged and pulled at it, but it was no use. Shrugging off the minor disappointment, she crossed her legs in front of her, still smiling. "She told you about us! I mean, who wouldn't? We're fabulous. But have you heard from Myra? How are she and her smoldering prince?"

Cal chuckled and continued to rub the back of his head. "They're fine, the last I heard. It's been a while since I last could write to her."

"Hold on, who are you? How do you know Myra, and… you're

pirates?" Rose asked. She handed Cal a container of ointment, and he took it so he could rub it on his aching head. Cal had told her bits and pieces about what Myra had been up to Oxare, and the phrase "pirate queen" sounded familiar.

Meanwhile, the three of them filled Rose in on how Ai and Finley met Myra in the Golden Palace in Oxare. Ai was posing as a contestant to win the hand of Prince Alvis, and Finley as her servant. They befriended Myra, Cal's adopted sister, who was also working as a servant in the palace. Oddly enough, Myra fell in love with Alvis, and the two of them helped her. Apparently, the purpose of Finley and Ai being at the pageant was to steal Amelia's mirror and help set her free as Finley was Amelia's cousin. Estranged cousin, though, since they had the mirror but didn't know where Amelia was and didn't care. All they'd wanted was the mirror. They hated Amelia almost as much as Rose did but didn't have the same drive to be rid of her. As long as Amelia stayed out of their way and they could sail the high seas, the pair were happy.

"So, how did you end up here?" Rose asked after their story was complete. "Why aren't you with your crew on The Mystic?"

"Because we knew we were being followed. The Oxarian guard is after us. What do you think?" Finley groaned and shifted her position as she answered, but the ropes prevented her from moving much. She pulled and shook at them with an animalistic growl and threw them back on the floor. She shifted again and stretched her legs out. "We escaped from the prison and got back to The Mystic and could sail north. But, by the time we got to the Marali and Cresin border right there, where it gets closer to the Dravian Islands, they ambushed us."

For the first time since she'd woken up, the light in Finley's eyes dimmed. She wore the same self-assured expression with eyebrows high and shoulders square, but Rose could see something haunted the pirate queen. A tiny part of Rose pitied her.

Ai patted Finley on the shoulder and gave it a gentle squeeze. "We have ways of making The Mystic disappear, or at least appear to. But all sides attacked us from the kingdoms surrounding us."

"It's too close to too many borders, but I thought we'd be able to risk it," Finley murmured.

"We could escape, but they got the rest of our crew and the ship. We wanted to go back and save them, but we got word that the crew were safe and to continue on our journey. Finley here wanted to ignore it and go back anyway, but I made her see reason. So we went on. Only this time, on land. Thankfully, we were at the edge of Eral Forest where it's easier to get lost and we could lose the soldiers who were after us. We thought we were in the clear."

Finley grunted again and crossed her arms in front of her. "Until we ran into a couple of ogres a few days ago, and here we are."

"But what would ogres want with two pirates?" Rose asked.

"Who knows why they do anything?" Rafe answered. The four of them turned toward Rafe, who was now circling around the ailing ogress like a predator seeing out his next meal. His yellow eyes glowed and dimmed again. He paused his circling and stared at the ogre lying there. "I do know they want respect and power. Maybe they knew who Ai and Finley were and thought having them in their possession would aid them in that. What we really need to determine is how we're going to get out of this."

Rose slouched in her seat and placed a hand on her forehead. He was right. For some reason, Kartek let Rose in with no harm, but she had a sinking feeling getting out would not be the same way. They originally were going to bring her there by force for deities sake.

She wrapped her arms around her knees and looked at the sleeping ogress. At least she was at rest for now. Who knew how long that would last? "What does she expect me to do? I said I don't know of a cure."

"She said to help, not cure," Rafe pointed out.

Rose pushed herself onto her feet. "Cal, can you help me?"

Cal nodded, then stood and helped Rose walk over to the bed and so she could look at their patient. Zorar appeared to be around the same age of Kartek, but ogre skin was so thick and leathery it was difficult to tell their age. A small plate of bland food sat on the bedside table with a glass of swamp water - untouched. Zorar must have been deep into the disease.

"She's been like that ever since we got here," Finley told her.

"Can I have my bag?" Rose asked, and Rafe handed it over. She dug through it to find her herbs and mixed them together like she had done for the pixie. She placed the concoction in Rafe's palm. "Put some on her forehead. She looks to be far along, so I'm not sure how much it will do."

Once she administered the medicine, there was nothing to do but wait. It was late into the evening, and they all were yawning. They determined it was for the best they all went to sleep and started on a plan in the morning.

Kartek didn't give any indication of giving Rose, Rafe, and Cal another place to sleep for the night, and there was only one extra bed. It was large enough where it would fit two ogres, so there was plenty of space for the pair of them. Perhaps even three if they dared. Which they did not. Rafe, who played by his own rules, vanished with a wisp of smoke. Then Finley and Ai made themselves as comfortable as possible and lay down on the ground.

Rose climbed into the bed next to Cal, space for a whole other person between them, and tried to sleep. The ogres outside were still enjoying themselves, and spending the night in their midst was not what Rose imagined for capturing the ashes of the phoenix. She closed her eyes, but thoughts and plans continued to run through her mind. Besides, Cal was as warm as the fire outside the tent. Having him sleep near her outside on their bed mats was entirely different from sharing an actual bed; especially after their kiss, he was particularly distracting. She threw off the blanket and turned on her side.

"Are you awake?" she whispered.

Cal murmured something indistinguishable, but Rose decided it meant he was.

"If we can't make Zorar well again, I don't know what we're going to do," she said in hushed tones. There was no sign Ai and Finley were awake and seemed to be in a deep sleep, but she didn't want to risk them overhearing their conversation. Cal seemed to trust them because of Myra, and Rose had no reason not to, but they were pirates. Their first loyalty was to themselves and their crew.

Cal groaned and turned over on his side to face her. "I'm not sure either. But while we're here, we can use the bird for your grandmother's recipe. And we're close to the swamp, I think, so maybe they'll be able to help us get to it, maybe even enter. But..."

"But what?" Rose urged.

"What about the Chalice?"

Rose blinked a few times. She hadn't thought about Gallis's Chalice at all since Father had gotten cured. "What about it?"

Cal paused for a moment before speaking. "How many people do you think it can heal at once?"

"I'm not sure," Rose answered and tried to think back to when she and Eira spoke with the Stulan priest all those months ago. "The priest didn't say how much to give to each patient. It's possible they may only need a drop or two and if that's the case, it could help many people. If they need to drink everything in the goblet, then only one. Rafe might know. We could ask him about it when he returns."

Cal propped his head up on his hand. "Have you considered using it for those falling ill to this blue skin disease with the mushrooms?"

It was Rose's turn to pause. It was an idea, but Eira and Aytigin kept the Chalice even more hidden than they did the weapons. She had a feeling it would be a challenge to convince them to let her use it. "I haven't. I've been so focused on getting to the swamp and Amelia, I haven't thought about much else. But the story the priest told us was only regarding the poison Father had. He said nothing else about other sicknesses or diseases."

"Perhaps not. However, once you have the Chalice, Attendants might use it to heal all these people who are falling ill."

Rose turned over onto her back and considered this while staring at the ceiling. "Galis's Chalice was taken away and hidden in the mountain because people abused it. Do you think we would do the same thing?"

"I'm not sure," Cal admitted. "I do wonder, though, if you could use it as a bargaining tool with Kartek. Tell her the truth of how you need the phoenix and to get to the swamp and, in exchange, you will return to her clan with the Chalice to heal Zorar."

Rose looked at him. "We need to find out what they want to do with the phoenix. Perhaps it is something we can help with, or they do not wish to harm it. Do you think it's possible we can get what we need and leave?"

Cal reached over and tucked a stray strand of hair behind Rose's ear. "With you? Absolutely."

Chapter Twenty

AMELIA

AMELIA NUDGED HER FEET ALONG THE EDGE OF THE SWAMP. THE LONGER she was there, the more her magic got to know the water. It splashed aside as she walked through, allowing snippets of dry land to appear before her so she could navigate the terrain. It knew she was its queen, and she barely needed to think or wave her hand for it to obey her wishes now.

Come to me.

Dusan's call whispered in her ear early in the morning, waking her from a restless sleep full of dreams of ogres and wolves and crashing ocean waves. The sound of his voice sent a ripple through her body she couldn't ignore. The way a stone dropped into a pond and it changed the surface of the water. She'd ignored the cries of protest from Charis when she walked through the cottage without instructions for the day or to help with the baby. Mother said little anymore, and only raised an eyebrow at Amelia's wordless mission to get out into the swamp.

She'd dipped her toes into the water but when she did, his call came again, telling her to not go to the swamp but further into the trees away from prying eyes and ears.

Seek me in the shadows, queen.

The shadows were not Amelia's forte or where she would choose to be found, but another ripple ran through her anyway. So, she did and stepped deeper into the trees and mist. She peered through the green fog that hovered and twisted through the trees and vines in the dark places no one else wanted to seek. Where an ancient sorcerer would haunt and spy.

A flutter of blue robes danced in the mist, and Amelia's breath caught. Then, out of the corner of her eye, the dark brown of his hair flashed past her. She whipped her head around to find Dusan, but he wasn't there. She shivered. He looked almost human when he'd come to the cottage, and she had to remind herself he wasn't. What, she wasn't sure. Corpse didn't sound like the correct word anymore. She didn't know what to do with Dusan. She'd never met a man she didn't know what to do with.

Her stomach twisted at this, and something rustled behind her. She spun around again.

You're not looking hard enough.

The whisper was a breath against her ear, and she shivered again. She closed her eyes then, when opening them again, Dusan appeared. His brown eyes stared unblinkingly at her, and she held back a gasp. There were no signs of mildew or rot on him. Where recently she could peer into his skull and see his exposed bones, there was solid brown flesh. Muscle that before was withered away and decomposed was full and flexed.

Amelia took a half a step back and lifted her chin. There was something still empty in those dark eyes.

"You look different," she said.

"It's because of you," was his answer. He continued to look at her and a tiny quirk lifted the corner of his mouth. "Ever since you answered my call, I've gained myself back. Not only my flesh, but I crave. I hunger. I desire."

Deep in Amelia's core, she warmed. His seductive words were dangerous ones, and she knew what effect they could have on a person. It was something she'd done countless times. She'd never let dangerous words get the better of her.

She lifted an eyebrow. "Good for you. But I don't see how that helps me. Did you wake me up just to show I put you back together? I have no interest in men who need to be repaired. Or should I say corpse?"

The word didn't sound right on her tongue, but it was the reminder she needed. Despite his appearance, he wasn't human. He hadn't been for the last millennia.

Dusan grabbed Amelia's hand and pulled her toward him, pressing her palm against his chest. It was warm and a steady thump pulsed underneath.

"Do corpses have a heartbeat?"

His black eyes met hers, and she couldn't tear her gaze away. A wave of her own traitorous desire flooded through her, and she felt her underthings dampen with want. She ripped her hand away from his chest. It'd been far too long since she'd been with anyone, let alone someone she was remotely attracted to. That was all this was. Maybe she'd disguise herself and go into a nearby village to find a prostitute to get it out of her system.

"And what does that mean for me?" she asked. "Rafe is on his mission, and the ogres have captured the princess and her companions. Soon, Kartek will be the new Minister and I can free your swamp. Whether you are a corpse or a human doesn't matter to me."

Dusan's fingers curled and straightened like he wanted to grasp something but didn't know what. "But don't you see? It's proof."

"Proof of what?"

"You are to be my queen."

Amelia barked out a laugh. "Your queen? I've had kings claim me as theirs before, and it didn't go well, in case you weren't aware. I have no desire to be anyone's queen but my own."

"But we could bring the water sorcerers into power. Don't you see it? You have the strength to bring us out of hiding and rule."

She shook her head. "You've been talking to my mother, haven't you?"

"This is bigger than your mother or your own petty vendettas. Together, you and I could rule the world. Aren't you tired of living in the shadows?"

The water flowing through Amelia's veins splashed and swirled at the idea and bits of scales appeared on her flesh, then vanished again. Of course, she was tired of hiding her true self. But everyone knew what she was now, so what did it matter anymore?

"I set you free, you help me take back Cresin and kill the royal family. That was the deal."

Dusan narrowed his eyes and shook his head. "And then what? There's more you can do, Amelia. More we can do. You're a beautiful and powerful woman. From the moment I found you, I could feel my heart beat again. Something it hadn't done in a millennium. Then when you finally came to us... to me." He licked his lips and took a step closer. She should have moved away from him. Should ignore everything he said. This was another man, and she vowed to never be under the power of a man again.

Only Dusan wasn't a man. Or not an ordinary one. He was magic and power, and her water magic flowed like a river within her when he was near.

Another step closer and their noses almost touched. His breath should have smelled like mildew and rot, but there was something fresh and salty about it, as though he'd come directly from clear ocean water.

He took her hand again and raised it so their palms hovered over one another like a piece of paper would hold between them. Instead, a thin oval of perfectly still water formed, then rippled like a breeze wafted through the thick mist. The ripples grew larger and larger and spread the oval out so it expanded far past their hands. From each of their palms trickles of water dripped out then into small streams and then even stronger in small rivers. Water cascaded and splashed around their legs in crashing waves. The moisture in the air collected together and created waterfalls surrounded them through the vines and trees. The world was a swirl of crashing and flowing water except for a small circle where Amelia and Dusan stood palm to palm.

"Your magic speaks to mine," Dusan told her. "You can't deny what we can do together."

His salty breath caressed her skin, and she drank it in. Even being a water sorceress, she was so thirsty, and had been for a long time.

Nothing ever quenched it. No matter how much water was around Amelia or how much she drank, nothing ever satisfied. Her magic, combining with his, filled her more than swimming in an open ocean had.

Amelia searched his face and through the dark depths of his hooded eyes, she recognized the glossiness of desire in them. She licked her lips and noticed how full and warm he looked.

It had been so long, and never someone whose power matched hers.

Their lips crashed together in a tangle of mouths and teeth and tongue. It wasn't slow and romantic but the desperation of two people who'd been thirsty for too long and nothing would satisfy but each other. Ready to drown in one another if that was what it took to be satisfied. They took and took from one another and the water splashed against Amelia's back, soaking through her clothes so they clung to her like a second skin.

She tangled her hands in his hair and clothes as though she could contain him and take what she wanted. He had his plans for her, but that didn't mean she didn't have her own for him. With a push, she shoved him toward a tree and he soared through the water and his back crashed into it. There was no sign of pain or struggle from him when he hit it, and he only gave her a wicked grin.

"I knew you would see my point," he said.

Amelia burned. Of course, he would make it about what he wanted.

"I have ideas of my own."

"Show me."

With only a few steps, Amelia stalked toward him and put her hand on his chest, feeling his heart pounding through it. She could feel his water magic coursing through him and knew she could reach her own inside and do what she wanted. Instead, she kissed him again, setting off an explosion of waves through the trees. She pressed herself against him and his stiff cock rubbed between her legs and she moaned. When was the last time she'd felt this, the way she could affect someone else, and not from fear?

The thin fabric of his ancient tunic tore when Amelia tugged at it and she trailed her kisses down his chest. Her hand grasped his trousers, containing his thick member, and stroked it with rough movements. He growled and moaned at her touch, then grasped her by the shoulders and shoved.

"You'll have that, queen, but I need more first."

She flew through the coursing water and crashed into a tree the way she'd done to him. The bark dug into her back and the shock of it ran down her spine. But when she saw Dusan walking toward her with the waves parting for him, the pain vanished and before she knew it, he was shoved against her. He ripped at her dress, exposing her breasts to him and the world.

He buried his face between them and licked the sensitive skin there, sending a shiver through her. She moaned.

"If I'm your queen, then you'll do what I say."

He licked and sucked at her breast, his teeth gripped her taut nipple. She gasped and clutched his hair in her fingers.

"And what is that?" he asked when he released her.

"Fuck me until I can't think anymore."

"I'm glad we're in agreement, because that was what I was planning."

He reached down and grasped at her skirt so he could reach beneath it and between her legs. She spread them enough for his fingers to find her already soaked womanhood. He rubbed two fingers over her core, and she let out a loud groan. She couldn't remember when someone had filled her with such desire before. Someone who navigated her body with such ease. Then he thrust those fingers inside of her, and she cried out. He kissed her neck, then whispered into her ear.

"I knew you desired me. I've wanted you for so long."

"Then show me."

If he didn't get inside of her immediately, she thought she might explode.

Dusan didn't need more encouragement though, and with a swift movement cupped her rear in his hands and wrapped her legs around his waist. Shoving her even harder against the tree trunk, he reached between them to guide his cock deep inside of her.

He went in once, then twice deeper, then with a loud groan he shoved himself fully into her, and Amelia saw stars behind her closed lids. He wasn't gentle, and she took each pound of his body, going deeper. She clawed at his back, giving him just as much as he was giving her. Dusan did as he was told, and with each wave of desire, the less Amelia thought and drowned herself in the sorcerer and their magic and power.

Chapter Twenty-One

ROSE

THEY STAYED AT THE CAMP FOR DAYS, BUT THE ONLY TIMES ROSE SAW Kartek was when she came in to check on Zorar. The chief typically spent her days hunting, hosting parties, speaking with Arag, but mostly defending her position of power. Ogres were infamous for the turnover of their chiefs, for they all were violent and power hungry. Particularly when drunk, which was most of the time. Almost each day someone challenged Kartek and one by one she took down her opposition, leaving little wonder why Arag was by her side nearly at all times. Not because he was a dear friend, but a bodyguard. Rose witnessed more bloodshed in those days than she ever had in her life. If it wasn't for how often they fornicated, it was a wonder their species was still alive.

Except for Kartek. While the others enjoyed themselves, she retreated to Zorar's tent. Zorar no longer screamed randomly through the day and night and took at least a couple of bites a day. But she plateaued and showed no sign of getting better. She remained in her dazed and fatigued state. Yet Kartek was devoted to her visits and whenever she saw Rose, the challenge was the same.

Make her well.

"How many people do you think the Chalice can serve at once?" Rose asked Rafe one afternoon as they walked around the camp during his patrol. Noticing how strong Cal was, and the way Rafe could change forms, Kartek was quick to enlist them in helping guard the camp. They'd quickly agreed, for it gave them more leverage with the chief. They were also slightly terrified of her and didn't want to see the reaction she'd have if they said no.

It was a comfort to know Kartek trusted them, at least to an extent. They'd had little luck in getting Kartek to loosen her restrictions on Ai and Finley, though. The pair remained tied, and the guards escorted them outside when they needed to relieve themselves. But they could negotiate with them being able to walk around the camp. Still tied up and escorted. Still, it was progress. Not that Rose wanted to give them much more freedom anyway, since she wasn't sure how much she could trust them. Her hope was Ai and Finley would be of help, though.

"I know as much as you do about the Chalice," Rafe said, and tossed Rose an apple. Thankfully, some apple trees grew nearby and the three of them had gathered some. It was far better than whatever gruel the ogres made each day. "When you visited the cave, it was the first I'd heard the story."

"Do you think we'll be able to use the Chalice to help heal those with this sickness?"

Rafe shrugged. "Perhaps."

Rose groaned. "You're a servant of the goddess of sickness. Aren't you supposed to know these things?"

Rafe tossed away his apple core. "The duties she has me attend to do not include my sitting besides sick beds."

"What is it she has you do?" To be honest, Rose was dying to know. Rafe was always so secretive about where he went when he wasn't with her and Cal and what being a servant of Stula entailed. Perhaps his contract with her prevented him from saying anything.

Rafe smiled. "I have a set of skills she finds valuable."

Rose groaned again. The same cryptic type of answer as always. Rafe laughed at her reaction, and they circled back to the camp entrance. The sun was setting, and it was nearly time for the nightly feasting. The phoenix in its cage cried out and flapped its wings, the sparks from its being mingling with that of the fire. Between the bonfire and the bird, at night it was so warm within the camp they almost didn't need blankets when they went to bed.

"I'll see you later," Rose told Rafe and walked toward the cage. It cawed and cried throughout the day and night. Trapped in the cage and unable to spread its wings the way it should and enjoy this life to its full extent.

Rose clasped a hand upon one of the metal rods caging in the magnificent bird. It quietly cawed when it saw her, and Rose gave it a weak smile. "I'm sorry you're in here. I'll find out what they want to do with you, I promise."

She moved her arm through the bars, and the phoenix rubbed its cheek against her fingers. The feathers were impossibly soft while still warm, like a fireplace in the palace. Soft and comforting, but never burning.

"A marvelous creature, isn't it?" Kartek commented as she stood by Rose's side.

Rose quickly pulled her arm out of the cage and stuffed it back inside her cloak. "It is. I'm amazed you could capture it."

Kartek smiled proudly. "It was my first act as chief. My predecessor sat on his ass all day, drank ale, and fucked whoever walked by, whether they liked it or not. A worthless piece of shit, if you ask me. When I defeated him, I declared I would do more for our clan and the next day we tracked this beauty. There's no denying we have a valuable bargaining chip."

Rose cocked her head in curiosity. "What do you need to bargain for?"

"A piece of Cresin, of course," Kartek answered as though it were the most logical response in the world. "The people are divided between the king and your sister, and they're all distracted and fearful of Amelia taking her revenge. Then there are others who will be quick to join with Amelia if she were to offer. This is the perfect time for us to make a better name for ourselves. With this beauty, ogres can establish themselves as more than mere barbarians. The phoenix has magic and power given to Ray. We would be quick to gain Oxarian support too, considering she's one of Ray's creatures. Don't you agree?"

Rose tried to keep the shock from not only these revelations but also

Kartek's confessions all of this hidden from her face, but some must have shown through, for Kartek laughed.

"Don't look so surprised, Red," she said. "What did you think was going to happen to the kingdom?"

"Is everyone unhappy with the royal family?" Rose asked.

"Oh, King Brennan is fine. He and the line before him have worked hard to maintain peace, it's all wonderful. But the family has been in power for so long. Now there's an opening and cracks in the peace. There will be people jumping to change things and claim their own power." She clapped Rose on the back and pointed to the phoenix. "And this bird is our ticket in."

When Kartek left her side, Rose rushed back to the tent where Ai, Finley, and Cal all sat sharing some apples. "They want to use it to barter for a place in court. Maybe even take over court."

Cal furrowed his brows and cut an apple into slices with his pocketknife. "The phoenix?"

Rose told them everything Kartek had said. Cal mused over the news while he took a bite of his food. "Amelia must know that things could be changing. She wasn't given it by birth, but by marriage. If she wants to put her new baby on the throne, she'll have to fight or gather supporters and allies. If the ogres come to the castle, either they'll take over, or Amelia might find it appealing to bring them to her side."

"I'm not sure about you, but I don't like either of those scenarios," Ai said.

"Ogres controlling Cresin? Me either."

"Or Amelia being back in power," Finley added. "Not that I want to get involved. We've already gotten ourselves in too deep as it is."

When Rafe returned, they filled him in on what Rose had learned and determined it was time. They approached Kartek with what brought them there.

That evening, Rose dressed in the cleanest clothes she had with her and had the guards by her tent escort her to Kartek. The chief eyes her warily, but eventually permitted her to sit during dinner. It was against their rules to speak of political matters during the meal, so Rose waited until the chief was happy and full. Most of the ogres approached her with their requests once the dancing started, and Rose made sure she was the first to speak.

"I have a proposition for you," Rose said.

Kartek raised a brow and took a swig of swamp water. "We already have a deal with you. Have you helped Zorar? You remember our agreement."

Command was more like it, but Rose only nodded. "I told you I don't of a cure for the sickness. It's something new Eral Forest has never seen. But Zorar is sleeping more peacefully than she once was. But if you grant my request, I might help more."

Kartek leaned back in her chair and lifted the cup to her. "Very well, you may present your case and I'll decide if you are worthy of it being granted to you."

Rose sat straighter and took her time. "We are here on a mission to find a cure for Eral from the Minister. Saving Eral from this water and the mushrooms would be for everyone living here, ogres and Zorar included. We're also searching for ingredients for a bread she wants us to make."

Kartek cocked her head to the side in interest. "Yes, the water and mushrooms have been unusual. Are you confident this causes Zohar's illness?"

"I am," Rose said, more confidently than she felt. If only Eira were here. She was much better at and well taught in how to bargain and negotiate these sorts of things. "But we need the phoenix for one ingredient for the bread."

Kartek extended her hand with an empty goblet and an ogre refilled it for her. "So you would have my bird, make your precious bread, then be the hero of Eral. And where would that leave me? The same place I am in now."

"I'm sure you've heard about Gallis's Chalice. The one we used to save King Brennan? What if it can cure those infected here in Eral? What if we promise Zorar is the first to drink?"

"And I don't get my bird back? I will have no bargaining chips to use."

"You know who I am. I'm the daughter of King Brennan and the granddaughter of Kutalous's Minister. You free us and help us. I can speak to them," Rose said. "We could give you and your clan credit for finding the phoenix and be sure they honor you for it. Grant you a place in court."

Kartek drank more from her cup and stared out into the fire. Its light danced across her face, making her orange eyes glow. She placed the cup down and rubbed the teeth on her necklace. How many of them did the chief collect herself? Which markings on her body showed how many kills she'd performed? The idea of someone such as this having a place in her family's beloved court made Rose's skin crawl. But there could be advantages to having this clan as allies.

"Do you need the bird outside of its cage? Or is it as simple as taking a feather?" Kartek asked.

"The ashes," Rose answered. "After it has burned itself and before it rises again from them."

"You would need to wait until the bird is ready," Kartek said. "I know the law of Eral, and considering how rare phoenixes are, Eral forbids us to harm them before their natural time to burn. Even we observe that law."

As if in response, the phoenix let out a weak caw. Even in the few days Rose had been there, the radiance of its feathers had faded. "We would wait until it is appropriate," Rose agreed.

Kartek crossed one leg over the other and swung it back and forth. "I am not guaranteed you would return, though. How do I know you will?"

"You have my word."

A dark chuckle emerged from Kartek's lips. "I am not so naïve." She looked about the camp with a mischievous gleam in her eye. "I could hold one of you here to serve me and my clan until you return. The wolf, perhaps. Or maybe the tall hunter?"

"There is no need," Rose snapped. "The bird deserves her freedom, though."

Kartek chuckled again. "We will determine this our way. You will fight for it. A duel. If you win, you may take your ashes, then bring the Chalice of Gallis here immediately to heal Zorar and grant our clan a rightful place in Faren Court. But we keep the mother. If you do not win…" A cruel smile crept across her face. "Well, you don't win."

Chapter Twenty-Two

ROSE

CAL STRUMMED HIS FINGERS UPON THE ARMREST OF A CHAIR IN THEIR tent. He'd been on observation for Zorar and she'd had a restless day, but with the herbs now lay silently. Ai sat in her usual place tied up while Finley's head lay in her lap as she took a nap. The pirate queen took more naps than anyone Rose ever knew, but she'd grown used to it.

"At least we have a bit of time to prepare you," Cal said. It had been several long moments since Rose told them of the outcome of her conversation with Kartek. "You've beaten me plenty of times, as well as those on the guard."

"That was on the training ground, and against other humans," Rose said. She sat on the bed she and Cal shared and unwrapped her straps. "This is entirely different. You've seen ogre brawls. There is no honor or rules. They simply fight to-"

"To the death," Ai finished quietly.

Rose nodded. The room was silent for a few moments while they all let those words settle in. How had she gotten herself into this mess? The negotiating and bartering she'd expected. It was foolish of her to imagine she wouldn't have to come to this.

"I've never killed anyone in cold blood before," Rose said.

"You've hunted," Cal pointed out.

"This is different."

"And you didn't seem afraid of killing with Amelia. Now, or when you tried to kill her back at Faren Castle."

That was true and wasn't even very long ago, even if it felt like an age. Amelia's actions had filled her with rage and anxiousness the day Rose tried to kill her, and when she thought about what the sorceress did, it all came flooding back. Yet, this was something else. Performing in a duel such as this wasn't for show and everyone was fine in the end, like during the tournament she and Cal fought each other in. Nor was this to defend her family or avenge wrongs or to do her duty to family and kingdom. It was the ogre's excuse for more violence.

"It's still different," Rose finally said.

"I know."

Ai sighed. "It's because you have a good heart, and this is not a bad thing, Rose. It is a gift."

The pirate may have had a point, but considering who it came from, Rose couldn't find courage from it. All of them there were fighters and warriors and did what they felt they needed to survive. Having a good heart wasn't particularly comforting at the moment.

Cal rose from his seat and approached Rose. He knelt, so he was at eye level with her, who wouldn't meet his gaze. His hand was gentle as he grasped her chin and rose it so she looked directly into his blue eyes and her entire body turned into hot molten lava. Sleeping next to him each night had been torture, knowing she shouldn't kiss or touch him. "It's never easy.. But there are moments we don't have much of a choice. We need to determine which is the lesser evil. The one we can live with. Do you see any other options?"

He removed his hand from her chin and placed it on his knee and waited patiently for her answer.

"We could steal the phoenix and the eggs when they aren't looking," Ai suggested, and Rose and Cal broke their gaze to look at her. "But if we're caught…"

They would be in the same situation they were in now. Or worse. But if Rose lost her duel… no. They may have had two pirates potentially on their side, but there was still too great of a risk. It wasn't an option.

"Do you want to steal them?" Cal asked.

Rose shook her head. "There is no way to guarantee we won't be caught."

Just as there was no guarantee she would win the duel. But if she won, would she be able to obtain the trust of the ogres? If she did, as brutal as they were, they could be useful to her and Eira in the future.

Cal grasped Rose's hands in his own. "We will find a way out of this, Rose. I promise. In the meantime, I will help you train. And you have the Shadowslayers. We'll train with those, and surely they'll help you."

"Maybe I could have a second? Someone to help fight with me or if I get injured," Rose wondered.

"Perhaps, but I doubt it," Ai answered. "They do not seem to fight that way. However, as much as I believe in you, if they allow you a second and you wish for one of us to fight in your place, it would be my honor."

"Mine too," Cal said.

"Not mine," added a sleepy voice. They all stared as Finley's eyes blinked open, and she pushed herself up to sit. "All of this 'I don't want to kill' and 'you have a good heart' bullshit is disturbing my sleep. Rose, your part of the royal guard, dedicated to the god of war, and the granddaughter of Kutlaous's Minister. Do what you need to do and move on. We've all had to kill someone at some point or another. But I'm not risking my neck for yours."

Ai heaved a heavy sigh. "Finley, how long have you been awake?"

"Long enough," Finley said with a groan. "But I say it's our best way out of here. You are taking us with you, correct?"

She raised a brow and stared down at Rose.

Rose shifted in her seat and looked at Cal. He looked as wary as she felt about Finley and Ai, but between the four of them - five, if Rafe showed up and helped - they had a better chance. She nodded. "Of course."

Rose slumped forward and let herself rest on Cal's shoulder. Cal put his arms around her in an embrace and let her stay for as long as she wished.

THE DAYS CONTINUED ON, BUT THE PHOENIX SHOWED NO SIGN OF wanting to burn. The straw it sat on continually grew warmer and glowed more brightly each time Rose saw the cage. The phoenix grew thinner. The bright color of her feathers faded away, and she did not flap her wings as often. Rose visited it each day and fed her berries and nuts found outside of the camp.

"When she burns and comes back to life, is it a new bird that rises from the ashes, or is it the same one?" Rose asked Rafe one day.

"How would I know?"

"Death. That's your realm."

Rafe tossed the bird a handful of nuts and she caught a few in her beak, but many fell to the ground. "From what I can tell, it's the same one reliving the same life repeatedly. She'll burn soon though."

"She will?" Rose asked.

Rafe nodded. "Don't you see her slowly fading away?"

"I can't decide if I'm looking forward to the day or dread it," Rose said.

"You don't think you're ready for your duel?"

"Is anyone ready to fight for their life?"

It was nearing Rose's turn to watch over Zorar, and they made their way to the tent. "We all do what we need in order to survive. I'm sure you find it cruel for me to say you get used to it after a while. Some are harder than others but, death is part of life."

"You've killed many?" Rose asked, hoping he would finally divulge what exactly it was he did for Stula.

He glanced at her out of the corner of his eye and looked forward again. "I try to see it more like lending a helping hand to send them to the next life. Although, she has me shove more than guide."

"Do you have a say in who you… help?"

"Sometimes she'll pick those I'm more willing to… help… but ultimately, no. The usual ones I assist are those who have been evading her for too long. It's not always polite."

Oh. Rose's stomach turned.

"I see."

They arrived at the tent, and Kartek was already sitting by the bed. Tears formed in her eyes, but she blinked them away before Rose discerned whether there was any truly there. Kartek held Zorar's hand, and she kissed it before she stood.

"She had a nightmare. You should watch more closely. It took me ages to calm her," Kartek said, her voice hard as stone. "I permit you to stay here because you said you would help."

"My apologies, Chief," Rose said.

"Do your job."

She pushed past them and exited the tent.

CAL SWUNG A CLUB ABOUT WITH ONE ARM, HIS SWORD OF AROS'S tattoo shining. He'd taken it from the camp and was almost as long as his arm and an ogre could wield it with one hand. Rose needed two to hold the one Cal had swiped for her. With his gifts from Aros, Cal was fine holding it with one. They'd found a small clearing near the camp where the ogres could monitor them, but far enough away where they could practice and speak with no one overhearing.

"It's a crude weapon, but they favor it, so you should get some practice in with it," he explained. He gestured for Rose to come closer to him and set his feet hip width apart to take a fighting stance. She walked over to him. "Usually, you need to be in close proximity for it to be effective."

He patted the end of the club. "This part will have the most impact, so if you can be close enough where only the portion closest to the hand will hit you, you can grab it and doge away, perhaps even disarm."

He swung at her, and Rose ducked, grabbing the handle and pulling it down. She elbowed him in the stomach and as he doubled over; she rolled out of his way, taking the club with her.

"Like that" she asked.

Cal gasped when he caught himself on the ground. He smiled, looking over at her. "Yeah, something like that."

Rose held the club with both hands and swung it back and forth. "Cadeyrn and I practiced with them sometimes, and I didn't hurt you that badly."

He propped himself up and knelt on the grass. "Perhaps not, but you surprised me, which could be useful to you."

Rose extended a hand to help him to his feet. He gripped her wrist and rose to stand and pulled her to the ground. Rose yelped as they fell. The club flew out of her hand and landed with a thud, and Cal laughed. Rose scowled and looped her leg around his, rolling him over, and his face planted into the dirt. A string of curse words poured out of his mouth, and it was Rose's turn to laugh.

"Serves you right," she said.

Cal sat and wiped his face with the back of his sleeve.

"I'm not sure it will work with an ogre, though," Rafe said as he stalked toward them.

Rose propped herself on her elbows. "And you know of a better way?"

"Surprise is good, since most ogres aren't clever," Rafe said. "But you'll need more than cleverness and speed for a duel."

He tossed the Shadowslayer dagger to her, and she caught it with one hand. The shining silver blade glimmered in the light.

"If you can stab your opponent with it when you doge away from his club, you'll at least wound him while you escape," Rafe said.

"Won't kill them, though, the blade isn't deep enough to hit anything vital under an ogre's thick skin," Cal pointed out.

"You'll need to be fast," Rafe added. He shifted into the wolf and jumped toward her.

Rose cried out and rolled out of the way, holding the knife before her. Rafe skidded across the ground, dirt flying around him, and he lowered his lower half, so his tail was in the air. He wagged it playfully. Something beyond Rose caught his yellow eyes. Rose looked behind her, and Cal was charging toward her.

Not fair. They'd teamed against her.

Rose scrambled to her feet and gripped the knife as Cal and Rafe stood side by side. A challenge.

Rose tossed the knife from hand to hand and ran. They ran to her as well as ran into her. Smashed between the two, they pushed her backward and knocked her on her ass. The hard ground sent a shudder down her spine, but she could roll and toss Rafe off her. Cal kept holding on, and she swung at him with her free arm. Rafe pounced and grabbed her cloak. She tugged at the strings, and it loosened, letting her wiggle free. She jumped to her feet and did a small dance.

Cal stood and took a step forward, but Rafe froze, his ears perked as though he were listening to something.

"Did I make you hit the ground too hard?" Rose teased.

He shifted back to being a man. Each part of him was stiff and alert.

"Are you all right?" Cal asked.

"I have to go," Rafe announced.

"Go?" Rose repeated. "Go where? You can't leave us here."

"I have to," Rafe said and walked past them in a rush. His shoulder bumped Rose's, and she scoffed.

"Hey!" she called and chased after him. She caught up and grabbed his arm, forcing him to stop. "What do you mean, you have to?"

"She's summoning me," Rafe said, his yellow eyes blazing. "When she calls, I don't have a choice but to go. I'll find you when she's done with me."

She? Oh. Stula.

Rafe shook her off and ran off. Within a moment, he was out of sight.

"Rafe!" Rose yelled helplessly. But he was gone. There weren't even footsteps left in the dirt to show the direction he'd gone. She spun around to face Cal. "He's gone."

Cal wiped the dirt off his tunic. "Apparently."

Rose sighed. "I'm getting tired of that. What if he's not back by the time of my duel? He knows Eral better than we do, and what if we get lost again?"

Rose closed the knife and slid it in her pocket and went to get her cloak.

Cal put an arm around her shoulders. "He'll come back."

"I thought you didn't trust him."

He shrugged. "I don't know if I do. But you like him and seem to trust him, so there must be something I don't see. And if he doesn't come back, I'll track him myself and make him answer for leaving."

Rose leaned into him, and they walked back to camp. "Only if I get to keep the skin."

Cal roared with laughter. "If you insist."

Rafe did not return. Each day, Cal and Rose trained and watched over Zorar, but there was no sign of their wolf friend. One day, there was a crack.

A stream of orange light erupted from the phoenix cage and cast a glow over the entire camp. A second and a third. Rose and Cal gathered with everyone else around the cage to watch the event. Her red feathers faded, and it wasted away her to almost the bones. The straw underneath her sizzled and popped and cracked from the heat.

"It will be soon," Kartek said. "Go get your weapons, Red. I want this done and over with."

Chapter Twenty-Three

ROSE

CAL PLACED A HAND ON THE SMALL OF ROSE'S BACK AND LED HER BACK to their tent so she could get ready. She crutched through the camp and in the trees saw a pair of yellow eyes watching.

Rose paused and tugged Cal's shoulder and pointed to them. But they were gone by the time he looked.

"What is it?" Cal asked when they were in the tent's shelter.

Rose found her fighting leathers and placed them over her tunic. "Those yellow eyes, they're back."

"Do you think it's Rafe?" Cal dug the straps out of the pile they were in and brought them over to Rose.

She sat upon the edge of the bed and extended her foot to him. He knelt on the ground and wrapped.

"Maybe. I don't know. I used to think it was, but I don't anymore. If it was, he would simply come into the camp, wouldn't he?"

"You know him better than I do." Cal carefully but tightly wrapped Rose's ankle while they spoke. Before this journey, he'd never helped her with it before, but had become a natural at it.

Rose rolled her ankle when he finished, to be sure she could still move. Sometimes when he first started where it was too tight, and she couldn't even flex. This was perfect. Even better than when Evony would do it.

"Whoever it is, I hope it's a friend."

Rose strapped the Shadowslayer sword to her back and placed the dagger on her belt. Lastly, she tied her road cloak around her neck. It was too warm for it. Already, a sheen of sweat was on her face and ogres were chattering outside about the upcoming duel. Yet, it was also to protect her from harm. Perhaps it would come in handy.

"Maybe she'll let me go in your stead," Cal said as they stepped out. It wasn't as though she wasn't capable. It was a simple fact. Even with being dedicated to Aros, Cal had more muscle, strength, and experience than she did.

The ogres circled around the center of the camp. They'd extinguished the usual bonfire, for the phoenix gave enough heat on its own. It also made more room for battle. Past the crowd, the yellow eyes appeared and disappeared.

Rose approached Kartek's chair and held her head high. No matter how nervous she was, the captain would never know. "Do I get a second?" Rose asked.

Kartek chuckled. "That's not how we do things around here. You should know this by now. You present the challenge. You must be the one to see it through."

It had been a long shot, but worth a try. "I am ready whenever you are, Chief."

"Oh, you aren't fighting me," Kartek answered.

"What? You said-"

Kartek gave her a smug grin. "I never said who you'd be fighting. Do you think I would risk my life and status on *you*?"

Rose couldn't decide if this made her feel better or worse. Kartek was clearly an excellent fighter, otherwise she wouldn't be sitting in that stone chair leading this clan. Not fighting her was a bit of a relief. Still, she didn't know who she *would* be fighting.

"Who will be my opponent?" Rose asked.

Kartek clapped her hands, and an ogre stepped forward. He was larger than Arag by at least a head. He wore no fighting leathers save for belts crossed in an X across his broad green chest and brown trousers. A club hung from his hand.

For a moment, Rose couldn't breathe. She tried to remember everything they had taught her on the practice field and what she and Cal had done in preparation, but it all vanished from her mind. This was it. She had to face him.

Rose nodded once and kept her face neutral while the ogres stomped and clapped, their blood lust palatable in the heavy air. She tried to channel Eira, who was always so good at keeping a brave face when inside she was falling apart. Rose could do the same now. She didn't have any other choice.

Cal was at her side and gave her hand a single squeeze. He couldn't be there with her in the battle, but he was still there.

"If I fail," Rose started.

"You're not going to."

"If I fail," she repeated. "Get the ashes anyway and tell Grandmother I tried. You'll finish it, won't you?"

Cal took in a deep breath. "I will."

Rose gulped and went toward him. She put her hand behind his head and kissed him. The ogres laughed and hollered behind them, but Rose didn't care. Pain jolted through her, and Cal groaned. If this was the last time she could kiss him, a little pain would be well worth it.

They broke apart, and both of them panted. She pressed her forehead against his and nodded. With another deep breath, Rose closed her eyes and dug for her magic. The power of Aros soared through her, and her tattoo glowed through the fabric of her leggings. She stepped forward and faced Kartek one last time. "Remember what you promised when I win."

Kartek raised her cup in a salute. "I am a woman of my word. As long as you are as well."

Rose barely stepped out when the warrior attacked. She hit the ground hard, and it knocked the wind right out of her. A faint glow emerged around her as the club struck her. The cloak. The blow should have done more damage with the force and strength behind it. Perhaps the cloak would come in handy after all.

The ogres surrounding them chuckled. Not even a minute into the fight, and she'd already fallen over.

Rose rolled and reached for the dagger as the ogre swung at her again. She lifted her cloak, so it covered her body, and it blocked the blow with a flash, giving her time to swat at his legs with the dagger. It caused minor damage but distracted him enough for Rose to get back to her feet.

She held out the dagger with one hand and with the other reached to unsheathe her sword. Her back ached already, but she pushed the pain aside. Get this done and she could moan and whine to Cal later on their way back to Grandmother's. This time, she'd let him carry her without complaint.

More bolts of light burst from the phoenix and the bird cried, making the camp even hotter than it already was.

The ogre growled at his minor injury and charged. Rose could block more attacks than she'd thought possible between her sword and cloak, but sweat was dripping in her eyes within minutes, and the blow that hit her took her breath away. She was defending herself more than causing any damage to him. She needed to disarm him if she wanted to make any sort of headway.

Closer. She needed to get as close to the beast as possible. Which would be difficult with the sword. Dagger it was.

She swung at the club with a hard enough blow it stuck in the wood and grabbed the dagger in her belt as he tried to swing the sword off the weapon, giving her an in. She propelled herself between the club and the ogre, stabbing him in the stomach with her dagger. He bellowed loudly enough Rose almost went deaf, and keeled over, his grip on the club loosening. Seizing the opportunity, Rose pushed her sword, so the club flew out of his hand, taking her weapon with it.

With a roll, Rose moved out of the way of the falling ogre and crawled toward the discarded weapons. Behind her, the ogre roared, and the ground shook as he chased after her. She reached the club, grabbed it and pulled her sword out. Something hit her bad leg, and she cried out.

The ogre used her dagger and sliced her leg. Blood seeped out through her trousers and leaked onto the straps. With both hands, she lifted the club and bashed his head with it. She tried to stand, but her leg wouldn't hold her. She propped the club onto the ground and used it as a crutch, and bit through the pain. The ogre only swung an arm and swatted it away, making her collapse again. He kicked her stomach, and Rose howled again.

What was she doing here? How did she think she could fight an ogre twice her size and strength?

She grasped at the hard ground and pulled herself forward toward her sword when the ogre stepped on her foot and a crack rang through the camp. The pain didn't hit her at first. Only the sense that something was terribly wrong. As though she could sense the gap in her bone. It was when the ogre moved her leg Rose cried out as searing pain roared through her body. Cal was screaming her name in the crowd, and she looked out at him. He was fighting to join her in the ring, but the ogres held him back. Rose peered more closely and past the crowd, the yellow eyes were staring at her. They blinked and a long vine slithered its way out from the crowd over the ground toward her.

Out of the corner of her eye, the ogre aimed to hit her again, but she grabbed the edge of her cloak to block the blow.

She needed to get to the vine. She didn't know why, but she had to.

Rose rolled and dodged each attack as she pulled herself forward to grasp at the vine, biting her lip to stop from crying out. Finally, she reached the edge and clutched her hand around it. A green glow poured from her hand and down the vine, and more strands grew out of it. Her fae blood line. Whoever's eyes those were knew about her heritage.

A cool sensation ran through her as she pulled at the vine and swung it toward the ogre, and it wrapped around one of his ankles. The pain didn't vanish but subsided to where she could move without wanting to die. She tugged it, and the ogre fell with such a thud the ground shook. More strands grew from it and wrapped themselves around the other ankle and wrapped his feet together. Rose used the plant to drag herself toward the ogre, who was twisting and flailing trying to escape. She pressed onto the vine more and the leaves and branches grew over his legs and up his torso, encasing him in a cage of green. He tried to fight and tear at the plant, but it only grew stronger and tied his arms as well.

Rose grabbed the club and her sword and struggled to stand, her head spinning, the blood draining from it. It hurt, but she could do it thanks to the vine magic coursing through her body. Using the club as a crutch, she hobbled toward the ogre. The vines covered his whole body and strapped him to the ground, unable to move. She looked over her shoulder at Kartek. The captain smiled and gave a single nod.

Rose needed to finish it.

It was the way of the ogres.

With a loud cry, Rose used all the strength she had and swung Shadowslayer upon the ogre, and his head rolled off, its face frozen in a silent scream.

The phoenix cried, and Rose dropped the sword. It wasn't glorious, and she didn't feel relief. It was only darkness and hate. Then she fell, and all went dark.

WATER SPLASHED ON ROSE'S FACE, AND SHE OPENED HER EYES TO FIND she was lying in the bed in her tent. Cal hovered over her and helped her to sit. Her leg throbbed but didn't have the sharp pain any more from the duel.

"What happened?" Rose asked.

"You passed out," Ai explained. She stood off to the side and was strapping weapons to her body. Finley was beside her, doing the same.

Cal sat on a stool next to the bed and brushed her wild hair aside. "I let you sleep so I could set your leg and wanted to let you sleep longer, but… it's almost done. The bird has begun to burn. It takes longer than I thought, but I think if we wait, we will have outstayed our welcome. Kartek will help us to the cage to get what we need, but the others aren't happy with a human killing on of their own."

A silly grudge to hold against her. They were killing each other off plenty.

"If it comes to stealing, we can get it," Finley said. She adjusted her hat so it sat primly on her head. "I have a feeling we have more experience in getting things out of unwanted places than you do."

Rose propped herself up on her elbows and narrowed her brows. "How are you untied?"

Finley wiggled her brows. "I have water magic and have been working on disintegrating the ropes for days."

Rose gaped at them.

"Sorry to have to fool you for so long," Ai said. She had a gentle smile, and her eyes were soft, as though she were genuinely apologetic. "It's better to be underestimated than over. We had to be sure we could trust you. The two of you go. We'll meet you outside of the camp."

Cal stood and helped Rose swing her legs over the edge of the bed. She wore a new set of fresh clothing, and they strapped her ankle into a splint made of wood and leather. It was sturdy and wrapped tight, so there was no chance of her leg moving.

"It's broken," Cal confirmed. "I mixed some herbs for you to help with the pain so we can at least get out of here in one piece. I'll try to carry you as much as possible once we're safe."

Rose's crutch and the ogre's club rested against the wall next to the bed so Rose could use both to walk. They strapped her weapons across her back and upon her belt, and Cal took on his own as well as their travel sack.

Out of the travel sack, Rose found some herbs she'd been using to help Zorar and placed them on the side table next to her bed. At least they could continue to help her when they were gone, even if it was only a bit.

Outside, ogres roared and yelled as Rose and Cal stepped out. Arag met them at the door and helped guide through the crowds toward the cage. More beams of light poured over the camp as though the sun were shining in the middle of summer. Rose squinted as Arag led them to where Kartek was waiting.

The burning phoenix cried and shrieked, hardly able to hold her own head over the climbing flames. The fire started small and slow at first. Glowing embers beneath her clawed feet. They rose her legs and over her stomach until she glowed, and the flames grew larger. She cried and writhed in pain. Rose wanted to look away but could not, mesmerized by the tragic event. It wasn't long before the whole bird was a pillar of fire so bright it nearly blinded those around the cage.

With a final caw, she exploded into fire and vanished. All which was left was a pile of ashes, black as night but had a faint glimmer. Cal nudged at Rose, who was staring at the sight. She pulled out a small container from her pocket, reached through the bars of the cage, and gathered what they needed.

It was just in time, for out of the silence came a tiny chirp. A minuscule beak poked from the ashes and there emerged a brand new bird.

"Now go," Kartek commanded.

"Thank you," Rose said as she hid the container in her pocket again.

Kartek stalked toward her with a sneer. "Now it's your turn to uphold the bargain. If you do not return, I'll track you and be sure you meet the same fate as your opponent."

Rose gulped, seeing the promise in the ogre chief's eyes. "Of course."

Rose and Cal nodded to her and went on their way. As they crossed the edge of the camp, Rose looked back at the cage to where the newborn bird was held captive. Although it looked more like a tiny beast with their bulging red eyes and mucus covered feathers plastered to their frail body. "When we come back, we take her with us," she said.

Cal squeezed her shoulder. "We'll make sure she's safe," he reassured her and they went off into Eral Forest.

Chapter Twenty-Four

ROSE

THE BEAMS OF LIGHT FROM THE PHOENIX DIED AWAY, BUT THE FRESH glow of the raging bonfire of the ogre camp reflected in the green haze hovering over Eral Forest as Rose and the others made their escape. Even with her Aros magic and the splint surrounding her broken ankle, the most Rose could do was bite through the pain and quickly hobble to keep pace with them. One ogre roared, and it shook the forest ground. Rose tripped over a protruding branch, the dirt covering it having been washed away from the water and mud overtaking the forest. She caught herself and bit her lip from the jarring pain in her ankle. She looked over her shoulder and something tightened in her chest. A small part of her worried for Kartek.

Which was ridiculous. She'd kept them imprisoned and wouldn't blink or hesitate to rip Rose's throat out if they betrayed her. But she helped them escape for some reason.

Rose shook her head and kept going. Kartek could take care of herself.

Finley and Ai raced ahead, but Ai looked around and paused. She put her hand on Finley's shoulder, who rolled her head around in a dramatic circle, the giant feather in her hat circling like a bird over its prey.

"Excuse me, did you want to stay in the ogre camp and have them slaughter you?" Finley asked.

The heat of the phoenix ashes in Rose's pocket only added to the burning through her at the question. Rose gritted her teeth and tried to catch up. It would be handy if Rafe would do one of his surprise pop ins and let her ride on his back.

Cal stopped his walking and waited until Rose was at his side. She paused and panted, trying to breathe through the throbbing in her ankle. The sharp pain from the initial break had subsided, and the brace helped keep things stable. But there was this feeling of *wrongness* coursing through her with each step. It was like a piece of her foot was out of place and missing and if she moved in the wrong way, it would fall apart. Rose had her fair share of injuries in the past, but usually had a day or so to recover before needing to get back on her feet. All she wanted was to sit for just a moment.

Cal leaned down closer to her. "Let me help. I can carry you."

Her face burned. It was one thing to be on Rafe's back when he was in wolf form and didn't feel different from riding a horse. It was another to have Cal carry her through Eral. She bit her lip and fought down the embarrassment burning in her chest. She slouched further on the makeshift crutch and club to relieve some of the pressure off her ankle. Oddly, the transition seemed to make it worse.

"I know it's not ideal," Cal told her. "But we need to get away. Let me help you get to safety."

Rose shook her head. No. She was a fighter and could do this. But the crutch and club wouldn't do.

Something flashed out of the corner of her eye, and Rose straightened enough to get a better look. Her heart dropped to the pit of her stomach. One ogre had come for them.

Leaves from the bushes rustled off to the side and a pair of yellow eyes peered out at Rose. She gulped and gripped the aids even tighter. "Help me," she said. "Give me something more so I can get to the swamp."

Cal took a protective half step toward her and looked out to where Rose's gaze had fallen. "Rose, who are you talking to?"

The yellow eyes continued to look out at her and narrowed as though it was considering her request. They blinked, then closed, vanishing into the dark forest.

Rose's lips tightened into a thin line and was ready to jump into the leaves to search for those eyes and gouge them out with her bare hands. Why did it help her with the fight, but not now?

Ai and Finley exchanged confused looks.

Ai cleared her throat. "Rose, is everything all right?"

But before Rose could answer, Finley's eyes grew wide and her brows rose so high on her forehead, Rose couldn't even see them under her hat anymore. "Um… what's that?"

The four of them turned to see a group of trees and bushes shaking and stirring. The green leaves swirled and spun off them into a twisted shape and branches broke off. They flew into the air and a cloud of fog and leaves, and branches spun around. They all instinctively reached for their weapons, and Rose felt ridiculous the moment they did so.

What were they going to use swords and arrows for against plants?

The branches spun around them in a circle and made the air whip through Rose's hair as though she were stuck in a storm. Her eyes watered from the wind and forced them shut. Then all at once, the wind stopped and the branches and the thuds of things falling to the ground filled the air.

Cal muttered at her side. "What in the deities' names?"

Rose blinked her eyes open and before her stood a tall creature that looked like a horse made of pieces of Eral Forest. Vines made its long mane and tail, with branches and twigs creating the body, head, and limbs. Moss-covered rocks were at the bottom of each leg like hooves. Then, dark brown acorns made up its eyes.

The wooden horse rocked its head back and forth and stopped its feet like it beckoned Rose to come near. She grasped her walking aids and moved forward toward it.

Deep breaths. It doesn't hurt that bad.

"Are you here to help?"

The vines and leads rustled as it shook its head up and down. This creature was nothing like Rose had ever seen before.

"Who sent you?"

The wooden horse stopped moving and only looked at her. Its dark acorn eyes bored into Rose's and yellow flashed through them so fast she almost didn't see it. Something stirred within her as she looked at the creature. Something she rarely touched or acknowledged, as though they buried it deep and were now sprouting to life.

Rose lay the club aside, extended her arm to the horse, and ran her hand over the viny mane. It came to life at her touch and wrapped itself around her fingers in a warm hug. A half laugh escaped from her.

"Amazing." She twisted around to talk to Cal. He, Ai, and Finley all gaped at the scene. "Cal, help me on?"

She gave him her aids and used his sturdy shoulder to jump onto the horse's back. It wasn't the same as sitting on an animal, but it was preferable to riding on Cal.

"Is this better?" he asked. His hand landed on her thigh, and he gave it a squeeze.

Then again, at least in this circumstance it was. She could think of a few other situations where she wouldn't mind.

Heat soared through Rose and she suddenly wished the others were around. She glanced up at him, and he had a playful grin on his face.

"I guess so," she answered. If only they could get some privacy and figure out how to help his own situation. Now that her ankle was in so much pain, she wondered if the jolts from Cal wouldn't be so bad. Maybe even fun.

Rose's face warmed, and by the way Cal's eyes hooded, she wondered if he was thinking the same thing.

A faint chuckle broke Rose out of her lust filled trance. Ai wore a knowing smile and Finley rolled her eyes.

"Should we give you two more privacy?" Ai asked.

Cal backed away as though lightning had struck him. "Where to next, Rose?"

Right. This wasn't the time or the place. She needed to get herself together. She'd never let a man distract her from her goals before and would not start now.

"The swamp. I think we're getting close."

She used the vines as reins and tugged them to guide the horse in the direction she thought they should go. Their time in the ogre camp made Rose lose her sense of where they were, but Eral changed so often even if she knew where she was going, it could still end up wrong. Off to one side, the mud looked thicker and the fog darker, so that was probably where the swamp water was coming from.

The rest turned to follow Rose; all but Finley, who looked over her shoulder in the opposite direction. "But what about the Chalice? Aren't you going to bring it back to Kartek?" There was a thinness to her voice Rose wasn't used to.

"We'll get it, but we've made it this far. I'm not giving up on my mission now."

The pirate queen's eyes met Ai's, and they seemed to communicate something to each other in a silent language only the closest of people could understand. It reminded Rose of how she and Cal had their own silent routines and communication. They nodded to each other.

Finley straightened her shoulders and tossed her hair to the side as though she were only deciding where to go to have dinner. Did nothing bother this woman? No matter what happened, she behaved as though these were normal occurrences in life. Maybe for a pirate it was.

"Fine, lead the way."

Once again, Rose ventured into Eral Forest. The horse maintained its footing, but the others struggled, slipping and tripping over the mud and the mushrooms that seemed to have grown thicker. They climbed and spread over the trees and ground like a lumpy multicolored and poisonous blanket.

The further they went, the darker and damper Eral became. And quieter. Too quiet for Rose's taste. Eral was usually full of sound and life with the flicker of pixies flying around, the rainbow-colored leaves on the trees, and creatures rustling and clawing about. This deep and this close to the swamp, everything was an odd glowing green, and the only sound came from their feet squishing through the mud and the occasional buzz of insects.

Moisture hung in the air and the green fog filled the space as though they walked through a cloud. Rose pulled her red cloak away from her neck to relieve some of the heat, but it didn't help. She considered taking it off, but with the luck she'd been having, she needed all the protection she could get.

The horse stopped. It happened so fast Rose nearly fell off and they bumped into Cal, who took a few steps to the side. She gripped the vines tighter to keep her balance. "Whoa! What's the matter?"

Then the ground shook. At first, it seemed like the tremors of a group of horses galloping through the area and Rose looked around, wondering who was there. The others searched too. Finley and Ai's brows both furrowed together, and they tightened their jaws as though on high alert. Rose knew soldiers had come through this area, but she didn't realize anyone remained.

But soon, the trees and bushes shook too. They trembled like the ogres had come back to shake something down from them. Rose reached for the knife hidden in her boot, but Eral went black and a harsh chill burst into the air. She gasped at the sudden cold and felt around for the horse or something to hold on to. She could barely see anything in front of her and only the faint shadowy silhouettes of her companions.

"Rose?" Cal's voice rang out in the darkness, and Rose extended her arm out to reach for him.

"I'm here, I'm okay," she reassured him, her hand flailing about until his firm grip grabbed hers. Her breath steadied, at least a little, knowing he was there beside her. "What happened?"

"I don't know."

In the distance, a faint purple glow shimmered in front of them. Once again, all four travel companions prepared to grab their weapons at any moment. It flew toward them then hovered in front of Rose, giving the space a soft purple hue, and allowed Rose to see everyone more clearly. She blinked a few times and saw it was the pixie she'd met earlier who'd been so worried about her friend Daisy.

"Oh, thank Kutalous I found you!" the pixie cried out. Her voice pitch was so high and shrill Rose almost covered her ears. Finley did.

"What are doing here?" Rose asked.

"They commanded me to find you as soon as possible. You must come quickly!"

Rose shook her head, but already her heart dropped into her stomach. The way the little pixie fluttered in panic, and she looked she was about to combust told her that this wasn't a pleasant command. "Come? Come where?"

"To your grandmother's house. But I'm afraid it may be too late."

Chapter Twenty-Five

AMELIA

AMELIA WAVED HER ARM IN FRONT OF HER FACE AND COUGHED FROM THE smoke that surrounded the usual chair Kartek sat in. A phoenix cage sat beside her, sparkling ash filled the bottom and a tiny wormlike chick perched on a bar inside of it. She curled her lip at the sight of its barely there feathers that made it look more like a naked rat than a bird. Amelia made the trek to the camp to see how things were progressing, and it was a pathetic sight they greeted her with.

"What do you mean, they're gone?"

The ogress seemed unbothered because not only Rose and Cal had left the camp, but they took Finley and Ai with them. Amelia hadn't planned on having Finley and Ai captured too. Then when she heard they were in Eral, she leapt at the opportunity to have them seized. All four being gone was not part of the plan. Water whooshed around inside of her, and she struggled to keep it contained. It'd been too long since she'd shown people what she was capable of and wondered if maybe it was time to let it go.

Kartek sat in her stone seat and counted the teeth on her necklace. She waved an arm toward some tents. "Exactly what those words mean. They're gone. Rose killed one of my best warriors, took what she wanted and the rest of them with her."

There had been a massive puddle of blood in the center of the camp. But this was a place inhabited by ogres. Amelia assumed it was nothing unusual. "And you couldn't stop them? With these ogres around, you couldn't handle four little humans? I thought I could trust you."

"Nothing has changed for our bargain." Kartek put her necklace down and took a long stretch like a cat. "The wolf has been gone for days, so I'm sure the task will be done soon. The bread will be made, and I'll enter the Trials as planned."

"But you were supposed to be sure Rose didn't enter them. If she's roaming Eral free, we can't stop her. How am I supposed to kill her if she's not here?"

Kartek raised and lowered a single shoulder. "I'll defeat her in the trials. If I don't kill her, I'm sure you'll figure out another way that satisfies you."

"That's not the point," Amelia snapped. "You have betrayed me and our agreement by not keeping her here. How am I supposed to trust you now?"

This was what she got for working with ogres. They hardly were loyal to each other, let alone to humans or sorceresses. The water in her veins swirled and crashed, begging to flow out of her and get rid of this smoke and show them who has the genuine power here. Amelia clenched, then unclenched her hand to calm her magic. She'd been building up so much power the last several weeks, thanks to Dusan and the swamp, that she could hardly contain it anymore. It would be so easy to flood this whole camp and remind Kartek who she was dealing with. But she needed to wait. Just a little more time, and she could release her vengeance. She needed to play nice with the ogres for a little longer.

Kartek scowled. "Rose killed one of my people. I will not fight for her to stay. Our agreement will remain the same. I'll win the Trials and then my people will team with yours to go beyond Eral. That has never changed, but my loyalty will always be for the ogres first. It's best you remember that."

Amelia's lip curled. It wouldn't hurt to show off a little. She balled her hands into tight fists as though she was prepared for a fight and felt for the water all around them. The ogre camp may have been smoky from the phoenix burning, but the rest of Eral surrounding them still had swamp water infiltrating it deeper and deeper each day.

Let's play a little, sorceress.

She was glad Dusan had the same idea.

Amelia felt for his power to join with her and directed it from her feet to the ground. Out of the dirt ground, little green bubbles floated and popped around them, and seeped out into small puddles. Mushrooms and through the cracks, tiny rivers flowed toward Kartek and her stone seat.

"And it's best you remember no one crosses me," Amelia told her. The water gathered and flooded the area, high enough to inch its way up Kartek's chair and slosh around her toes.

Kartek's orange eyes flashed at Amelia. "You have nothing to fear, sorceress. But keep your poison away from my clan. The infestation of this water has done enough damage around here."

Really? Now that was interesting. The ogress was keeping something from Amelia, but there was a hint of fear there. Which was the way she liked it.

She stretched her fingers out again, and the water soaked back into the dirt from where it came, like it was being sucked away. It slurped and bubbled until the ground was dry once again. "Then you'll be careful to not cross me. I'll see you at the Trials."

Amelia turned on her heel and sauntered out of the camp like it was her own castle. It was almost funny how a mere few weeks ago she'd snuck into it using Charis's flute and sleeping song. Now she could sashay herself in whenever she wanted. Little by little, she could feel herself coming back to herself.

Dusan stood outside of the camp, looking stronger and more human than ever. At his feet, a tiny stream flowed, and mushrooms popped up around the trees. He held his hands behind his back and watched her approach with an unreadable expression on his face.

"And what was the purpose of this brief visit?" he asked.

Amelia sashayed her way over to him and twisted her hair off her neck and on top of her head. "It's important to check in and be sure they remember who's in control."

He took a step toward her and traced a single finger down her neck and across her collarbone, making her shiver. "And why do you need them?"

"*We* need them, unfortunately," Amelia told him. "Or at least having them on our side will be helpful. The more allies we have, the stronger we'll be. It was a mistake I made in Cresin, and one I won't make again."

He moved his fingers behind her neck in a way that felt like they took tiny steps over her skin, then grasped the back of her head and pulled her toward him. "We're powerful enough."

"We are. But that doesn't mean we can't have more."

"Ambitious, aren't we?"

She tried not to get distracted by the way Dusan was touching her and kept herself from melting into him. He made her feel powerful and would help her get what she wanted. He was the best fuck she'd had in ages, and he kept her guessing. It was the most fun she'd had in years. But that's all he was, fun and a means to an end. She couldn't let him distract her from what she wanted.

"I know what I want and know what I can have. I'll do whatever I can get it." She took a step back and went back in the swamp's direction and cottage, leaving him standing behind her. It was time Dusan followed her around instead of her always going after his call. Remind him who he was dealing with.

Chapter Twenty-Six

ROSE

E RAL KNEW ROSE NEEDED TO HURRY. AS THE PIXIE LED THE WAY, TREES parted for Rose and the others to get through. A red path appeared before them and cleared out the mud and mushrooms. Within minutes, the fog thinned, and Eral looked more familiar than it had in days. It was always said that anyone who needed it no matter where they were in Eral would find the Minister's cottage. Only, it never happened this quickly before. At least not to Rose. And even though it was familiar, something was off about her surroundings. Everything was still so dark, and an empty cold filled the air.

It wasn't the crisp cold of autumn and winter, but of something else. Something Rose wouldn't let herself consider. She gulped and held onto the vines of her horse so tight her knuckles were white. Things must be dire.

Rose looked over her shoulder and Cal was a few paces behind her, with Finley and Ai even further behind. He waved her off.

"Go, Rose. We'll catch up."

She nodded, then flicked the reins. Just like one of the royal horses back at home, this horse followed her command and ran. The pixie zoomed ahead to guide her with a trail of purple dust glimmering in her wake.

Before long, Eral Forest cleared to reveal the grove where Grandmother's cottage stood. The forest was silent around Rose and not so much as a light breeze blew through the tree branches. It was like the world had paused and held its breath.

They trotted up to the home, and Rose slid off. She removed her crutch from the holding around her back to walk, not wanting to bother with it and the club. Her ankle had rested long enough. It was tolerable to walk on it a little with only one aid.

She paused at the door. There was something wrong, and the silence was deafening. The outdoors should never be so quiet.

A crash from inside brought Rose back to her senses. Of course, something was wrong. It was why she was here. She clasped the doorknob, and it opened almost as though it read her mind.

The cottage was a disaster, with furniture turned over on their sides and herbs and plants scattered across the floor. Then blood. Blood splattered everywhere. It was like someone took a bucket of crimson petals and scattered them across the cottage in some sort of grand gesture. But it wasn't a gesture Rose liked or wanted.

Her mouth went dry and her heart beat so fast she thought it would burst out of her chest.

"Grandmother?"

A rumble came from the other side of the room where the exit to the hall was. Rose limped her way there and pushed debris away with her foot to make a clearer path.

Bloody handprints and long claw marks covered the walls, and foot and paw prints led the way to Grandmother's room. Rose's breath grew shallower with each step and the crutch shook so much she was afraid it wouldn't hold her weight.

"Grandmother?" she called out again when she reached Grandmother's room. Her voice cracked on the name.

Another dark rumble came from the other side of the door. She pushed it, and it swung open with a loud creak to reveal a large lump on the bed, covered in a green quilt.

But it wasn't Grandmother who slept there.

It was too large. With ears too pointy. And a long tail. The lump turned and faced her. The eyes were far too yellow.

"Hello, Princess," Rafe growled. His pointed teeth dripped with blood.

Rose gripped the hilt of her sword but couldn't get herself to move forward. This wasn't happening. He couldn't be there, covered in blood. Covered in…

He slid off the bed and sauntered toward her. As the green quilt crumpled to the ground, another large lump appeared on the mattress.

Grandmother lay there, her empty eyes stared at the ceiling and her throat ripped open. Everything spun and the world turned blurry.

No. This couldn't be happening. Grandmother couldn't be lying there like that.

"I had to do it."

The sound of Rafe's voice made something inside of Rose snap. Every bit of logic and sense vanished, and all she wanted to do was rip the world apart. Rose screamed at her worst nightmare come to life. Her magic from Aros roared to life without her even needing to think about it, sending a red glow across the room from her tattoo.

"How dare you," she seethed. She unsheathed her sword and stalked toward the wolf. Her ankle throbbed with each step, but Rose didn't care anymore.

Rafe didn't cower away and stepped in her direction. Blood lust and a mix of something else Rose didn't care about swam in his yellow eyes. "I had no choice."

"There's always a choice."

She swung her sword at him, and he dodged away. With each swing, Rafe jumped as graceful as a dancer into the air and escaped her blows. He circled around her like a hunter with his prey. "And soon, you'll be next, Princess. You can fight and run all you want, but I'll find you too."

Rose kept her sword pointed at him. "Not if I kill you first."

"What's stopping you?"

With a yell, Rose charged toward him, and the wolf jumped over her head and across the room. He snapped his fangs and lunged at her. Rose fell to the ground and rolled, the sword flying out of her hand and under the bed. He snapped his jaws and growled. Rage and terror roared through Rose, and she screamed and yelled. But something inside told Rose she couldn't let him get to her, too. No matter how devastated she was, she couldn't let him.

Rose kicked her uninjured leg and shoved Rafe off her body and he hit a trunk with a thud. It only took him a moment to recover and shook his head. "Kill me if that's what you want to do, Rose, but listen to me."

She shook her head and found the knife in her boot. "You don't deserve to be listened to."

"But you need to, anyway." Rafe bowed his head low. It couldn't be in submission. Rose was smarter than that now. It must be so he could prepare to pounce again. "If it's worth anything, I performed her final ritual to go to Stula."

Rose yelled wordlessly and lunged toward him again, and he snapped and snarled at her. His head rocked back and forth like he couldn't control it, and he forced each word out. "Bake the bread and enter the Trials. You're next. It has to be you."

She shook her head. Whatever he was saying was nonsense. He needed to die before she had to listen to anymore of his jabber. She moved to stand over him, but he bit and snarled again, his mouth closing around her wounded ankle.

Rose cried out at the sharp pain and fell to the ground. Losing her knife now, too. Fine, she would kill him with her bare hands if she needed to. Skin the wolf limb from limb and make a fur coat out of him.

They fought and scratched and clawed at one another, and Rafe pinned her to the ground. Then, with a loud howl, he fell. Rose looked over at the wolf and saw Cal at the door with a bow in hand. Rafe whimpered on the ground beside her and little by little, he faded.

"Remember what I said," he told Rose, and vanished, leaving the arrow that wounded his shoulder there on the cottage floor.

Within moments, Finley and Ai joined Cal, and they both gasped at the sight.

"Fuck," Finley breathed.

Rose pushed herself up and looked around the carnage of what was Grandmother's room. Blood splattered everywhere. Tufts of fur scattered about. Then the bed.

She crawled over to it and pulled herself to her feet. Grandmother lay there as she had before. Empty open eyes without a single breath.

Rose's chest cracked and ripped open, and, with a last scream, she collapsed onto the mattress and wept.

Chapter Twenty-Seven

ROSE

ROSE BLINKED HER EYES OPEN AND GROANED. IT TOOK HER A MOMENT to realize she was in her bed at the cottage and only recognized it from the red quilt laying over her. Her throat was as dry as the Khadi desert, and the muscles in her ankle pounded like a drum. She felt like she'd been to Stula's realm and back.

She snapped her eyes closed. Stula's realm. Even thinking about it put a heaviness on her chest that made Rose think it might crush her. All the memories flooded back. The blood, Rafe, Grandmother…

And all too familiar feminine voice forced Rose to open her eyes again.

"Rose? Are you awake?"

Rose turned her head to the side and slouched in an armchair next to the bed was Eira. She'd wrapped a blue blanket around herself, and her usually brighteyes were red and puffy, as though she'd been crying. She looked at Rose and her shoulders relaxed.

"You are awake. You've been sleeping for hours. I was getting worried."

Rose blinked a few times and pushed herself into a seated position. She must be dreaming. Eira was supposed to be in the Paravian mountains. "Eira? What are you doing here?"

Eira straightened herself and rubbed her eyes. A thin layer of frost skimmed the floor beside her. "A pixie came to us. I don't know how they got there so fast, but they said I needed to come right away. Something told me I shouldn't ignore her." She shrugged. "I can't explain it, but I knew something was wrong, and I needed to come to you."

"I'm glad."

They sat in a comforting silence for several moments. There was nothing to say and nothing they could do but be together. Rose scooted over on the bed and made room for Eira to sit at her side. Her sister crawled in, and Rose lay her head on Eira's shoulder. When they were children, they snuck into each other's rooms and did the same thing. When Rose would get in trouble with their governess, or Eira didn't do well in her training with the priestesses. As they got older, of course, they learned to comfort themselves. But there were still times when the only one who would understand was a sister.

The weight of it all still lay on Rose. Amelia, Eral forest, the ogres, Cal, Rafe, and now… this. It was a gaping wound opened months ago and no matter what she did, nothing could close it. Now, she may as well bleed out there on the bed.

"I failed," Rose finally said, breaking the silence.

Eira stroked Rose's hair and pressed her cheek against her head. "What do you mean?"

"I trusted Rafe when I shouldn't have. I couldn't defeat Amelia, and she trapped me in that mirror. Without Cal getting captured or breaking my ankle, I couldn't defeat an ogre. Then we didn't get to the swamp and now… it's too late. Maybe I should just go back to Farren and let the rest of you take care of things like you were before."

"From what I've been told, none of that is true. You saved Cal and killed an ogre while with an injury. I wouldn't have been able to do any of those things." Eira shifted in her seat and Rose propped herself so she leaned against the headboard. "And I don't think any of us would have known about Rafe and what would happen. You couldn't predict what he would do."

"That's the problem, though. I think Grandmother knew."

This silence that followed wasn't a comforting one. This time, a dark and tense cloud hung between them. The quilt turned to a light frost, green and chilled. Noticing what she did, Eira removed her hand from it and the quilt went back to its usual deep red and warmed the bed once again.

"What do you mean, you think she knew?" Eira asked.

Rose made to turn and cross her legs in front of her when a sharp pain attacked her ankle when she turned it. For a moment, she'd forgotten about that. Eira gathered one pillow at the end of the bed and helped Rose prop it up.

"She didn't seem to trust Rafe much," Rose explained and fluffed the pillow. "And when we were here, she kept wanting me to read these things, and she told me about how she became Minister."

Rose shared about all the books she'd read, and the way Grandmother insisted they found ingredients for this special bread and how tired she'd been looking. The more she spoke, the more Rose convinced herself that Grandmother knew something was coming.

"Do you think she knew?" Rose asked when she was done.

Eira sighed and rubbed her temple. "I don't know. Maybe. She always knows when something is different in Eral and when people come and go. I suppose it's possible." She rubbed Rose's knee. "And no more of this failure talk."

Rose nodded. She still had a sinking pit in her stomach and felt like she could have done something more, but at least sharing this with Eira helped.

A knock came to the door and Cal's head popped in. "I don't mean to disturb you but, I think you better come downstairs."

The wood steps creaked and groaned even more than usual with each step Rose took down them. If it was possible, the stairway was darker than usual thanks to the pitch black that had befallen Eral when the Minister departed from their world. But when they arrived back in the great room, the fireplace roared and illuminated the cottage as though they were in the middle of the brightest spring day. Rose's eyes widened and her jaw dropped at the sight before her.

Tiny men and women, barely reaching Rose's waist, bustled around the cottage. They picked up the discarded and broken furniture, scrubbed blood off the floor, and dusted every surface they could find. It was a flurry of dark hair and patched clothes with thimble hats and pointed ears. In the kitchen, Ai and Finley were sharing a bottle of rum, leaning on the table with their elbows, watching the scene with amusement. By the fire, Aytigin reclined on the couch with a book.

"Where did they come from?" Eira asked.

Cal shrugged. "The brownies came while Rose slept. They have the whole cottage looking as though nothing happened at all. I don't know how they knew we needed help, but… here they are."

"Can we get these for The Mystic?" Finley asked Ai.

Ai shook her head. "We need to give the crew chores or else they get too restless and cause mischief."

Finely only grumbled wordlessly and took another swig of rum straight from the bottle.

"That's not why you needed to come, though," Cal continued. He led them to the front door and opened it to reveal Cadeyrn meeting with a tall fae man with pointed ears and a long black braid. All around the cottage were creatures from Eral. Centaurs, fae, pixies, brownies, birds and squirrels, wolves and gnomes, and creaturesRose didn't even recognize were all there. Even Kartek stood in the back with her bright orange eyes boring into Rose's. She gulped. Those with hands and arms held candles and lanterns, illuminating the pond around the cottage to make it look like stars shone in the water.

Rose and Eira stepped out of the cottage and gaped at the scene. Who were they? Where did they come from?

The fae man shoulder's straightened and stopped speaking to Cadeyrn. "The granddaughters, they're here." He unsheathed his sword and set the point on the ground, then knelt on one knee with his head bowed. The other creatures behind him all followed suit. One by one, they each bowed before Eira and Rose in waves.

Cadeyrn turned and when he saw the sisters, he went to Eira's side and put his arm around her. "They want to pay their respects to the Minister. But he said something else about trials?"

Rose's mouth went dry. The Trials. They were going to start already? Her heart pounded and jumped into her throat. Hearing the replacement Minister needed to be chosen right away sent a strange panic through Rose. It couldn't be happening. Not yet.

The fae man stood again and approached Rose and Eira. Rose had to crane her neck to look at his dark and handsome face. He appeared young, but there were centuries in his deep brown eyes. He wore brown leather clothing and a sack that looked like a giant leaf. She tried to stand as tall and straight as she could but flinched when she put too much weight on her ankle.

"It is an honor, granddaughters of the Minister," he said and bowed his head. "My name is Asher, and I have known Renata and your family for many years. I wish we could have met under happier circumstances."

Eira, who didn't seem to have any of the same nervousness Rose did, bowed her head to him and gave him a small curtsey. "Thank you for coming, Asher. I'm sure our grandmother would be most grateful."

Asher placed both hands on the hilt of his sword in front of him. "We need to put the Minister to rest, and let the Trials begin. I know it may seem sudden but . . ." He stretched one arm behind him to show what Eral Forest looked like. It was still as dark as it was when the pixie came to fetch Rose, and they could only see the falling leaves due to all the candles and lanterns. They detached themselves from branches and fell to the ground like autumn had arrived several months early. "Eral cannot last long without a Minister in place. As it already has been ill, the process of it dying is going faster than usual. I trust you have the ingredients for the bread?"

Rose sought Cal among the group, and when she did, saw he wanted to see her too. His jaw clenched. No one told them what the bread had been for, and Rose's chest ached. Grandmother must have known. "Yes, we received the last ingredient only recently."

Asher nodded, and two brownies popped out of the crowd and rushed into the cottage. "Good. We'll have it prepared right away."

A flurry of activity happened around them. Creatures went in and out of the cottage, carrying and preparing various things. Birds flew over to Rose and Eira and lay purple robes to symbolize Stula over their shoulders. They all gathered around the pond in front of the cottage in a giant circle illuminated by their candles and lanterns. Eira waved an arm and scattered what looked like a thousand stars into the air.

From the circle, a hooded Stulan priest stepped forward. He lowered his hood, and Rose recognized him as the one who helped her and Eira and gave them the ingredients for the potion to cure their father. He beckoned to Eira and Rose for them to step forward.

"I'm sorry for your loss, your highnesses," he told them. His voice was still thin and cold, but it didn't frighten Rose the way it had back then. "Renata was a wonderful woman, and all of Eral will miss her."

He raised his right arm, and the cottage door sprung open. Through it, a cloud of pixies fluttered through, carrying a large purple cloth, and Grandmother lay upon it. The blood was gone now, and even her neck looked to be in one piece. Her eyes were closed, and someone had sprinkled flowers into her long gray hair. It almost seemed like she smiled in her eternal sleep as they floated her out to the center of the pond.

At Rose's side, Eira let out a tiny gasp and tears like diamonds glimmered in the corners of her eyes.

The ceremony went by in a blur, and Rose didn't grasp any of the words the priest spoke. What did it matter anyway? Rafe said he'd already performed the ritual to escort Grandmother into Stula's arms. This was only a ceremony. Rose blinked a few times.

Wait. He said he'd performed the ritual. Why would he do that? He murdered Grandmother. The last Rose checked, murderers wouldn't take the time or care to do that. Maybe it was because he served Stula, and it was part of his job.

That had to be it.

Then again, Rafe said a lot of things while she attacked him. She'd been so angry, she had put no thought into it until now. The bread and the Trials. He wanted her to go into the Trials. But why? Grandmother also talked to her about the Trials and how she became Minister, which was something she never did before. Rose shifted her weight from foot to foot and leaned further on her crutch.

They wanted her to be the next Minister. Rose tried not to blanch or vomit at the thought. Especially during her Grandmother's funeral. The idea was ridiculous. Rose didn't want to be heir to the Cresin throne, and she didn't want to be Minister. Why couldn't anyone get their minds around that? She just wanted to...

Well. She didn't know anymore. If someone asked even a few weeks ago, Rose would have said to remain in the palace guard. But now, the idea of going back to court put her stomach in knots. She hated court.

Rose shook her head. Her grandmother's funeral was *not* the time or place to be thinking about such things. She blinked the thoughts out of her head and put her focus back on the priest, whose arms were now raised, and Grandmother's body floated horizontally over the water.

Across the pond stood Kartek. Her orange eyes gleamed in the candlelight and a cruel and thin smile crept across her face. She was hungry and greedy, and there was something sinister behind the look on her face. Rose gulped.

Kartek wanted to be Minister. That had to be it. Why else would she be there? The ogress was power hungry and wanted to give the ogres a better name. They hated their treatment and held a grudge against Rose's family for years. Of course, that's what Kartek wanted. How could Rose not see it sooner?

The ogres could not be the ones to lead Eral. That Rose knew for sure. She peered around the pond at the other creatures who stood around it. Fae, centaurs, pixies, they might all be fine as Ministers. At least Grandmother was related to the fae, or some of them must have been. Even if distantly.

The stars shone even brighter around Grandmother, and a bright light glowed from her fingers and toes. A lump formed in Rose's throat, and she tried to swallow it down. Little by little, the glow spread through Grandmother's body, and she disintegrated into tiny pieces of dust. It went from her toes and fingers, then traveled up her arms and legs until less and less of Grandmother's body was visible. The priest moved his hands in a circle over his head, and as the last bit of her hair vanished, the particles of stars and dust swirled around in a giant circle. He spread his hands wide and shot them out in front of him, and the particles flew toward the cottage and formed themselves into a willow tree with shining green leaves. Grandmother would forever be a part of Eral.

Eira choked out a sob next to Rose, and she put her arm around her older sister. Rose knew she should cry. But she couldn't bring herself to. She couldn't even bring herself tobe sad. All Rose felt was emptiness. Grandmother was in Stula's arms now, and her body would rest in Eral for forever. It was the way Grandmother would have wanted it. Maybe she'd already shed all her tears.

Or maybe the worst of the grief was still coming.

Rose took in a deep breath as she looked at the glimmering tree with its hanging branches. Her chest tightened, and her fae magic stirred. Out of the corner of her eye, she could see the green grass beneath her feet wave and dance as though feeling her magic. She knew what Grandmother wanted now. But was it what Rose wanted, too?

Chapter Twenty-Eight

ROSE

THE OTHERS WENT INSIDE THE COTTAGE, BUT ROSE LAGGED BEHIND while the creatures of Eral scattered and talked among themselves. When Cal noticed her, he walked at her side and took slow steps so they had a little more privacy. He lowered his head and spoke in a quiet, concerned voice.

"How are you doing?"

"I think I need to enter the Trials," Rose answered in an equally quiet tone. She didn't want anyone else knowing what she was considering. She hardly wanted to know about what she was considering.

He blinked a few times, but as Rose didn't stop walking, he didn't either. She was glad he could tell she wasn't ready to join the group again yet and keep the conversation between the two of them. "Why do you think you need to enter?"

Rose explained to him about Grandmother's behavior and what she taught them, then about her theory about Kartek wanting to be the next Minister. Cal frowned and his eyes darted toward the ogres, then back to Rose without moving his neck so no one realized he was thinking about them. He took in a deep breath.

"Just because you don't want Kartek in power, it doesn't mean you have to do it."

Rose nodded. "I know. Trust me, I know. But I can't explain it, Cal, there's something about it that sounds right. I can tell it's what Grandmother wanted, and I've felt my fae magic more here than I have any other time in my life. It's like Eral is telling me I need to be its Minister."

Ahead of them, Eira stood at the entrance of the cottage and waved them in. Her brows furrowed when they didn't take the invitation. Rose looked out at her and put one finger up to let her know it would be a moment. Eira nodded, then closed the door behind her.

There was a bench next to the cottage, and Rose and Cal sat on it side by side. She let her leg rest against his and she savored the warmth and comfort of the feeling.

"Rose, you know I think you can do whatever you want. I've seen you here in Eral, and it fits you. Even at home, I know you hate being the heiress, but you'd be an amazing queen. But is it what you want?"

That was the question of the day, wasn't it? Rose slumped against the side of the cottage and looked up into the branches with all its bright green leaves and the remnants of the ceremony glistening on them. If she went through with it, and she succeeded, this would be her home. Forever. Rose never wanted to be in a leadership position. At most, running the royal guard and protecting her sister.

She shrugged. "I wish I knew. My whole life I've seen the burdens of leading Cresin weighed on Father and Eira. They'd have to leave things they wanted to do, leave me, in order to fulfill their duties. I remember there was this one time when I was younger, maybe a year or two before you came to court, the three of us were supposed to go on a hunt. It was at the start of autumn, and it was our family tradition. I looked forward to it every year. But then, Father couldn't come. There was an emergency, and he had to go away. He was so sad and felt awful. I was never mad at him, but at his being king and the Council. I knew it wasn't what he wanted to do, but it was what he had to do, and I promised myself I would never be in that sort of position. And seeing Eira struggle with Alvis and Cadeyrn, and now losing her title…" She trailed off, trying to gather her thoughts. So much had happened this past year, she hardly had time to comprehend it all. She couldn't think past what would happen once Eira could return to the throne.

If she could return to the throne.

"If I become Minister, I'll have to live here forever, and I couldn't leave for long. I'd be leaving so much behind." Cal put his arm around Rose and let her lean against his shoulder. Something inside of her chest broke at the slight gesture. "I'd have to leave you behind."

They were silent for a few moments, the unintelligible conversations of the other creatures still there the only sound. Maybe they all were having similar talks and ideas, wondering which of them would step up and enter the Trials.

"You wouldn't have to leave me behind. Not if you didn't want to."

Rose stilled at Cal's proclamation. She sat straight up and stared at him. There was a resoluteness in his face that told her he was serious. "You'd join me?"

He nodded. "If that's what you wanted."

"But what about Faren Castle? And Myra? And… everything?"

"I've never liked court, and I only stayed because you were still there. Myra would understand and visit when she could. If you became Minister and I didn't join you, I'd go find another place and position, anyway. But I would rather be here with you."

Rose's chest tightened, and tears threatened to escape from the corners of her eyes. It was like pieces of her broke and then put back together again all at once. She knew, no matter where she went and made her life, if Cal was there, she was home. She sniffed back the tears and nodded.

"I'd rather you were, too."

The biggest and brightest smile Rose had ever seen appeared on Cal's face. He cupped her face in his large hands and placed a kiss on her lips. It was home.

A small zap shot through Rose, and they broke apart. Right. There was that minor detail. They both chuckled.

"I guess we'll need to figure that part out," Rose said.

"I guess so."

"Saving Eral first."

The turning in Rose's stomach calmed, and her shoulders relaxed. Whatever she'd come across, they navigate it together.

"I love you."

Rose blurted the three words out before she could think to stop herself and they slurred together. She wasn't even sure if he could understand them. Maybe that would be a good thing. Or maybe it. She needed to think before she opened her mouth. And it was moments after her grandmother's funeral. Her cheeks burned. Timing had never been her strong suit.

"What?"

Diar bless it. He was going to make her repeat it? She swallowed the lump in her throat. She may as well get it out there and let everything fall where it wanted.

"I love you."

Cal wove his fingers through hers and rubbed the back of her hand with his thumb. How he could make her so calm and relaxed but set each nerve ablaze with only his hand touching hers she's never understand. Not that she was complaining.

"I love you too, Rose."

Yet another weight lifted. He said he will pick up his life and live in Eral for the rest of his days with her. It should have made her confident that would be his response. But hearing him say it was still a comfort. Words spoken out loud had a way of making things more real.

Cal kissed her again, and another shock went through Rose. But she didn't mind. Maybe she'd get used to it.

Rose squeezed his hand. "Now for the real trial. Telling Eira."

THEY SAT AROUND THE FIREPLACE and ROSE WATCHED EIRA'S FACE FOR her reactions, which went from blank from what Rose assumed was shock, to tight and furrowed with pursed lips, to now the corners of her lips tugged downward and eyes drooped.

"You would have to live here," Eira said. "Is this truly what you want?"

Oddly enough, even though it had only been a short time since she'd put this together, the more Rose thought and talked about it, the more confident she became. Already she could see herself in this cottage and how she would arrange it for herself and Cal. Where they'd store their weapons (there was wonderful space for a trunk and rack by the door), and the way they could organize and set up the garden outside.

Rose nodded. "It feels right."

Eira pushed herself further back on the couch she and Cadeyrn shared and let her shoulder relax against his. Rose's heart warmed to see how comfortable her older sister was now. Before, the only times she would see Eira fully relaxed was when the two of them were in private, and even then, she more often than not had a tense and proper stance about her. Now, it was as though a veil lifted off Eira and she could show her true self and feelings. There was nothing to hide or prove.

"I almost hate to admit it, but I have to agree," Eira said.

Cadeyrn's hand was on Eira's knee, and he made small circles on it with his thumb. "But what would happen to Cresin? Who's next in line for the throne?"

It was an excellent question. There were some distant relatives, but the ins and outs of who ranked as what got lost sometimes. Especially when there'd been a Luana's and Ray's Chosen's. Now those were out of the question… it could be open to several possibilities.

"Amelia's baby, of course."

They all blinked and stared at each other at the sound of Aytigin's voice. He'd been off to the side, still paging through the various books in Grandmother's library and had said little since he arrived.

The dragon rolled his shoulders and closed the book he was reading. "That was her plan all along. Put the baby on the throne and she would be regent until he came of age, thus ensuring her place in power."

The flutter of hope in Rose's chest at the idea of becoming Minister and saving Eral faded and her stomach clenched. Of course. She'd been so concerned about getting rid of Amelia herself, she'd completely forgotten about the baby, who would be a few months old by now.

Aytigin rolled his eyes. "And you all expect to rule kingdoms and forests someday."

"But we don't know if King Brennan is the father," Cadeyrn pointed out. "Amelia is infamous for her affairs."

"We also don't know he isn't," Rose said. "It all depends on if Father will claim him. If he has no evidence that the child isn't his, there would be no reason for him to disown them. Besides, even if the baby is on the throne, the Council would never allow Amelia to act as regent."

Eira craned her neck to look back at Aytigin. "Also, I intend to take my crown back. Once I break the curse, I have full intentions of returning to Faren castle."

A tiny scowl came across Aytigin's face, then it vanished and turned back into his usual bored and superior expression. Rose wondered if maybe he'd gotten used to the company in his lonely castle.

"Fine. But if Rose abdicates and becomes Minister, the way things stand now, the baby would be next in line, which was my point."

Which, if Rose became Minister, she may more easily be able to track down Amelia and save Eral. Maybe even retrieve the baby and get them back to Cresin, where he was in a safe environment, away from Amelia's influences. Rose shuddered. She hoped the poor thing wasn't trapped in a mirror the way Nell had been for so many years.

But that was another issued they'd have to deal with later. For now, Rose had to focus on the Trials and what she was going to do about Kartek. She frowned. Kartek. She hadn't even mentioned the deal she'd struck with the ogress.

"What's wrong?" Eira asked.

Rose grimaced. "There's something else we need to talk about. It's the ogres."

She dove into the story about their time in the ogre camp. When she got to the part about her deal with Kartek and their escape, a thin frost covered the floor and stardust fluttered from Aytigin's wings. He seemed to grow at least a foot taller, and Rose thought he was about to fly through the ceiling.

"You promised her *what*?"

Cal pushed himself forward in his seat as though he was about to attack the dragon, and it tempted Rose to do the same thing. There wasn't any reason for him to get so upset. Yet. Or at least not much to be upset about.

"We have the Chalice. Why shouldn't we use it to help those who are sick in Eral?" Rose asked.

Eira pushed her hair aside and shook her head. "It's not ours to determine who gets to use it and who doesn't. Gallis wanted Luana to hide it for a reason. We can't allow people to use it whenever they want and go against Gallis and Stula. Besides, we don't even know what ingredients we would need."

"But we used it," Rose argued. "No one gave us permission, and you intended to steal it to save Father."

Eira pursed her lips and paused for a moment before replying. "I know, and if there had been any other way… but we still need to be careful."

Aytigin still fumed and more frost formed at his feet, spreading through the cottage. "You humans, thinking you're entitled to whatever you want." He pointed at Rose with his long claw. "Stealing the Shadowslayers and now placing a claim on the Chalice when it's not yours to give. The world is not at your leisure to take whatever you want, Princess. There are some things you shouldn't mess with."

Rose scowled at him. Eira and Cadeyrn may have grown used to him, but Aytigin was a selfish and out of touch creature who'd been locked away in a castle for too long. Her face burned. "And what do you know about it rotting away in your castle? You sit there with the wealth and magic of the world, hoarding it all for yourself, and never using it to help anyone. What good is it to have weapons and tools and power if you never use them?"

His lip curled, and he crossed his arms over his chest. "Because I know the consequences of what happens when foolish people get their hands on them. Perhaps you can cure this mushroom disease. But what then? Do you truly think this ogre chief will let you take the Chalice back and you'll be on your merry way? It will get into the wrong hands."

Eira looked back and forth between Rose and Aytigin, a tired look in her eyes. "Rose, I know it's difficult, but he has a point. We need to think more clearly about this."

Rose clenched her fists and released them with a loud huff. "Then what do I do? If I betray the ogres, they'll turn against us. I don't imagine that would be an intelligent way to start as Minister."

"We'll figure something out," Cal whispered.

A flurry of applause came from the kitchen, followed by the small, high-pitched cries of a group of brownies. The oven door opened and from it, four of them pulled out the sweetest smelling bread Rose's nose ever experienced. They lifted it over their heads to show off to everyone, and one cried out, "The bread is prepared! The Trials can begin!"

Through the window, those who'd gathered for the funeral still awaited outside. Various groups clustered together, and each had one being standing in front. Maybe they were the ones to enter the trials along with Rose. If she succeeded, they would all be in her charge. Rose swallowed and thought she might hurl. She could do this. If Grandmother didn't think she was capable, she wouldn't be here.

Rose groaned as she stood from the chair she was in, her ankle barking in protest. Why couldn't the Trials have waited until *after* her bones knit themselves back together?

Eira stood up along with her and pointed to Rose's injury. "I'll get you something for that."

Meanwhile, Rose found her crutch and made her way to the door to gather the Shadowslayers. At least she had those at her disposal if she should need them. Except they weren't there where she'd left them. There was only her red cloak hanging on a lone hook. A cold panic ran through her as she searched the area. She'd sworn she put them right there. Hadn't she? Maybe Cal moved them for safekeeping.

"Cal, did you move the Shadowslayers?"

He was busy preparing his own sword and shook his head. "No, I thought they were with your cloak."

Rose's stomach clenched as the dread set in. It was impossible. Someone had been here the whole time and would have noticed if anyone had moved them. She tried to remember the events of the day, but it was such a blur with the funeral. Protecting the Shadowslayers was the last thing on her mind.

Someone pinned a small white note to the red cloak like a feather that clung on after falling off a bird. Rose ripped it off and opened it to read the contents.

It appears our paths are going in other directions, and we will no longer be useful to one another. We have other tasks and adventures to seek and needed the extra help. We plan to return the Shadowslayers another time.

And tell Cal, our promise to Myra stands if she still wishes it.
- Finley & Ai

Rose crumpled the note in her hand. "Damn them to Stula's realm! Fucking pirates!"

A pair of brownies squeaked in surprise at Rose's outburst and the platter they carried clattered to the floor. Another almost dropped the bread but caught it before it joined the platter.

"They stole them! Finley and Ai took the Shadowslayers!"

Everyone paused and the already tense atmosphere grew stronger and colder. More frost covered the floor and if Rose hadn't been so angry, she would have shivered from it. Aytigin hovered inched above the ground and white puffs of air snorted out of his nostrils.

"They stole *what?*" he seethed.

The room spun, and Rose propped herself up with the wall. Injured and did no idea she was doing. The Trials would be impossible without the Shadowslayers. "What am I going to do?"

Cal put his palm on her back and rubbed it, and while Rose appreciated the thought, this time it didn't help. "You're a powerful fighter, Rose. You'll be fine. Besides, you don't even know what's in the Trials."

Which was the point exactly. Since she didn't know what was coming, she wanted every tool and weapon available.

Cadeyrn had both arms extended out, one toward Aytigin and one toward Rose, as though he was preparing for a battle between the two of them. Maybe Rose should have been more afraid of the icy glare coming from the dragon. But there were too many other things to be concerned about at the moment.

"Aytigin and I will go search for Finley and Ai. You just worry about the Trials."

Rose nodded. Right. Maybe with Aytigin on the hunt, they'd found sooner rather than later.

With a farewell kiss to Eira, Cadeyrn followed Aytigin out of the cottage and within moments, the sound of a dragon's wings flapping in the wind could be heard, followed by the gasps of those waiting outside.

Eira gave Rose a small tonic to assist with the pain, which she took in one gulp. It was sweet and in moments she could feel her muscles relaxing. Then Cal helped her wrap the enchanted straps around her foot. The tonic helped with the transition of her foot from warped and twisted to straight and sturdy, but she still bit her lip from the pain. Her foot wouldn't be nearly as strong if she had them on while uninjured, but it was better than nothing, and she didn't need as much help from a crutch with only a small limp.

The world was unsteady under Rose's feet as she made her way out of the cottage. The brownies scampered ahead of them, holding the bread high over their heads, then lay it at Asher's feet who stood before them. He knelt to their height and bowed his head as reverently as he would to a king or queen. The brownies bowed and curtsied respectively and with happy chatters trooped off to the side with the others.

A circle closed in with Asher in the center, and Rose moved in place with Eira and Cal on either side of her. She grabbed their hands in hers and squeezed as hard as she could. They wouldn't be able to be at her side for much longer, and she wanted to hold on as long as possible. To keep her upright and not pass out from the stress.

Asher looked around the circle and rotated around so all could see his face. "I was present the last Trials when the mantle was passed to Renata. It was my honor to be chosen to conduct the ceremony today as well. May all of those who wish to compete, please step forward."

Oh, Aros curse it. Here it was. Eira and Cal both squeezed Rose's hands one last time, and she stepped forward, and the single movement alone made her feel like she was about to lose whatever little was in her stomach. Deep soothing breaths calmed her stomach, and she could see who else was there with her to compete.

Kartek, which was no surprise, stood in the direct opposite side of the circle as Rose. The tooth laden necklace gleamed like they had shined it for the occasion, and her chest stuck out proudly, bearing her warrior trophies. Next to her was a centaur with tattoos covering his bare chest, and a shining brown fur coat. He looked at all in presence with narrow eyes, like he was surveying and judging each of them. On the other side of Kartek was a stout dwarf with a long blond beard that trailed to his knees and braids throughout his hair. He held an ax over his shoulder and wore a slightly bored look, as though there were other places he could be rather than here.

Rose tried to hold her shoulders straighter and not shift her weight back and forth too often when her ankle ached. She assumed they were all natives of Eral and knew the forest far better than she did. Beings who had their own right and claim to the title of Minister. Except for maybe Kartek, but even the ogress at first glance deserved to be Minister more than Rose. A spoiled princess who always got what she wanted must be what they thought of her.

Asher took the bread and broke it into four pieces, one for each contestant. The bread Grandmother knew would need to be prepared to find her replacement. It felt oddly heavy in Rose's hand.

"Are there any who will choose to step in as partners if any of these beings succeed in their endeavors?" Asher asked the crowd.

Rose turned back to face Eira and Cal and extended her arm out to him. Eira's jaw dropped, and tears pooled in her eyes, but there was a smile on her lips. Cal kissed Rose's knuckles and when she dared to peek at the others, a woman had joined the dwarves, but the centaur and Kartek stood alone. There was a deep sadness in Kartek's eyes, and Rose had to look away. Her stomach twisted in guilt. If Eira and Aytigin wouldn't let Rose use the Chalice, there had to be another way to save Kartek's lover.

Asher nodded as he saw the expanded group. "Your partners will not partake of the same Trials as you, but if you succeed, they will undergo their own joining with Eral." He extended his arms. "Now, you may eat."

Rose gulped and bit into the bread. The outside crunched, but the inside was softer than a cloud and its sweetness danced on her tongue. It was a delicacy delivered straight from the deities themselves. Then Rose gagged and coughed. The sweetness turned bitter and hot. The ashes from the phoenix burning as she swallowed it. She clasped her throat and kept swallowing, hoping whatever moisture was in her mouth would cool the sensation.

"Rose! Are you all right?" Cal's desperate voice rang in her ear, but she couldn't reply. When she tried, the burning fell into her stomach and she collapsed to her knees and saw darkness.

Chapter Twenty-Nine

ROSE

When Rose opened her eyes, Cal was gone. The forest creatures were gone. Eira was gone. She was alone. There was cool smooth grass beneath her, and she grasped at its blades. It was real, and she was real, too. At first, she worried this was a dream, but the soft throb from her ankle proved it wasn't.

She pushed herself into a seated position with her injured foot stretched in front of her and tried to grasp her surroundings. There were still trees all around her, so a forest. Eral still, perhaps. But instead of a cottage or animals or creatures, there stood a wall built of giant stones and vines growing on it. To each side it stretched so long either ending vanished, and so tall only a sliver of blue sky and treetops were visible above.

Rose fell to her back and looked at what was before her. Huh. Well, this wasn't what she expected. Was she supposed to climb it? Go around it? Tear her way through it stone by stone? None of them seemed to make much sense, but there weren't any other options. There didn't seem to be any other contestants either.

She pushed herself onto her elbows and looked around for more. Using the dagger, she might dig through it a bit. With the hint of an idea on hand, Rose got up and went to the towering wall.

Rose pulled the dagger out of her boot and struck the mortar, holding the stones together with all the strength she could muster. It clanged against the wall and fell to the ground, making no difference in the wall. She picked it back up and tried again with the same result. With a sigh, Rose tossed the dagger into the air and caught it a few times while thinking of what to do next. The dagger had been a long shot anyway, but it didn't hurt trying. Maybe there was a door hidden somewhere in the vines.

Putting the dagger back, Rose now went for her sword. It swiped through the vines with a whispered swish, revealing more dark gray stone underneath. She pressed her hand against the wall and moved it along the stones, searching for hints of a doorway or gate. When she did, the vines pieced themselves back together and closed in on her arm, wrapping themselves around her like she was part of the wall.

Rose let out a frustrated grunt and yanked her arm out of the vines before they trapped her in. She stuck the sword into the ground and leaned against it like a crutch and strummed her fingers against the hilt.

"Well, I guess the only way to go is up," she said, fully realizing there was no one there to respond, but didn't care. She couldn't handle too much silence. It made her mind go foggy.

She sheathed the sword and made sure she strapped it tight around her back and grasped onto a vine. Of course, she would have to climb a wall with a broken ankle. It was just her luck. Whoever designed this must have known Rose's weakness and made sure the Trials were as difficult as possible for her. At least there were the vines she could use to pull herself up.

She had to try, though.

Rose closed her eyes and summoned her Aros magic. Her tattoo glowed through the fabric of her trousers and the warmth of Aros's strength and agility ran through her body. It tingled through her, and adrenaline coursed through her veins. She prayed it was enough to get her over the wall and through whatever was next.

"Here goes nothing, I guess."

She wrapped her fingers around the thickest vine she could find and pulled herself onto the wall, using her unbroken foot first to take most of the weight. The other ankle tightened and throbbed, but thanks to the tonic Eira made, the pain was bearable. Rose nodded to herself. Good. She could deal with that.

It was a long track up the wall and after what felt like forever, Rose's arms and legs ached. She'd climbed in the past, but rarely. And when she did, there were places to stop and rest - even if they were dubious locations you wouldn't want to stay in for long - but here there was no such option. Only a long wall that didn't seem to end. Above, it still towered over her and felt as far away as ever. She didn't dare look down, though. It would only make her already uneasy stomach want to execrate itself from her body.

"Gah!" Rose's sweaty hand slipped from the vine, and her body swayed.

Kartek, with her long legs and muscular arms, was probably already over the top and onto whatever task was next. Keeping this in mind, Rose gritted her teeth and continued to pull herself along the vines.

Her ankle grew stiff and throbbed. She tried at every opportunity to not put weight on it but using it couldn't be helped. Rose gripped one particularly thick vine and could wrap her uninjured foot around another to give herself some relief. She rested her forehead against the wall and tried to catch her breath.

"Kutlaous, you must enjoy torturing your people. A little help would be nice. Unless you want the ogres taking over Eral," she muttered. Not sure if it counted as a prayer, considering she was complaining, but had to put it out into the universe that the god of nature wasn't her favorite deity at the moment. She didn't expect him to respond anyway since the whole point was for her to prove herself worthy to be the Minister.

Yet, moments after she uttered the words, vines moved. They floated and twisted around her and created a narrow ladder so narrow it was doubtful anyone could climb it. It would be a challenge still not to lose balance and fall to her depth, but it was worth a try.

Rose looked up at the sky like Kutlaous was there, looking right back. "That was it? I just had to ask for help? Do I lose points or something?"

Naturally, no one answered.

"Ridiculous obscure deities," she muttered.

With careful movements, Rose inched her way forward and across to the ladder. She tugged the vines a few times, and it hardly moved. When it did, it bounced back to its original form. This would have to do. The climb was hard work, and Rose's muscles yelled and moaned, but this was far preferable to the other method.

Finally, Rose made her way to the top, and she pushed herself onto the ledge of the wall and stood. Wind whipped her red curls across her face, her braid falling out in places during the climb. Before her stood a forest, Eral perhaps, and she towered over the tops of its trees. She put her hands on her hips and surveyed the area. There were no vines on this side of the wall or stairs. Not even a slope she could slide down.

"Well, fuck. Now what?" She looked back up at the sky. "Any suggestions?"

Silence.

She waited for a few moments in the vain hope that Kutlaous would come to her aid again. But there was no such luck as everything remained perfectly still save for the soft movements of the treetops in the breeze. Then something rumbled beneath her feet. Something rumbled in the distance like a thunderstorm rolling in. The wall beneath her shook, and Rose knelt to hold on.

On either side of her, the wall crumbled and the crashing of the stones onto the ground roared in her ears. Unless she wanted to fall with the pile, Rose needed to get to the trees.

Rose tilted her head to the side and narrowed her eyes in observance of them. There were only a few feet between the wall and the line of trees. Too far for Rose to reach on her own or jump to. But…

Rose closed her eyes, and the glow of her tattoo faded, the strength of Aros leaving her. Now, she reached further down inside of herself and felt for her fae magic. It was softer and wilder at the same time. It wasn't the intense speed and force of Aros like an arrow aiming for its target. Instead, the fae magic was like the vines climbing up the other side of the wall. Going in all directions, growing and moving. She opened her eyes and reached an arm out to grab a branch. Focusing on a tree in front of her, she willed it to come forward.

"Come to me. Bring me off this thing."

After a few long moments, the tree closest to Rose stirred and moved. The branch, like an arm, rose up and down and, with a loud creak and groan, moved toward her. Her fingertips brushed the end of the twigs and leaves, then she grabbed on.

Rose crouched low and took tentative steps onto the branch, holding on with both hands until she was next to the thick trunk. Behind her, the wall crashed to the ground, and it shook the tree she now found shelter in. She coughed and wrapped her arms around it and held on as gray clouds from the broken stones filled the air. The entire world shook while she buried her face in the tree, and she let go when it subsided.

It was gone. The entire wall she'd just climbed and escaped from was gone, as though nothing had ever been there. Even on the ground, no stones were in sight. She clenched her jaw. All of that for it to just fall apart and vanish. If she ever met the god face to face, he was going to get a piece of her mind.

She sat on the tree branch and propped her injured ankle on it and let the other dangle. Her muscles relaxed inch by inch during the moment of relaxation. Not that she should rest long. There was still no sign of the other contestants and for all she knew, they were all far ahead of her at this point. Even she wasn't the one to be minister, she at least needed to be sure it wasn't Kartek.

Out ahead, a tiny glimmer of light shone through the forest. Considering there was nothing around but trees, that must be where she needed to go next. Branch by branch, Rose came down from the tree, and still seeing the light from below, she went toward it.

The light came from a small clearing with a single tree in the middle. It wasn't an impressive tree, as it was thin, with only three branches protruding out from the top. Perched on the lowest of the tree was a golden owl with a snowy white face. Its feathers glinted in the sunlight, making it seem like the bird came from Ray himself and its deep black eyes stared at Rose unblinking.

"Hello?" she asked.

The owl lowered its head to her. "Welcome."

His voice was lighter and gentler than Rose expected, if she expected it to speak at all. But it was friendly and made her shoulders relax. "I'm in the right place, then."

"There are many paths you could have taken. This is one of them." He tilted his head to the side and Rose felt like she was under observance. After the wall climb, Rose was sure she didn't look like much of a Minister. She tucked a strand of hair behind her ear. "Are you ready, Rose?"

It felt like a bit of a silly question, and she was taken aback that the owl knew her name. But maybe nothing should surprise her anymore. "I don't really have much of a choice about that, do I?"

The owl tilted its head to the other side now. "Perhaps. But you always have a choice."

"In your reactions maybe," Rose pointed out, not entirely sure why she felt like debating the point, but it felt like the right thing to do. "But whatever is going to come next, you can't control. It'll come whether you're ready or not. The only choice you have is how you react."

There was a smile in his eyes now, and the black depths of them glimmered at Rose. "Valid point. I have a puzzle for you. Do you *choose* to answer it?"

"Oh." Rose wasn't sure how to respond to that. When she'd heard the word "Trials" to become the next Minister, puzzles weren't the next thing that came to mind. Mind games and riddles weren't her strong suit. "I'll give it a go."

He lowered his head to her again. "Very well." He raised his right wing, displaying layers of golden feathers. They rustled when he moved, and shimmers of light danced over the blades of grass like flecks of fairy dust. As though the light removed a dark veil over the grassy area, a pile of wooden blocks, bones, and furs. "Put this together, and your next task will reveal itself."

The vague directions continued. Maybe Kutlaous wanted to know how well she could problem solve on her own. Whatever the reason, she needed to get to it.

Rose lay everything out in front of her one by one in hopes they would give her a better idea of what she was looking for. As children, sometimes their governess would find a wooden puzzle for them to work on, and many times there was an illustration to go with it, so they had something to base it off. Eira always had better concentration than Rose did and lasted far longer on the task, while Rose would grow frustrated and bored and wander off to another part of the room to find other toys to play with or a sewing project. Oddly enough, needlework Rose had taken a liking to. To start off with, she had patterns to go off that made sense. Then, when she became more experienced, Rose understood the mechanics of it enough where she could make her own designs and be creative.

She preferred making holders for her knifes and sewing small tapestries depicting battles more than decorating pieces of clothing, but that was no matter. It was something she could do with her hands that was more productive than playing with a sword in her governess's eyes.

With this puzzle, there were no directions or image to go off for this puzzle, and one piece seemed to have an obvious fit or pattern. At least she could sit on the ground and kneel for a while to give her ankle a break. She sat on the grass and examined the array of pieces and rested her chin on her knee.

"Am I allowed any hints?" she asked the owl who watched over her from above in the tree. "Is it supposed to be a scene? A person? A creature?"

The owl blinked its black eyes a few times and his head tilted so far to the left she worried it would fall right off his neck. "It's something in the forest."

Rose frowned and continued her observance of the pieces. "So, it could be almost anything. Wonderful."

A few pieces lay in front of her, and she turned them back and forth and twisted them around. For what felt like hours, Rose experimented with the pieces sticking them together. Little by little, they fit together. It was a being she figured out, eventually. There was a head, and some bones created arms or legs (she hadn't figured out which yet), and the pieces of fur could be a tail of some sort. Oddly enough, it was almost as though she could make whatever she wanted with them.

She only hoped it was good enough. It had taken her long enough, she almost quit. But remembering Kartek was still out there and picturing Grandmother's tree outside of the cottage, she kept going.

Even if she was woefully behind the others, she wouldn't give up so quickly.

The puzzle shaped into a part human, part fae creature with a long oval leaf-shaped head. It had long spindly limbs and thin fingers and toes. She used the fur pieces to give it a covering like clothes. Then, nothing happened. Because of course it didn't.

Rose curled her lip and crossed her arms. It was supposed to show her what was next and here the humanoid creature was just lying there. She looked up at the owl, who still sat on the top of the tree. "Now what?"

"Are you sure you have all the pieces?"

Rose's frown deepened. She thought she had everything. But there on the ground were two long oval stones. She held one in each hand and there was a strange warmth about them, like they'd been near a warm fire for a while. Then, she placed them on the face for eyes. Something rumbled beneath her, and Rose stepped away.

The creature trembled and shook, and the two rock eyes flashed in a yellow so light it was almost clear. Its head rocked back and forth like the ticking of a clock, counting down to when it would go after Rose. She unsheathed her sword and took another step back, wanting to give it a wide berth but prepared to strike if needed.

Back
And forth
Back
And forth
Tick
Tock
Tick
Tock

Then it stopped and looked at her. The thin fingers clasped around the blades of grass and pushed itself to stand, the bony knees creaking and clacking together. Its eyes glowing and staring without blinking.

Rose's mouth went dry, and she held the sword out in front of her. The creature walked toward her with arms outstretched like it wanted to give her a bone-crushing hug that would surely suffocate her.

The owl hooted overhead, and it echoed off the trees. With a flash of light and a crack like thunder, he flew into the sky and vanished, leaving Rose alone with the creature she created.

She gulped and gripped her sword even tighter to stop herself from shaking. The creature stalked toward her, and Rose swiped, and it dodged to the side. Another swish and it dodged the other direction. Its arms still raised in front leaves and vines extended out from its fingertips, growing out from the creature's body and fell to the ground like a green waterfall. But it didn't stop when it hit the ground and instead kept crawling along toward Rose.

The vines darted and shot at Rose's feet, and she skipped backward to avoid it. With her sword, she swiped and chopped away at the vines. With each cut they only grew thicker and stronger until they backed away Rose against the three branched tree. She grabbed the edge of her cloak and swung it forward, and as she crouched to the ground, it covered her whole body.

The creature cried out, and something rustled and creaked. Rose peeked out from around the cloak, and when it hit the foliage, it sprang back and broke apart.

Thank you, Mother.

For once Rose grinned, and she dug deep inside for her fae magic again. She'd never used it so often before and hoped it wouldn't grow tired. She put her hands on the ground and felt for the roots and life-force beneath the grass. Little by little, the ground glowed a gentle green color, and it spread to the area around Rose. Now, instead of going after Rose, the vines and leaves and branches protruding from the creature aimed toward the ground. They dug into the grass and dirt flew about the area like someone had jumped into a lake and made a giant splash.

The creature's head looked back and forth in a frantic motion, and a pathetic and high-pitched cry came from it. Rose raised her head, and it pinched together the large and glowing oval eyes in fear as the ends of its arms and legs became trapped and. Her chest tightened.

This thing was trying to attack her. It was getting what it deserved.

But was it? She'd made it, after all. This thing didn't ask to be built. Did it? It was just a pawn in the Trials.

The argument she and Eira had back in Luana's castle rang in

Rose's ears. How Rose was too thirsty for revenge and violence and how it wasn't always the answer.

So, what was the answer here?

Kartek had probably pounded whatever her creature was down to stubs in an instant with her club. But the idea didn't sit right with Rose.

She pressed her hands deeper into the ground, and when she did, hidden in the shadows of the tree, was one more stone. It was round and red and had a faint glow that faded in and out. How hadn't she seen it before? She crawled toward it, releasing her grip on the magic deep in the earth and, in doing so, releasing the vines.

The red stone had an odd warmth to it the way the eyes did, and there was a slight pulse to it. Like a heartbeat. Rose looked over her shoulder, and the creature had now gained control over the vines again, and let out a delighted cackle. It walked toward her, arms outstretched again and the vines crawling to her like an army of snakes.

The creature needed a heart.

Rose swallowed and as much as she didn't want to, let the creature come closer. She yelled and kicked away the vines that threatened to wrap themselves around her limbs. Swishing her cloak back and forth, they flew away and crumpled in on themselves. But it didn't stop the creature.

Good.

"Come here, friend, I've got something for you."

She braced herself and it laid its long fingers on her shoulders and grabbed tightly. Leaves and vines crawled and swarmed around her arms and body, threatening to crush her. Rose yelled and with as much strength as she had, threw her arms out and shoved the red stone into its chest.

The creature let out a surprised cry and staggered back. It looked down at its chest. It glowed red now, and the vines fell away from Rose's body. The creature looked up, eyes pinched together in a confused expression. Then, bit by bit, the leaves of the vines warped into tiny buds, then exploded into large radiant red roses.

It stood next to the tree, and its legs rooted into the ground. It raised its arms like it was about to dance and more red roses bloomed all over its body until the creature had become a beautiful rose tree. The creature sighed and relaxed.

Rose took a step forward toward it and touched one flower with her finger. It swayed and danced at her touch. She smiled. They were like the roses that grew outside of her and Eira's rooms back at Farren Castle, that was planted in honor of their mother.

"Thanks again, Mother," she whispered.

Behind her, something rustled, and she whipped her head around to find trees parting their way in the forest, creating a path full of red petals. Rose took one last look at the tree and the new rosebush, and the creature she'd built let out a small sigh and petals fluttered around it as it relaxed. She could have sworn there was a small smile made from the veins of its oval leaf face.

Rose followed the rose laden path, limping only slightly. In time, she came to a large tree stump set in the middle of the path. It was a perfect and smooth wooden circle. On its surface was an empty emerald vial, mixing and crushing tools, and a piece of parchment attached with an arrow. She pulled the arrow out of the stump and picked up the parchment. A flowing script filled the page with sketches of flowers and leaves bordering around the words.

The source of life from thine own hand
The same shade and soft as silk
With faith and trust and dust
But careful to be sure the next is safe, as they deceive
Stir with what nourishes all
Then consume to your will, but watch for the fall

Some of the ingredients were simple. Rose's blood was the first, then petals the second. Pixie dust was next. But what was after that? Something that would be hard to discern.

Rose thought and tapped the side of the tree stump. Mushrooms. They'd been the most mistrustful thing she'd encountered lately. Even in normal circumstances, you had to be careful which ones you consumed.

Then water would be the last thing.

She placed her hands on her hips and nodded. The petals and mushrooms were easy enough, considering there were petals all over the place, and after walking off the path a little, she came across several tiny fairy circles. She only hoped this alternate world version of Eral didn't have poisoned mushrooms the way the Eral she knew did currently. Drops of her blood were obvious, and she could prick her finger for that. Water and pixie dust, though, would be a little trickier. She had heard no running or flowing water nearby for a creek or waterfall, and there had been no pixies flying around anywhere so far.

"Why couldn't I just fight something off?" Rose mumbled as she wandered around the forest. "Or hit something with my bow and arrow? Something that resembled what I'm actually good at."

She battled the leaf creature she'd puzzled together. At least it seemed like whoever was running this thing liked her solution. Assuming the rose petal path and the concoction she needed to make didn't lead to her death, of course.

Eventually, Rose came across a small creek and filled the vial with its sparkling water. Then on her way back to the path and tree stump, in the middle of a fairy circle, was a tiny pile of pixie dust. She added it to her collection of ingredients and hurried back. Kneeling in front of the tree stump, Rose went to work at crushing the petals and mixing the ingredients.

"Now, that wasn't too hard, was it?" Rose asked no one as she corked the vial and shook it up. She sort of missed the owl from the previous challenge. Even though he hadn't been helpful, it was nice to have another living thing around to talk to. Hopefully, she could get this done soon and be back with Eira and Cal.

Rose lowered the vial once she was done shaking it, and her heart sank. Eira. They'd spent more time apart than together the last few years with the different directions their lives had taken them, but becoming Minister felt different. If she went through with this, Rose couldn't come and go from Eral as she pleased. They would write to each other, of course, and Eira could come visit Eral, and Rose could leave for brief periods of time. But Rose knew how life worked. As good of intentions people have of connecting, sometimes the separation couldn't be helped.

She rubbed the side of the vial with the pad of her thumb to try to ease the thoughts from her mind. This wasn't the time to think about that now. Rose and Eira were sisters and would never truly let each other go. She had to believe that.

With a deep breath, Rose uncorked the vial and took it in one gulp.

Like the bread, the concoction was sweet on her tongue and slid down her throat with ease. It almost seemed to dance and tingle in her mouth, and her head grew fuzzy and dizzy like she'd had one drink too many. Her eyes grew heavy until she couldn't keep them open anymore, and everything went dark.

Chapter Thirty

ROSE

Rose opened her eyes and found herself transported yet again. Now, flowers surrounded her. They ranged from every color Rose could ever imagine, from red to purple to yellow to blue to some she couldn't even describe or had seen before. Fountains flowed with waterfalls of water, large orange fish swam in a nearby pond, and a few trees scattered throughout the space with tall branches launching into the air where an expanse of blue sky with puffy white and glittering clouds drifted overhead. When Rose pushed herself up into a seated position and grasped the green grass, puffs of shimmering green dust filled the air floated around her.

It was the most beautiful garden Rose had ever seen.

A rustling came from the bush ahead. Its branches rocked back and forth like it was saying hello. Rose crawled over to it and looked into the leaves.

"Hello? Is anyone there?"

Something squeaked from below and out of the bottom of the bush walked a tubby little yellow creature. It had a heart-shaped face framed with white fur, long pointed ears, and tiny twigs stuck out of their head like antlers. The little thing waddled out on their stubby hind legs and squeaked some more in a forest creature language Rose couldn't understand. It came up to Rose and placed its front paws onto her leg and squeaked some more.

Rose chuckled. "I'm sorry, I can't understand you."

They wagged their short tail and pushed off Rose's leg, then on all fours scampered away into the garden.

"Wait, I'm coming!" Rose scrambled to her feet, her ankle twitching at the sudden movement. She gave it a rub and calm down the aching muscles and went after the creature. The concoction Eira gave her was wearing off.

She followed the creature through the garden filled with winding cobblestone paths and floating starlight lanterns. They stopped in front of a large pond with water so clear the fish and multi-legged crawlers at the bottom were visible. A waterfall poured from a statue as tall as the Minister's cottage depicting a fae woman holding a large jug. The yellow creature hopped onto one stone circling the pond and wagged its tail. Rose had to hold back a giggle. The tail was so short it mostly looked like it was shaking its entire rear end.

Rose took a seat on another rock next to them and dipped her hand in the pond. The water was shockingly warm. "Can I put my feet in?"

The creature waved their hands and squeaked and chattered in a way that Rose interpreted as a yes. She slid off her boots and stockings and rolled up her trousers, then debated if she should remove the straps. It wouldn't hurt them if they got wet, and with no one there to help, putting them back on would be a literal pain. So, she kept them on and deal with them being wet.

With each inch her feet went into the water, she could feel the muscles relaxing. She sighed in relief. Who knew what sort of challenge would come to her next in this place? But she would at least enjoy the peace while it lasted.

The water of the pond rippled as though someone threw a stone into it. Small waves rolled through it, splashing Rose's legs. Then it stopped and was perfectly still, like a sheet of smooth glass. Something tugged at Rose's chin, as though an invisible hand guided her gaze, and made her look at the center of the pond. She tried to turn her head back and forth, but the invisible hand forced her to stay staring at the water.

On the surface, an image appeared. A woman lay in a grand bed filled with pillows and blankets with a green canopy overhead. Her long red hair plastered to her head, wet with sweat. She was pale and eyes drooped, but she smiled. Attendants bustled around the room and one of them carried a baby to her side. The woman took the child into her arms and rocked them back and forth.

The attendant said something to the woman, but Rose couldn't hear the words. The woman pinched her brows together and unwrapped the swaddle and examined the baby's feet. One was twisted.

Rose gasped. This was her and her mother. It must have been the day she was born. At Mother's side, Grandmother appeared, and she stroked Mother's hair and said something that made Mother laugh. Soon, Father was at her side also and in his arms was a toddler version of Eira. Tears pooled in Rose's eyes. It was a moment Rose never thought she would see. Her whole family was all together. Let alone Father and Grandmother appeared to be getting along.

Then Mother's eyes drooped, and her head wobbled back and forth. *Oh no.* They couldn't possibly be showing her this moment. Rose wanted to close her eyes, but found she wasn't able to. She had to watch her mother die.

Tears blurred her vision as Attendants hurried around the room. Rose's chest cracked open as Father wept and clung to Eira and Grandmother collapsed onto the bed sobbing. The scene faded as the late Queen Lennox's life did, and the last thing Rose saw of it was an Attendant handing Rose as a baby to Grandmother, who kissed the top of her head and whispered something Rose couldn't hear.

To Rose's dismay, it didn't end there. The pond showed her scenes of her life, from when she was a child all the way to her recent days. She saw every tantrum, every rash decision, the moments Eira and Father had to leave her alone because of some duty the needed to perform, the times she lost battles, and the heartbreaks of the few and brief affairs she'd had. She didn't sit in her own shoes again and experience everything like she relived it, but as an onlooker. Someone from the outside looking in who not only saw the best in Rose, but the worst.

Rose saw the moments when she was left out because she didn't have her straps yet and wasn't able to play the same games as other children. There was the time shortly after being chosen for the guard she overheard courtiers whispering about how they thought it was out of pity and because she was the king's daughter, they let her on. She saw her first kill. And the ones following. Then those weeks trapped inside Amelia's mirror. Finally, her time in Eral and ending with Grandmother's death and her fight with Rafe.

The tears came in earnest now, and there was nothing Rose could do to stop them.

But there was more. Whoever determined what Rose watched gave her the blessing of the happy memories too. All the time she and Eira spent together, the day she met Cal, days spent wandering Eral Forest, the tournaments she'd won, and times she'd helped other people and Rose didn't even remember.

The last image went away, leaving only the still pond. Her tiny companion hopped to her side and rested their chin on her leg and let her stroke their head. Rose's whole life was before her. All of where she came from and what made her and who she was. She was impulsive and selfish and never knew when to keep her mouth shut. She was weak and stubborn. There was no choice but to face it. Every part of her was exhausted.

Rose swallowed a lump in her throat and wiped her face with the back of her sleeve. It came back soaked from all the tears she'd cried. "It wasn't all bad, though, was it?"

The creature wagged its tail and squeaked.

"But I've failed so much…"

The water rippled again, and Rose braced herself for what was to come next. It rolled and waved, then parted in the center, and she almost expected a Stulan priest to come out, as this was almost exactly like the scene when she and Eira encountered one that autumn. She pushed herself back, ready to jump and leave. That was the case. But it wasn't a priest who came out of the water. Instead, a head of long silvery white hair appeared, with soft green eyes and a gentle smile.

She gasped and covered her mouth with her hands. It couldn't be. But it was.

"Grandmother?" Rose's voice cracked on the word, and she pushed herself to her feet, unsure if she wanted to run into the pond to her, or run the other way in case this was a trick. It didn't matter either way because once she was standing, Rose couldn't get herself to move in either direction like something had reached out from the ground and held her feet in place.

Grandmother walked across the water to the edge, looking as dry as a summer's day, toward Rose with arms outstretched. "My dear girl, I'm so proud."

Rose choked out a sob and found herself in Grandmother's arms, sobbing. Grandmother stroked her hair like Rose was a little girl again, needing comfort after a nightmare. "How is it you? You died. I saw…"

"Shhh. I know. I'm not here for long. And I'm not even really here."

Wherever here was. Rose still didn't know. Grandmother looked and felt and sounded real. She wasn't a ghost she could see or walk through. She was truly there with her without a single scratch or scar on her. Rose sniffed and wiped away more tears as she took a step back to look at Grandmother better. "I failed you. I'm so sorry. Rafe, I should have known. I thought he was my friend. I never should have trusted…"

"Shhh." Grandmother looped her arm through Rose's and guided her on a leisurely walk through the garden. The grass was cool and soft beneath Rose's bare feet, and she didn't have as much of a limp now. "My time has been coming for a long time. It surprised me Stula didn't commission Rafe sooner. Deities know I've been avoiding her for years."

"What do you mean? You knew?" Rose suspected Grandmother knew what was coming but hearing her confirm it was more disconcerting than the thoughts floating around in her head.

"I wasn't sure of the exact timing of it all, of course. But when Rafe had brought you to the cottage, I had my suspicions."

"And what do you mean by Rafe being commissioned?" She had to spit out the wolf's name. Even the thought of him brought a rolling heat through her and needed to fight the desire to rip something apart.

"It's his job," Grandmother said, as though it was as simple and normal as there being a baker who lived down the road. "There's a reason they call him 'The Prince of Death.' As I'm sure you know, Rafe serves the goddess Stula, and is commissioned to send people to her realm when the time is appropriate. Usually, it is for cases such as me when we've avoided death for too long and it warps the ways of nature."

She sighed and plucked a white rose off a bush, then twirled its stem between her fingers. "I was far too stubborn and didn't want to go until I knew Eral would be in the best hands. Each time I could see myself going toward Stula, I fought against it. I'm not sure who commissioned Rafe, but once he has a task set upon him, he has no choice but to carry it out. While he can avoid it, and I truly believe he tried, in time, his victim will meet their end. Not that I let him win without a fight. It's not entirely his fault. Don't be too hard on him."

Rose gripped Grandmother's arm and looked at the ground. She shook her head. "I hate him."

Grandmother patted Rose's arm. "I know. And I can't say I don't blame you, but I need you to know it is not entirely his fault. But... you should be wary."

"What do you mean?"

She tucked the flower into Rose's braid. "While I don't know for certain who commissioned Rafe, I have my suspicions, and I wouldn't be surprised if his commission extended to a pair of sisters."

Rose stopped in her tracks, which didn't seem to surprise Grandmother, who stopped in stride losing no balance. "Do you think he's going to come after me and Eira?"

"I think it's possible, and likely."

"Then why didn't he kill me when he had the chance?"

Grandmother smiled, and beautiful thin lines crinkled in the corners of her eyes. "Because he's avoiding it. And I don't know if my theory is correct, but I wanted to tell you in case it was. If you and Eira are his next victims, unless his bond to Stula can be broken, in time, there will be nothing anyone can do to stop him."

The words were like heavy stones inside of Rose's chest. If this was true, there had to be a way to stop it. But how did someone break a bond with a goddess? And she thought the Trials were to be her biggest challenge.

"But, while I wanted to tell you all of that, it is not why I'm here."

Rose's heart dropped into her stomach. How could there possibly be more? Grandmother stood in front of her and took both of Rose's hands into her own.

"Then why are you here?" She was almost afraid to ask.

"Because you did it. You succeeded in the Trials. If it is your wish, you are Eral's next Minister."

The ground fell out beneath Rose, and she felt like she was floating and the only thing keeping her steady was Grandmother's hands in hers. No. It was impossible. "But... but how? I hardly did anything!"

Grandmother placed a soft hand against Rose's cheek, and tears pooled in her eyes. "Rose, I am so proud of you. The deities permitted me to be the one to tell you and escort you to Kutlaous, if it is what you wish."

Rose's stomach twisted, and she thought she might hurl. Escorted to Kutlaous. It made sense. The Minister would encounter the god, but it was an event Rose never considered happening. What did someone do when they met a deity? She should have asked Eira who had experience in such things.

"But... but I... really? It's me? Are you sure?"

"I always knew you could do it. Are you ready?"

She could have laughed. Was she ready? Was anyone ever ready for something like this? But somehow, here she was. She'd done it. Amidst the feeling of nausea, her heart swelled. The idea of being Minister was the most terrifying one she'd ever experienced, but she couldn't remember the last time she'd ever been so excited either. Maybe when she'd joined the guard, but it paled in comparison.

"As much as I'll ever be, I guess."

She'd never seen Grandmother smile so big. They linked arms again and kept walking through the garden until they reached an ivy-covered archway.

"This is where I leave you."

Rose's hands shook, and her chin quivered. No. Not yet. Grandmother couldn't leave her again. "Were you scared when you were done with the Trials?"

"Terrified." Her eyes glazed over, and a quirk of a smile played on her lips as though she relived that moment. "But the best things in life sometimes do."

Grandmother pulled her into one last embraced and Rose held on as tight and as long as she could. I couldn't think she could do this without her, but here she was.

"Give Eira all my love," Grandmother whispered into Rose's ear.

She nodded. "I wish she could have been here."

"I do, too, my darling."

"What am I going to do without her?" Rose asked. "My whole life, all I wanted was to serve Cresin and be in Eira's court. Now I'll be in Eral…"

For this was what frightened Rose the most. Everything she'd ever done was about Eira and helping her become queen and protecting her and Father and serving Cresin. She didn't want to be them or have the same status or power, but she wanted to help and serve. As much as it pained it, that was why she agreed to Eira's plan to sit as heiress to the throne. Her tattoo even was a testament to her dedication to her sister with the roses that wound around Aros's sword.

Grandmother squeezed Rose's shoulders and looked at her straight on. Her green eyes were as bright and clear as the leaves of the strongest trees in Eral. "And now it is your turn. What you have done for Eira and your father and Cresin are admirable. But you are so much more than that. It is time for you to live your own life and do everything we all know you are capable of."

Grandmother kissed her forehead one last time, then faded away into tiny flower petals and floated off in the wind.

Through the archway, the little yellow creature sat there waiting for her. They wagged their tail and hurried off on all fours. Rose stepped in, wincing at the ache in her ankle, and looked around. It looked at the rest of the garden with all the flowers and trees and fountains and statues. A light brown pathway led to a circled clearing where a gigantic creature sat on a wooden throne.

Rose gulped. The god of nature, Kutlaous.

He was as tall as an ogre with long horns coming out of his head and pointed ears. His skin was green and brown and looked like some sort of cross between a faun and a tree. He looked at her with intense yellow eyes.

Wait. Yellow eyes. She'd seen those before. Her lip curled. "You!"

Kutlaous blinked a few times. "Excuse me?"

Rose pointed a finger and marched toward him. "You're the one who's been stalking me this whole time!"

The god crossed one leg over the other and raised a brow. Rose knew she should have been embarrassed for yelling at a deity, but the damn eyes kept showing up out of nowhere, making her think it was Rafe, and never revealing themselves. It was rude.

"I prefer the terms 'protecting' and 'watching over.' Didn't I help you when you needed it?"

She opened and closed her mouth a few times. "Well… yes."

"And did I ever cause you harm?"

"No… I guess you didn't."

"So, what is your complaint? I don't watch over just anyone, you know."

The two of them stared at each other for a moment, both with their arms crossed over their chests. "Well, it would have been nice if you'd introduced yourself. I don't enjoy being so confused."

"It's not in my nature to be forthright. Nor is it in any deity's nature."

"Faith and trust and something like that?"

He smirked. "Yes, something like that." He stood and towered over her. Rose wanted to cower away but kept her shoulders straight and head tall. If she was going to be his Minister, she needed to at least appear to be brave. "So, future Minister, if you're finished chastising me, shall we get this started?"

She shifted her weight back and forth, trying to ease some of the pressure off her ankle. "Yes, I suppose so. Have any of the other Ministers yelled at you?"

He cocked his head to the side, an oddly casual and unsure stance for a god, Rose thought, as though he was trying to go through his eons of life trying to remember. "A few."

"Did my grandmother?"

"A few times after she'd met me a few times, yes," he answered with a chuckle. The sound rumbled through the garden and shook the flowers like thunder.

"But not the moment she was supposed to take on the mantle of Minister?" Rose figured she may as well know now how much she'd messed up in doing so.

He shook his head. "No. But I wouldn't expect anything less. It's part of why I like you."

The god walked off with the yellow creature prancing around his feet, trying not to be stepped on like it was a game. Assuming she should follow, Rose jogged a bit to catch up with him. "You like me? And how did I win the Trials? I hardly did anything!"

Kutlaous looked over his shoulder and down at her. She was probably annoying him with all her talking back and questions, but they were valid. If she was going to be Minster, she should know how she got there.

"I've watched you for some time." He looked straight ahead again and kept walking. "I always look in on the descendants of current or previous Minister to see if they have what it takes to be next. You were outspoken, foolish, impulsive, and brave. It impressed me with the way you handled yourself in court and your dedication to your sister. When you and Eira came into Eral in seek of the Stulan Priest, I knew you may wander into a dangerous situation. Especially when Rafe was involved. So, I monitored you, and I felt your connection to your fae heritage."

"Eira has fae blood too and has been training to be a leader her whole life. Why not her?" Rose pointed out.

He nodded. "She does, but her powers with Luana were stronger than most people's and she'd been honing in on it for years. While she could still access her fae magic, it was weaker than yours. This is especially true since her encounter with Luana. Besides, the deities agree Eira belongs to Luana, and I would never overstep that." He looked over his shoulder again. "She doesn't have the right temperament for Eral, anyway. Not like you."

Rose's cheeks burned. She and Eira were vastly different people, and they each had their own strengths, but for a position such as this, Rose never would have considered someone picking her over Eira. "I'm dedicated to Aros, though. I'm assuming I need to be dedicated to you to be Minister, but I've never heard of being dedicated to two deities. Is it even possible?"

"I'm a god. I wouldn't be much of one if I couldn't change the rules periodically."

Fair point. "Then what about the Trials? They were challenging, of course, but… I don't feel like I did much."

"You did a great deal," Kutlaous said. "You showed endurance and strength on the wall, being willing to climb it despite your injury. Then in asking for help, that showed you understood it is all right to do so. Too many leaders try to do things on their own and don't each out for help when needed. Eral is not yours to command or control, but to partner with. You were clever and brave in escaping the collapsed wall. Then, with the puzzle, you proved you could solve problems, and when the creature attacked, you responded with peace and life instead of destruction. Those are all things that are important in being Minister. When you put together the potion, you proved you understood how to search the Forest for what you needed and understood how to put it together."

Rose supposed it made sense. She wasn't a deity, so maybe it wasn't her place to determine what he would need to pick a new Minister. "Then what about the pool? Was that just to torture me?"

He shook his noble head, and the leaves and a tiny nest tucked into his antlers shook and rained miniature twigs onto Rose. "That was the most important of all and where most fail. You faced yourself. You saw your whole life and everything of what makes you who you are and didn't back away. You accept yourself the good along with the bad. Many don't realize how truly challenging that can be."

Her cheeks warmed again. She hadn't thought of that.

Kutlaous stopped walking and Rose stood at his side, her head only reaching his chest. "Questions?"

She smiled up at him. "I'm sure I'll think of some more eventually."

He chuckled, and the ground trembled again because of it. "I'm sure. If you're done for now, the time has come. And you have someone waiting for you." He extended an arm out and before them lay two rectangles made of flowers with fluffy cloud pillows at the top of each. Between them stood -

"Cal!"

He stood there in front of Rose, still in his travel clothes, but with no weapons. His long blond hair was brushed and tied back, and beard trimmed closer to his chin than it had been in weeks. His blue eyes were bright, and Rose couldn't help but smile at the sight of him. She rushed to his side, wincing, and biting through the pain in her ankle and into his arms. He lifted her off the ground with his powerful arms and held on as tight as he could.

"I knew you could do it," he murmured into her hair.

"Is this your chosen partner?" Kutlaous asked.

Cal set Rose back onto the ground, and they faced the god. Rose nodded. "Yes."

Kutlaous grimaced and stepped toward them, the yellow creature hopping and squeaking at his side. "He has a curse on him. That could be problematic."

Rose squeezed Cal's hand, and her gaze drifted to his chest. She couldn't see the dark cloud through his clothes, but she could almost feel its presence. "Is there anything you can do?"

The god rubbed his chin and tilted his head to the side in contemplation. "Perhaps. I may not cure it, but there might be a way I can help." He outstretched his arms toward each of the flower beds. "Each of you please lay down and close your eyes."

She took in a deep breath and squeezed Cal's hand one more time, then they both picked a bed and lay on them. The sun was so bright in her face, Rose didn't mind closing her eyes as instructed. At first, it seemed like she would take a relaxing - and much needed - nap. Then, something crawled up her leg and Rose screeched, thinking it was a snake. But it didn't have scales, and she realized it must have been a vine or ivy. They wrapped around her legs, then arms, tying her to the ground.

It pulled and tugged on her body, and Rose wanted to cry out but found she didn't have a voice. Thorns pricked at her and dug into her skin, awakening her fae magic. Something sprung to life inside of Rose and burst open in her chest like flowers blooming in the spring. Yet on the outside, it felt like she was being pulled and poked and prodded at all sides.

A bright green light glowed behind her closed eyelids and after what felt like hours, someone grasped her hand. She didn't need to see anyone to know it was Cal. The contours and callouses of his hand were as familiar as her own. Their fingers intertwined, and she felt some of whatever plants trapped her travel over to him, and some of his energy spread through her. It was a solid comfort to know he was there despite the pain. He was there and always would be. And she would be there for him, too.

Then, all at once, all feeling vanished and again the world turned black.

Chapter Thirty-One

ROSE

RoseRose opened her eyes, and she lay on solid ground with no flowers or thorns or vines or thorns jabbing at her legs. She patted her torso and all the way down her legs to her ankles, which the injured one was now freed with the wraps folded neatly to the side. It was back to its usual twisted state, but there was none of the aching and pain from the broken bone. She moved it side to side, and nothing hurt. It was like there'd never been an injury.

But never mind the broken - or not broken anymore as it was - ankle. Rose stared at her left arm that now had a green and glowing tattoo whose thorned stem wound around it and rose flowers blooming from it.

"At least it's pretty," Rose said to no one in particular.

At her side, Cal stirred and sat. His hair and beard were as perfectly trimmed and maintained as it had been in the garden. Only now, he had his own rose tattoo etched around his left wrist. He pushed himself to a seated position and looked to Rose.

"Are you all right?" he asked.

Rose moved her ankle back and forth to show him. "Great. You?"

"I'm fine…" But there was a pinched look on his face, and he patted his torso with both hands. "My chest. There's something different." He unceremoniously untied his shirt - which should have had all the ceremony in Rose's humble opinion - and examined the spot where the black cloud was.

It was still there, but now covered in leaves. Branches and vines covered the dark cloud like they were reining it in unable to escape. He ran his hand over it like he was trying to convince himself it was real.

Rose crawled over to him and put her hand over his across his chest. It wasn't empty and cold like a cloud anymore. Instead, it was warm with bristles and the leaves brushed against her skin. Or maybe the heat was from touching Cal, even if it was just his hand. And his chest, in a way. She didn't know how it was possible, but as Kutlaous told her, he wouldn't be much of a god if he couldn't bend the rules a bit.

Cal's new tattoo glowed brighter, and Rose felt hers send a warm tingle up her arm.

"Do you think it'll help?" she asked.

"Only one way to find out."

Keeping their hands clasped together over his chest, he used his other hand to hold the back of Rose's head with fingers tangled in her unkept braid. Rose quietly moaned at the feel of his soft lips and a hot jolt soared through her. It was a faded version of what had happened before when they kissed, but instead of it causing her pain and distracting Rose from the kiss, it heightened it.

Hoots and hollers and cheers surrounded them, and they broke apart. It was only then Rose realized they were back in Eral at Grandmother's cottage.

Or rather, Rose's cottage.

Her cheeks flushed and Rose looked around to see everyone was still there, and they clapped for Rose and Cal. The dwarf was yelling and throwing his ax, the centaur was a puddle of tears and surrounded by his clan, then there was Kartek. As though they had done nothing since eating the bread, the ogress stood tall and stared at Rose like she was ready to rip her limb from limb. Rose was going to have to deal with her, and she didn't look forward to it. But she had a few ideas.

"I guess we should greet everyone," Cal said. He stood and extended his hands to her and let Rose use his hands and arms to pull herself up and lean on.

The cheers from the crowd grew even louder, and they all bowed before her. Even Kartek lowered her head. Albeit reluctantly. They all stood straight again. A shriek and cheer came from behind her.

Eira ran toward Rose and engulfed her in a bone-crushing hug that almost made Rose fall over. "We did not know what was happening!" Eira said. "You ate the bread, and you screamed and then you were fast asleep. We could see you moving some and you'd cry out or mumble something we couldn't understand, but for all we knew they had poisoned you or something." Eira stepped back and examined her sister. "Are you all right? Are you hurt?"

Rose swayed a little since she didn't have her straps and couldn't put her full weight on her ankle. Cal grasped her arm right away and steadied her. "I'm fine. We're fine. A little overwhelmed."

"Understandable."

Rose wasn't sure what it was, but something clicked inside of her and there was a new clarity. She could sense everything in Eral. Even if she couldn't see it all clearly, there was a sense of the entire forest running through her mind. Creatures being born in the northern corner, a fae was hunting toward the west, and there was something wet and sinister in the southeast. It was the swamp and Amelia, and Rose knew it even more certainly now. She couldn't explain it, but she knew the sorceress was there, and she had to stop her.

All the surrounding creatures were shouting and celebrating, and towering over them, Kartek talked with other ogres. Rose needed Kartek on her side. She leaned into Eira and brought Cal in closer so others around them couldn't hear. "We need to talk to Kartek, and I might have an idea. But I need you to be on board, Eira."

"Of course. What are you thinking about?"

Rose would have preferred to bring them all into the cottage to talk and was sure Eira would have wanted Cadeyrn and Aytigin there. But a party was beginning around them, and she was getting the sense other creatures and various groups wanted her ear and time. So she hurried with the plans she was forming. As suspected, Eira wasn't entirely keen on the idea. But in time, she nodded and agreed.

It was just in time, too, because the brownies brought Rose her crutch and the clan of centaurs approached Rose with deep bows. The rest of the night - or maybe it was day now, Rose wasn't sure how much time had passed - they passed her and Cal from group to group and clan to clan. They gave her drinks and food and blankets and baskets of gifts. Vial of sparking dust from the pixies, a basket of uncontaminated mushrooms from the gnomes, a large shining ax from the dwarfs, and a shining ruby necklace from the fae. She did not know where she was going to put these gifts but was grateful just the same.

A pair of fauns were giving Rose and Cal a warm wool blanket that would be of use in the winter months when she saw her opportunity to talk to Kartek. Rose nudged Cal and pointed to Kartek, who stood on her own for once. She had a tall goblet in her clawed hand and took a deep drink.

"Kartek," Rose said, and the ogre chief turned to face her. "I need to speak with you."

She gave Rose a mocking bow and tossed her goblet aside. It fell with a thump to the ground. "Of course, oh wise Minister."

Rose grimaced but said nothing in response. She didn't need Kartek to like her or be happy with how the Trials turned out, but she didn't need her for an enemy either. "I have a new proposition for you."

Kartek raised a single brow. "You don't have the Chalice, do you?" She snorted and pursed her lips. "Of course, you don't. I knew you wouldn't keep your word. Can never trust humans."

Rose shook her head. "No, I don't. But I think we can still help Zorar and give you even more of what you want. You're working with Amelia, aren't you? You want the ogres to have power. You've been unhappy with my family for years, and Amelia hates us too. The two of you figured you could work together to get rid of my family and put the ogres and sorceresses in power. Am I right?"

Kartek crossed her arms, and her face was unreadable, but there was a slight flash of recognition in her eyes. It was all Rose needed to know. She was on the right track. "And what can you offer?"

"Land," Rose answered. Karate's expression was as still as stone, but her orange eyes were glued to Rose. "You're right about one thing: the ogres haven't been treated as equals the way they should be. Our ways might be different, but you are citizens of Eral as much as everyone else. And your people had an agreement with my family when one of yours wanted to marry my mother, and she went off and found her own solution that didn't give you what you wanted. I've already spoken with Princess Eira, and she has agreed to give your clan a piece of Cresin."

Cal pulled out a small map from his satchel and unfolded it. He pointed to a small portion outside of Eral. "No one has inhabited it for years. It's not much, but if you agree to help us, Eira says it's yours."

Kartek bent forward so she could see it better. "That's all very well and good, but Eira is not to be the next queen anymore. It's not guaranteed."

"You're right," Rose agreed. "While we're confident Eira will get her crown back, we can't rely on that alone. If Eira cannot fulfill her end of the bargain, I will offer a piece of Eral."

There was a light in Kartek's eyes that hadn't been there before at the idea of this. "Is Eral yours to give?"

Cal pulled out another map, this time of Eral, and pointed at various portions of the forest. "The centaurs have their own settlement, so do the fae. Why can't the ogres? You wouldn't have to move camp from place to place and create your own stake. You could establish your clan in the forest, you already know. It's not the same as having territory in one of the kingdoms, but still respectable. And it would still be under my protection," Rose added.

Kartek stepped back and kept her arms crossed as though they were stopping Rose and Cal from jumping and attacking her. Rose felt like her heart was in her throat but couldn't help but wonder if their offer was wearing her down.

"And if you help us," Rose went on as a last-ditch effort. "I think we might heal Zorar."

The ogre chief's body went stiff, and her orange eyes glued to the map Cal kept open. She swallowed and nodded. "What's your plan?"

Chapter Thirty-Two

ROSE

THE CELEBRATIONS WENT LONG INTO THE NIGHT. OR MAYBE IT WAS morning. Rose still didn't have a sense of what time of day it was. Maybe it was the next evening already, and the Trials had taken far longer than she'd thought. But, little by little, the residents of Eral scattered and went on their ways. Kartek was one of the first to leave as she and those who joined her went to gather the others to help Rose the next day.

At least, it was what Kartek told her.

When the last had gone, Rose and the others dragged themselves back into the cottage. Aytigin had drank a bucketful of the fae wine and was singing a sad song about Luana and Ray and the stars and was being held up by Eira and Cadeyrn on either side of him. He kept flapping his wings to fly, but his companions kept him safe on the ground. Rose didn't want to think about what it would be like to have a drunken ice dragon flying around Eral without supervision.

The three of them said goodnight to Rose and Cal and went up the stairs to their rooms, leaving them alone with a flurry of brownies who stayed to clean the kitchen. In time, Rose could bribe them away with bowls of milk and cream, which they took with delighted chatters and high-pitched squeals.

The last one left and Rose shut the door, then barricaded it with the long wooden bolt. It latched shut with a satisfying thud, and she pressed her forehead to the door for a moment to take in a deep breath.

Peace and quiet at last.

Cal waited for her on the couch, and Rose made her way over to him. She collapsed half onto it and half onto Cal and his open arms. He kissed the top of her head and let her snuggle in like he was her personal, giant pillow. It amazed her at how natural it all felt. The switch from friends to…

Partners?

Lovers?

They hadn't quite figured that part out yet. But whatever it was, the transition to it was like they'd been this way forever. Rose always imagined love was a roller coaster of emotions filled with tension and longing and excitement. Maybe for some people it was. It certainly seemed that way for Eira and Cadeyrn and their journey. While this was exciting and terrifying in its own way, loving Cal wasn't like that for Rose. Loving Cal was finding the piece of the puzzle she'd been searching for when all along it was right there and fit perfectly into place.

It was a relief. Rose had enough dramatics in her life as it was. She didn't need it in her relationship.

His arm wrapped around her, and he stroked the top of her thigh with the tips of his calloused fingers. "How are you holding up?"

"I think I've plateaued," Rose answered. "Nothing has set in yet, I don't think. It's been a long day."

Long was too simple of a word for it, but she didn't have the energy to think of another one.

"I'm sure the Trials took it out of you."

Rose nodded and snuggled closed into him. He smelled like earth and bonfire and a hint of rain. "They did. Not what I expected, though."

"Oh?"

Reluctant to move from her position, Rose adjusted herself so she could still cuddle with him but look at his face while talking. She told him all about the Trials and the way they were a challenge but felt as though she hadn't done much of anything. The worst of it had been the pond, which wasn't even a physical challenge. He particularly enjoyed the part about the little yellow creature but was silent and stone cold when she mentioned the conversation she had with Grandmother about Rafe. He gripped her thigh so tightly she wondered if it would leave a bruise.

If he was going to leave a mark on her, it was going to be for very different reasons.

"I knew we shouldn't have trusted him."

Rose put her hand on his, and he released his grip. "There's no way we could have known. We'll deal with him, but one thing at a time."

And if she thought about it too much, there was a good chance Rose would burn the world down trying to find the wolf and avenge Grandmother.

"And now this whole place is yours."

Hers. Rose didn't have many things that were really hers, let alone a home. Even if she'd stayed at Farren Castle and became queen, it never would belong to her. A home she could put her own mark on. A place for her and Cal to live their life together. It warmed her all the way to her toes.

"Ours," she corrected.

"Ours."

Rose lifted her face up so she could see him even better. His blue eyes shone down at her, glistening with want. He cupped her face in his palm and kissed her. His grip on her thigh tightened, and this time in the way she hoped for. Rose grasped onto his shirt and melted into it, wanting to drink and soak Cal in. Now that she could and there wasn't anything to stop them, it was like Rose realized she'd been in a closed room blind to the only door. But the door was open and gave her a brand-new world she could go through, and it was better than anything she'd imagined.

Cal groaned as he opened his mouth further and her lips explored each other. His chest rumbled and a small wave went through her body. Rose gasped and broke the kiss.

"Are you all right? Does it hurt?"

She pressed her hand against his chest, feeling the rumbling beneath.

He nodded. "I'm fine. It's… different."

Rose raised her brows. "A good different?"

"Absolutely."

She rubbed his chest and could feel the bumps and contrasts of the vines and leaves that now encased the cloud inside him. "I feel like I should check. Just to be sure. For your health."

His kiss-swollen lips tugged into a small smile. "For my health?"

She gave him a single nod while she fingered the laces of his tunic and pulled them out inch by inch. Cal leaned back against the couch and watched her through hooded lids as she opened the tunic, revealing a triangle of skin showing off his muscled chest. She slid her hands underneath the fabric and lifted it up and over his head.

The dark cloud hovering over where his heart should be, and encased in foliage, rumbled, but where before there were black streaks like dark lightning, green vines shuddered and radiated as Cal licked his lips. It hypnotized Rose.

"Do I look healthy to you?"

"I think you'll survive."

"Praise the deities."

He pulled her into a deep kiss, and the vibrations from the curse radiated through Rose. She climbed onto his lap and pressed herself against his chest, letting the waves roll onto her as though if they shared them, it would calm it down more. He kissed her with the greediness of a starving man, and she was the only thing that would satisfy. Heat pulsed through Rose and yet she still shivered when his hands found their way under her shirt and up to her breasts.

"I should be sure I'm not hurting you either," he said into her ear.

"For my health?"

Cal pressed a kiss to her neck and murmured something wordlessly. In a flash, he pulled up her shirt and ripped it off her body, her undergarments following soon after, so her breasts were free and revealed to him. He cupped the pale and freckled skin. "So beautiful."

A moan escaped her lips as his mouth closed in around her taught nipple. Another shock went through her, and she grasped onto him, urging him to keep going. A low rumble came from his chest in response and moved to the other side with a playful lick and bite.

"More," Rose groaned. "I need more of you."

Cal's tattoo glowed and in a swift movement, he smacked her rear and flipped Rose over, so she sat on the couch and Cal knelt in front of her like she was the deity he worshiped. It only took a single tug and her trousers ripped and pulled off, so Rose was bare before him.

Those weren't her favorite clothes anyway.

He knelt before her, eyes wild with desire and his muscles taught. Rose met his gaze and with slow movements spread her legs wide for him. Cal licked his lips and rubbed a calloused thumb over her. "Is this what you wanted?"

Rose panted and nodded. "Yes."

"Already so wet for me, darling."

"Yes." It was more like a cross between a squeak and a groan than a word, but Cal understood, his fingers pressing harder into her core.

"I can't wait to taste your sweet pussy." He placed a kiss on the inside of her thigh. Rose shivered. She'd never heard him talk like this before, and she liked it. Cal removed his hand and clasped her thighs in each palm like she needed to be anchored down and under his control.

Rose never wanted to be under someone's control. But laying bare and spread out before Cal like this, she relished the feeling of letting go for him to do with her as he wanted. She ran her hand between her legs, and she was even more wet than she'd expected.

What almost sounded like a growl came from Cals's lips and he gripped harder onto Rose's hips and pulled her to the edge of the couch. She gasped, then moaned when his mouth met her core, his tongue sliding inside her, lapping up her wetness. Her fingers tangled into his hair, and her back arched to grind against him.

Diar bless it.

"Yes, Cal, please. I need you more." It surprised Rose to hear herself beg, but she couldn't help it. He looked up at her with wicked eyes as he licked her, and she thought she might explode.

Cal took his time and let Rose ride the waves of pleasure until she felt like she could die from it. He pinned her down to the couch, keeping her in place until he had his fill, and her body shook.

With one final nibble to her inner thigh, Cal lifted his head and kissed Rose on the lips so she could taste her desire for herself. She leaned into him and pulled against him so tightly she toppled off the couch and they collapsed into a heap on the floor with Rose on top of him.

His chest tumbled with laughter, and Rose descended into a fit of giggles along with him. This was happening, and Rose could hardly believe it. They should have been doing this for years.

Rose took in a few deep breaths and calmed herself while Cal grabbed her legs and adjusted them, so she sat straddled around his hips. She sank back and ran her hands over his chest and wiggled herself so she could feel him throb against her body.

"Seems like I'm not the only one ready to go," Rose mused.

Cal's hands wrapped around her waist and landed on her rear, which he gave a tight squeeze. "It's what you do to me, Rose."

As much as she enjoyed this position, she shifted enough to reach between their bodies and tug his trousers down his legs. His swollen shaft emerged free, and Rose rubbed her hand up and down the smooth skin.

Cal squeezed her rear even tighter and let out a guttural sound. "Diar bless it. I've been imaging you for so long."

Rose felt herself growing wet all over again and grasped the tip of him and rubbed it against the bud between her legs. Deities, he felt amazing.

"Ride it, Rose."

She needed no more encouragement. Rose leaned forward and pressed a kiss to his mouth, pushed herself back up, then positioned herself to lower onto him. It'd been a while since Rose had been with anyone, and he was so large she almost worried she wouldn't be able to handle him. But as she slid down his shaft and felt herself wrapping right around him, small joyful cries came out of her mouth. The two puzzle pieces coming together to fit just right. "Oh, gods."

"Are you all right?" Cal's voice was tight and quiet, but that he wanted to be sure she was fine warmed her heart.

Rose nodded. "You're amazing."

She leaned forward to kiss him again, then rocked against his body, bracing herself against his chest with her hands as he watched her breast bob up and down. He held them in his hands and groaned.

Cal pushed his hips up, shoving himself further inside of Rose with each thrust. He slapped her rear with a loud smack, then with his tattoo flashing, flipped her around so he was on top; her legs wrapped around his waist. His hands grasped hers with fingers intertwined and raised them over her head.

Rose's bare body rubbed against the hardwood floor as Cal slammed into her, making her see stars, but she didn't care. She bit her bottom lip so as not to scream and wake the others upstairs.

Cal pressed his mouth against her ear and with one hand rubbed her at her most sensitive spot. "Come for me."

Rose could only nod and softly moan.

He rammed himself into her once, twice, three times, each one deeper and harder than the last. His fingers pressed and circled around her, and she ground herself against him.

"Come for me, Rose," he commanded again.

She wrapped her legs tighter around his body and nodded, wanting to be closer, deeper. Nothing would be enough. "Yes," she said. His demands did something to her she couldn't explain and drove her wild.

"I'm coming soon, love," he panted.

Yes. Deities, yes.

Rose reached down and held her hand on his between their bodies and rocked against him, their fingers rubbing her in unison. She couldn't hold in a cry anymore as her body exploded, and Cal joined her. He pulled himself out, so he spilled over her leg, as they hadn't even thought about finding a tonic for him to take.

Cal collapsed onto the floor next to Rose, his chest heaving. She rolled to her side and curled into him, and his arm warped around her. They lay there for a moment to catch their breath.

"We should have been doing that for years," Rose said.

Cal chuckled. "I agree."

Chapter Thirty-Three

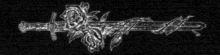

ROSE

Rose jolted upright out of bed. At her side, Cal still slept soundly on his stomach, the blanket half off his naked body as it was so warm in the bedroom from the summer heat. When they'd finally went to bed, they originally went upstairs to where Rose had slept before. But the image on her door had vanished, and the door locked. The cottage already had turned Grandmother's old room on the ground floor into hers. Grandmother's furniture was gone and replaced with brand new pieces just for Rose and Cal. A piece of Rose was sad Grandmother's things were already stored away somewhere, but also grateful she would not have to climb up the steps every night.

She coughed and panted and waved away at the green haze that had seeped into the room. Even before she'd opened her eyes, Rose knew there'd been a shift in the atmosphere. She couldn't describe it, but something in her sleep stirred and told Rose she needed to get up. Out the window there was the smallest hint of light. Early morning then. At least they'd gotten some rest.

Her stomach twisted, and there was a heaviness on her chest. Even without the haze, she knew something wasn't right in Eral. It was like Kutlaous had gifted another sense to Rose after the Trials, and she knew there was something amiss the way you could smell a change of seasons in the air.

All around the room the fog seeped in through the windows, and along the walls mushrooms popped out one after another, puffs of green dust spreading out with each of them. Rose pushed herself over to the edge of the bed to get her crutch.

She let out a high-pitched screech at the feel of the damp floor.

Cal stirred at Rose's side. "Rose?"

She pressed the pads of her palms to her eyes and shook her head. "Something is wrong. Amelia, the swamp…"

It was Amelia. Something deep inside of Rose knew it. Not just her gut instincts, but as though through the magic flowing through her, Eral was crying out for help and told her who was to blame. It was Amelia, but someone, something else with her.

The words had barely escaped her mouth before Cal sat next to her. His blue eyes bulged at the sight of the room. "Amelia."

"We need to go."

Without hesitation, the two of them were up and moving to get dressed to see what the rest of the cottage and Eral looked like. Cal helped Rose wrap her ankle, and within moments, they were out in the kitchen. Eira and Cadeyrn clamored down the stairs in their own simple tunics and trousers, prepared for a day of travel.

Rose gasped and clasped her hands to her mouth. Green haze poured in through the cracks under the windows and doorway, and trails of mushrooms sprouted across all the surfaces.

"What's happened?" Eira asked. She tugged a brown belt around her waist and tied it tight.

Rose could only shake her head. "Amelia, and someone else. I don't know who, but it's her. Eral told me."

"Told you?"

It wasn't the best way to phrase it, but it was all Rose could think of to describe what she was feeling. It was like when your own body spoke to you. Your body couldn't use words or phrases, but when it was sick or felt good or needed something, it still communicated. Eral was the same way.

"Sort of," Rose answered and made her way to the door to where she and Cal had discarded her cloak and their weapons the night before. She swung it over her shoulders and clasped it around her neck. Another layer of clothing sounded awful with the heat and the sticky humidity, but she could use whatever protection was available. "We're going to go find her."

Eira followed close behind her sister. She picked up a sword and helped Rose strap it to her back. "Where is she? We'll go with you."

Rose shook her head. "I don't know for sure. I think…" She paused and took in a deep breath, then closed her eyes to search through her magic for where Amelia might be. It took a moment, as she was still learning how it all worked. Sensations of what the forest dwellers were experiencing flooded through her, and she pressed her hand to her forehead as it thudded in pain. Grandmother didn't tell her about this part. Maybe it just took some getting used to. After a few minutes, Rose found the source. "I think Amelia knows Kartek partnered with us now. And she's coming."

When she opened her eyes, a concerned and shocked look was on Eira's face. Eira handed Rose a dagger with a slight shake of her hand. "How do you know? Did you see it?"

"I can sense it. It's like Eral is calling to me for help and is showing me what's going on." Rose took the dagger and slid the holder onto her belt, nothing. Her hands had a slight tremor to them too.

"Then we're coming too," Eira announced. She crossed the room to where another cabinet stood with additional weapons. Cadeyrn was already there and handed her a sword. "We'll do this together."

The cottage shuddered beneath their feet, and Rose placed her hand on the wall to brace herself. Cal and Cadeyrn's tattoos glowed to keep their balance and Eira grabbed onto Cadeyrn, almost falling to the ground.

They were here. Who they were exactly, Rose couldn't tell. But it wasn't a friendly visit that she could tell.

Someone pounded on the front door, and Eira yelled. They all jumped, then took a step back. An unfamiliar male voice beckoned Rose from outside. It was deep and rumbled the house. It sent a shiver down Rose's spine. "Come out, little Minister, don't you want to play?"

Rose unsheathed her sword and stepped in front of the others. They all could protect themselves. Cal and Cadeyrn were two of the strongest fighters Rose knew, and Eira had the powers of a goddess. If Aytigin was outside, he could freeze them all to death with a single blow. But this was her forest, and her cottage. Whoever it was, out there wanted her, and everyone in the cottage was under her protection.

"Oh, little princesses with your enormous powers and vigorous men." Rose gripped her sword even tighter at the sound of the fresh voice that joined in. Amelia. "The cottage might be warded against us, but you can't hide in there forever. And we have our ways of getting to you."

Every window of the cottage rattled, then green water trickled in from under the door. It was just like in Farren Castle when Rose discovered Amelia was a sorceress. Swords and daggers wouldn't help them now against the flowing water. Rose sheathed her sword, and Cadeyrn and Cal did the same. The four of them huddled together and scurried backward. They weren't fast enough. Green swamp water rose higher and higher until it was almost to their knees.

"We need to get above the water," Cal said. His tattoo glowed, and he jumped onto a table, then outstretched his arm to Rose. She took it and let him pull her onto the table. "And whatever you do, don't drink it," he instructed Cade and Eira. "It's been infesting in the mushrooms and could poison you."

The cottage continued to shake, and Rose had to crouch and hold on to the furniture so as not to fall off. There were another series of quakes inside the cottage now, and a deep rumble close to Rose's ear. A loud male yell rang through the house, and Cadeyrn shifted before them into a giant bear. He nodded to Eira, who climbed onto his back, then onto the table next to Rose.

Waves of water pounded against the outside walls in deafening hits. Whoever it was out there had said nothing in a while. They could be planning their next move. Or harming others out there. Others who were in Rose's care.

Speaking of, where was Kartek? She and the ogres were supposed to meet them here to go after Amelia. Unfortunately, Amelia beat them to it.

"Any ideas?" Rose asked to any of them who would listen.

"I can go after Amelia and whoever is out there with her," Cadeyrn said. His voice was an octave deeper than usual and only added to the trembling of the cottage.

Cal nodded. "I'll go with him. Depending on who's out there with her, swords may not do much good. But we can distract them."

"I can use my ice, but I don't want to freeze and trap us all in here," Eira added.

No, that wouldn't be helpful.

They needed to block or drain or soak up the water somehow before the whole cottage flooded.

Before all of Eral flooded.

Something crashed against the cottage with a loud boom sounding like thunder.

The three of them all looked to Rose for guidance, and her stomach twisted. Her first day on the job, and she had no idea what to do. She racked her brain to think of all the things Grandmother taught her and what she'd learned while traveling in Eral. But they kept pounding on the doors and it blocked all thought from her. The bookshelves shook and books slid off the shelves. Rose's eyes widened.

The books. There was a spell Grandmother had been working on when they arrived in Eral to help with soaking up water. Something to do with dirt and sand…

Rose jumped off the table and ignored the cries of her family behind her. She slogged her way through the green water to the shelf and frantically searched for the book Grandmother was using before. It was thin and green. "Cal! What was that thing Grandmother was working on when we got here? Do you remember the book?"

Cal's brows furrowed as he tried to remember. "There was silver lettering, I think."

Yes. That was it. Rose continued her frantic search and there on the shelf above her head it was. She stood on tiptoe, something not easily done with water sloshing around her waist that threatened to knock her over, and after a few tries grabbed it.

"She was working on something to help soak up and block the water from infiltrating Eral more," Rose explained and flipped through the pages as fast as her fingers allowed until she found the correct page.

Dirt, of course, vines were easy enough to find, and most of it came from Rose tapping into her own magic. "If I can do it, I can get it to the swamp and block the water from drowning Eral. Maybe I can start it here."

Cal tilted his head to the side. "In theory, that's wonderful. But how are you going to get there?"

Something slammed their hand against the window next to Rose. She yelled and jumped. Through the glass was a green hand pressed against it. Mushrooms and algae, with rotting flesh dripping off the bone. Behind it a face appeared, just as grotesque as the arm with slimy black hair and empty eyes. The face snarled at her.

A scream caught in Rose's throat. Who or what in Kutalous's name did Amelia ally with?

Then, as fast as the zombie appeared, another shudder went through the cottage and a shot of ice blew past the window. The zombie now stood frozen outside of the window. Rose smiled. Aytigin was here.

"I think I found my way."

Chapter Thirty-Four

ROSE

Rose repeated what she needed repeatedly under her breath, so she didn't need to bring the book with her. She shoved it back onto the shelf, then climbed onto Cadeyrn's back. He could get her outside, and from there, get to Aytigin and make him fly her to the swamp. It wasn't much of a plan, but it was all she had at the moment. It would work.

It had to work.

"Are you ready?" Cadeyrn asked. His deep voice shook, and Rose tightened her grip on his fur as Cal climbed on behind her. He would stay there with the cottage to ward off Amelia and the zombies, and meanwhile, Eira planned to do what she could with her ice and star magic.

"No time like the present."

Cadeyrn roared and charged at the front door. He knocked it over with a single blow and plowed out into Eral. Zombies surrounded the cottage and ran after them, but Cadeyrn ran them down, slipping and sliding in the green water and mud. Mushrooms flew all around them, followed by the puffs of pixie dust from the tiny beings who lived underneath them. The zombies he didn't get Rose and Cal did with their swords.

A green haze hovered over the forest outside of the cottage door

Leaves on the trees wilted under the oppressive heat, and fresh new mushrooms sprouted over the whole ground like it made a fresh path. Even more surprising was who stood on the other side of the pond before her.

It'd sounded as though the voice was just outside the door, but he stood so far away. The man was dressed in ancient blue and green robes with light brown skin and dark braided hair. At his side stood Amelia, her blonde hair pulled on top of her head in a bun that would have looked like a mess on anyone else, but on her was the image of power and regality. Her thin blue dress floated around her like a cloud. To the side was Kartek, whom they'd gagged and tied to a tree.

Rose expected to find Amelia, but the others were a surprise.

Whoever they were.

But they were the least of their worries. Amelia and the man joined hands and water spun and flowed in a circle around their wrists. They closed their eyes and raised their free hands into the air, muttering words Rose couldn't hear or understand. Then out of the pond, bony hands with skin hanging off them rose out of the pond. Equally bony heads and bodies followed them. It was as though the swamp had attached itself to the undead beings who rose out of the water. The slime and muck was as much a part of them as the bits of flesh that hung off their bones.

"Watch out!" Eira cried from behind them.

Rose's sister ran out of the cottage. Sheets of ice formed underneath her, so she had a path to walk on instead of the mud. Oddly, Eira was better at walking on ice than the mud. She stretched her arms out and daggers of ice shot off out her hands toward the zombies. One by one, they hit the beings, and they fell back into the pond.

A dragon cry roared overhead, and Rose felt a cool breeze break through the humid air. Aytigin, still in his part of human form, swooped down over them with ice that poured out of his hands and shot down into the pond. He aimed a few at Amelia and her companions, but they didn't break their concentration.

Rose cupped her mouth with her hands and shouted up at him. "I need you to take me to the swamp!"

Aytigin hovered over them, and his white wings made a slight breeze. "And leave here? I don't think so."

"You'll go, old man," Cadeyrn growled.

Aytigin's lip curled. "What have I told you about calling me that?" He jerked his head toward Amelia and the man. "And what is Dusan doing here? He's supposed to be dead."

Rose blinked a few times. "Do you know him?"

Aytigin scoffed. "I'm not *that* old. He's an ancient Colman sorcerer. Even when I was young, he was a character in old tales about sorcerers and sorceresses who would lure children into their waters and eat them for lunch."

"Maybe I should eat *you* for lunch."

They all turned to see Amelia and Dusan watching them, their hands still intertwined. The sorcerer had a cruel smile on his face and twisted his free hand. Out of the forest and through the trees, more undead sorcerers stalked toward them.

Rose shuddered. As if that was all they needed now, a dead evil sorcerer. "Were the stories true?"

"Let's not wait to find out." Apparently not needing anymore convincing, Aytigin shuddered and shifted into his full dragon form.

Cal wrapped his hand around Rose's wrist and turned her toward him. He gave her a single kiss. "I'll see you soon."

Rose dug inside of herself and found her magic from Aros. While Kutlaous said she would magic from both gods it still surprised her to find it there. But pulling from its strength, she jumped from Cadeyrn's back onto Aytigin. She grasped onto the dragon as tightly as possible and they shot up into the air. She sent prayers to Kutlaous and Aros that the others would stay safe while she was gone.

There was so much Rose wanted to know and ask Aytigin about Dusan and these undead sorcerers and sorceresses. What other terrifying stories were told about him? What were the different legends about how he died? Where was this burial ground? Then, most of all, how did he end up working with Amelia? They didn't have time to go into these questions, even if Aytigin could hear her over the wind of his wings as they flew over Eral.

Rose leaned over to see how far down into the forest she'd be able to observe. Thankfully, at least from what she could tell, the area around the cottage was the only one flooded. That didn't mean it couldn't spread to the rest of Eral, though.

She made Aytigin swoop down periodically to gather dirt and leaves and the other items she needed. When he went at a slower pace, Aytigin's back was large enough she could balance and mix the ingredients together and create a long shape like a log or thin tree trunk.

It was obvious when they came closer to the swamp as the trees grew more crowded together, moss and vines hung from every branch, and the sounds of bugs and frogs filled Rose's ears. Aytigin lowered them to the ground, and Rose jumped off before he turned back into his human form.

Death hung in the air like a dense fog.

The remnants of skeletons poked out of the shrubbery and discarded pieces of armor scattered across the ground. A shield bobbed in the green water, and the hint of a crescent moon glimmered in the bit of sun that peeked through the trees. Rose's heart sank. This was where soldiers who were after Amelia came and died.

"So, what else can you tell me about this sorcerer? Were the stories they told about him true?"

Aytigin shrugged. "Who knows? What I know is he was obsessed with immortality, and according to the legends, that's why they ate children. They thought it would make them youthful and live forever."

Rose strummed her fingers on the log she made. "Clearly he did it if he's as old as you say."

He shook his head. "But he died. How it happened, there are different tales. But they all say he died almost a thousand years ago and was buried in one of Colma's sacred sites."

A ball of dread rolled around in Rose's stomach. This was wonderful. An undead, cannibalistic sorcerer. "And he's teamed with Amelia." It was a pairing made of someone's worst nightmare.

Now, where to place the spell where it would work best before Amelia and Dusan could impart anymore damage to the cottage. Or harm anyone. They'd partnered with Kartek before, and Rose was sure her not winning the Trials put a twist in their plans. Which meant they must have known the Trials were going to happen. And knew Grandmother was going to die. And Rafe…

The pieces fit together the further Rose journeyed into the swamp. So Kartek knew too. That must have been why the ogres wanted her captured and took her and Cal. It was all a distraction to keep Rose away from the cottage and finding the swamp. Her Aros and Kutalous magic burned and coiled inside of her. All of it had been for nothing. She let Rafe and Kartek lead her astray, and now they could take over Eral.

And maybe kill Eira and the others in the process.

"All right, let's get this done," Rose said. Aytigin hovered overhead, and stars and snowflakes circled around his hands like he was prepared to attack at any moment. She gripped the log tightly and slammed it into the muddy ground. Her eyes closed, and she summoned all her magic gifted by Kutalous. Rose reached for the green threads inside of her that connected to Eral Forest and searched for anything dry that left to draw it to her.

She felt like she was being pushed and pulled from all sides, broken, then put back together. Drowning, then breathing free. The ground shook beneath her feet and little by little; she felt the moisture pulling itself out of Eral and back into the swamp. It bubbled and boiled as the rest of Eral healed.

Then, a green light shone in the water and an ear-piercing shriek exploded out of the swamp. Boney hands and water-soaked skulls shot through the surface as the agonized undead beings screamed. Rose froze in place in shock. She was saving Eral but didn't think about what the effect it would have on the rest of the swamp.

The wind from Aytigin's wings blew around her, and she shivered from his ice.

"I'll freeze them, that'll take care of things." He raised his armed over his head but Rose shook her head.

"No, we can't destroy it."

Technically, it wasn't part of Eral, which meant it wasn't part of her jurisdiction. The swamp was on the border of Marali and was part of their kingdom. The screams made Rose's skin crawl, and her stomach pitched. This wasn't right.

"What are you talking about? These are ancient and evil beings. If we don't, they could take over Eral again."

"But we've trespassed first," Rose said. Soldiers attacked it in search of Amelia. Nestled in the trees were nests of Eralian creatures. "Don't you get it? This is supposed to be a resting place for them, and we've been the ones interfering. If we destroy it, they'll only get worse. This swamp isn't mine to regulate."

Aytigin's chest heaved, and ice poured out of his nostrils. He swore. "Humans. Don't know what's good for you."

He had a point. This log helped for the moment, but what was to stop Dusan and Amelia from taking over Eral again? She needed to protect it.

"Get me into the sky," Rose directed.

Aytigin scowled at her but shifted back to his dragon form. Rose dug even deeper for her magic and focused it on the log. With all the power she possessed, she pressed it toward the log and let go. It floated into the air, a deep forest green glow around it. Rose jumped onto Aytigin's back and they flew high over the swamp. The log followed them, its green glow spreading out around it.

The trees quaked as the light expanded through the air. The log spun in circles and a light filled shield formed. Then, everything outside of the shield went dark. So much so, Aytigin had to wave one of his claws to give them starlight to see. Through the shadows, the faces of Amelia and Dusan formed.

Hand in hand, they floated toward Rose and Aytigin.

"So, this is the famous warrior princess turned Minister," Dusan said. He spread his arms out like he was presenting a grand gift and gave her a mocking bow. "Apparently those powers aren't what they used to be or Kutlaous is getting weak in his choosing for my power to spread so far into Eral."

Rose's magic coiled and stretched like newborn sprouts wanting to emerge, and her lips pressed together into a thin line.

Amelia's upper lip curled into a crooked and arrogant smile. She lifted a blue and green scaled hand to the man and placed it on his arm. "I told you she wasn't much, Dusan. She can't even face you and had the others fight her battle for her." Amelia's mocking voice rang through the forest, and Rose's heart burned.

She wanted to reach out and strangle Amelia, but knew it wouldn't be any use, and she'd lose her focus on the shield. "I was just expecting something a little more than a dead guy. You're losing your touch, Amelia."

The former queen sneered back at Rose. "You do not know what we're capable of, girl."

Maybe, maybe not. Rose guessed she was about to find out.

"What do you want?" Rose yelled. She wanted to skip the banter part and get to saving Eral and finally kicking Amelia's ass.

"You weren't supposed to be Minister," Dusan answered. His voice was surprisingly human. Rose would have expected something haunting and broken. "Now we'll have to take Eral the hard way; or hard for you, at least."

"Looks like you're a little late," Rose said. "I won't destroy your swamp, and you can have your space in peace. But leave my forest alone."

Rose lowered one arm and felt for the roots below, deep in the dirt. She curled her fingers like she grasped a large ball in her palm and branches shot out of the ground. Rose and Eral were the same. If she wanted the Forest protected, it would do so.

Dusan and Amelia floated on the other side and created a wall of water. Rose's plants, and their water, warred against one another with the glowing shield between them. Sweat poured over Rose's face as she focused her magic on protecting Eral. She thought she might collapse from the effort of it. Then stars shone around her. More than the ones Aytigin already provided. Then ice cracked and formed along the ground.

Rose looked down. And there were Eira, Cal, and Cadeyrn. Eira raised her arms over her head. Her moon tattoo glowed from her chest, as stars and ice poured out. Cal and Cadeyrn took hold of branches in their hands, their own tattoos shining out, and a red glow pulsed through their bodies into the branches. They were sharing their Aros strength with Eral. Combined, the plants, the strength, the ice, and the stars created an even more powerful and strong shield that pushed away the water.

Seeing them there with her gave Rose the extra strength she needed. With one final push, Rose yelled wordlessly, and light exploded around them. Dusan and Amelia cried out and were shoved away. They fell into the swamp with a giant splash.

Then, all was still, as though they'd never been there.

Light returned to the forest, and Aytigin lowered them back to the ground. The dirt was solid and dry, and mushrooms shrank away from the trees and forest floor like it pulled down them. The puffs of pixie dust poured around them, changing from green and blue to vibrant shades of purple and pink and red and yellow all around them.

Eral came back to life.

Chapter Thirty-Five

AMELIA

AMELIA AND DUSAN STEPPED OUT OF THE SWAMP WATER AND TOWARD the cottage. Rage boiled inside of her, and the water bubbled in response. Rose already had more to her power than Amelia expected. They tried to get through the barrier into Eral Rose created, but thanks to the additional magic, no matter how much water they used, they couldn't get through. Dusan swore and stomped up to the cottage. He yelled wordlessly and water splashed around him so he could walk on dry land.

Things hadn't turned out the way either of them planned. Her power was stronger combined with his. It was true. But when others brought their magic together, too, she still needed more.

Damn Kartek. If she'd stepped up and won the Trials and became Minister, Amelia would have all of Eral and an ogre clan at her fingers. Now she couldn't even get inside the forest. At least not that way. She would need to go into Marali and enter Cresin through their borders. Her mind swam, thinking of how she could make her way.

One good thing about Rose being Minister was that now there was no heir to the Cresin throne. It wasn't the ideal outcome, but one Amelia could work with.

Mother burst out of the cottage, her usually perfect hair now a tangled mess around her hair. "What was that? Did you create an earthquake?"

"Not exactly," Amelia answered as she walked up the steps. "We don't have the ogre's aid any longer, and they blocked Eral."

Mother's face turned as red as blood, and her blue eyes bulged. "What? How could you fail? Again? Have I taught you nothing?"

Amelia raised a hand and felt for the water inside Mother. Mariah choked and sputtered as water trickled out of her mouth. "You have done nothing." She released her hand and Mother coughed and gasped for air. With a flourish of her skirt, Amelia turned to go into the cottage.

The swamp gave Amelia her strength back, and she didn't need its refuge any longer to rest. It was time to stop playing games. The ogres were a decent try, and she managed to get Renata out of the way. Even better, Rafe's next target was Rose. Which only left Eira and Brennan now.

With each step, Amelia let go of her confrontation with Rose. One thing she learned in her favor was that Rose no longer had possession of the Shadowslayers. If she had, Amelia was sure the confrontation would have been even worse.

Which meant someone else had the weapons. The one thing she wondered could be her demise. She had a hunch about who it was. That wretched and traitorous cousin of hers, Finley. She now had the mirror and the Shadowslayers, and if Amelia could get to her, she could get to them too.

She stalked through the cottage until she reached the bedroom. Charis stood there in front of the crib and held the baby, who quietly cried. He was calming down after a tantrum, Amelia could tell. Charis rocked him back and forth and groaned.

"Just go back to sleep," she moaned.

Amelia held out her arms. "Let me take him."

Charis stopped her rocking and stared at Amelia with wide eyes. "You… you want to hold him?"

Amelia raised a brow. "He *is* my child."

Charis looked back and forth between Amelia and the baby a few times, but eventually relented and handed the child to Amelia. She took him in her arms and rocked him the way Charis did. He was surprisingly heavy. Were all babies this heavy? No matter. It meant he would be big and strong someday. Exactly what she needed.

She took the baby back outside, who slowly calmed, and took mental notes of all she needed to bring with her. The swamp had been a suitable home for Amelia these past few months, but now it was time to move on. Someday she would come back, though.

Mariah still fumed when Amelia returned to the porch. Her hands clutched at her sides, and she paced back and forth. "How dare you treat me that way! After all I've done for you. After everything we've been through!"

"Shhh," Amelia whispered. "You'll disturb him again. Unless you want to hear him cry more?"

Mariah pressed her lips together in a thin line and looked down her pointed nose at Amelia. "You've never cared before."

Amelia stroked the soft black hair that grew over the baby's head and cooed. It was so rude of them to assume she didn't care. Like they didn't realize she'd gotten pregnant on purpose. This child was the key to her plan. The black in his hair was exactly the color Amelia hoped it would be. It matched Brennan's.

Dusan stood before the porch now. He was no longer swearing, and he wore a calm look on his face. He really was handsome now that he was fully human. Amelia could do far worse than this powerful sorcerer. "They're awake, and they're angry."

Amelia smiled. Good.

"Did you plan for things to go the way they did today?" he asked.

She took in a deep breath and looked down at the baby. He peered up at her with ocean green eyes and blew tiny bubbles in his mouth. "Sometimes things just work out, I suppose."

"Well, I think you have an army prepared to fight now."

The swamp water bubbled and rippled. Small waves splashed along the shore and bumps like tiny hills appeared over the surface. Row after row, the undead sorcerers and sorceresses of old rose out of it. Behind her, Mariah gasped.

They were an ugly troupe, and Amelia would need more allies than this. But an entire army was a good start.

Amelia turned the baby, so he faced Dusan and the army. He cooed and gurgled in reply.

"Well, Xanth, are you ready to meet your father, the king?"

Chapter Thirty-Six

ROSE

ROSE STEPPED OUT OF THE COTTAGE, LEANED HER CRUTCH AGAINST THE porch rail, and looked out over the pond water. It was already a scorching morning, but the humidity had lifted, and she didn't feel like her clothes stuck to her skin the moment she went outside anymore. Her forest made horse, Gale, she'd named him, was taking a lazy walk around the pond. She leaned against the rail and took a sip of coffee from her clay mug.

Eral Forest was back. Or at least on its way.

After her encounter with Amelia and Dusan, Eral had been going back to normal. It didn't take long for the mushrooms to vanish, and the forest ground returned to being dry and walkable. She, Cal, Eira, and Cadeyrn, over the last few days, scattered through the forest and placed smaller logs Rose had made to the locations that had trouble healing. Once they did, the healing was almost instant. Pixies returned to their normal colors, and those who'd been ill already were on the mend.

Rose rolled her head, releasing tension from her neck. She must have slept oddly the night before. But taking care of an enchanted forest paid its toll. All day creatures from Eral came and went from the cottage asking for help, or to greet and welcome Rose and Cal if they'd been unable to attend the Trials and funeral. Many of them wanted to pay homage to Renata, and they'd gathered a collection of flowers and gifts at the foot of the willow tree. Rose loved having them there, but it made her tired.

A caw rang through the trees. Out of the top of the forest canopy, a bright orange bird flew overhead. It sang the most beautiful song that reminded Rose of freedom.

A pair of travelers appeared through the trees, and Rose stood straight once again. First thing in the morning and she already had visitors. But it wasn't a surprise. Rose knew someone was coming, and it was why she went outside. The others were still sleeping, and she didn't want to wake anyone. She didn't know who it was. She hadn't gotten good at figuring out those details in her premonitions yet but figured that would come with time and experience.

It was Kartek. Which, in other circumstances, Rose wouldn't be happy about. But with her was Zorar. Her green skin had a slightly pale color, and Kartek had to walk slower than usual for her to keep up. Still, Zorar was upright and had a smile on her face. Kartek didn't, but she wasn't scowling either, so Rose considered it a win.

"Early morning for you," Rose called out from the porch once they were closer on the red path. "No late celebration last night?"

The pair of ogresses stopped at the foot of the steps, giving Rose the benefit of standing at their eye level. They had their usual clubs and knifes attached to their belts, but their stance was relaxed, so Rose didn't feel the need to be prepared to grab her own weapons.

"We wanted to see you before other distractions came your way," Kartek answered. For the first time, the chief looked uneasy. She fiddled with the laces of her shirt and avoided losing at Rose in the eye.

Rose tried not to look smug. Served her right to be nervous. They hadn't spoken since Rose created the barrier and untied Kartek from the tree, so while she assumed their alliance was still in place, it didn't mean they were on friendly terms.

"You look well, Zorar. Good to see you on your feet," Rose said to break the ice and create peace.

Zorar looked at her, her orange eyes curious. They'd never spoken, considering Zorar had been sick the whole time was at the ogre camp.

"It's good to be up. And I'm glad to see you aren't some fever dream I had," she answered. It surprised Rose how gentle her voice was.

Kartek cleared her throat. "We wanted to thank you for helping. Your theory worked. Once Eral was drained of the swamp water and the magic lifted, Zorar returned to health almost right away."

"I'm glad to hear it," Rose said. And she was. Ogres weren't her favorite creatures, but they were still under her care.

The three stood in silence for a few long moments. They needed to address their alliance, and Rose wanted to know the extent of Kartek's involvement with Amelia. Yet, she didn't want to know at all. Ignorance was bliss, after all. But she had to.

"Did you know Renata would leave us?" Rose asked finally.

Kartek's shyness vanished, and her orange eyes hardened. "Yes. But I had nothing to do with it. By the time Amelia approached me, the wolf was already commissioned."

Rose took in a deep breath and nodded. At least there was that. "Did you know about the undead? How much of her plan did Amelia tell you?"

Kartek crossed her arms. "I didn't. Amelia hardly told me anything and instead barked orders. In case you haven't noticed, I don't take kindly to that." She flashed a toothy grin and lifted her chin.

"And the Trials? Did you always want to be Minister?"

"No. That was Amelia's idea. She promised me she had a way for me to win, which I know now was a lie."

It didn't change the fact that Kartek once allied with Amelia, and they didn't agree on ways to handle leadership. Knowing these small details lifted a weight off Rose's chest. Rose nodded again. "Amelia is taken care of, but only for now. I'm sure she'll be stirring up some sort of trouble and we'll need help. Can I depend on your clan for aid when that time comes?"

Kartek and Zorar exchanged glances, an oddly intimate moment between them where Rose almost wanted to look away. The pair knew each other so well. The way Rose and Cal did. Kartek took in a deep breath. "Do you still promise us land?"

"Eira and I are women of our word," Rose told her. "In fact, if you want your piece of Eral now, while you wait for Eira to return to Cresin, you're welcome to it. We can create the guidelines now if you wish."

They exchanged another look. "Very well. If you need help, we will come."

"Then let's get started." Rose welcomed the pair of them to the porch and got a map from inside, and they sat down and got to work.

When Kartek and Zorar left, Rose made her way back into the kitchen. Inside, Eira and Cadeyrn were carrying their bags down the stairs. Rose's shoulders slumped. "You're leaving?"

Eira's bag slid off her arm and fell to the ground with a thud. "We've been away from the castle for too long. I'm sure Malle is unruly, and I can't imagine Cynth and Evony would appreciate being in charge for much longer. Besides, I think you have a handle on things around here."

She was right; Rose knew she was. It didn't make the sadness of her sister leaving ease at all. Rose'd gotten used to having Eira around. The cottage was going to fall so quiet once it was just her and Cal.

They spent the rest of the morning getting Eira and Cadeyrn prepared to return to the Paravian Mountains. There wasn't much for them to pack, but Rose and Eira stretched out any task they needed to do so they could savor these last moments together. Eventually, there was nothing else.

Rose hugged Cadeyrn while Cal hugged Eira. Then they each shook Aytigin's clawed hand.

"Thank for your help," Rose told him. "I couldn't have done it without you."

"Eira would have cursed me to Stula's realm if I didn't," was his response. "I'll be glad to be done with your human problems." But he'd been stalling as much as the others all morning, so Rose knew he secretly was enjoying this new life with them.

Eira gave Cal a hug, then went to Rose. "I'm going to miss you so much. But you'll be the best Minister. I know it."

Rose squeezed her back as tight as she could and almost lost her balance. She grabbed onto the crutch and set herself right again. "Come visit soon. I don't know what I'm going to do without you."

Eira raised her brows. "I'm sure you and Cal will think of something to do when you have the cottage all to yourselves."

Rose felt her cheeks turn pink. Evony was rubbing off on her. "You know what I mean." She shook her head. "You know, it didn't happen the way we thought, but you gained allies through all of this."

Eira tilted her head to the side and smiled. "Yes, I guess you're right. An entire forest full. Although, we didn't capture Amelia."

No, they hadn't. It still stung Rose they hadn't succeeded on that end, but the desire for vengeance had faded. She wanted justice served and for Amelia to be captured, but Rose already had blood on her hands, and wasn't eager for more. "But we will. Together."

"Together."

THAT EVENING, ROSE AND CAL SAT TOGETHER OUTSIDE. ONLY A FEW days into living there, and they already behaved like they were elderly and wanted to sit side by side on the porch. There was a long swing where it was easy to curl up and cozy next to Cal. A flurry of pixies sparkled and danced in the distance. An array of light and color filling the dark forest. Overhead, the phoenix continued to fly and sing its song. It gave the sky a beautiful red and orange glow like a glorious sunset.

"So, we'll go see your father soon?" Cal asked.

Rose nodded. "Sooner rather than later. I'm sure he's heard that I'm Minister by now, and I want to talk to him before rumors spread. And we need to gather our things to move here. It'll be short, though."

The times Grandmother had visited Faren castle only lasted a day or two, and Rose expected any of her visits anywhere outside of Eral would be similar lengths of time. She dreaded talking to Father and telling him he officially had no more heirs to the throne, and his second daughter wanted to abdicate. She only hoped he would understand.

"Do you think you'll miss it? Our life in Cresin?" Rose asked.

Cal took in a deep breath. His chest moved up and down in a heave and made Rose's head move with it since she was resting on his chest. "Honestly? No. I feel at home here. You?"

It took Rose a little longer to think of her answer, and she ran her hand up and down his torso. "Maybe I will a little. I'll miss my friends and family. This will be different, but I think in a good way. It feels right. It's going to be so much quieter, though. Just us two here."

Cal chuckled. "Oh yes, with forest dwellers knocking on our door all the time, Amelia still out there, the ogres, and an army of undead sorcerers, our life will be very quiet."

Rose laughed. All right, so maybe it won't be so quiet. He had a point. She pushed herself up and stretched her arms out wide, then wrapped them around Cal's neck. With a loud smack, she gave him a wet kiss on the cheek. "Although…. It is quiet now. Whatever will we do?"

A wicked glint appeared in Cal's eye and in a flash, he stood, then picked Rose up and slung her over his shoulder like a sack. She laughed as he carried her inside and slammed the door shut with his foot.

To be in their home together.

Epilogue

FINLEY

THIS WAS THE BEST SWORD IN THE WORLD. NOT JUST THE WORLD, BUT the universe. Finley swung and hit the soldiers attacking her and Ai with glee as the Shadowslayer hit each target she aimed for. She didn't even need to be dedicated to Aros to feel like she was stronger and faster with the weapon. She turned to see Ai with the dagger, and from the smile on her face, Finley knew she was having just as much fun.

All right, fine.

Maybe being attacked by royal guards when they'd started a brawl in a Cresin town wasn't exactly *fun*. And Finely didn't intend to start the brawl. But a man had touched her without permission, and she was tired and hungry and just wanted to get drunk, so… things happened.

It's not like anyone died.

That Finely was aware of.

A yawn overtook her, and the edges of her vision went blurry. She'd only napped once that day, and the exhaustion was hitting her.

"Finley, behind you!" Ai called.

Finley spun around and slashed Shadowslayer at the soldier behind her. She didn't understand why they were so intent here. It was rare when a simple breaking up of a tavern fight went to such extremes.

In Oxare, where her ship was more notorious, Finley was used to being tracked by soldiers and law enforcement. Or on the coast in the more northern kingdoms. But here in the middle of Cresin, where no large bodies of water were to be seen and pirates weren't a concern they had often? No. This was highly unusual. Finley never would have caused trouble if she'd been concerned about soldiers being after them.

Most likely she wouldn't have.

Maybe.

They must have known who she and Ai were and what they possessed. Not the Shadowslayers of course. No one knew about those. But the mirror. The one they'd stolen from the Golden Palace and left on The Mystic. She'd hoped when they met Rose in Eral Forest, they would have been able to get their name cleared and get access to Gallis's Chalice. Alas, it didn't happen that way. The likelihood Rose would let them anywhere near the Chalice were slim, so the two of them decided it was time to part ways.

It was a shame. Finley was warming up to the princess.

She yawned again and this time, her eyes closed, and she raised her arms over her head. She was getting dizzy, and it was a struggle to keep her eyes open. It was happening more often lately, and this wasn't the time for the sleeping curse to go into action.

"Finley? Finley! Wake up!"

Something hit her in the back and Finley startled awake. Right. Eyes open. She was in the middle of a fight.

But it was too late. Once the curse took its course, there was no stopping it. Finley mustered up as much energy as she could and dug inside for her water magic. If she was going down, the rest were going down with her.

Water poured out of her hands and splashed across the cobblestone street. It hit soldiers in the chest and sent them flying in all directions. The world faded around her, and her head grew heavy.

Damn. There was nothing soft to land on. Oh well, by the time she hit the pavement she'd be asleep and wouldn't feel any wounds until she woke again. She could count down the moments at this point.

Three...

Two...

One...

Thud.

FINLEY BLINKED HER EYES OPEN, JOSTLED AWAKE BY SOME SORT OF movement. There was wood all around her, a dark ceiling, and barred windows that shown bright blue sky beyond. Pieces of something stuck at her arm and she brushed it off. Straw. A carriage of some sort.

She pushed herself up with a groan and pressed a hand to her pounding head. Every part of her body ached and cracked when she moved. How long had she been asleep, and how many injuries did she get in the process? Off to the side sat her hat with its feather sticking out. She breathed a sigh of relief. Praise the deities, she still had her hat.

"Ai, where are we? How long was I out that time?"

"I'd say a day or two, and she's not here."

The male voice was a familiar one, but Finley couldn't place it. She'd met a lot of men in her life and couldn't be expected to remember all of their voices. Especially when she'd just woken up from a two-day slumber. But who he was didn't matter. What mattered was his reply.

Finley's heart stopped. Ai wasn't there.

"Where is she?" she dared to ask.

"I'm not sure. I've been in here for a while, and they brought you alone. I figured you knew they had separated you."

Finely rubbed her eyes and shook her head. No. No. That couldn't be possible. Maybe there was another cart, and she was in there.

And who was that voice? It was husky but playful at the same time. She turned around to the rest of the cart to find out who her companion was.

It was a lanky man with shaggy dark hair that hung in his yellow eyes. He wore clothing that looked to be made of leaves and had bare feet. A wave of fury ran through her.

"Rafe." The name came out of her mouth in a snarl.

He bowed his head. "At your service."

"You killed Rose's grandmother."

"Well... technically..."

Finley didn't wait to hear the rest and launched at him.

Thank you for reading! Did you enjoy? Please add your review because nothing helps an author more and encourages readers to take a chance on a book than a review.

Find more from E. E. Hornburg at www.emilyhornburg.com

And discover THE LAIRD OF DUNCAIRN, by City Owl Author, Craig Comer. Turn the page for a sneak peek!

You can also sign up for the City Owl Press newsletter to receive notice of all book releases!

Sneak Peek of The Laird of Duncairn

BY CRAIG COMER

Effie exposed her hand to the growling bear. Her fingers found Rorie's head and gave him a few soothing strokes behind the ears. A rumble came from deep in his gullet, as fierce as his wee body could muster. Frigid wind blasted them as they hid behind a large boulder atop the crown of Ben Nevis, the highest peak in the Highlands. A stranger had come to speak with her employer, Thomas Stevenson. Not an odd occurrence, but for a fortnight Rorie had groaned and whined, pawing for her attention as if disturbed by dark thoughts, trying to plead with her that something was amiss. And now that the stranger had come, Rorie's discomfort had turned into malice.

"If only I could peer into that head of yours and see what the fuss is about," she said, planting her hands firmly on her hips.

Rorie squatted on his haunches with a big huff, turning his head away. Though preferring the wild of the forest, he behaved himself around others when she asked. And only because it was she who asked. The bond had something to do with her Sithling blood, but Effie couldn't explain how it worked. It was as much a mystery to her as any of the uncanny bonds she'd made with woodland creatures, lazy housecats, and goofy hounds over the years. As much a mystery as why the queen and all the lords of London abhorred her kind, though she'd done nothing to warrant their wrath.

Rorie had been loyal to her ever since she'd convinced Stuart Graham to rescue him from a carnival the prior year, saving him from a brutal—and probably short—life of baiting. But he'd never acted so ill-tempered. Had the stranger come to take him away? Or was it she who should be fearful? By sight alone, the stranger wouldn't know her for a Sithling. Short of stature, with a young woman's curves and chestnut locks clipped about the shoulders, she lived her life amongst the Scots all but unnoticed, the truth of her mixed fey blood hidden.

Yet such reliance on appearance was a false safety.

Her hair whipped about her face, blinding her until she swept it back. The lodge of the Scottish Meteorological Society perched only a short distance away, a cozy, timbered house well-weathered from years of driving gales. Its chimney puffed white smoke, teasing her with thoughts of hot tea and honeyed biscuits. But that was where Mr. Stevenson had taken the stranger, and he'd instructed her not to return until he bade her. She blew into her hands for warmth, vexed by the riddle of the strange visitor, unable to contain her curiosity any longer.

"I'm going for a closer look," she said to Rorie. "Wait here." Hoarfrost crunched as she shifted her weight and slunk forward. The frozen dew crusted the fern and bracken around the lodge, radiating a cold that sank into her bones. Her olive-colored dress and drab woolen coat were serviceable enough, but they did little against the cutting winds atop the mountain, winds that drove in the damp air as if she wore nothing as all.

She understood why Mr. Stevenson wished her to hide. He was a man who believed in prudence. He would not jeopardize one of his great works, nor his reputation nor her safety, on the off chance a stranger would find her out. There were some who could recognize her fey nature if they stood close enough. The scientists of the day, many of whom had their pockets lined by London's coin, said fey blood corrupted the flesh, giving off an odor that some could smell. Catholics and Protestants alike said it was the sins of the fey that radiated a cloud of evil around them, allowing those pure of heart to perceive them. Other tales held that a fey's eyes glowed in the dark or that they would burst into flame if they touched iron. All of it seemed foolish to Effie. She drank her tea and let it pass the same way as anyone she'd ever met, regardless of their blood. How some knew her for a Sithling while most did not was as random as why some seeds took root and others wilted.

A whistle shrieked, drawing her attention. Next to the lodge, Mr. Stevenson's plans for a great observatory were coming to fruition. Steel beams braced half-raised walls as masons slathered on stone and concrete by the ton. The pipes of a steam crane shuddered, and a burst of gas exhaled as another beam was lifted into place, soaring thrice the height of a man to the workers waiting above. The construction was what had brought them to Ben Nevis, and Effie guessed the stranger would not have come if he weren't involved with the great project in some manner.

She stalked forward, half-crouched so the wind wouldn't stagger her, and reached the sill of one of the lodge's thick windows. Grabbing the smooth, lacquered wood for support, she peered through the glass into the lodge's main room. It held several tables of a dark and sturdy teak, and a stone hearth large enough for a royal estate.

The stranger stood with his back toward her. His coat and polished shoes bespoke a city, but not the odd leather cap with its flaps that clung tight around his ears. She didn't recognize the tartan on his trousers: blues, greens, and purples all jumbled together as if shouting at her. She recalled he'd driven his own steam carriage up the winding road, working the levers and knobs as if he were used to the task, an odd thing for a wealthy man.

"I will take your concerns into account, Mr. Crofter," said Stevenson. The window's frame had warped over the years, allowing her to hear him clearly. He stood by the hearth. A dark coat fit snugly around his stout frame, its wool threadbare from years of rugged service. His balding head held tufts of hair around the ears, yet they served to dignify his face rather than embarrass it.

"They are not just my concerns, Mr. Stevenson. They carry the weight of the Society. It is time to distance ourselves from such relations. Lord Granville will have his way, and you must choose where your loyalties lie—with the Society or with your fey friends."

Stevenson's face darkened. "We have pushed back these threats before and should not wilt so easily to tactics of hatemongering. Parliament has no grounds, and Lord Granville not enough allies."

A shadow moved from the corner of the room, and Stuart Graham's stocky frame came into view from where she crouched outside. The man's knee-length boots were coated in mud, a workman's badge he wore proudly, and his white locks curled in ringlets atop a face as cheery as it was round. "Bah, let us speak plain, Mr. Crofter. You knew of Mr. Stevenson's associations before you funded the observatory.

It was his name alone which brought in enough benefactors to ensure the completion of construction."

Mr. Crofter grunted. "Do you think any of these benefactors will stand against the threat of an Inquiry? No, Mr. Graham, they will scatter like rats." The stranger turned to Stevenson. "You will do as we ask, or we will sever ties and throw you to the wolves. One noted engineer is easily replaced by another. Now I bid you good day." He slapped his gloves together and strode for the door.

Effie recoiled. The news from London must be dire for Mr. Crofter to speak to Stevenson as he had. She crept to the front corner of the lodge and watched the small yard of trampled grass where the stranger's carriage sat. Graham emerged from the lodge's main door. He pulled a worn and battered watch from his pocket and studied it before casting his gaze to the skies. Mr. Crofter came out on Graham's heels, walking cane thumping the dirt as he ambled. The pair exchanged a cordial nod, similar to one shared by passing gentlemen in a city street. Effie didn't understand such manners. It was clear Graham was in a foul mood and Mr. Crofter the cause of it, but they pretended like nothing cross had occurred between them.

Rorie wasn't as polite. A low growl came from behind the boulder where she'd left him, and the bruin's head popped into view, teeth bared. She waved at him to stay back, but the noise had already drawn Mr. Crofter's attention. He peered at the boulder, his eyes growing wide. He muttered something, a scowl on his face, before clambering into the waiting steam carriage. Graham stood stiffly while the other man brought the boiler into action. The carriage's engine was a monster of steel and wood, with copper tubes lashed in a lattice across its flank and a charred snout thrusting upward from its roof. With a parting nod, Mr. Crofter threw open the valve, and the carriage sputtered forth with a burst of burnt coal perfuming the air. Only when the squeaking of the carriage's axles had faded down the mountain road did Graham turn to stare right at Effie.

As he beckoned her, brooding clouds rolled over the surrounding hills, darkening the sky. The wind gusted, flapping his leather coat about his legs. Neither were good omens. She stood and crossed to him, her cheeks flushed in embarrassment. He greeted her with a grin forced from pursed lips, and he spoke in a rushed manner, barely taking a breath.

"Och, lass," he said. "You took a risk. If my waistcoat weren't as round as an ox, ye'd surely been seen. It's like to piss down any moment. Let's get into the warmth before it does. Mr. Stevenson wants a word."

Effie nodded sheepishly as the steam crane's whistle shrilled again. Black smoke belched from its boiler, the engine fighting the strain of the wind. But she needn't watch the work progress to know the shape of the observatory. Its structure had long been affixed in her head from the drawings she'd rendered of the project. That was her place in the endeavor. Stevenson had discovered her talent for depicting his designs years before when she was just a lost girl sheltering under his protection. She'd sought him out after the death of her mother, the famous lighthouse engineer who designed edifices powered by stardust—the glowing azure silt, forged by Fey Craft, that burned hotter than oil and slower than coal. Her eyes grew glassy. The time was a blurred memory that still haunted her dreams. She'd come close to starvation and almost succumbed to exposure. Worse, she'd been captured and beaten by the queen's Sniffers, those who hunted fey, and only managed to escape by sheer luck. Yet none of those trials compared to the sorrow of isolation, the sense that all her warmth and cheer had fled. That she was alone, the last of her family, nearly the last of the Sithlings.

Alone and yet not alone. She glanced at the dark shadows of forest sprouting from the hills ranging beneath the peak of Ben Nevis. How many of the other fey races hid there watching them? Pixies and brownies, gnomes and hogboons all still dwelt within the Highlands. The remnants of a Seily Court existed, yet her mother had taught her to be as wary of it as of the Scots. She could count on a single hand the number of fey she'd ever met, and none were likely to take her in if the need arose. Such was the way for many Sithlings. Despite their appearance, they lived between races, not quite human and not quite fey. Their blood derived from a sect of the Daoine Sith interbred with the Votadini, an ancient human clan whose might had receded under an onslaught of Scoti tribesmen. What remained centuries later could claim neither as kinsfolk.

Effie followed the man she considered an uncle into the lodge. Heat from the hearth enveloped her the moment she stepped inside, soothing away the bite the cold wind had left. Laid out on one of the tables were Thomas Stevenson's plans of the observatory, his lines and notes as formal and stiff as he was. On another perched the casing for one of his famous screens, a protective box for meteorological instruments. Its sides were angled slats designed to keep moisture from the instruments contained within, allowing them to collect data for weeks on end unattended. Her own worktable rested in a corner. A collection of colored charcoals, neatly arranged within a tin, sat atop a rendering of the observatory. Her drawings always held more flora than the bleak locations Stevenson chose to build on, and the observatory was no exception. Ben Nevis' crown boasted none of the hearty pines and spring flowers her depiction held, but that never seemed to bother her employer.

Stevenson greeted her with a curt nod and gestured to a chair by the hearth. He didn't make her wait long, once settled. "Our caller was Mr. James Crofter, a noted engineer whose father worked with Thomas Telford on the Great Canal." Effie's lips tugged at a smile. To Stevenson, names were always linked to matters of accomplishment. His own noted a long family line of engineers. "He came to us in haste with news from the coast. Murder has been done in the village of Duncairn."

Effie started. If given a dozen guesses, it was not the news she'd expected to hear. She read Stevenson's face, but it remained a stone mask. "Was it someone you knew?"

"A fisherman," answered Graham, bringing her a cup of tea, "An Ewan Ross. His boat capsized in the Bay of Lunan."

She took the cup, piping hot and full of sugar the way she liked, and breathed in its sweetness.

"The importance is not whom but the how," said Stevenson. "Fishermen in the area swear a host of rabid seals tipped Mr. Ross' boat, accosting it in unison. Not normal behavior to say the least."

She stifled a laugh. The poor fisherman deserved better, but the image of a group of seals harassing his vessel, barking and slapping the water with their flippers, was comical to her. "Surely these fishermen are mistaken in what they saw, or perhaps Mr. Ross agitated the seals in some manner. Perhaps they were trying to help the man." She glanced between the two men, wondering if they were jesting with her. "Yet I fail to see how one could call it murder."

"That's what I did say," said Graham. "The Scottish folk are long known for tales of fancy. Any dark bed of kelp becomes the Kraken in their minds."

Stevenson cleared his throat. "Putting Mr. Ross aside, there is a second account Mr. Crofter related. A week ago, a young lass was accosted on the road to Montrose, just outside of Duncairn. She suffered woefully and is much delirious, but describes her attackers as hairy imps slight of stature, with sharp ears and wicked fangs. They battered her as she fled. She recovers now from a fractured skull and other wounds." Stepping to the table, Stevenson rested his fingertips on it. "Short, devilish imps with pointed ears. These creatures have a name. The Shetland folk call them trows."

"Bah, bollocks," spat Graham.

Effie blinked, taken aback by the certainty in Stevenson's gaze. "I had not believed trows real." Her cheeks flushed at the admission. Her knowledge of the fey races, and of Fey Craft, were scarce at best. Much that she knew had come from Stevenson.

"Real enough," said Stevenson, "though not seen in the Highlands for centuries. They are fell creatures not of the Seily Court."

She frowned. "I thought all fey were bound to the Seily Court, before the Leaving at least. The binding is what gave Fey Craft power in this world." That power had dwindled ever since the Daoine Sith abandoned Sidh Chailleann, their ancestral home.

"There are some fey the Seily Court cannot control. They form their own covenants, Unseily Courts they are called, though decades have gone since the last rumors of one's appearance."

"Oh," she said. She stared into her cup, feeling a bit lost. It seemed, every time matters of fey lore arose, she understood the least.

Graham read her expression. "Don't fret, lass. You still ken more of your blood than all of us together. Mr. Stevenson's just got more years of hearing tales than you." He winked. "Many more, by the top of his head."

She forced a smile. Graham often reminded her how young she still was. For all her curves, she was still recent to adulthood by human standards, let alone fey. Thinking on the accounts of Duncairn, she drew the simple connection. "You believe the two attacks are linked, and if these trow creatures did the one, then the seals were really—"

"Selkies," affirmed Stevenson.

"But that doesn't make any sense. Selkies are not wicked creatures. They shed their sealskins in favor of human form to lure men and women into loving them. They don't work in packs, nor accost fishermen at sea."

"I have never heard tale of such a thing either," said Stevenson. "Just the same, fey sightings have grown in past weeks across the Highlands, enough to reach the ears of Her Majesty's Fey Finders, and now with these attacks it is almost certain there will be an Inquiry."

Effie blanched. There hadn't been an Inquiry by the Sniffers in almost fifty years. Most in London called the fey hunters relics, the funds used to support them better used elsewhere. Yet as dire as the news was, it did not follow why Mr. Crofter had spoken of such immediate threats. There was more to the stranger's visit Stevenson wasn't telling her, something she hadn't overheard. She studied his face. Her foot tapped impatiently. Cheeks growing red, she forced herself to still and sip her tea. She could be more stubborn than a stone when it fancied her, but secrets foiled her patience. As much as anything else, curiosity had driven her into the world of man after the passing of her mother, the need to explore the enigma of their society. Yet even as a girl she had always quested after knowledge. Her mother had often scolded her, reminding her life wasn't a puzzle to be solved but a great riddle to be savored.

The lesson had rarely stuck.

She would need to pull the truth out of the man. "Rorie is in a foul temper," she said. "He wants to warn me of something, but I can't understand what. I thought it might be Mr. Crofter."

Graham traded a glance with Stevenson. "She's a woman more than twenty years grown. There's no sense as treating her like the girl she was."

Running a hand over his chin, Stevenson worked at the muscles of his jaw. "Parliament pushes for legislation to formally outlaw any association with the fey. That would include the use of Fey Craft— stardust, precisely—and the harboring of those with fey blood."

"Bah!" Graham cursed. "That kind of nonsense comes up every odd year. They'll make no ground with it. We've still friends enough in London."

Pain flashed in Stevenson's eyes. "That is not the worst of it, you well know, Mr. Graham." He turned to Effie. "The Society feels a sacrifice is in order, something to appease the crown and end talk of an Inquiry. They instructed I draw up a document listing the fey I am in contact with and hand it over to the crown."

Stevenson drew up his weight into a rigid posture, clasping his hands behind his back before speaking. "That is why Mr. Crofter came to us— to demand I betray dear friends."

Effie's blood ran cold, and she had to swallow hard to keep the tea in her stomach from surging upward. So that was it—the missing piece. To protect their investments, the Society wished to send her and Stevenson's other fey allies to the gallows. It was not strictly illegal to harbor pro-fey sympathies, but neither was it fashionable, and those who did often found themselves in prison or their fortunes waning. She sensed Rorie's seething hatred for Mr. Crofter and felt a fury of her own spring to life.

"Do they all know of me, then?" she asked.

"Not directly," answered Stevenson. "But they know I have enough involvement with the fey that I could perhaps influence the crown's good graces."

"You wouldn't!" Effie exclaimed.

"Of course not," Stevenson snapped. He turned from her to cool his temper, yet she thought nothing of his outburst. His benefactors had placed him in a horrible position. They would not let their investments fail; they had too much money at stake. Either he sacrificed the fey known to him, or they would find an engineer to run their projects who would. She had heard Mr. Crofter threaten as much, she now understood.

"It's a fool plan," spat Graham. "I should've skinned the man alive for suggesting such a cowardly thing. The Fey Finders would hang the fey and still seek an Inquiry in Duncairn. Better if this observatory falls to ruin."

Stevenson shook his head. "The Society will not allow that. But they do underestimate the devastation of an Inquiry; they see only what it would mean in London. Her Majesty's Fey Finders care naught whether a fey is good or fell, peaceful or sinister of purpose. Their aim is to demonstrate their own worth. Without check, they'll scour the coast and put to the question all they find, as they did during the Potato Famines a few decades ago. They'll use the Inquiry as a grand stage and propel these legislations through. From there, their wrath would spiral out of control." He pressed his palms against the table, though it appeared he would rather knock it over. "We cannot let that happen. We must strive to show the world that fey and human can coexist."

"What will you do?" Effie asked, eager to hear his thoughts. Part of what drew her to Stevenson was his work, always seeking to blend science with nature. He was a pure naturalist who used stardust to power his famous lighthouses, promoted harmony with the fey, and sought to canonize their lore.

"We must sap the hatemongers of their advantage," said Stevenson. "I will stall them as best I can, but we must find the true motive and intent of these attacks before their Inquiry can come to bear. If the truth is known, there's a chance the Fey Finders will find no allies north of Edinburgh. The Scots have no fondness for London's authority."

Effie considered his words. She had no stomach for politics. Large crowds and public debate went against every fiber of her nature. But that did not mean she would wither away like some English violet. She could not let innocent fey fall victim to such a scheme as the Society planned. If Stevenson meant to unravel the truth of the attacks rather than appease his benefactors, it would take all his resources to hinder their enemies in Parliament, leaving nothing for Duncairn.

So to there she must go.

She rose, her mind settled. "If an Unseily Court exists in Duncairn, we must know of it before the Inquiry. It may be our best chance of gaining leverage, and our only chance to forestall Mr. Crofter's designs." Her words were heavy, but she stiffened her back against them. "I will go there and uncover the truth of the matter."

"What!" Graham barked. "You can't mean to go near that village. The queen's bastards will be crawling over it before the fortnight is through."

Effie swallowed to keep her voice from trembling. "There is danger, but to do nothing is to guarantee more fey will suffer." She faced Graham. "I can do nothing here to help; my presence might even bring greater danger if Mr. Crofter returns."

"You can do less against an Unseily Court!"

"If one exists," she reminded him. She tried to keep herself steady despite the knot forming in her gut. Graham and Stevenson had risked their lives and the fortunes of their families to let her in and give her a sheltered life. She would not balk at doing the same for them. "You are both needed here. At the least you cannot be seen in Duncairn. The scandal would link your names to whatever judgment the Inquiry handed down."

"There are others," huffed Graham. "I ken a man near Montrose who often trades with the fishermen of Duncairn." His tone was more tired than she had ever heard. "He knows much of the fey and has befriended a few in the area. I would have him handle this."

"If you could reach him," said Stevenson. "The man is a drunkard and hasn't responded to your missives in weeks."

"I'll speak with the fishermen and the girl's family," said Effie, "and if an Unseily Court exists, we will throw them to your benefactors and limit the crown's hand. It is the least either party deserves. Please, Mr. Graham, I must do something to protect the lives of the fey. I will not run and hide when I can offer aid instead."

"Bah!" Graham stammered, but his shoulders sagged in defeat. He spun on a heel and stormed out, slamming the door behind him.

The cold gust that rushed in made Effie shiver. She smoothed her coat and stepped closer to the hearth. Stevenson's face fell as blank as unmarked parchment, and he bent to scour over the observatory's designs. Effie knew Stevenson well enough to leave him be. Silent brooding was his nature, and she didn't take offense. To others it might seem he didn't care, but she knew he cared perhaps too much.

"Mr. Graham left his coat," she said. "I'll go after him."

She found Graham watching as the workmen set the observatory's giant lens in place. It was a moment they had planned for weeks. She knew a few of Graham's crew by name, but they all recognized her, giving her a cheery nod or word of greeting. Mr. Stevenson thought it a risk, yet she took that sentiment with a grain of salt. Where Stevenson placed prudence above mirth, Graham naturally exuded an honest warmth. He treated the crew like family and didn't employ a man he didn't trust.

"He should be seeing this." Graham had his arms folded across his chest. His cheeks and nose were rose-colored, as if he'd been nipping a few drams, but it was only from the wind.

"He has more pressing matters on his mind," said Effie, handing Graham his coat. She was not in a mood to speak in circles. "How dangerous are these creatures?"

Graham raised his eyebrow and stared at her askance. "If they're real? Dangerous enough you shouldn't go messing with them. It's a thick lad who pokes at a badger and doesn't expect to get bit."

"But you doubt trows exist?"

Graham stomped his boots for warmth. "I think Stevenson's nose has sniffed after funding for so long that it doesn't know a fart from a flower." Her eyes narrowed, and he held up a hand for her pardon. "This observatory is funded by landowners hoping its weather data will lead to better crop growing. They don't give a cuss about Acts of Parliament or the stars or the fey or any other bit of science that doesn't put more money in their pockets."

He pointed down the road. "That man, Crofter, is from Newcastle where the Hostmen lord over the coal trade for the entire empire. They aren't the type of men one should meddle with, and I wouldn't doubt the bugger is afoul of them."

"And Mr. Stevenson has been led down this path before." Effie finished Graham's thought. The affair with the lighthouse engineer, John Wigham, had left Stevenson accused of reckless slander, his name tarnished forever in the eyes of many in the scientific world.

"He's blinded by his own interests," said Graham.

"It is the fey's interest too," said Effie. "We are also his benefactors and have no other voice. The constabularies will not defend us. The magistrates of Edinburgh are bought and paid for by men who proclaim us the offspring of Black Donald." She stopped short of mentioning Graham's own interests, those of the French merchants who stocked his warehouses full of goods.

Graham gave her a cheery smile, but she saw the doubt and fear behind it. "We have enemies, lass. Too right. Some we know of, some we don't. I can't say as I understand what's going on myself, and that's what frightens me most. There's a strange feeling to this whole ordeal." The smile dropped from his face. "Robert Ramsey is a good man and no drunkard."

She rested a hand on his arm. "I will inquire after him."

He squirmed in frustration. "The tale of this Mr. Ross being killed by selkies is foolishness, and no doubt the other attack was carried out by some drunken rogue. The lass is just mistaken in what she saw or embellishing the tale for some reason." His skepticism made her love him more. It was the concern of a father not believing night had fallen, if only so his child could play in the sun a little longer.

"I've lived a happy life these past years, sheltered from those who would do me harm. That was your doing, yours and Mr. Stevenson's. It's time I repaid you the favor."

Graham's eyes grew moist. "Be careful, lass. The queen's appointed a new Fey Finder General, the man called Edmund Glover. I fear you know him, and he knows you."

Effie's stomach dropped to her toes. The name made her skin crawl. The last time she had heard it, she'd almost died.

Don't stop now. Keep reading with your copy of <u>THE LAIRD OF DUNCAIRN</u>, by City Owl Author, Craig Comer.

And find more from E. E. Hornburg at www.emilyhornburg.com

A Guide to the Deities

LUANA, GODDESS OF THE MOON
Other influences: stars, darkness, winter, ice, night
Color: blue
Common Symbols: moon in various stages, stars, snowflakes
High Temple Location: Farren Castle in Cresin
Appearance: slender woman with long dark hair and pale skin

RAY, GOD OF THE SUN
Other influences: clouds, light, summer, fire, day
Color: yellow
Common Symbols: sun, fire, sand, cloud, phoenix, dragon
High Temple Location: Cyre Palace—the Golden Palace—in Oxare
Appearance: large, muscular man with golden skin and flaming hair

KUTLAOUS, GOD OF NATURE
Other influences: forest, jungle, agriculture, animals, plants
Color: green
Common Symbols: vine, stag, horns, leaves, flowers, animals
High Temple Location: Eral Forest
Appearance: human man with horns on his head and hooves for feet, green skin with vines wrapped around his body

AROS, GOD OF WAR
Other influences: hunting, fitness, athletes
Color: red
Common Symbols: sword, arrow, snake, lion
High Temple Location: Khadi Desert

Appearance: tall, almost giant man with white skin, red eyes, and shaved head

COLMA, GOD OF WATER
Other influences: water creatures, other liquids, drinks
Color: blue or green
Common Symbols: waves, fish, pitcher, ship, mermaid tail
High Temple Location: Dravian Islands
Appearance: lanky yet muscular man with translucent skin, long blue hair, often wearing blue robes

STULA, GODDESS OF DEATH
Other influences: sickness, disability, change, maturity
Color: purple
Common Symbols: skull, bones, rose, clock, raven
High Temple Location: Underworld
Appearance: woman with dark skin, purple hair, and black robes

YLA, DEITY OF BIRTH
Other influences: fertility, childhood
Color: pink
Common Symbols: footprints, lotus flower, baby animals, egg
High Temple Location: Oxare Coast
Appearance: no one knows their "true" appearance, as they come as they are needed. A middle-aged woman to be a midwife; a young man preparing for fatherhood; a pregnant woman; a grandparent, etc. The commonalities are brown hair and a tattoo of the lotus flower.

DIAR, DEITY OF LOVE
Other influences: beauty, desire, charity
Color: red or pink
Common Symbols: rose, heart, ribbons intertwined or tied together, doves
High Temple Location: Belovian Islands
Appearance: a nonbinary being containing anatomy of both male and female, long and flowing pink hair and light-brown skin

EFARAE, GODDESS OF INSPIRATION
Other influences: the arts, keepers of the deities' tales
Color: Lavender
Common Symbols: music notes, a quill, paint brush, owl, scroll
High Temple Location: Kingdom of Marali
Appearance: petite woman with blond hair, purple eyes, and often wearing glasses

GALLIS, GODDESS OF RESTORATION
Other influences: healing, health, fitness, building
Color: gold
Common Symbols: a chalice, building tools, bandages, tonic bottles, hands
High Temple Location: Kingdom of Imare
Appearance: a round and plump yet strong woman with brown hair and golden robes

Don't miss more of the The Cursed Queens series, and find more from E. E. Hornburg at www.emilyhornburg.com

And discover THE LAIRD OF DUNCAIRN, by City Owl Author, Craig Comer!

A war is brewing between the worlds of fey and man . . . but only one can prevail. Find out which in this fantasy featuring nefarious plots, dashing knaves, and militant gnomes.

When Sir Walter Conrad discovers a new energy source, one that could topple nations and revolutionize society, the race to dominate its ownership begins.

But the excavation of this energy will have dire consequences for both humans and fey. For an ancient enemy stirs, awakened by Sir Walter's discovery.

Outcast half-fey Effie of Glen Coe is the empire's only hope at averting the oncoming disaster. But she finds herself embroiled in the conflict, investigating the eldritch evil spreading throughout the Highlands.

As she struggles against the greed of mighty lords and to escape the clutches of the queen's minions, her comfortable world is shattered.

Racing to thwart the growing menace, she realizes the only thing that can save them all is a truce no one wants.

Please sign up for the City Owl Press newsletter for chances to win special subscriber-only contests and giveaways as well as receiving information on upcoming releases and special excerpts.

All reviews are **welcome** and **appreciated**. Please consider leaving one on your favorite social media and book buying sites.

For books in the world of romance and speculative fiction that embody Innovation, Creativity, and Affordability, check out City Owl Press at www.cityowlpress.com.

Acknowledgments

I've been waiting to write Rose's book and share her story for almost as long as I did for Eira's back in *The Night's Chosen*. When readers loved her just as much as I did when they met her back then, it filled my heart! Because of that, I wanted *The Forest's Keeper* to live up to what Rose, and you all, deserve.

First, I want to thank God for giving me the words even when I thought they'd never come.

Thank you to my editor Tee Tate. You've believed in me and these books even when I haven't, and your support and guidance mean everything.

Tina, Yelena, and the rest of the City Owl team, you are some of the best people to work with. Your love and passion for books and your authors shines in all you do. Thank you!

All the other authors with City Owl, I love the little family we are. I'm honored to be a part of such an amazing group of talented writers!

My Royal Readers who share and read in advance and like and comment and read. Books, and me, are nothing without you!

Thank you to all my friends who read and show up to events and share and listen to me talk about books all day. You've always supported my dreams and believed in me.

Dale, thank you all your love. We're in this together, and there's no one else I'd rather be on this journey with.

Mom, Dad, Natalie, Tim, Elsie, Patrick, and my whole family. You are the world to me, and wouldn't be anywhere without you. Thank you for always being there.

About the Author

E. E. HORNBURG is a Chicago South-sider, consumer of nachos, dog mom, aunt to the greatest niece ever, and owner of far too many mugs and travel cups which hold her coffee. When not creating or devouring books you can find her pretending she can rap along with the *Hamilton* cast and plotting how she can get to Disney World (again). *The Night's Chosen* is the first in the *Cursed Queens* series and her debut novel.

You can follow along and get free stories by signing up for her newsletter at

www.emilyhornburg.com

 twitter.com/eehornburg

 instagram.com/eehornburg

 facebook.com/EmilyEHornburg

About the Publisher

City Owl Press is a cutting edge indie publishing company, bringing the world of romance and speculative fiction to discerning readers.

Escape Your World. Get Lost in Ours!

www.cityowlpress.com

facebook.com/CityOwlPress

twitter.com/cityowlpress

instagram.com/cityowlbooks

pinterest.com/cityowlpress

tiktok.com/@cityowlpress

Made in the USA
Columbia, SC
09 July 2024

83f132e9-4e6a-4878-bf97-99de0e33796eR01